PRAISE FOR L

Praise for *West with Giraffes*

"A delightful read."

—*The New York Times Book Review*

"*West with Giraffes* is truly a fun read . . . I [can't] imagine a reading list that would not contain Lynda Rutledge's astonishing novel."

—*Old Naples News*

"Every year I find at least one book that soars above all the others. This year *West with Giraffes* is that book."

—*Florida Times-Union*

"A flawless novel."

—*Austin American-Statesman*

"A perfect balance between history and fiction."

—POPSUGAR

"[A] larger-than-life story about the power of both animal magnetism and human connection . . . witty, charming, and heartwarming."

—*Booklist*

Praise for *Faith Bass Darling's Last Garage Sale*

"Incredibly engaging . . . a powerful first novel."

—*Booklist*

"This solid debut is a fascinating character-driven story of misconceptions, family, and tragedy."

—Library Journal

"Paints a colorful portrait of a larger than life Texas matron."

—Publishers Weekly

"Reminiscent of early works of Larry McMurtry and Edward Swift . . . In her wry and witty voice, Rutledge has given the tale, if not greater power, at least a contemporary twist."

—Texas Observer

Mockingbird Summer

ALSO BY LYNDA RUTLEDGE

Faith Bass Darling's Last Garage Sale
West with Giraffes

Mockingbird Summer

A Novel

LYNDA RUTLEDGE

LAKE UNION
PUBLISHING

Published by Lake Union Publishing, Seattle

www.apub.com

Amazon, the Amazon logo, and Lake Union Publishing are trademarks of Amazon.com, Inc., or its affiliates.

ISBN-13: 9781662504501 (hardcover)
ISBN-13: 9781662504518 (paperback)
ISBN-13: 9781662504525 (ebook)

Cover design by Jarrod Taylor
Image: © hackerkuper / Shutterstock

Printed in the United States of America

First edition

To my brother, Rick,
because those we love early never truly leave us

Each friend represents a world in us, a world
possibly not born until they arrive, and it is only by
this meeting that a new world is born.

—Anaïs Nin

May you live in interesting times.
—Ancient Curse

The times they are a-changin' . . .
—Bob Dylan

In 1964, a small miracle of a summer happened in Kate "Corky" Corcoran's tiny segregated town because of a softball game, a pastor feud, a drugstore sit-in, and a girl named America, who Corky saw run as fast as Olympic champion Wilma Rudolph, the fastest woman in the world.

Corky had just turned thirteen. During her short life, the country had already experienced the Cold War, Cuban Missile Crisis, Kennedy assassination, and Martin Luther King Jr.'s "I Have a Dream" speech. In the decade ahead as she grew into an adult, it would see school integration, the Vietnam War, hippie counterculture, and women's lib.

That summer, the last of her childhood, forever marked a moment in between as plainly as the railroad track running through her Texas town separated its citizens. It would change her in ways she wouldn't fully understand until she'd lived a long lifetime . . .

And, as life-changing stories sometimes do, it all began with a book.

SUMMER 1964

1

"Corky, sugar! Happy belated thirteenth birthday!" said Miss Delacourt, the town's librarian, to young Kate as she came through the big doors of the public library in High Cotton, Texas. "I've got a grown-up book idea for you to read this summer."

The librarian and Corky had a special relationship. She actually called her Corky, the nickname her ponytailed, tomboy self preferred, not Kathryn, as her mom called her, or Katie, as her dad called her. And never Miss Kathryn Kay Corcoran, as most adults did when vexed with her, which happened more than she thought necessary.

"I think you're going to like it," the librarian added. Book in hand, Miss Delacourt came from behind the library's fancy marble circulation desk. The public library was deeply ostentatious compared to other buildings in town. It was a two-story Italian Renaissance–style Carnegie public library, one of the twenty-five-hundred-plus libraries steel baron Andrew Carnegie helped plant across the country at the turn of the twentieth century. Corky, though, loved it. She had roamed its dark aisles and squeaky wood floors, reading everything she was allowed to read, since the moment she could put ideas to letters to make words. So, if her favorite librarian was excited about a book for her, she was excited.

"Here you go." The librarian handed her *To Kill a Mockingbird*, a novel about a family in 1930s small-town Alabama reckoning with childhood, a trial, and racism. It had won a Pulitzer Prize and was made into an Oscar-winning movie still showing in Fort Worth thirty miles away. Within a few years, it would be required reading for high schoolers, yet right then, since it was considered an adult book, it was a bit like forbidden fruit.

Glancing behind Corky, Miss Delacourt sighed. "Corky, sugar, I've told you we can't have Roy Rogers in here, as much as I like him."

Corky turned around. There sat Roy.

Roy Rogers was Corky's dog, a huge mutt that was a cross between Rin Tin Tin and Old Yeller, a mix of German shepherd, Labrador retriever, and mastiff. Named by her older brother, Mack, when he was ten and a fan of the '50s cowboy TV star, he tended to follow her everywhere, including somehow through doors. "Sorry, Miss Delacourt. He showed up after I walked to the drugstore. I just started my new summer job there helping behind the soda fountain. Everybody in the store watched him trot across the main street to stare in the front glass doors at me, and Dad said I needed to take him home."

"You're working at your daddy's drugstore already?" said Miss Delacourt. "That's why you're so dressed up on a summer day?"

"Yes, ma'am, just at lunch." Corky beamed, straightening the dress her mother had made her wear along with her Sunday-go-to-meeting dress shoes that pinched her toes. It was part of the deal her parents had made with her after she'd begged incessantly to work behind the store's soda fountain. Dresses were still expected for female outings, even for tomboys. Although, to feel better about the deal, Corky was secretly wearing her shorts underneath.

Miss Delacourt smiled. "Well, okay, sugar, but you've got to remember. You need to leave Roy outside from now on."

In 1964, there were no real leash laws in most of Texas, much less in Corky's tiny town. The town's dogs could roam anywhere, anytime, and did so with relish. The best part was that everybody knew everybody's dogs. It was an "it takes a village" sort of thing, but with canines.

Even Miss Delacourt knew about Roy Rogers's one trick, which Mack had taught him long ago.

"Roy, how are you doing today?" she said.

Roy bared his teeth in a big doggy grin.

Mack had taught him that trick for various occasions. If Mack said, "Roy, how ya doing today?" his teeth meant all things nice. But if Mack was being bullied or in some kind of perceived danger, he'd yell, "Roy! Want a *bite?*" and his smile became bared teeth with an added little growl that had dastardly types quickly backing away.

At the sight of Roy's sweet smile, Miss Delacourt chuckled and stamped the due date inside the library book's front cover with a decided flourish. Snatching it up, Corky headed out the door with Roy Rogers in tow, excited to rush home and start reading.

They bounded out of the library just as the town's only policeman, Tommy Tilton, was passing in his police cruiser, a 1955 black-and-white Ford Customline with a hood-attached siren that had seen better days. "Hello, Young Miss Corcoran," he called to them. "You and Roy Rogers need a lift home? Going that way."

"No, thank you! We'll walk," Corky answered and the cruiser cruised away.

The entirety of Corky's young world revolved around the drugstore, library, church, and school, all of which she'd pass to get home, the town being that tiny and laid out as straight as the railroad line that ran through it. She and Roy turned in front of the school . . . and stopped. Standing suspiciously by one of the school's windows was Dwayne Bumgardner. Spying them spying him, he hid a crowbar behind his back. Dwayne was the official bully of the eighth grade due to the fact he'd failed it twice and now was a head taller than his classmates. He and his brother, Darryl, the bully of his own three years spent in the eighth grade, were perpetually up to no good.

Roy trotted over to sniff his crotch.

"Hey, get this dog away from me!" Dwayne yelped.

"Roy!" Corky called, running over. "Wanna *bite?*"

Growling, Roy Rogers bared his teeth.

Stepping to the safe side of Corky, Dwayne hissed, "You tell anyone you saw me, and you're dead meat, you and your dog." Then he disappeared around the corner, giving her a full view of the hidden crowbar.

"Good boy," Corky said, hugging Roy Rogers, and they headed on home.

Although some things never change about growing up, the time in which you grow up isn't one of them. It's forever changing, shaping you in ways you can't control or anticipate. As each year passes, the only wild card is you.

In the very same way, the place you grow up shapes you as well.

In 1964, High Cotton, Texas, was a place you drove through without thinking, a one-stoplight town forgettable by your second blink, no different from any other town except in the specific ways that everywhere is different from everywhere else.

The town claimed to have a population of twenty-five hundred souls, but that was probably on the high side. At its height in 1914, right before World War I, High Cotton had boasted a population near fifteen thousand, with five cotton gins, three lumberyards, four banks, six bars that closed permanently with Prohibition, a newspaper, and stores and churches galore. Even a Jewish temple congregation once met on the second floor of the drugstore, complete with a Torah, or so Corky's father, Cal Corcoran Jr., was told when he bought the store in the '50s. The town had no famous native sons to speak of, save for Aloysius Homer Dowd, who played for the 1908 Pittsburgh Pirates by way of the minor-league Fort Worth Panthers, according to the old-timey bronze memorial plaque set on a sturdy pole and erected in front of the high school, with Aloysius's etched likeness. In the years to come, the town wouldn't even be there, swallowed up by the Dallas–Fort Worth metroplex. Nothing would be left except the shell of the drugstore Corky's dad owned, which would be turned into a yoga center. And that surely would have made her dad grump: *What the hell is a yoga center?*

And maybe the town being gone was fitting. Depending on who was asked, the only reason High Cotton, Texas, was in existence in the first place was either because of an 1870s poker game in which a dirty carpetbagger named Noah Ulysses Boatwright won a thousand-acre pocket of rich land surrounded by otherwise rocky, rattlesnake-infested soil that was good for little more than driving cattle through to get to the Chisholm Trail. Or he'd been an ousted member of the Civil War–era Texas Confederate legislature who claimed he fought "injuns" with Republic of Texas President Mirabeau B. Lamar in 1841 to make the land safe for "decent" White settlers. That's the way of lots of origin stories in Texas. They have to be big and slightly sketchy to be told well and long.

Either way, in 1872, when the railroad came through, Noah Ulysses Boatwright started what would have been called a plantation before the Civil War in that pocket of rich soil and named the place High Cotton, prophesying his success. Soon, he'd made his cotton-picking fortune; married a young, nubile wife; built a mansion; and started popping out prodigies to start a little High Cotton dynasty. And perhaps that's why Blacks—or, as they were called by polite White folks in Corky's youth, *Negroes* or *colored folks*—came to live in High Cotton at all. Noah Boatwright had to have somebody who didn't mind the back-breaking, heat-stroking work of picking all that "high" cotton, and in the 1870s that usually meant freed slaves and their progeny. Plus, the new railroad track offered a convenient little dividing line for every-one to live "separate but equal." Nobody questioned it, or if they did, nobody was listening. The railroad went straight through town, angling northwest from Fort Worth, High Cotton's White population living on the Northside, its Black population on the Southside. So, the good citizens of High Cotton never referred to it as the *wrong side of the tracks*, deeming it rude. They always said the *Southside*, and everybody on both sides of the track knew what that meant.

By the 1960s, since manual cotton picking was no longer an option, most of the town's remaining working class, Black and White, was employed by the railroad. If lucky. If not, they had to work for the sole remaining cotton gin, a nasty, dangerous job that had lost more than one High Cotton citizen an arm or hand over the years.

As for High Cotton's fading downtown, it hugged those railroad tracks, spread out for five blocks along the two-lane Fort Worth–Decatur highway. Among lots of empty storefronts, it still offered a bank, a hardware store, a feed store, a barber and beauty shop, a gas station, a grocery store, a shoe store, a dress shop, and a five-and-dime where nothing was any longer a nickel or a dime but offered most anything you couldn't get at the other stores, including underwear. However, while the Southside's Black citizens had their own barber and beauty shops, along with their own separate public school, the town only had one drugstore. Southsiders had to cross the tracks and patronize Mr. Cal Corcoran Jr.'s drugstore for everything from hair straightener to ice-cream cones, all of which the store offered in great supply to everyone.

With one hitch.

Since early-1960s Texas was still in the last-gasp throes of Jim Crow laws segregating every last little thing, ice-cream cones or anything else Southsiders might desire from the soda fountain had to be fetched for them while they waited at the main counter. One of the permanent employees Cal Corcoran inherited when he'd bought the store did the fetching. Usually that was Earl Shively, a tall bag of bones who always smelled faintly of whiskey. If not, it was one of the redheaded Stamper sisters, sweet Velma, who wore her patience as long as her skirts, or spunky Velvadine, who wore glasses almost as big as her face. That summer, more often than not, though, it was Corcoran's young daughter, Corky.

Despite the segregated status quo, High Cotton citizens got along surprisingly well in the best small-town way, with most everyone willing to help their neighbor, whatever side of the tracks that neighbor happened to call home. Just that morning, Velma came into work describing how a neighborly Southside man named Rayford Willcox had come out of the store the night before just as she was trying to start her car, saw she was having trouble, and fixed it. "Such a nice man. He just stuck his hand in under the hood, wiggled something, and it started right up!" Velma told Corky and Velvadine.

The only other drugstore employees were the delivery boys, a pack of ever-changing teenagers who drove the drugstore's truck as a "Service to the Sick," the drugstore's motto, to deliver prescriptions. Every boy with a driver's license not only knew Corky's dad but hoped to work for him, not the best situation for a thirteen-year-old girl about to burst from tomboy into full-blown teenage boy-crazy.

Of course, it wasn't just the delivery boys who knew Corky Corcoran's father. Everybody in town traipsed through the store on a regular basis for needed sundries, a cold drink, ice cream, or a grilled cheese lunch, including one of Corky's first customers that day, her minister, Pastor Pete of the First Baptist Church.

"Corky, look at you working here!" he said upon seeing her. "A Dr Pepper, please. I've got a bone to pick with your brother!"

His full name was Reverend Peter J. Hockenheimer. It was such an unpleasant mouthful for most High Cotton Baptists—any attempt at using it sounding like a bad case of throat clearing—that he was called either *Pastor Pete* or *Brother Pete*, depending on how deeply Baptist you were. "They've now beaten us ten years in a row!" Pastor Pete went on as Corky handed him the ice-cold Dr Pepper bottle out of the soft-drink cooler. "We needed Mack. He promised he'd be home for the game!" Corky's brother, Mack, had been an All-State baseball pitcher for the High Cotton Boll Weevils and had always played on the church softball team for the big summer Baptist versus Methodist rivalry. "What *happened?*"

When Corky shrugged, Pastor Pete went over and asked the same question of her dad, who wasn't a fan of Pastor Pete or the Baptist church or anyone else who had the gumption to presume to preach hellfire at him on a consistent basis, which Baptists seemed to do more than most.

But Pastor Pete wasn't worried about saving folks from hellfire that day. He was upset about losing yet again to the Methodist church's

Reverend Douglas D. Gifford. Reverend Doug had played minor-league baseball before receiving the call to ministry and took every chance to remind skinny, hawk-nosed, bespectacled Pastor Pete of it. Both of them had come to High Cotton right out of their respective seminaries and had already stayed maybe a little too long.

A rivalry played out via the sport of baseball was not uncommon in small towns, its significance as American as ballpark hot dogs. What was uncommon about the High Cotton rivalry was its particular in-town churchy element: a pastor feud.

While High Cotton was struggling to maintain at least a single store of every type the residents needed, it had, like most small towns, a wide variety of churches to choose from. A decade before, after both young pastors had started their ministries in High Cotton at the same time, the former-minor-leaguer Methodist minister, Reverend Doug, posed an idea to the Baptist minister, Pastor Pete. Since the town wasn't big enough to have a summer youth softball league, he suggested that the two biggest churches, the Baptists and Methodists, start a friendly little summer slow-pitch softball game for the elementary and junior high kids right after the school year ended, the assumption being, as with most things in the railroad-track-divided town, a game for the kids on the town's Northside. Pastor Pete had agreed. So, both churches invited every boy and girl on the Northside to play, which meant that over the years the game had players from each local religious persuasion: Pentecostal, Episcopal, Presbyterian, Church of Christ, Jehovah's Witness, Catholic, and No Church at All. The umpire was always High Cotton's policeman, Tommy Tilton, judged by the two pastors to be the most likely to be impartial. And since the Baptist church had a larger membership than any other church, the original consensus was that the other churches' kids would play with the Methodists. At the start, this seemed only fair since their smaller membership supposedly put them at a disadvantage. Ironically, it had turned out to be no disadvantage at all. The Methodists had a perfect record of wins, year after year after year. For a while, all went well. However, when the Baptists kept on losing, some hometown hang-arounds and even some Baptist men started playing, denominational pride upstaging Christian benevolence or any other concepts of brotherly love and friendly competition. Naturally the older Methodist "boys" started playing, too. That year, though, to Pastor Pete's sky-high delight, the best Methodist team players had moved or graduated before the big game. To make this year finally the end of the painful softball losing streak, Pastor Pete *had* needed Mack. So they'd lost. Again.

That left the Baptist girls' team to break the losing streak. But the girls' softball team only consisted of actual girls, since the town's ladies considered such rivalry silly and its boy-crazy high school girls were not interested in looking un-girly. The odds of preventing another losing year looked mighty grim.

However, that very afternoon, the first day of that unusual summer, things would change.

For softball.

But, also, for High Cotton.

2

Corky, back in just her shorts after ditching her drugstore dress the moment she got home, was sitting at the dining table near the kitchen, reading. She was already halfway through *To Kill a Mockingbird*, Roy Rogers splayed out near her feet, when the phone rang. It was her dad. He was calling to tell her mom to expect a new helper. Corky could hear everything, the kitchen phone being one of those bulky, loud things all phones were in the '60s, and the voice of Cal Corcoran Jr. being the kind you could hear across a big, noisy drugstore.

"Her name is Evangeline Willcox," his voice boomed. "Her husband, Rayford, is a good man and wants to pay off a loan I made him last night after he got laid off from his railroad job. Since he's out of town looking for a new job, she offered to help. So, Belle, I want you to make a real effort to make this one work, all right?"

Corky's mother, Belle, had a reputation for running off the helpers that her husband hired for her. She was a hard woman to work for, the scuttlebutt went, picky and particular. Corky couldn't argue with that, having had her as a mom. Since it was such a small town, though, her mother was running through the candidates pretty fast.

"Cal, we've been over this," her mother said. "I don't need help."

"Yes, you do, you *know* you do," her dad's voice went on. "You can't do it all."

Corky's mother seemed to resent the whole idea of needing help, although she didn't seem to mind making Corky help her. "You're not helping, you're *doing*. You live here, young lady, and no spoiled children live here," she'd said enough times for Corky to be able to perfectly mimic her, which she knew definitely never to do, at least not in front of her mother.

"It's only temporary, Belle," Corky's father went on. "And she's bringing her daughter with her."

"What?" her mother said. "Why?"

That answer Corky didn't quite hear, but whatever it was, it made her mother sigh. "Fine," she said, flicking her hair in the way she did when peeved. Her mother was quite a stunner, a true dark-haired, dark-eyed, porcelain-skinned beauty. Even Corky had noticed it, and she never noticed such things. Maybe because she didn't take after Belle, being pug-nosed, sandy-haired, and freckled like her dad, Mack getting all their mother's good-looking genes. But as beautiful as she was, her mother had contracted polio as a child, leaving her with one leg weaker and skinnier than the other, a phenomenon that happened quite a bit with the scourge before Jonas Salk's vaccine was developed. Since the 1964 Olympics were that year, everyone knew about a famous Black woman named Wilma Rudolph, who had survived polio to win gold in the 1960 Olympics, earning the label of "fastest woman in the world." Corky's mother, however, wouldn't be winning any footraces, the house's stairs, both the ones in the front hallway and in the back near the kitchen, being enough of a challenge when she was tired. And big houses like the Corcorans' all had stairs.

Hanging up the phone, Belle pursed her lips and looked over at Corky. "Kathryn, there's a girl coming along with the new helper your dad is sending over right now, and we need to see what that means. So, don't run off."

Corky started to protest. She was planning to go back to the library and ask Miss Delacourt important questions about the novel she was reading, but the look on her mother's face stopped her cold. "Yes, ma'am," she said. "Mom, what's *rape?*"

Her mother, already halfway back to the kitchen, whirled around. ". . . *What?*"

"It's a word in this book I've never heard: *rape*."

Her mother suddenly appeared right by her chair. "Is that a library book? Let me see."

Corky showed her the cover.

"Where did you get this? From Raynelle?"

Corky nodded.

Her mother picked up the phone receiver and dialed. "Raynelle? Belle. The book you gave Kathryn—she just asked me what *rape* was."

Corky leaned near so as not to miss a word.

"Yes, the word *rape* is in it," she heard Miss Delacourt's muffled voice answer, "but it's a rape that didn't happen, Belle, a trumped-up charge against a Black man by a white-trash woman. Remember? You read it."

"Doesn't matter, Raynelle," her mother said. "She shouldn't know about such things yet."

"But you know the story's not about that," Miss Delacourt's voice went on. "It's about racial injustice. And considering what's happening with the Civil Rights Movement now, don't you think she should read it? If nothing else, it shows we're doing better than they were thirty years ago. Plus, the movie with Gregory Peck was *soooo* good. You should go down to Fort Worth to see it. It won three Oscars."

"I don't like having my child reading about such things," her mother said next.

"She's thirteen, Belle," Miss Delacourt's voice answered. "That child is older than you think she is."

Now Corky was really interested.

At that point, her mother realized Corky was overhearing everything and decided she'd heard enough. "Go in the other room, Kathryn."

Taking her book, Corky went through the door to the living room and slipped behind it to hear what she could. But it was little more than her mother saying, ". . . I don't know, Raynelle. Yes, she's already into it. Well . . . all right."

Hearing her mother hang up the phone, Corky popped back into the room, and Belle gave her a look that said she was too tired to argue about it. And that meant Corky had a fighting chance to get her way.

Corky tried again: "What is it?"

"What is what?"

"Rape."

"We'll discuss that later," Belle said. "Right now, help me straighten up a bit. They'll be here any minute. And put Roy Rogers outside."

Corky could tell she wasn't going to get an answer right away. But with courage borne of eavesdropping on Miss Raynelle Delacourt's perceived level of her maturity, and since she couldn't ask her librarian friend, she decided to ask her mother the other questions bugging her as they strode through the house. "In the book, the townspeople believed the lying white-trash woman over the nice Black man," she said to her mother as she picked up a pair of her sneakers. "Why?"

Belle didn't answer, straightening a stack of *Life* magazines on the coffee table.

"And even weirder," Corky went on, "there was this mob of White men wanting to bust him out of jail. I mean, where were they going to take him if they did?"

"Kathryn Kay Corcoran, *stop*. I said we'll talk about this later. Now, behave, hear me? No nosy questions. And put Roy Rogers out right now, young lady."

At that moment, they heard a knock on the back screen door. Standing on the steps were two slim Black women, one Belle's age, the other only a few years older than Corky. The mother had on a flowery housedress. The daughter was wearing pedal pushers, a tucked-in blouse made out of the same fabric as the mom's housedress, along with a pair of Sunday-go-to-meeting dress shoes of her own. And she was fidgeting in them as if her shoes pinched like Corky's. They both had their hair pulled back in ropelike braids Corky had never seen before, the mother's shoulder-length hair in a short one, the teenager's in a long one down her back, finished off with a piece of curled red ribbon. The way they held themselves impressed Corky's little tomboy self, who had slunk around like a boy her whole life, to her mother's consternation. They radiated a quality Corky couldn't quite put into words at the time, but later thought of as *poised*. The only time they looked less so was when both of them jumped slightly when Roy Rogers bounded through the door to sniff them before giving his approval and trotting out to the backyard, the screen door slapping shut behind him.

Opening the screen door wide, her mother asked them to come in. As the two followed her mother into the kitchen, Corky stared. She was used to seeing a parade of Southside women her dad kept hiring to help her mom, and she knew she was expected to act mannerly with them all, keeping her curiosity's questions in check. But sometimes she couldn't help herself. Squelching all her new questions, she stood clumsily in their way. They had to move around her, probably wondering why this little White girl was staring at them. Corky had never seen them before. That seemed strange until she realized it was also strange that she had never been across the train tracks to the Southside, especially since the tracks were only three blocks from where she stood.

She scrambled to follow them into the kitchen.

They all stood there uncomfortably for a moment, except for Corky, who was still staring the way only a thirteen-year-old can. Finally, after giving Corky the eye, her mother launched into what Corky's dad had told her. "Forgive my rude daughter. Your name is Evangeline?"

"*Oui*, yes."

"My husband said English is your second language?" Belle said.

"That is right," Evangeline answered.

"And you're from Haiti?"

"*Oui*. Yes," Evangeline repeated.

"But you do speak English fairly well?"

"Sometimes I still don't understand words, but yes, okay—okay. If not, she will explain," Evangeline said, nodding to her daughter. "This is my *pitit fi*, my daughter, America," Evangeline said proudly.

"You named her *America*," Belle said with a hint of a smile.

Evangeline nodded. "America Evangeline Willcox."

"Well, it is a beautiful name," Belle said to America.

And that made America respond with her own hint of a smile.

Corky eyed her. *She's either shy or stuck-up.* In Corky's experience, older girls were usually the latter. She decided to find out which. "Hi," she said to America. "I'm Corky."

"Hi," America said back, still smiling the same slight smile.

"Do you like baseball?" Corky blurted.

America looked a bit surprised, as did their mothers.

"Kathryn . . . ," Belle began.

But America quietly answered, "Sure."

Suddenly, Roy Rogers started barking up the devil. The front screen door slapped open, and they heard: "Anybody home?"

Corky's brother, Mack, strode into the kitchen, finally home after his freshman year at the University of Texas. With Roy Rogers wiggling and waggling and dancing all around him, Mack kissed their mother on the cheek and cocked his head toward Corky.

"Well, look at *you!*" he said, reaching out to poke her in the arm. Puberty had just kicked in. Since the last time her brother had seen her, Corky had grown four inches taller and lost all her baby fat. Mack nodded politely at Evangeline and America, knowing the odds were low they'd be around long enough for introductions to be necessary. Then he held out a record album in his hand until Corky took it. "Sorry I missed your birthday, Bug. Figured this might make up for it." It was *Meet the Beatles!* That was the year the Beatles would tour America for the first time. Within a few months, Corky would know every line of every song by heart like every other teenager in the world, but at that moment, she was more impressed with what was happening in front of her.

Their mother, arms folded, was talking. "Your father is angry at you, young man. We got your grades. Where have you been?"

"I had something I had to do. I'm home now, and for the whole summer, just like he wants."

"You're supposed to call him the moment you get in."

Instead of doing so, Mack headed back to his old yellow '57 Chevy, the kind with the fins, to get his bags, Roy Rogers tagging along.

Corky set the album on the table. "Mom, I need help practicing my batting for softball practice. Can America come help me for a few minutes?" Corky said, turning toward America. "Want to?"

America looked back at both their mothers.

Already talking to Evangeline about the chores, Belle waved them on. "We'll come get you if we need to."

Corky headed toward the front door, motioning America to follow, slowing only to grab her bat, ball, cap, and glove from the hallway closet.

America, though, stopped in her tracks as she walked into the big front hallway. Under the stairs, the house had a built-in bookshelf. On it were the *Encyclopedia Britannica*, years of *National Geographic* magazines, *Reader's Digest Condensed Books*, and other such important publications the modern '60s family would have. America was gaping at them. Seeing that, Corky was about to burst with questions, so she glanced around to check whether her mother and Evangeline could hear. From the hallway, Corky spied them in the adjacent living room near their baby grand piano.

"You play, then, yes?" she heard Evangeline ask Belle.

"I wish," Belle demurred. "My husband found it secondhand for the kids to take piano lessons. The lessons didn't quite take. But I so like looking at it that I just couldn't part with it. Do you play?"

As they disappeared back into the den, Corky heard Evangeline say, "A little—*nan zòrèy*—by ear."

Corky figured she was now safe to sneak in a few questions, especially since America was still staring at their bookshelf. Glancing at America's unusual braid, she decided that was a good place to start. "I like your braid."

America didn't seem to hear her, entranced by the bookshelf.

Corky said it louder: "I like your braid."

America glanced back at her. "It's Mamà's way, Haitian style."

"Oh," Corky said, not having a clue what that meant. She'd never much cared about her hair, in fact was almost clueless about it, having a lot to learn, since she was beginning to care what she looked like. She had always let her mother cut it off short-short for the summer and let it grow out during the school year into a ponytail. But after seeing America's braid, she decided she might not cut hers off this summer. "So, your mom is from another country?" Corky tried next. "Haiti, that's a country, right?"

America, looking at the books again, absently nodded.

"And she was talking Haitian?" Corky went on.

America nodded again. "Creole."

"And your name is really America? Why did your mom name you that?"

"Mamà always says she loved being in America," she mumbled over her shoulder, "and thought naming me that might give me a chance for an easier life."

Easier life? Corky wondered what that meant. So, she asked. "Has it?"

America didn't respond, her attention riveted on the books in front of her.

Corky, rarely one to take a hint, just moved on to her next question. "Is your father from Haiti, too?"

"No."

"Where's he from?"

"Galveston."

"How'd y'all end up in High Cotton?"

"Papà's railroad job."

"Been here long?"

"About a year."

"Did you move from Galveston?"

"No."

"Where'd you move from?"

At that, America turned and gave Corky a puzzled look that Corky had seen many times before. "You sure ask a lot of questions, anybody ever tell you that?"

"All the time," Corky answered, "but how else are you going to learn stuff?"

For a second, Corky thought America was going to smile. Instead, she just turned back to the bookshelf as if she still hadn't gotten enough of looking at it, which then had Corky wondering what *that* was all about.

"You like books? Me, too," Corky said. "I have more upstairs in my room that are mine. What books do y'all have?"

America paused. "None."

Incredulous at the thought, Corky blurted, "You don't have any *books?*"

In 1964, most homes had some kind of reading material, since that was the only way to get information, even if it was just a phone book, a Sears, Roebuck, and Co. catalogue, or a *Farmers' Almanac*. Nobody said *none*.

Still gazing at the bookshelf, America said, "My father doesn't really like to read anything but the newspaper, and Mamá can't read English." Then Corky watched America reach out and touch the encyclopedias, her hand brushing the entire length of the beautifully bound volumes, lingering on their leatherlike binding. "One day, I'm going to have a fine, full bookshelf," she suddenly murmured as if making herself a promise. "Full as this one."

"Well," Corky tried, "you can always check out books from the public library, right?"

Stiffening, America shot Corky a look as if her head had just swiveled off. And that made Corky realize she'd never seen any Black people in the library. Ever. From America's pained look, Corky grasped it might not be because they didn't want to go. Sensing she was about to either embarrass herself or anger this interesting older girl she'd just met,

Corky quickly changed the subject. "What grade are you in? I'll be in the eighth. I just turned thirteen."

"I'm sixteen. I'll be in the tenth," America answered, "but I may not go if we stay here."

May not go? That *really* got Corky curious. She'd never known anyone who just stopped going to school. "Why not?"

America shrugged. "I'm the only girl in my class with six boys, and they're full of nothing but foolishness."

That surprised Corky. She knew the Southside's school was tinier than her Northside school, but that sounded tiny-tiny. "No girls? Really?"

America shook her head. "All the older girls have already dropped out and gotten jobs to help their families get by. Mamà won't let me, though, least not yet. She won't even let me get a summer job, since we'll be moving again soon as my father finds a new job. I offered to help her here, but she won't let me do that anymore. I'm just supposed to help with her English."

"You don't like school?" Corky asked.

"I like it. But here it's just the same teachers in the same classrooms, with most grades lumped together. They've got no choice but to teach the same things over and over. Besides," America went on, "I've already read the textbooks through senior year, and there's never any new ones. They're just hand-me-downs from your school."

Corky thought she didn't hear right. "You don't get new textbooks every year?" Corky actually liked the first day of school because of the smell and feel of the fresh, uncracked textbooks and the nice, long time they spent protecting them with manila covers made especially for their school. "You're saying you get our *used* textbooks?"

America made a face. "They've got student names and doodles in them and are worn out. Last year, I found a piece of gum stuck in my English book."

Corky wasn't great at picking up on signals from other people, even those from a girl only a few years older than her, but she knew *sad* when she saw it. So, quickly changing the subject again, Corky said, "Ready to play?"

That seemed to make America brighten. Which made Corky brighten.

Clutching the rest of the softball stuff under an arm, Corky headed out the door with America. Outside, she dropped the baseball equipment on the grass to adjust her cap over her ponytail, realizing this was the first time she'd put it on in months. It was a little too small. But it still made her happy because she was going to get to play a real game on a real baseball field very soon. Just like Mack. For as long as she could remember, Corky had wanted to play baseball like Mack and was miffed in elementary school to be forced to play softball instead of hardball because she was a girl. So she'd done the next best thing. She'd imitated her older brother's every baseball habit. She watched Mack tap the Aloysius Homer Dowd bronze memorial plaque in front of the school, knowing it was Mack's way of prophesying his own sign one day. And she did it, too. During his high school games, she saw Mack pop the bottom of his baseball shoes with his bat to knock dirt from his cleats when he approached the plate, and even though she didn't wear cleats, she did it, too. Most of all, though, she saw how Mack worked his baseball cap. In the '60s, you worked your baseball cap just as hard as your baseball glove, putting a rubber band around the cap's crown to make the brim roll over on both sides. Corky thought Mack's was a thing of beauty and begged him to make hers like that. When he did, she wore it everywhere for her entire fifth-grade year.

As Corky adjusted her baseball cap, she noticed America was staring toward their side lot.

"You have a horse," America said.

"That's Goldy," Corky explained.

This being Texas, the Corcorans' side lot between their house and their next-door neighbors, the Poindexters, had a horse corral. There, an old palomino paint bought for young Mack right before Roy Rogers joined the family was living out her last years, enjoying the view and the pampering, only occasionally being ridden bareback by Corky down the dirt streets behind the Corcoran house.

"Want to meet her?" Corky asked.

"Sure," America answered.

Just then, though, Mack dropped his last bag from the car in the grass and grabbed up Corky's glove, bat, and ball. "Here," he said, tossing Corky her glove and motioning for her to start running toward the open field across the street. "Catch this."

Except for Goldy's corral lot, houses stretched all along the west side of the street, but the Corcorans' front yard faced a fenceless field several acres wide that Mack and Corky had used for this sort of thing their entire childhood. Except for a large live oak sixty feet away, it was just a big, long patch of sandy soil, and the wind that day was kicking up the loose dust.

"Catch it in the air or we'll never get it back from Roy," Mack reminded Corky.

Glove up and ready, Corky started jogging across the street, Roy Rogers by her side. Mack gave her a few steps, threw the ball in the air, and smacked it toward the open field.

The ball was going farther than Corky thought it would because of the wind. She turned on the jets to try to get there in time . . . and suddenly America was beside her and then *way* ahead of her . . . *barefoot*. She had ditched her Sunday shoes and still beat Corky to the ball, catching it with her bare hands and throwing it back. Hard.

Mack whistled in clear appreciation as the softball smacked his hand. "Got a good arm on you, and you're pretty fast barefoot," he called to America. After being outside and playing with Roy just a few minutes before, the only reason Corky had put on shoes was by mother-edict before Evangeline and America arrived. So, going barefoot was not impressive. Running as fast as America did *while* barefoot was. And Mack knew it. As they all trotted back to him, he asked America, "Why'd you kick off your sneakers? Bet you're even faster in them."

"She kicked off her Sunday shoes," Corky explained.

"My sneakers don't fit anymore," America said. "Just grew outa them."

"Oh." He turned to Corky. "Give her your glove, Bug." Handing Corky the bat, he stepped a dozen steps back, readying to pitch to Corky. "Hit it as far as you can. Let's see what you got this year."

Mack pitched, and Corky whacked it, the ball heading toward the tree. Roy Rogers was already on his way, ready to snatch it up when it hit the ground. Instead, America caught it in the air and was back so fast that Mack and Corky could only gape. Even Roy seemed surprised.

Mack studied her another moment and pointed to the tree. "Want to race?"

America answered by dropping the glove and turning toward the tree.

Mack lined up beside her.

"*On your mark . . . get set,*" Corky yelled in true Olympic fashion, "*GO!*"

America beat him to the tree. By a lot.

"What the hell . . . ," Mack said to America as they walked back to Corky. "Do you run track at school?" This time, it was Mack's turn to get the look from America as if his head had swiveled off. "Sorry," he said. "I forgot."

In 1964, neither of High Cotton's high schools had a track team or any other kind of team for girls. Rare was the high school of the era that did, although some larger schools offered girls' tennis, deemed more ladylike and easier on delicate female parts. In a few years, a 1972 piece of legislation called Title IX would decree that girls should have the same opportunities as boys, forcing public schools and universities to offer sports teams for girls along with other expanded educational opportunities. But this was not yet 1972.

That, however, didn't stop Mack. "Bet you can't do it again," he said, egging her on. "Race me to the tree and back."

America lined up next to Mack. They raced. She beat him soundly again. And, this time, she broke into a smile so big and wide on the way back to where Corky stood that she looked like a different person—and Corky could tell the smile was less about besting Mack and more about the sheer joy of running.

Finally back beside them, Mack bent over his knees to catch his breath. *"Damn!"* he wheezed. "I'm not slow. How fast *are* you?" Straightening up, he paused. "I need to use the phone. Stay here." He trotted toward the house, but then turned around and came back. "Hold still," he said to America, placing his foot up against America's. Next, he picked up one of her Sunday shoes and held it up to the bottom of one of his shoes. And back to the house he went. As soon as America had put on her Sunday shoes, she and Corky followed, catching up just as he finished dialing the phone.

"Coach?" Mack said into the phone receiver. "It's Mack Corcoran. Yeah, home for the summer. Got a minute? Meet us at the track and bring your stopwatch. And some track shoes, maybe size nine and ten. I'll explain there."

Looking around for their mothers, Corky heard laughing coming from upstairs. "Is that . . . Mom?"

Mack grabbed the two girls by the shoulders, whirled them around, and hustled them out the door, yelling up to Belle, "Mother! I have to go to the school for a minute, and I need the girls' help!"

Belle's laughter stopped. *". . . What?"* she called down.

But Mack hustled them out before their mother could stop them.

A few minutes later, they were at the high school's football field and running track, the breeze swirling around them. Coach John Trumbull, who coached every sport offered at tiny High Cotton High, was waiting.

"Mack, what's this about?" called Trumbull, striding their way.

"Coach, this is . . ." Mack turned to America. "Shoot . . . I'm sorry. I don't know your name."

"America."

"Your name is America? Nice," Mack said. "America, this is Coach Trumbull. Let's see how fast you are. Want to?"

Hesitantly, she nodded again.

The coach looked down at America's Sunday dress shoes. "Where are her track shoes?"

"Don't have any," America said. "Never ran track before."

"She beat me barefoot," Mack said. "That's why I told you to bring some cleats."

"Ah." The coach took off the bag hanging on his shoulder, pulled out several pairs of track shoes with small metal cleats, and laid them before her.

America just stared at them.

"Well, try them on," Mack coaxed. America sat down on the cinders and tried them on until she got a good fit. Getting to her feet, she trotted around.

"Okay," Coach Trumbull said. "Let's try the hundred-yard dash. Come with me." He marched toward a line across the track a hundred yards away. "Know how to use the blocks?" he asked as they walked. "Just lean down, put your feet in the blocks, with your fingers touching the ground. You'll get it."

She did. And the coach walked back to the rest of the group, where another line crossed the track.

Out on the street, they heard a screech of brakes. Jumping out of his Chevy Nova, Pastor Pete adjusted his horn-rimmed glasses and marched straight for them. "Dang it, Mack Corcoran, where *were* you? The only way you can make this up to me is to help me coach the girls' team for *their* last chance to not lose for a decade."

"Fine, Pastor Pete, fine," Mack said, looking back at Coach Trumbull.

But Pastor Pete wasn't finished. "If you'd been there, we could've won!"

"Put a sock in it, Preacher. We're doing something here," the coach interrupted. "America, you ready?"

Waiting on the blocks up the track, America nodded.

"Ready . . . set . . . GO!" the coach yelled.

As she sprinted straight for them, America looked self-conscious at first. Then suddenly her face relaxed, her head went back, and she was smiling so wide again that Corky wondered how she could breathe. In the decades to come, when Corky thought about America, it was that euphoric look she'd always see. It was as if America were feeling some sort of bliss in the sheer joy of movement.

As America passed, the coach clicked the stopwatch.

Pastor Pete stood staring at America, who was now walking back to them, hands on hips, barely breathing hard at all. "That was . . . *beautiful,*" he said. "She runs like the wind! Who is she?"

"That's my new friend," Corky said. "She was helping me practice for the softball game, and she beat Mack in a footrace. She can catch good, too." But Pastor Pete wasn't quite listening, still thunderstruck at what he'd just witnessed.

As for Corky, breeze in her face, she was thinking about rushing wind and moving grace, busting with pride that she knew someone who could look that good running that fast. She had always wanted to be her elegant mother because of Belle's beautiful face. But, right then, Corky was thinking maybe she'd rather be America Willcox, who looked elegantly beautiful running at the speed of liquid lightning.

Coach gawked at the stopwatch: 10.1 seconds. "I'll be damned."

Mack and Coach Trumbull stared at each other. They knew the windy day affected her time, but she was already faster than anyone on the High Cotton boys' team had been for years.

"What was Wilma Rudolph's Olympic time, do you remember?" Mack asked.

"Eleven seconds, but that was for a hundred meters."

"And that's longer, right?" Mack said.

"Let's step off a hundred meters," Coach ordered. "Look in my bag for the tape measure." Mack rummaged in the coach's equipment bag until he found it. "The extra marks are in meters. Go start at the blocks up by the hundred-yard line and come back this way until you get to a hundred meters."

Mack jogged back to the hundred-yard blocks, walked off the extra amount past the group, and waited, stopwatch in hand.

"Have you caught your breath?" Coach asked America.

America nodded.

"Okay. Walk back to the blocks, save your sprint," he ordered.

America walked back to the blocks, got set . . . and waited for the coach to yell: *"GO!"*

And go she did.

When she passed Mack, he clicked the stopwatch.

"Eleven!" Mack announced. "An actual eleven seconds!" he repeated as a hard-breathing America jogged back to him.

Pastor Pete gasped. "Ho-ly Moses—"

Coach rushed over and grabbed the stopwatch. "Let me see that!" And they all had to see.

Mack turned to America. "Do you know what this means?"

A bit overwhelmed by all the sudden attention, America slowly shook her head.

"You've heard of Wilma Rudolph? Fastest woman in the world?" Mack asked her.

She nodded.

"It means"—Mack could barely find the words to go on—"if that stopwatch is right, you're already so fast you're as fast as *her*. And even if it isn't, you're still right there at *Olympic* speed . . . With training, you just might . . ." Mack swiveled his head back to Coach Trumbull. *"Coach?"*

Coach Trumbull was still gaping at the watch. He even shook it.

And that made Mack look at his own watch. "Oh, *crap on a cracker.* We'll talk later, Coach," he said, gesturing to Corky and America, "but right now, we've got to go!"

As America quickly switched out the track shoes for her Sunday shoes, Pastor Pete grabbed Corky's arm. "Did you say a minute ago she could catch?" he asked.

Corky nodded.

"Hold on . . . Hold on," said Pastor Pete. "Oh wow, do I have an idea." He turned to America and put out his hand. "Let me introduce myself. My name is Pastor Pete. What's yours?"

"America."

"Your name is *America*?" Pastor Pete said.

"Yes," they all answered.

Pastor Pete grinned ear to ear. "America, do you like softball?"

"Pastor Pete, we gotta *go*." Mack grabbed the girls' shoulders again and steered them firmly to the car. "We have to get back to the house before Mother explodes into little pieces. She's probably about as mad as you are at me right now."

"Well, let's go," Pastor Pete said.

Mack paused. "What?"

"Let's go! Let's go! Don't make your mom madder!"

Within a couple of minutes, they were back at the house, everybody tromping into the kitchen where Evangeline and Belle stood.

Belle began laying into Mack the moment they came through the door. "Mack Corcoran, where did you take the girls without permiss—" Then she saw Pastor Pete. "Oh, hello, Brother Pete. What are you doing here?"

Pastor Pete was already talking. "Dear ladies! Please forgive us," he said and stepped over to Evangeline. "Ma'am, I don't know if you're aware, but your daughter has incredible God-given athletic abilities. I'm Reverend Peter Hockenheimer of the First Baptist Church. And I'd like to ask your permission to let your daughter play on our church softball team for our big game with the Methodists next week. She'll love it! And so will we!"

As taken back as you'd expect, Evangeline looked from Pastor Pete to America to Belle and back to America. While the group waited, Evangeline and America spoke in rapid-fire Creole. Then Evangeline frowned and hesitantly began to answer. "Well . . ."

Pastor Pete jumped back in before she could say no. "You go to church, ma'am?"

Evangeline nodded.

"Would it be Mount Olive Baptist, ma'am?"

Evangeline nodded again.

Pastor Pete beamed. "Ah, a fellow Baptist! What if Reverend Washington says it's okay?"

Evangeline thought for a moment and nodded again, if slightly.

Asking Belle to use the phone, Pastor Pete called Reverend Moses P. Washington of the Southside's Mount Olive Baptist Church.

"Brother Washington, this is Brother Hockenheimer. How are you doing this fine day? Good, good. One of your parishioners is very talented . . . Oh yes, all of them have fine spiritual gifts from God, no doubt. I mean athletically. Her name is America. Yes, a fine, fine girl. We'd like her to come to our softball practice tomorrow. And if she likes it, we'd love for her to play with us at our game with the Methodists next week. Her mother said she could if you felt it to be as potentially beneficial to her spiritual growth as I do. Oh yes, I do! I think it would be very good for her, and very good for our girls, too. We'll come get her, and we'll take her straight home afterward, right to her front door, I promise. Good? *Good!*" He hung up the phone, turned toward Evangeline, full of hope, and waited.

Evangeline cocked her head toward her daughter. "*Èske ou vle*, America Evangeline?"

Corky worried a bit hearing that, since her own mother never used her own middle name unless she was in trouble.

Still a bit overwhelmed, America glanced at Corky, who was now nodding enough for both of them, and turned to her mother. "Yes."

"O-K," Evangeline agreed.

"Wonderful!" Pete crowed, happily straightening his glasses. "Shall we come get you?"

America shook her head.

"Okay! We'll see you at practice tomorrow at the high school baseball field. It's right across from the highway and the railroad tracks, but I'm sure you know," Pastor Pete said, all but bouncing on his heels.

"Ladies," he said, nodding goodbye to Belle and Evangeline as he headed toward the front door. "Mack, a word?" When Corky saw Pete and Mack talking low as they walked through the front hallway, she hurried close to catch what they were saying. "We help Mount Olive financially. I knew he'd be fine with it," she heard Pete whisper to Mack somewhat smugly as he left. "But you gotta help me coach—and when I say help, I mean *you* coach."

Corky glanced back at America. America was looking Corky's way. And she was smiling.

The Baptist girls' team had a chance.

Later that night, when Corky and Mack's dad, Cal, came home from work, he ordered Mack to a sit-down-at-the-table-right-now talk, and that was never good.

Corky and her mom headed to the living room.

"Why are your grades so bad this semester?" they heard Cal ask Mack.

"They're required classes. I haven't liked any of them."

"Then find ones you *do* like. What the hell have you been doing? You sure aren't going to class."

"I've had things on my mind, that's all."

"Like what? Like how you're going to pay me back my wasted money on your tuition, room, and board if you flunk out? You have no idea how lucky you are. I had to work my way through college against your grandfather's will. He figured sharecropping for the Boatwrights was good enough for him, so it was good enough for me. Nobody dreamed big during the Depression. You know what I ate for a treat as a kid? Sorghum on white bread." Which was true. He still did it, the nasty stuff being his comfort food, and it always made Corky deeply happy that her future comfort food would be Frosted Flakes and Snickers bars. "But I dreamed big, anyway," Cal went on. "I had to work three jobs at UT all through college and pharmacy school, and now I'm able to pay for your chance to do better. I swear, if I could, I'd make you sharecrop like your grandfather to know what real work is. Instead, you're going to stock all summer just to show you why you're going to college. Got it?"

"Yes, sir." Mack started to get up.

"Sit back down." Cal went on: "Why were you late coming home?"

"I . . . was trying out for the team again," Mack admitted.

Hearing that, their father sounded as if he were about to pop a blood vessel. "You already tried this UT baseball thing last summer! Even after you injured your arm!"

"My arm feels good again, Pop. I think it's healed," Mack said. "I got my fastball up a notch this spring, and the head coach invited me to try out again. I really have a good chance this time. Coach said he'd let me know if I made it by the end of June, in just a couple of weeks."

Cal fumed. "When are you going to grow up?"

To that, Mack fumed his own fume. "I should've taken that Jacksboro Baptist College scholarship. They sure thought my arm would heal."

"Use the brain your mother and I gave you, son. What would that diploma be worth compared to one from the University of Texas? And don't even think about telling me you'd have gotten a job playing in the pros!"

"You dreamed big! You saying I can't?"

At that point, things got loud.

"*That's it!*" their father said at the top of his voice. "You will stock for me all summer. Then you will go back to school, forget this baseball nonsense, and get those grades up, or you are on your own."

"That's not fair! Don't you care what I want?" Mack hollered.

"Not when you're acting like a child!" their dad hollered back.

With that, Belle put her favorite classical music piece, "Clair de Lune," on the living room's hi-fi record player, sat down on the couch, and closed her eyes. Corky went on up to her room, where, to the sound of "Clair de Lune" and angry male voices, she went back to reading *To Kill a Mockingbird*.

Finally, Mack stomped past her bedroom at the top of the stairs and slammed his own bedroom door.

Putting her finger in her book to mark where she was, she walked down the hall and knocked on his door.

"*What?*"

"It's me."

"What do you want, Bug?"

"Stop calling me that."

"I will when you stop bugging me."

He and Papa Cal—her grandfather Cal Corcoran Sr.—thought it a hoot when Mack started calling her that as a kid after hearing her parents say she was *cute as a bug,* and even Papa Cal began calling her *Cricket* to have a nice little joke with young Mack. She never liked it. And that made teasing her even more fun for them, of course.

Corky started to leave. But then she heard her brother sigh. "I'm just mad, Bug. C'mon in. What do you want?"

Opening the door to see a still steamed Mack flopped on his bed, she asked, "What is *rape?*"

Mack sat straight up. "Why are you asking that? Did something happen?"

"No, it's in this book."

"Book? What the hell are you reading? Let me see it."

She handed it to him. "Miss Delacourt says it won a prize and was made into a movie still playing in Fort Worth. Have you read it?"

He looked at the back cover and said, "Heard about it. Let me borrow it tonight. I'm not going to sleep, anyway, and God knows I need something else to think about."

Corky didn't want to do that. After all, she wasn't finished with it. She just wanted him to explain a word to her. But she said, "Okay," and slowly left.

"Close the door, will ya, Bug?"

As she did, Corky saw him open the book and start reading.

3

The next morning, Corky found the library book on the edge of her bed when she woke up. Her brother must have stayed up most of the night reading it.

Throwing on a shirt and shorts, she looked in his room for him, thinking she might finally get an answer to her question about the word in the book. But he wasn't there. So, she thumbed through the book to find her place again and saw pencil marks . . . Mack had underlined things! It was a library book! You didn't mark up a library book! Flipping through the pages, she saw he'd underlined half a dozen passages. She'd recall that moment years later, remembering one passage over all the rest. Atticus Finch, the lawyer hero of the book, was telling his son, Jem, that he wouldn't see the laws change before he died, and if Jem did, he'd be an old man. Maybe it was just the shock of her big brother marking up a library book, which was close to a sin in her young world. Maybe the memory would stick because the laws really were starting to change. Or it could just have been the way powerful words linger in a well-told story. But none of that was on Corky's mind at the time as she scrambled for an eraser. She had to clean up the book before Miss Delacourt saw, and she used almost the entire eraser end of a #2 pencil trying to make it look new again.

Just as she finished, she heard voices downstairs.

"But, Cal, today's newspaper even says the new Civil Rights Act will include women."

"That's for women without husbands who have to work, Belle. It's not normal. And it'll look bad for business, as if we need the money."

"It's not about money. Whatever job I find will just be part-time until Corky's out of school and—"

"You already volunteer at the library. Why do you want to be a working girl? Why isn't taking care of us enough? It was for my mother. Do you want another baby?"

"What? No! It's not about that."

"I'm late for work, Belle."

Hearing the back screen door whap shut and her father's drugstore truck pull away, Corky started to go downstairs. But she heard a familiar sound out front.

Whack!

The sound was coming from across the street.

Whack!

Going down the stairs, Corky saw Mack through the front door's glass panel. He was over in the sandy, fenceless field across the street with Roy Rogers, pitching at the big oak tree. He'd dropped a bucket of old hardballs in the place he'd marked for a pitcher's mound long ago and was whacking the hell out of the tree, Roy running after each and every ball.

Whack!

It was what her brother had done all through elementary and junior high school, spending hours out there, trying to hit makeshift targets he'd carved in the wood to mark the strike zone, catcher high.

Whack!

Over the years, as his aim got better, he'd worn a place in the bark, wearing out baseballs and the bark of the poor tree until their father finally noticed and, at the risk of evoking the Wrath of Dad, made him go to the school's baseball field to do damage to the school's property instead.

Whack!

Today, though, Mack didn't seem to care about the Wrath of Dad.

Corky scooted out the front door and over to him. "Hi," she tried.

He didn't answer, winding up and letting another one go.

Whack!

Roy Rogers loped over and scooped up the ball.

"Did you like that book?" she asked.

"Liking it is not the real point, I don't think," Mack mumbled, picking up another ball and winding up.

Whack!

"You shouldn't mark in a library book," she said.

He picked up another ball in response.

Corky didn't know what to say at that point. So, she said what she was thinking: "Are you still mad at Dad?"

WHACK!

She decided she'd better change the subject since her brother still seemed pretty mad. "Is Coach Trumbull going to help America get to the Olympics?" she tried next.

Mack picked up another ball. "No track coach is going to see what he saw and just let it go. It'd be a feather in his cap if he helps her get a chance to *train* for the Olympics, much less go." Instead of throwing it, he clutched the new ball hard enough to turn his knuckles red. "I hope America does play softball with your team. I hope she burns up the bases. She needs to see what she can do and show everybody else. Everybody's got a right to try filling their God-given potential, *right?*"

Corky wasn't sure whether they were still talking about America. As sympathetic as she could muster, she answered, "Right."

And he turned and threw the ball.

WHACK!

Seeing him throw it that hard, Corky decided it might be wise to change the subject back to the book. "I haven't finished the library book yet. I like it so far, but I'm sure glad I don't live back then."

Mack was fuming, his emotions roiling. Like so many college students in the '60s, his freshman year was an education far beyond the classroom. After growing up in High Cotton, everything he'd heard and seen on campus had opened his eyes. He learned about the recent sit-ins where Black students requested service at lunch counters across not only the city but the country. Soon, most counters opened to all. He heard about the even more recent stand-ins that integrated the campus's movie theater: Both Black and White students lined up to ask if the ticket seller sold to Blacks. When the answer was no, students got back in line to keep real customers from entering by showtime. Soon, the theater opened to all. And yet he'd learned that while the university had been integrated for years, it still had no Black scholarship athletes.

He picked up another ball and studied his little sister. "I'm going to tell you something I didn't tell Dad," he said. "With my arm feeling good this spring, I started practicing my fastball as much as I could, getting ready to try out again. One day, I went to do some pitching at the intramural fields with a buddy. A Black guy was already there doing the same thing on one of the fields with his buddy. We started to move on to another field, but I saw the guy pitch. He had a knuckleball you wouldn't believe, like a fluttering butterfly, so we sat down and watched for a while. Then he threw a beauty of a slider. And that did it. I told the guy he should talk to a baseball coach for a tryout, too. Somebody's got to be first. I mean, hell, Jackie Robinson broke into the major leagues in 1947!" Mack shook his head. "You know what the guy told me? He'd already asked for one—the UT coaching staff wasn't 'ready,'" Mack fumed. "I'm telling you, that guy's knuckleball was a frigging fluttering *butterfly*. The whole thing's nuts." He picked up another ball. "It's been over thirty years since the time of the story in that book. Things should be better. Everybody's got a right to try filling their God-given potential! *Everybody!*"

And he threw the ball. *WHACK!*

Blowing out a big, cleansing breath, he started picking up the loose balls and dumping them back in the bucket, all but the one that Roy Rogers still had in his mouth. Roy dropped the ball at Mack's feet. Mack picked it up, wiped at the slobber, and instead of dropping it into the bucket, he turned and hurled it so hard at the tree, the ball left a dent in the old dent, right in the heart of his target mark.

Corky didn't understand most of what her brother had said. But she noticed he hadn't answered her original question, so she thought she'd try one more time. "Yeah, okay, but what does *rape* mean?"

To that, her big brother sighed. "Bug, you need to go ask Mother. I don't think I'm the one to tell you about that. I've got to go feed Goldy before going to Papa Cal's." He picked up the bucket and walked toward the corral.

Confused and a little frustrated, Corky headed back through the front door and made her way to the kitchen. Her mother was sitting at the table staring at her plate of cold, untouched eggs.

"Mom?"

"Good morning, dear. I'll make you breakfast," Belle said, getting up and moving toward the stove.

"Is something wrong?" Corky asked, sitting down at her place.

"No, dear. Everything's fine," her mom said as she began cracking eggs.

Loudly.

Sometimes even Corky knew not to ask her mother anything. She stayed tight-lipped even though she was bursting with questions. And not just about the word in the book. As she watched her mother prepare breakfast, she was replaying her parents' fight she'd overheard a few minutes ago. And she was even more confused. Her dad had stated the only truth Corky knew about working women. If you were married, you were a housewife. "A woman's place is in the home," the saying went. Unless, of course, your husband wasn't a good breadwinner and you had to work to make ends meet—or unless you had the misfortune to not even have a husband. If you were single after the age of twenty, you were on the verge of being considered an *old maid*, so you were expected to be husband-hunting double-time. If you weren't married by thirty, you were pretty much relegated to spinsterhood. This was the world Corky had grown up in. And the world you grow up in always feels like the way it has always been and will always be. Until it isn't.

As Corky watched her mother, she couldn't picture her doing anything but being her mother at home waiting to cook her eggs. The only time she saw her mother show any talent for anything beyond mothering was Corky's Girl Scout Cookie sale years. Belle got into it more than Corky did. She seemed to enjoy surveying Corky's handwritten list of sales after Corky spent her Saturday knocking on the neighbors' doors. More than once, when Corky had missed a neighbor, Belle would actually call and sell them cookies over the phone, and get a bang out of adding them to Corky's list. Once, ten-year-old Corky had accidentally on purpose skipped their next-door neighbor Mrs. Poindexter, who was famous for her cluttered lawn ornament collection with boring accompanying stories. ("What do you think of my new garden gnome? It just showed up one day! Mr. Poindexter said somebody dumped it here, but I think the little gnome knew I'd give it a good home. And did you see my little garden fairy? And my pink flamingos? And I bet you can see my glow-in-the-dark American flag lighthouse all the way to your house! I bought it at a Stuckey's on our way to visit my sister in Waco because it just called to me! Oh, the stories my lawn can tell!") When Belle perused Corky's sales list that night, she'd noticed the omission. "Didn't you try Mrs. Poindexter, Kathryn?" Being only ten at the time, Corky nodded, at first, until the nod turned into a headshake.

"Well, we'll just call her." Corky's mother picked up the phone, called their talkative neighbor, and got an order of five boxes of Thin Mints for the price of hearing one of her lawn ornament stories.

Belle placed a plate of scrambled eggs, sausage, grape juice, and cinnamon toast in front of Corky. Corky didn't know what to think. Her usual summer breakfast was just a bowl of Frosted Flakes to go with her grape juice. She watched her mother closely as Belle went to the sink to pick up a dish towel, because once she had it in her hand, she just stood staring out the kitchen window. Corky gobbled down the eggs and started on the rest. But, glancing back at her mother, she paused. Belle hadn't moved, still staring out the window, dish towel in hand.

By the time Corky finished the rest of her breakfast, Evangeline and America appeared at the back door. Corky popped to her feet. "I'll let them in."

Corky opened the screen door. As she followed them into the kitchen, she noticed they matched again: Evangeline's house smock and America's blouse were made from the same fabric, this time a deep-blue paisley.

"I like your dress and America's shirt," Corky said to Evangeline, figuring she was the one who was creating the matching clothes.

Evangeline grinned proudly at America. "Her papà brought home a machine that sews, and now she dresses *me*! My America is very talented, yes? She will be rich and famous. *Tann epi wè*—wait and see!"

Corky's jaw dropped. Her one attempt at making a dress was for a six-week home economics class that she was forced to take with the high schoolers—and what she made was so ugly that Corky played hooky the day all the girls were slated to wear their creations to school. "You sew *that* good?" Corky said.

America just smiled her shy smile as they all stepped into the kitchen.

"I don't think we'll be needing America today, Evangeline. We're doing just fine," Belle said, finally putting the dish towel back on the sink. "Mack can take her home. Tomorrow, though, do please come back, America, will you? You can help Kathryn and me with the church women's group, if you don't mind."

"I'll go with them," Corky announced, rushing up to change into her dress. "I can be early to the store."

"Oh, and, Kathryn," Belle said, "your father wanted me to remind Mack to take Roy Rogers over to Papa Cal's this morning. Papa Cal asked for him. Tell your brother, please."

Corky ran up to her room and threw on a dress for the drugstore over her shorts. Then, eyeing her sneakers and realizing a great opportunity to sneak them by her mother, she slipped them on and rushed down the stairs and out the front door.

In a few minutes, America and Corky were both settled into the back seat of Mack's '57 Chevy, Roy Rogers already in the front. Part of Mack's summer job was to check in on Papa Cal before stocking the store every day. And that was fine by Corky. That meant she might not have to see Papa Cal as much, because whatever familial responsibility lessons she was supposed to be learning by being around her cranky old grandfather, they weren't taking.

After Mack backed his old Chevy out of the driveway, though, instead of turning left to hit the main road that would lead them over the railroad tracks to the Southside, he turned right. Corky panicked. She thought for sure that meant he was going to make them all go to Papa Cal's first. She didn't want America to meet Papa Cal, and certainly not the other way around. As cranky grandfathers went, Papa Cal was Olympic material of his own. He had lived his whole life in allegiance to Jim Crow laws, and yet his constant companion was a Black man named Willy with whom he'd worked for sixty years sharecropping on Boatwright land. At eighty, both Papa Cal and Willy had been born in the nineteenth century and lived their entire hardworking lives inside the confines of the High Cotton city limits with all that would exclude. Plus, Papa Cal was now legally blind, seeing nothing but blurs and shapes, yet refusing to wear Coke-bottle-thick glasses, and that just magnified his crankiness. So, after a lifetime of tenant farming, he spent his days gazing toward the window at the land he'd farmed his entire life that he could only see in his memories. Most mornings, Willy was dropped off by the drugstore delivery boy to sit with Papa Cal and watch Texas Rangers baseball on TV, Willy turning down the TV sound and turning up the radio for the play-by-play. Every Sunday, though, Corky had to go. Since Papa Cal was also unable to read the newspaper anymore, and Willy didn't like reading out loud, Corky's dad brought her over to read the Sunday paper to him. And once a week with her grandfather was quite enough.

So, Corky was about to object loudly to this change of plans when Mack pulled up to the church instead. He looked back at America. "We need to get you a pair of gym shoes for our softball practice tonight. And don't say you'll go barefoot, America, you just can't."

"But I can't buy anything right now," America said. "Not until my father gets a new job."

"We'll figure out something, don't worry," Mack answered. "It's just that you've got to have some shoes to play in *today*. Let's go check with Pastor Pete."

As they all walked into his office, Pete looked up from cleaning his glasses. "Why, hi, Corcorans—and America. Oh, and your dog, I see. Hello there, Roy. What can I do for you this morning?" he said, putting his glasses back on his nose. "The practice is at 5:00, right? Everybody excited?"

"We need to get America some shoes to play ball in tonight," Mack said. "She's outgrown her gym shoes."

Pete shook his head. "We don't have anything in the budget for softballs, much less shoes. Everybody's got to bring their own gear, you know that, Mack. But I guess we can look in the missionary barrel, although I don't recall seeing any canvas shoes in there."

Mack frowned. "Girls, let's go. I got another idea."

"Well, okay," said Pastor Pete. "We'll see y'all at five at the ballfield. And don't forget to bring your gloves, balls, and bats!"

Downtown, one of the handful of still-in-business shops was a shoe store that had done quite nicely for over fifty years and would continue to do so until Fort Worth grew too close to ignore the better footwear deals there. An older couple, the Daniels, manned the store every day, all day, by themselves. They had inherited the store from Daniels's father, who first opened it in 1910 during High Cotton's prime. And that explained why the store's setup was different from the other remaining downtown stores along the tracks. The Daniels had maintained the throwback design of its heyday era's Jim Crow laws. The storefront facing the main street was the Northside folks' entrance, and the Southside folks' entrance was in the alley along the railroad tracks. Much like the segregating track itself, it was just the way it had always been. But in 1959, after attending a shoe convention in Chicago, Mr. Daniels came home and closed the back entrance, putting up a big sign directing Southside customers to the front, much to the consternation of Mrs. Daniels. For a while, no Southside customers came at all. When they finally did, both Northside and Southside shoppers were openly uncomfortable with his newfangled idea. So, to satisfy both types of hometown customers, he was forced to return to the segregated status quo inside. But he refused to open the railroad-track back entrance, forcing all his customers to use the front door, together. And that was the way it was the day Mack, Corky, and America visited to find America some softball practice shoes.

As the door chimes announced their presence, Mr. Howard "Dan" Daniels looked up from rearranging a display. He was grandfatherly charming, ready to hand anyone under twelve a lollipop, and invited people of every age to call him Mr. Dan. His wife, Mrs. Daniels, however, was tetchy and had been for as long as Corky could recall. It was like she had been going through "the change of life" for most of Corky's life—which was Cal Corcoran's usual wry comment about tetchy women of a certain age. Not even commanding a stash of lollipops seemed to make her happy, Corky had thought as a kid.

So, as Mack, America, and Corky entered the front door, leaving Roy in the car with the windows rolled halfway down, they all moved toward Mr. Dan as Mrs. Daniels poked her head out of the stockroom.

"Dear, I'll handle these customers," Mr. Dan said to his wife. "Hello, Mr. Mack and Miss Katie!" he said, using Cal Corcoran's name for Corky. "How may I help you this fine day?"

Mack spoke up. "Mr. Dan, let me introduce you to America."

"How do you do, young lady?" Mr. Daniels said, bowing ever so slightly. "Have you been here before?"

America shook her head.

"She doesn't talk much," Corky offered. "She's shy, not stuck-up."

Mr. Dan smiled. "I see."

"We need to get her some gym shoes," Mack said, eyeing the large display of all kinds of canvas shoes that, at the time, were called anything from *tennis shoes* to *gym shoes* to *sneakers*, Keds being the brand seemingly every kid in the '50s and '60s wore.

America, staring nervously at the display, motioned to Mack. Mack came closer. "I promise I can buy some new sneakers when my father gets home," she whispered.

"But you need them now," Mack whispered back to her. "How about this—if we find some, I'll pay for them, and you can pay me back when he gets home, okay?"

That seemed to satisfy her.

"Okay, Miss America," Mr. Dan said. "I assume you'll be more comfortable through here." And he guided the group through the stockroom to the Southside customers' area.

Mack hesitated, not liking it, but followed.

As soon as they were in the Southside area, Mr. Dan said, "Please have a seat. Now, athletic shoes, you say?"

"America's outgrown the sneakers she has, and she's going to be playing with our church softball team starting tonight," Mack explained.

"Ah yes. So I heard."

That surprised Corky. "You have?"

Mr. Dan didn't even answer, as if the fact that news traveled fast in a tiny town went without comment. "Let's see what size you are. I like to guess. It's a game I play. If I'm wrong, we'll use the sizer and everybody gets a lollipop. So, let me see. Oh my, you're surely a women's eleven! This might be tough." He picked up a pair off the discount rack. "These are tens. We could try 'em."

Mack frowned, glancing back at the stockroom, where Mrs. Daniels was peeking through the curtains. "Got anything else?"

Mr. Dan thought for a moment. "Well, not in her size. You have large feet, my dear, for a young lady!"

Better to run like the dang Wilma Rudolph wind! Corky thought.

"Well, we could try a boy's shoe, maybe size nine or ten," Dan was saying, turning back to the discount rack.

At that, Mack got up, trudged through the stockroom past Mrs. Daniels to the Northside area, and came back with a nice pair of men's Keds the same size as the track shoes America had used. Mack unboxed them and told America to try them on.

She did. They fit.

"We'll take these," Mack said, reaching for his billfold. "What do we owe you?"

Dan smiled again. "They're on me."

Glancing back at Mrs. Daniels watching from the stockroom, Mack bristled. "Why would you do that?"

"I heard she's so fast, she could be good enough to make it to the Olympics," Mr. Dan answered. "If true, I want to be the one who put her in her first pair of good athletic shoes. I'll also order some women's track shoes for the same reason, on the house, as well," he added, looking at both America and Mack. "Just say the word."

Breaking into a grin, Mack shook hands with Mr. Dan and even nodded at Mrs. Daniels, who, while still looking mighty tetchy, had at least come out from behind the stockroom's curtains to see them off.

Outside, Roy was still in the car's front seat, so Corky and America climbed into the back. America was holding the box of sneakers in her lap. But she wasn't happy. "He didn't have to do this."

Mack climbed into the driver's seat and looked back at her. "America, it isn't charity. He'd heard how fast you are."

"Still, would you just bring them to the practice tonight for me?"

Mack frowned, puzzled. "Sure, but why?"

America glanced Corky's way for help. Corky realized she didn't want Evangeline to know about them for some reason. "She just wants you to, okay?" Corky blurted.

Mack's eyebrows popped up. "Whatever you girls think is best. You sure we can't pick you up for practice, America?"

America shook her head. "I know where the ballfield is."

"Well, all right. We'll see you there. But, remember, either Pastor Pete or I will be taking you home afterward like we promised," Mack said, putting the car in gear.

Steering the car to the drugstore a block over, he pulled to a stop under the big sign announcing "Corcoran Drugs—Service to the Sick."

"Here you go, Bug. Jump out."

Flashing America a big smile, Corky slammed the car door and headed inside. But when she heard Roy bark and another door slam, Corky whirled around to see that America had hopped out, too, and was already trotting across the railroad tracks to the Southside.

"What happened?" she called to Mack.

"Nothing. She just said she could make it from here and left. Look, it's fine. I gotta go check on Papa Cal," he said and pulled away.

On the other side of the railroad tracks, America looked back. Watching Corky enter the drugstore and Corky's brother and dog drive away, she paused a moment to consider all the things that had occurred since yesterday. Something new was happening, different than ever before, and she wasn't sure what to make of it.

Walking down the Southside's dirt streets, she thought about her mother at the Corcorans' big house with their full bookshelf . . . about racing Corky's brother and rushing to the Northside school's track to meet the White coach . . . about putting on track shoes for the first time and stepping into what the coach called blocks . . . about hearing she was fast, maybe very, very fast . . . about the First Baptist preacher, out of the blue, asking her to play softball with his church's girls' team . . .

And now the downtown shoe-store man had *given* her a pair of sneakers?

America sighed as she passed the Mount Olive Baptist Church. *Mamà won't like the free shoes, because Papà won't like it,* she thought. But her father wasn't there . . . and that was new, too.

Pausing at the picket-fence gate of their cream-colored rental house with her mother's rocker on the front porch, she glanced back toward the railroad tracks and downtown. She still didn't know quite how to feel about it all. Something told her she should be uneasy. But as she opened the gate and went into the house, she realized she was smiling.

4

Having a drugstore daddy was, for Corky, like having her own weird wonderland of comic books, candy, Band-Aids, liniment, and strange bottles galore. The store consisted of four walls like any other store. But the two that fronted the main and side streets consisted entirely of big plate-glass windows showing off display cases of King Edward cigars; Lucky Strike cigarettes; pocketknives for all occasions; and carousels of comics, magazines, and paperbacks—along with the town's only cosmetic corner, loaded with face powder, mascara, lipsticks, and perfumes, complete with a powder-puff-pink chair where the town's beautiful women, or beautiful-to-be, could park their derrieres and test the testers to their faces' content. Several aisles over, nowhere near the padded chair, was the lone shelf of Black beauty products—hair straighteners, Afro Sheen, Satin Sheen, and such. The other two walls featured the entire length of the soda fountain, with its dozen seats, and the main counter, fronting a raised employees-only prescription area with floor-to-ceiling medicine shelves and a place for Cal Corcoran to stand and see the entire store while typing Rx labels two-fingered on his manual Underwood typewriter. That included a clear view of the soda fountain, where, this summer, Corky was learning the joys of creating banana splits, malted milkshakes, fountain Dr Peppers, and grilled cheese on the griddle for the customers.

And Corky thought it heaven itself.

After Mack let her out of the car, she'd gone in through the store's side entrance. Remembering her parents' fight that morning, Corky glanced hesitantly up at her father on the raised prescription area. Cal noticed and motioned her to him, pulling a coin from his pocket. "Got something for you, Katie." It was a worn 1898 Indian Head penny. The two of them had been doing this since she started first grade, her father deciding that since a steady stream of coinage was always coming through the store, coin collecting, at least the casual jar-filling kind, was something his creative, curious little girl would like. Not to mention that coins were literally money. Corky beamed, rubbing her finger over the still visible headdress on the penny. But since her dress didn't have pockets, she gave it back to him to bring home that night to put in her jar.

"Ah yes, of course," he said and pocketed it. "You do look very lady-like. Remember, now, you're working, and the customer is always right."

"Yessir," she said, straightening her dress. With her parents' fight still on her mind, though, she felt deeply confused about other things her dad had told her over the years. In third grade, when her little tomboy self had jumped on a boy who was making fun of her for being chubby, her father had belly-laughed and said, "Good girl. Don't you take guff from anyone." Did he like her being a tomboy, or did he agree with her mother that she should be a lady, too? If so, did being ladylike mean taking guff at the store if the customer really is always right? And there was the other thing: About the same time as the no-guff fight advice, she'd told him she wanted to be either a baseball player or a librarian or an astronaut. He'd belly-laughed again and said, "You can be anything you want, and don't let anyone tell you different." But that very morning, she'd heard her mother and father fight about what her mother wanted to be. How could Corky be anything she wanted if her mom couldn't?

Earl, standing at the front counter, turned toward them. "Katie, honey," Earl said, using the name her dad called her, just as Velma, Velvadine, and Mr. Dan did. "Will you please make this little boy a strawberry ice-cream cone?"

A seven- or eight-year-old Black boy was standing there with his fist clutched around his quarter. Corky pushed all her confusion down deep, trusting she'd figure it out one way or the other, and happily went to fulfill the boy's order.

As she scooped and delivered the ice-cream cone to the boy, in walked Mr. Noah Ulysses Boatwright IV, the eldest living Boatwright. A big, doughy specimen of a man with an awkwardly receding hairline, he nodded curtly at her dad up on his prescription area, who nodded curtly back. Then he sat down on his usual fountain stool and ordered his usual lunch: a grilled cheese and three bottles of Coca-Cola, which he'd consume one by one while reading the *Fort Worth Star-Telegram*.

To say Corky's father, Cal, did not like him was the truest of understatements, and the feeling was deeply mutual. They'd gone to school together. He was the fourth-generation High Cotton Boatwright. By 1964, the one thousand acres of land owned and cultivated by Noah I in the 1870s had been sold off piece by piece. So, all that was left was the money, the town's only mansion situated on a slight rise northwest of town, and Noah I's wastrel great-grandson Noah IV, who found a mousy wife with whom he'd had two sons Mack's and Corky's ages—Noah V, who the family called Bubba, and his younger brother, Thaddeus, who the family called Tad. The story went that, years ago, right after Cal had bought the store, he saw a tipsy Noah IV slap young Bubba in front of Tad after bringing them in for ice cream. Corky's dad stepped down from his prescription area perch and gave Noah IV a tongue-lashing in front of God and everybody. Since the elder Boatwright was drunk, the upbraiding didn't take. So, when it happened again, her father not only read him the riot act but called High Cotton's cop, Tommy Tilton. Noah IV was so sauced, he actually waited around for Tommy to arrive, telling Cal to mind his own business and turning to slap Bubba again. This time, though, Earl stopped him, grabbing Noah IV's hand before it hit young Bubba, twisting his arm behind him, and shoving him onto a fountain stool. After that, whenever Belle would comment on Earl's whiskey breath, Cal would always remind her of that day. As a Boatwright, though, Noah IV wasn't about to go to jail, even if High Cotton had one. So, when Tommy arrived, Tommy called the new Baptist minister, Pastor Pete. And at the very sight of a preacher, as if he were a stand-in for the Judgment of God Almighty, Noah IV crumpled into a weepy mush. After that, he went to a Billy Graham crusade, found Jesus, got sober and religious. Next thing everybody knew, Noah IV was in the Baptist church choir belting out hymns in his off-key baritone louder than anybody else and, just as quick, was made a deacon.

In the Southern Baptist tradition, there are no bishops or the like, no hierarchy exercising authority over church members. Every church can do whatever they want . . . inside the teachings of the Bible, the leading of the Holy Spirit, and, when it suited them, the Southern Baptist denomination leaders, as any Baptist would take pains to explain. What the First Baptist Church of High Cotton had, instead, was a board of deacons, all God-fearing married men of good moral character who thought their true job was to keep the preacher in line. Or, as they'd formally put it: to assist the pastor in doing the church's work of budgeting, serving, and saving souls. Of course, the problem was that there were only so many souls to save; therefore, many of them got re-saved quite a bit, which made for a fine system to keep the congregation on the straight and narrow, but only when it continued to work. So, having a shining example of a dramatic conversion, like Noah Boatwright IV's, was witness to all that the Baptist church members held dear. Hence him quickly being voted onto the deacon board.

All Corky's father would ever say when the subject of the elder Boatwright came up was that there was nothing more irritating than a rich born-again boozer.

Noah IV stopped hitting the boys, as far as anyone could tell, so the conversion seemed real. Tad, the younger son, was sweet, with wavy blond hair and big water-blue eyes, and stayed more that way than his older brother, Bubba, perhaps because he got the back of his father's hand less. Bubba, though, was another matter. Such acts of violence

imprint a child deeply in ways no amount of apology or redemption
can fully wash away. Bubba had begun bullying other boys in elementary school, and that didn't stop after his father found Jesus. Being big
and doughy like his father, he'd pick fights with anybody who looked
crossways at him all through school, and that was pretty much everybody, including, and perhaps especially, Mack Corcoran. Bubba was
the bully who had made eleven-year-old Mack teach Roy Rogers the
"Roy, want a bite?" trick of baring his fangs. And he seemed to have it
out for Mack, day in and day out, calling him Miss Goody Two-Shoes,
probably because Bubba couldn't call his father Miss Goody Two-Shoes,
no matter how much he wanted to. By high school, Bubba was well into
his own drinking problem, wrecking his Corvette half a dozen times
on the two-lane road between High Cotton and Broke Spoke Tavern
fifteen miles up the Fort Worth–Decatur highway, where no one ever
bothered to check his or anyone else's ID.

So, Mack and Bubba had as little love lost between them as Cal
Corcoran and Noah Boatwright IV, as if the sins of the fathers were
carved somewhere on the family trees.

But, after Noah IV finished his soda fountain lunch that summer
day in '64, Corky saw him stop by the drugstore's main counter and
call Corky's father down to talk, which was a deeply strange thing to
behold. Corky had never seen them do more than the curt nodding
they'd done when Noah IV had arrived. But now they were talking quietly and seriously, both glancing back at the soda fountain . . . straight,
it seemed, at her.

Corky tensed. *Are they talking about me?*

Moving behind the candy rack at the end of the fountain, she
inched nearer to eavesdrop.

"That can't be true," Corky heard her father say. "Where'd you hear
that?"

"I've got my sources, Corcoran. You know how things are right
now, what with all this Civil Rights Act crap stirring up trouble. You
better be ready."

Ready? Corky thought. *Ready for what?*

"Katie, want to help with these banana splits?" Velma called to her.

By the time Corky finished squirting whipped cream on top of the fountain creations, Noah IV had left.

Not fifteen minutes later, just as she was delivering an ice-cream cone to another Black boy at the main counter, she noticed her dad up on the prescription area talking with the town's Black doctor, Dr. Ambrose DuBose. The good doctor, dressed as always in a dark suit and tie, was round as a bull with a crinkled-hair mane he wore like a crown. He was a frequent visitor to her father's prescription area perch, just like Drs. Alexander Sr. and Jr., the town's White doctors. That alone wasn't enough to make Corky curious. It was the way they were talking low, like secrets . . . exactly the same way her dad had been talking to Noah IV. To her thirteen-year-old eyes, unless they were belly-laughing or telling their corny jokes, all adult conversations looked serious and boring. But something about those two very different men talking to her father in whispers on the same day made her take note. The adults in her life were always a mystery, but today they seemed more so than usual.

"That's what Boatwright just said," her father was telling Dr. DuBose. "You heard anything about it?"

At that, the big doctor, no longer whispering, all but boomed, "Not in my town!"

With that, everyone looked around as Dr. DuBose stormed out the side door.

And Corky began to wonder if she was missing something big.

After begging her father to stay longer, since she wasn't coming the next day, Corky left the soda fountain with plenty of time to make softball practice at 5:00 p.m. Mack had already left for Papa Cal's to take Willy home. So, after making herself an ice-cream cone, Corky headed home on foot.

Just about the time she was finishing the last of her cone, where the ice cream had melted into the little grooves, Tad Boatwright appeared out of nowhere on his bike.

"Hi," he said.

"Hi," she said, swallowing the rest.

As much as Bubba and Mack hated each other, Tad and Corky were pals, at least in the way that kids in a tiny town are always being thrown together. They'd been in Sunday school and nursery school and grade school together. He'd sat in front of her in every classroom, due to alphabetical order, and she'd kick his seat when she was bored. On Sundays, since Tad and his mother always sat behind Corky and Belle in church, he'd return the favor when he was bored. If the school desks still had inkwells and Corky wore pigtails, Tad would have been the boy behind her, dipping her pigtail into the ink, which would have probably made Corky punch him, and they would have made up until he did it again. In short, he was sweet on her. And, while she'd never admit it, she liked it.

Over the spring, however, some mighty puberty-driven things had happened to him, too. Pleasantly plump Tad was now as skinny as Corky, a few inches taller, and cute as the dang devil. And Corky had noticed, her attraction to the way he now looked being more than a little confusing. It was as if they'd both changed into entirely new people. He'd had a bit of a hormonal head start on Corky, though, and that was about to become obvious. He stood there for a moment, grinning at her. That was all. Just grinning. It was a new grin, a half grin, cockeyed and full of new meaning.

She stared at his grin. "What's wrong with you?"

He just kept grinning. "Hop on. I'll take ya home."

She did. Instead of turning toward Corky's house, though, Tad biked them to the school and pulled to a stop out of sight around the building's far side.

"What are you doing?" she said, getting off.

Getting off, too, he popped the kickstand and said, "Want to kiss?"

Want to kiss, her brain repeated, staring at this new Tad with his new grin and his new idea. ". . . Sure."

He leaned in and planted a kiss right on her lips. It was Corky's first kiss. Then he did it again. This time, though, he stuck his tongue in her mouth, which was about the strangest thing she'd ever felt.

She pulled back.

"Like it?" he said.

"I don't know," Corky mumbled.

"It's called a French kiss."

He leaned in again, but he kissed her like the first time, just longer. Much longer. Corky stepped back, breathing hard. And there was that half grin of his again. She melted, a dizzy new feeling rushing through her. For the next few minutes, the two practiced, trying out different positions for their noses between breaths . . . until a car rumbled by, popping Corky out of her kissing daze.

"What time is it?" Corky gasped. "Quick, get me home!"

They both got back on the bike, and Tad pedaled them away.

As soon as she could see her house, though, Corky made him stop and she hopped off.

"Hey," Tad said as she started to rush away, "Mollylynne Morehead's parents will be out of town getting a divorce Thursday, and she talked them into letting her stay by herself. And she's having a party soon as it gets dark. She only lives around the corner from you. You gotta come."

Mollylynne Morehead was a stuck-up ninth-grade girly-girl, the wild-child granddaughter of Mrs. Etta Mayweather, a sour church lady Papa Cal's age. So, Corky had no reason to hold a conversation with her, much less care whether she was invited to the girl's teenage party.

Until now.

"I dunno. Mom probably won't let me."

"Just sneak out!" Tad went on. "We're gonna play Spin the Bottle."

"What's that?" Corky said.

"You spin the bottle, and whoever it points to, you go in the closet and kiss."

"You mean, other boys? And you, other girls?"

"Yeah, but it'd be *you*! I'll rig it, you just wait," he said, his half grin going full as he sped away.

As Corky rushed up her driveway, Mack was putting the equipment bag in his car. "Where've you been? Dad said you left the store a long time ago."

"Nowhere . . . *None* of your *business* . . . *Stop bugging me*!" she spit, feeling her face flush as she smoothed her dress, which was crooked and wrinkled from running.

Mack's eyebrows popped high. "O-kay. Well, we're late for practice. Go change fast. I have to stop for a fill-up."

A minute later, as she rushed back down the stairs in her shorts, shirt, and sneakers ready to go, Belle called after her, "Take the dog! He's going to follow you anyway if I let him out. And I can't keep him in. I've got to cook dinner, and that would be torture for both of us."

"He grabs the balls, Mom!" Corky complained.

"Just tell him not to. I'd rather him be with you than roaming all over town trying to find you if he gets a mind to."

Roy Rogers, as if he'd understood every word, and perhaps he had, came bounding out behind them.

As they pulled into the town's only gas station a few minutes later, out came the station's attendant, Clifford Dean, who had lost an arm working at the cotton gin as a teenager. "Well, hi there, Mack and Corky," he said as Roy leaned out the window to get his usual ear rub from Cliff. "Fill 'er up?"

"Thanks, Cliff," Mack said.

Corky was usually mesmerized by how much Cliff could do with only one arm. But today, she had other things on her mind, and not all of them were about softball practice.

As Cliff finished, Mack handed him some cash, and they headed toward the baseball field. "Did you get your glove?" he asked Corky.

"Sure, I . . ." Corky looked around. She'd forgotten her glove.

"What is up with you today?" Mack asked as they entered the base-ball field's parking lot. "We're already late. Use one of the extra ones I brought. We don't have time to go back for it."

The high school's baseball field was rudimentary, to say the least. Immediately behind the field was the Northside's High Cotton school system, elementary through high school, spread across two blocks. But the football and baseball fields, along with their shared parking lot, lined the Fort Worth–Decatur highway just up from High Cotton's downtown area. In other words, the school athletic fields were at the heart of the town, but so was everything else, all bunched together along the same straight-arrow stretch of two-lane highway and railroad line. The high school's baseball field was shorter than average due to its location, sandwiched between the school and the much larger football field—football being, as the saying goes, a Texas religion. But it was still bigger than the usual softball field, if you didn't mind less home runs than the usual softball outing. Both fields' lights had been turned off for the summer. But that had never been a problem for the church teams' use, since their games were played in the early evening after the worst of the June heat, and had always finished long before dusk.

As Mack, Corky, and Roy Rogers got out of the car, the girls on the baseball field were chattering away. But when they saw Mack and Corky, they hushed in unison. Word about America had obviously spread to the members of the softball team, too.

Pastor Pete strode up to Mack, beaming. "Let's get this practice going! Mack Corcoran is our new coach, girls. Take your places!"

So the little ragtag team, along with Roy Rogers, rushed onto the field to start practicing for their one-and-only game. This being a town with no leash laws, other dogs had also followed their girls there, most aiming for litter patrol, hunting for dropped snacks under the metal stands where a few of the parents were sitting. Only Roy trotted out among the players, ball crazy and deliriously happy about his prospects.

The annual girls' softball game was an exercise in *can-do* for the girls—or, more to the point, *can I do*—one of the few chances that most of the tiny town's girls, on both teams, would ever be invited to try something beyond what was expected of them or what they expected of themselves. The girls on the Baptist team who could usually catch the ball were put on each of the bases. But no one ever wanted to be pitcher, probably since the entire game rested on the pitcher's ability to actually make the ball go where the thrower wanted it to go. So, early on, the two pastor-coaches had decided they'd fill the pitcher position for the girls' slow-pitch softball game each year. And, so far, that had fixed the problem.

This year, the 1964 summer Baptist girls' team consisted of one fifth grader, three sixth graders, two seventh graders, and two eighth graders.

The two seventh graders were the Birdsong twins Edith and Ethel, who, saddled with their grandmothers' names, chose to be called by their family nicknames, Onezy and Twozy. Onezy Birdsong was the first baseman. She never missed a catch. Throwing, however, was not her strong suit. Pastor Pete had put her on first base, since most of the time she didn't have to throw it anywhere except back to the pitcher, which she was working on.

Second baseman Lily Sue Wooldridge, a sixth grader, had about a 50 percent catching average when it was thrown to her. God forbid, though, if she had to throw it much farther than back to the pitcher's mound.

Shortstop was Corky, who every year lobbied for the position because that was where the action was.

Third base was sixth grader Prudence Macintosh. She did what she could. That was about all you could say.

Left field was Twozy Birdsong, her skills identical to her twin, Onezy—that was, great catching and not-so-great throwing.

Center field was sixth grader Sadie Springer, who was famous for running away from the ball until it hit the ground.

In right field was little fifth grader Thelma Lee Ledbetter, called Peanut for good reason, using what looked like her daddy's glove, which was almost as big as she was.

And playing catcher was squatty eighth grader Marilou Moon. Beyond the advantage of her squattiness making her closer to the ground, she also was relatively capable of catching the ball. Only one out of five times did it get by her in practice, which was good odds for this group.

As a team, the Baptist girls weren't any good. In fact, they were terrible. Roy Rogers was a better player than most of them. If he'd ever give the ball back, Pastor Pete might have thought about adding him to the team. The girls had all played scrub softball in elementary school during recess, but, beyond that, they barely knew the rules, much less how to play. Plus, even with their pastors taking the pitcher positions, most years they had to scramble to have enough players. Corky and the other girls had not been above pressuring a few girly Baptist girls to show up and stand there so they could play a game, often to the point of bribing them with free ice cream or toys or whatever it took. During Corky's first year on the team in fifth grade, little Prissy Larue arrived in a frilly pink dress and plastic play high heels and stood out in right field to earn the bribe Corky had offered: a Christmas gift Barbie doll that Corky hated. But this year, for the first time, the Baptist team had the exact right amount of willing players. So, if America showed up, the girls believed someone would have to sit on the bench, and that would probably be little Thelma Lee "Peanut" Ledbetter, who played right field because that's where the worst fielder was historically put. And Thelma Lee knew it.

So, everyone but Thelma was pumped up about the possibility of actually winning for the very first time with the help of a girl named America, who they heard could run as fast as the wind.

The minutes ticked by with no America in sight. And then there she was, hurrying across the tracks and highway toward the baseball field.

She was wearing a T-shirt and a pair of cutoff overalls, her hair pulled back in her usual long braid. Mack handed her a glove and the tennis shoes from Daniels' Shoe Store. And, as she put on the shoes, everybody, including Roy Rogers, gathered near to meet her. Except Thelma Lee.

"C'mon, Thelma, you need to meet our new player!" Pastor Pete coaxed.

Thelma pursed her lips, hugging herself. "My daddy said she shouldn't be playing with us."

Pastor Pete fumed, "He did, did he? Well, maybe your daddy needs to rededicate his life to Jesus if he can't open his heart to such a thing. And that goes for you, too, young lady. God's watching."

At that, Mack sighed and stepped over to her. "Thelma, is this about you worrying over not playing?"

Thelma nodded, lowering her head.

"Don't worry, okay?" said Mack. "I promise you'll play."

Deciding to believe Mack, Thelma went to meet America, too.

For a warm-up, instead of going back to their positions, the first thing Mack had the girls do was pair off and throw to each other, back and forth, back and forth, which would have been boring if everybody could actually catch, but since catching was always a toss-up, literally, anything could happen. Corky was paired up with America. The two of them were doing just fine until Onezy Birdsong decided to throw a hard one that her partner, Twozy, missed. The stray ball was headed straight for the back of Corky's head until America dashed over and caught it an instant before it whacked her. As Corky gawked at what might have been, America only smiled that shy smile, which now seemed less shy and more sly. And then she tossed Corky the ball.

As they warmed up, a few spectators appeared, which was very unusual.

First to arrive was a gaggle of high school girls. The word had spread that Mack Corcoran, hometown heartthrob, was home for the summer.

"Yoo-hoo, Mack! Mack Corcoran!" the girls called to him. Mack didn't acknowledge them, which just caused more giggling and *yoo-hoos*.

As the giggling gaggle kept it up, Thelma missed a throw from her partner, Prudence, that bopped Mack on the shin. Scooping it up,

Mack gestured to the waiting baseball diamond and said, "All right! Take your positions. America, why don't you play rover?"

This was exciting. The team had never had enough players for a rover, an added field position for softball. A rover, by definition, was an outfielder who could rove anywhere needed, so if fleet-footed America could catch, and she surely could, then she should surely rove.

Mack began hitting softballs all over the field, one after the other. And as America roved, Roy Rogers began to run after America, his first worthy opponent, barking with joy. Corky had worried that America might not like dogs when she flinched on first seeing Roy bounding out of the Corcorans' back door. But now America seemed to like Roy being there, even egging him on to keep up with her. America would catch a ball, pitch it to Roy, point to Mack, and, to everyone's surprise, Roy would trot to Mack and drop the ball at his feet.

America liked her dog.

And her dog liked America.

For that alone, Corky already loved her.

As they got fully into practice, Pastor Pete fed the balls to a bat-wielding Mack to keep everyone hustling, and all the girls did better than ever before, even little Thelma, who actually caught the only ball that Mack whacked out there.

The whole team was jubilant.

Meanwhile, even more spectators arrived.

"Mack! Yoo-hoo!" the growing girl gaggle started up again. The girls calling the loudest were sisters Sunny and Sandy Beach, a senior and a junior, whose parents thought it memorable, if not altogether wise, to name their children after beach adjectives. Although, seemingly proving the Roman expression *nomen est omen*, "name is destiny," the two were true visions of their names, blonde, svelte, and a touch bubbleheaded. And, now, hovering near them was Bubba Boatwright, who was there only because of the Beach sisters. The two had both dated Bubba, and their flirting Mack's way had Bubba worrying what Mack's return meant for Bubba's long-shot chances of getting back with either sister. So, he'd made it his summer pledge to pretty much stalk the Beach sisters, who thought nothing of it, since they and their giggling friends would be doing the same to Mack.

But the other new spectators came for a different reason. Since word had clearly spread beyond the team about the Baptists' "ringer," some were there just to see if the scuttlebutt about America was true. On the far side of the stands was the Methodist team's star player, Anna Mae Mulroney and, from the huge looks of him, her father. She was huge, too, with wild hair and a scowl that cowed most kids, especially since she could whop the whey out of any softball ever made. Year after year, long after the other high school Methodist girls turned boy-crazy and quit, Anna Mae kept playing in the church softball game. Now in the tenth grade, she was the only high schooler who still played. Until America. For the last several years, left-handed Anna Mae had almost single-handedly won all the Methodists' games for their team, knocking the leather off one home run ball after another, summer after summer, relishing her status as big dog. And for the very first time, here she was scouting the Baptist girls' team practice. Corky looked back and forth between Anna Mae and America. Anna Mae was usually both the biggest and tallest girl on either team. America was taller, but graceful in contrast to Anna Mae's bulk. And that made Corky smile. *Hey, high school girly-girls, you want to look graceful and athletic? Watch my new friend, America!* Corky wanted to yell. And she punched her glove in delight at the thought.

In the stands, another spectator arrived to scout the Baptists' new player. Sitting down by Anna Mae and her dad was the other team's coach, the Methodist minister, Reverend Douglas Gifford.

Reverend Doug was as chunky as Pete was skinny, looking the very picture of a minor-league player gone to seed. He was usually chewing gum, as he was now, which hinted at a past habit of chewing tobacco, like most ballplayers of the time. Except for pastoral visits to the sick and shut-in, the only time he wasn't chewing either a wad of Wrigley's Spearmint or Dubble Bubble was when he was at the pulpit, and, even there, he looked as if he should be. With all that gum experience, as one might imagine, he was also quite accomplished with his gum, able to chew, snap, smack, and pop, sometimes all in the same couple of chomps. The longer he watched America, the more serious his gum-chomping became.

Then he saw America do something remarkable. Roving near right field, she watched Mack hit a high pop fly to left field over Corky's head at shortstop. When left fielder Twozy began to run toward it, she tripped. Seeing that, America sprinted from right field all the way to left, getting there just in time to catch the ball before it hit the ground without even slowing down. And that did it. Reverend Doug stormed onto the ballfield straight for Pastor Pete.

"Hold on!" he said between agitated chews. "What's this all about?"

"Why, whatever do you mean?" Pastor Pete responded, straightening his glasses. "You don't have a problem with our new player, do you? I would never have considered you racist, Reverend Gifford."

Reverend Doug looked like he might implode. "Of *course* not!" he said, menacingly smacking his bubble gum in Pastor Pete's face. "But if you can have a Southside girl play for you, we can have one playing for us. Fair is fair," he said, fairness being one of the Christian values the game was supposed to be ingraining.

Pastor Pete leaned into Reverend Doug's face until the two looked like they were going to bite off each other's noses. "Be my guest."

Reverend Doug said, "I will." Giving his gum one last snap and roll, he marched off the field. From what the town would hear, he'd soon be calling all of High Cotton's Southside churches, even Mount Olive Baptist Church. But, if there were more Americas on the Southside, none were willing to play.

At the end of an hour, Mack and Pastor Pete figured the girls had practiced as much as their abilities could take. So, Pastor Pete waved everybody over to the Dairy Dip, High Cotton's ice-cream stand right by the field, for soft-serve curlicue cones all around. "My treat!" he announced, and the girls happily lined up under the giant "Smiling Swirl-Top Cone" sign to order at the stand's walk-up window.

For a few minutes, the team went quiet, enjoying their cones. When they all finished, Pastor Pete said, "America, a promise is a promise. I'll take you straight to your front door now."

"Corky and I'll do it," Mack called over as he stuffed the equipment bag into his car's trunk.

America suddenly tensed, looking at Corky. Her eyes said, *Don't come.* Corky hesitated, unsure if that was what America's look meant, since she was awful at taking hints. But she had to go. She just couldn't help herself. This would be her first chance to see what there was to see across the tracks. Her curiosity about the Southside, therefore, bested any sensitivity she was supposed to be nurturing.

"In," Mack commanded Roy Rogers. Roy jumped into the back seat and then immediately into the front, so America and Corky again got in the back.

Turning south at Corky's street, they bumped over the railroad track, and Corky felt a new, strange sensation, as if she were doing something forbidden. Because she was. Not once had her parents ever taken her across the tracks. Southsiders were always coming over to the Northside to work or shop, but while it was never said out loud, Northsiders weren't all that welcome on the Southside. Corky strained, trying not to miss anything, and immediately noticed differences: The city cemetery was situated where her own street hit the highway, but she had never noticed that there were two parts to it, one on her side of the highway and one on the other side. As for the street itself, on her side, the street was paved, but it wasn't on the Southside. In fact, while only some of the Northside roads were dirt, Corky noticed that *all* the Southside roads seemed to be. And while none of the houses on the Northside of the tracks were mansions, save for the Boatwrights', they all looked different. Not here. Almost all the houses they passed on the Southside were the same size and even the same color. Except for some scattered square-shaped homes with cream-colored siding, the

Southside houses all looked the same—twelve feet wide, bright-white, one-story rectangles. And there was a reason. They'd been built back in the town's boom days by Noah Boatwrights I and II to accommodate their cotton farm's growing labor force.

When the first structures of such design were built across the South and Southwest, the long, skinny, high-ceilinged clapboard houses, designed to help keep the inhabitants cool, were tagged *shotgun houses*. Since the houses had no hallways, just one room leading into another, if the front and back doors were opened, a shotgun blast fired from the front would zip straight through and out the back. Or so the story went. The Southside houses weren't the first shotgun houses Corky had seen. Tenant farmers on Northside patches of Boatwright land had the very same kind of housing. Papa Cal had sharecropped the land around his house on the far side of High Cotton for the Boatwrights his entire adult life, and his land's shotgun house was like these. She'd just never seen this many, all in one place, lining entire streets.

After they'd driven by four blocks of shotgun houses, with different lawn trinkets and furniture and barking dogs, they passed a small, single-story, redbrick school building that housed the entire Southside's public school with a dusty bit of playground and an even dustier little sandlot baseball field beside it.

And, there, directly across from the school, was a tall, pristine, white wooden building with a steeple and rows of clear windows, its sign announcing it to be "Mount Olive Baptist Church."

As Mack passed, America told him to stop.

"We promised to take you to your front door," Mack said.

"This is fine, thank you. It's right that way," she said, pointing, and began to take off her new tennis shoes. But she stopped herself and, instead, smiling shyly, got out.

She's going to keep playing with us, Corky thought and said a little softball prayer of thanks.

"America, you did great," Mack called after her.

America, embarrassed, smiled again.

"The game is going to be fun with you playing with us. Everybody's glad you are," Mack went on, making America smile broader. "Remember, Monday's our next practice."

"Oh wait!" Corky called out the car window. She reached under the seat for her library copy of *To Kill a Mockingbird*. "I just finished my book. Want to borrow it? It's not due until next week."

America's eyebrows popped high. "Sure."

Corky held it out. America took it, waved, and jogged away.

"See ya tomorrow!" Corky called after her.

"Ah, damn, Bug," Mack said as he put the car in gear. "I don't think that was a good idea."

"What? Why?" Corky frowned. "She likes books and she doesn't have any."

Mack sighed. "Never mind. Let's go."

Back at the house, the sounds of the hi-fi greeted them as they came in the front door. Their mother was playing "Clair de Lune" again.

Alone.

Mack went on up the stairs, but Corky paused, gazing into the living room. "Mom, we're home," she called. "Everything okay?"

"Yes, dear," her mother said, getting up and turning off the music. "I'll start supper."

5

Bouncy in her new sneakers, America opened the picket-fence gate of her cream-colored rental house a block from the Mount Olive Baptist Church, where Mack and Corky had just dropped her.

Her mother was sitting at the table in the tiny kitchen, staring out the window, something she'd been doing a lot since America's father had gone looking for a job. They'd lived in four towns since she was born, her father always being transferred somewhere else, but this was the first time he'd had to go job hunting. And this time, he was worried. He'd tried to hide it when he left, hugging them both and waving big at her as he drove away, but she'd overheard her parents whispering about it.

"I'm home," America said as she entered the house. "Practice was fun."

At first, Evangeline seemed not to hear her daughter. Then, as if shaking out of a daydream, she looked around. "Oh, hello, *chéri*. Fun?"

"Yes, Mamà, fun."

"Okay?"

"Yes, Mamà, everything was okay."

America waited for her mother to notice her sneakers. She'd been practicing her explanation for them, since she'd been told they couldn't buy anything for now. In fact, she was so focused on that, she forgot she was holding the book Corky had loaned her. She'd planned to hide it behind her back, not wanting to worry her mamà over having a "public" library book from the other side of town. America braced for her mother's disapproval of both. Evangeline, though, didn't notice either shoes or book. She just turned back to stare out the window. So, America went on to her room. After a while, hearing her mother close the door to the house's other bedroom, America was so excited to start reading Corky's library book that she didn't even get ready for bed first. She just plopped on her bed and began to read. And she kept reading into the wee hours of the morning, reading slow, relishing the sound of the author's voice. It sounded like right now. She wasn't used to that. She'd read as much as she could find in the Southside school's "library," a single solitary bookshelf at the end of the school's hallway. But past such classic children's books she'd read long ago like *Swiss Family Robinson* and *Treasure Island*, the few adult novels the school offered were boring old books about boring British people's problems from a boring old-timey century, like *Wuthering Heights* or *Jane Eyre*, ones she couldn't finish if she tried because they were seriously, seriously boring. Especially since none of them ever had people in them that looked like she did. Corky Corcoran's public library book, though, did. And boring was the last thing it was. Instead, it made her feel too much. Because as she kept reading, something ominous threatened to happen on the pages of the story, a potentially horrible something. And the dread of it felt personal, as if it were happening in front of her . . . as if it could happen *to* her. The magical way that characters of a good novel seem alive in a reader's mind was what she'd always liked most about the few she got to read. She enjoyed waiting for the people on the page to come to life, excited for the chance to feel deeply what they felt.

But not this time.

Oh . . . please, not this time.

In the book, the White mob was at the jail, threatening to bust out the Black man. And, even with no mention of a rope, she knew what they wanted to do with him.

Tears welling up in her eyes, America jumped up, dropping the book to the floor. For minutes, she just stood there, her heart beating double-time. Pent-up and nervous, she needed to move. It was 2:00

a.m., though. She lay down and closed her eyes. But she just couldn't settle down, still seeing the story in her head.

Her entire being was yelling: *Go.*

Knowing her mother was a sound sleeper, she pulled on her sneakers and slipped out the front door to run, just run, as fast as she could. Fast as the wind.

In less than a minute, she found herself at the railroad tracks. Breathing good and hard, she threw her hands on her hips and stared toward High Cotton's Northside across the highway. First, she looked straight ahead, where she and her mother had met the Corcorans in their big house with their big bookshelf . . . Then she looked left toward the baseball field, where only a few hours ago, she'd had more fun than she'd had since moving to town . . . Then she gazed toward the football field's track, where she had been told she was special, maybe extra special. And she couldn't help but wonder what being special, maybe extra special, meant. Or, more scary than exciting, what it *might* mean for her future. She was sixteen, no longer naïve, and less so every day. Despite her parents shielding her from the worst as best they could, she knew about the past, the centuries-long struggle of people that looked like she did, which included the dread that made her drop the library book. Plus, it was impossible not to know what was happening across the country the last few years, what with the marches and the sit-ins and all. It was just somehow harder when a book, something you love and covet and admire, throws you, on the strength of words alone, *into* a dangerous past world—one in some ways not past at all—stirring up roiling emotions and fears you cannot handle all at once.

It was too much.

The deeper she felt it, the more urgent her need to keep running. She trotted into the middle of the empty highway, right on the yellow line. She knew not to run down the highway at night. She was hoping to make herself cross over. The Northside of High Cotton had many more miles of streets to run on compared to her side. She took a step forward. But with the library book's dark threat still weighing on her mind, she immediately swung around and sprinted back into the Southside until she was at the front steps of her church, where she plopped down to catch her breath.

As her breathing slowed, America sighed. For a long moment, she sat listening to the chirping sounds of the summer cicadas in the night. *I should go home,* she thought, standing up. But she couldn't make herself do it. So, instead, she tried the church's door, and like most doors in High Cotton, it was unlocked.

She pushed it open and went in.

As her eyes adjusted to the sanctuary's darkness, she started to slip into the pew near the back, where she and her mother always sat. But she didn't. Wandering down the aisle, she eased onto the front pew to stare up at the baptistry's river mural painted across the entire wall. Sitting in the hushed dark, moonlight streaming through the rows of windows, making the painted angels above the baptistry seem to glow, America began to feel herself calm down.

And as she gazed up at the angels so near, she noticed they all looked like she did. Why hadn't she ever noticed that before? And she couldn't take her eyes away.

She didn't know how long she sat there. Time passes differently in the middle of the night. It felt like a long time and yet no time at all.

Finally, when the calm of the sanctuary became her own, she got up to leave. With a last look back at the angels, she eased the church door closed behind her and walked back to her house.

Sneaking through the front door and into her room, she saw Corky's book where it had landed on the floor, and started feeling too much again. So, shoving the unfinished book under the bed, away from her mother's sight—and her own—she lay down to wait for either sleep or dawn.

6

By the next day, everybody in town had heard that a girl from the Southside was playing with the Baptist girls' softball team, and *everybody* included the Baptist Women's Missionary Union ladies about to descend on the Corcoran house.

After helping Mack feed their palomino paint, Goldy, Corky cleaned up and pulled on a nice Sunday dress for the WMU crowd, minus her shorts underneath this time. Excited about being around America again, since she was coming to help with the WMU group, too, Corky rummaged around in her mother's sewing machine cabinet until she found a strand of red ribbon, and wrapped it around her ponytail to look like her new speedy friend. She met America at the back door with the ball and bat, despite the fact they were both wearing Sunday dresses for the church ladies. They had some time before they had to help Evangeline and her mother serve the ladies. Since Mack had already left, Corky figured she'd get America to help her practice hitting for a few minutes.

America, though, wouldn't do it, and it had nothing to do with wearing a dress. She followed Corky and Roy Rogers out the front door and just stood there with her arms crossed. Even Roy Rogers wagging his tail at her wasn't helping.

"What's wrong?" Corky finally asked.

With a glance back at the house, America said, "How could you give me a book with a *lynching?*"

"You already read it?" Corky said. "Boy, you and Mack are fast readers. Wait . . . *what*? There's no lynching . . ."

"There was *about* to be. At the jail. I had to stop reading."

And Corky knew suddenly, stupidly, what the mob at the jail wanted to do with the nice Black man in the book. She was at a loss for words, and she was never at a loss for words. "But there's no lynching . . . I . . . I . . . promise!" she finally stuttered. "It gets better! I mean . . . it gets a little worse, but then it gets a lot better! A lot! At least *I* thought it did," Corky said, now doubting herself.

America didn't move.

So Corky blurted what she feared most: "Are you still playing with us?"

America composed herself. "I'll bring your book back soon as I can," she said so quietly Corky almost didn't hear. "I don't want the library police after me."

"But you're still playing with us, right?" Corky repeated.

America took the bat from Corky. "Throw it."

Corky stepped back and pitched one. America smashed it into the open field across the street.

"Another."

Corky threw another. America smashed it.

Corky had five more softballs. And five times, America smashed it, banging them all to roll across the street and past the tree in the field, making only Roy Rogers happy.

"Girls! *Stop* that!" Belle called from the house. "You'll get sweaty and mess up your dresses. Time to help us. And, Kathryn Kay Corcoran, put on your Sunday shoes. You've got on your sneakers!"

As they both headed inside, Corky kept glancing at America, who was clearly mad and trying hard not to show it. But America wouldn't look at her.

Soon, the Women's Missionary Union ladies trickled into the Corcoran house and took their repose on the living room furniture.

"Kathryn, you and America take in those trays that Evangeline and I just filled," Belle said, looking down at her shoes to make sure that her daughter had obeyed her.

So Corky and America both headed into the living room, holding trays of finger foods and iced tea, offering them to the WMU members sitting on the Corcorans' sofa and chairs.

"Well, who do have we here?" said one of the ladies to America. "Are you the one who is going to play softball with our Baptist girls?"

"Yes, ma'am, she is," Corky said, jumping in. "This is America Willcox."

"Your mother named you *America*? How lovely!" another said. "And don't both of you look nice in your dresses, wearing matching red ribbons for us!"

Corky glanced self-consciously at America and saw that America had not noticed Corky's red ribbon addition until that moment.

Belle joined the group, sitting down on the unoccupied side chair. There that day with Corky's mother were five church women: Mrs. Etta Mayweather; Miss Cordelia Bass; Miss Agnes Doolittle; Mrs. Gertrude Solomon; and Mrs. Noah Boatwright IV, who almost never used her own given name, which was Dorothy.

"Let's get down to business," said Miss Bass, president of the little group. "We've raised over three hundred dollars for foreign missions. That money will go straight to Africa!"

The women clapped.

For the next thirty minutes, the group did all the usual things that such groups do, including reading the last meeting's minutes and planning the usual good deeds at the church and out in the world. After that, the meeting was adjourned, allowing the women to chitchat while finishing off the finger sandwiches and tea. By the top of the hour, the drugstore delivery boy drove up the back driveway in the delivery truck to take America and Evangeline home. So the two left, Corky following them outside. As the truck pulled away, America finally glanced back at Corky. But it was a different look now. Instead of seeming mad, it was the look from the day they'd stood in front of the bookshelf—the sad one.

Inside, Corky slowly untied the red ribbon from her ponytail and dropped it into the kitchen catchall drawer.

Returning to the living room, she could hear the ladies still chatting as they finished off the last of the refreshments.

"Belle, what's this about the girls' softball game? This colored girl is going to play for our church?" said Etta Mayweather, the grandmother of Spin-the-Bottle-party planner, Mollylynne Morehead. "What are you thinking?"

"I don't have control over the girls' softball, Etta," Belle answered. "You should speak to the preacher about that."

"Oh, I have. But she's your daughter. Are you really going to let your daughter play with her?" Etta Mayweather pressed.

At that, Miss Cordelia Bass, Corky's third-grade schoolteacher, chimed in. "Oh hush, Etta, what's wrong with that? And don't say it's never been done before. It's just softball."

Etta Mayweather harrumphed into her teacup, making Miss Agnes Doolittle chuckle into hers.

"What do you think, Dorothy? Gertrude?" Etta Mayweather said to Mrs. Noah Boatwright and Mrs. Gertrude Solomon, hoping for some support.

Before she could answer, though, a horn honked. They all glanced out the front windows. It was Bubba Boatwright coming to pick up his mother in their big, shiny Cadillac. And there, in the back seat, was Tad. Mrs. Boatwright didn't drive, and in Texas, everybody drove. You almost had to drive if you didn't want to be a shut-in. That was weird in itself and underscored the weirdness of the entire Boatwright clan living in the mansion on the rise west of town, the kind of eccentricity that every extremely rich family in Texas, or anywhere else, for that matter, seemed to display after the first few generations.

As Bubba and Tad waited for their mother to take her leave from the WMU ladies, Corky popped out the front door, only half understanding why she was doing it: her pal Tad was out there . . . her pal Tad . . . who'd kissed her . . .

Bubba yelled Corky's way. "Hey, c'mere."

Corky casually went over, staring at Tad in the back seat, who was grinning his blue-eyed new half grin at her, obviously thinking the same thing she was.

Just then, Bubba noticed the delivery truck only now turning the corner with America and Evangeline. "That's the colored girl from your softball practice. You got your maid playing with our church team?"

Corky didn't hear, too busy grinning at Tad, who was still grinning at her.

"HEY, I'm talking to you!" yelled Bubba. "Where's your brother?"

"At the store," Corky answered.

"Tell him I'm looking for him," Bubba said. "Don't forget. Tell him."

Instead of asking her usual *Why?* Corky was still looking at Tad. A year ago, with both of them short, chubby little kids, everything was completely normal. Now, not so much. *What the heck's happening?* Corky wondered, feeling a nice, little confusing tingle at the thought.

Mrs. Boatwright appeared, stepping daintily down the front steps, and the Boatwrights were off. That signaled the end of the party, as the other women streamed out of the front door, too, chattering their goodbyes.

When Corky went back inside, her mother was waiting for her, sitting on the living room couch. "Kathryn, come sit down with me."

Corky stopped in her tracks. "What's wrong?"

"Nothing's wrong."

Something is definitely wrong, Corky thought, easing onto the couch.

Her mother took a deep breath and said, "Maybe you shouldn't play in this summer's softball game."

Corky jumped back to her feet. "But we might win! I gotta play!"

"Maybe you shouldn't this year."

"Why? Because America is playing? Because Mrs. Mayweather said what she said?"

"No, no, it's just that you're growing up. Perhaps it's not ladylike anymore."

"*Ladylike?*" Corky said. "It was Mrs. Solomon, wasn't it? She's never liked me."

Belle cocked her head at her daughter. "Perhaps that's because you ask too many irritating questions." Which was true. Long-suffering Mrs. Gertrude Solomon had good reason for reservations concerning Corky's ladylike potential. Sunday school with Mrs. Solomon, who had taught grades three to six in their small church for thirty years, had been like a game of Twenty Questions for Corky since she was eight.

Mrs. Solomon would say, "The world was made in seven days."

Third grader Corky'd say: "But how?"

Mrs. Solomon would answer, "Because God did it. Our Father in Heaven can do anything."

Corky'd say: "But why seven days? Why not one day if God can do anything?"

And Mrs. Solomon would cringe.

Mrs. Solomon would say: "God took a rib from Adam and made Eve."

Fourth grader Corky'd say: "He made Eve from a rib bone?"

"So the Bible says, Miss Corcoran."

"But why would God do that? He was God, so why did He need the rib bone to make a girl? He made a boy just fine without one."

And poor Mrs. Solomon would cringe.

In Corky's fifth-grade year, Mrs. Solomon had hung a holographic 3D picture of Jesus on the Sunday school class's wall, wearing his customary Galilean robe while knocking at an English cottage's door. If you leaned left, Jesus's hand dropped. If you leaned right, Jesus's hand knocked. Corky had been deeply intrigued, but not for the reason Mrs. Solomon hoped, which had been more about inviting Jesus to come into her young students' hearts than how cool the graphics were. After a few weeks of Corky fidgeting left and right to get the holograph to work, and by bad example inciting Tad and the other children to do the same, high-minded Mrs. Solomon gave up and took 3D Jesus home.

Belle was still talking. "All right, if you want to play so much, we'll discuss this next year. In the meantime, maybe it's time for you to start being more sensitive about what you say to others, young lady," she was saying to Corky. "You've really got to stop asking too many questions, especially at Sunday school."

Corky flopped into a chair. "But *why*? Why can't I ask questions?"

Her mother sighed. "Because people won't like you, and as a grown-up, you've got to have people like you to do anything as a woman. And you're on your way to being one very soon."

Corky paused, thinking perhaps being a grown-up was not going to be all that fun. Being her budding teenage self wasn't much fun that day, either, since she'd just upset America. With that, Corky was suddenly miles away, deep in thought, thinking about America instead of listening to her mother. Corky knew she had to find a way to make it up to her new friend, but first she had to grasp what, exactly, it was that had made her mad. It was a book, a story. Stories weren't supposed to make readers mad. Were they?

Corky got to her feet.

"Where are you going?" Belle said.

"Are we through, Mom?"

Belle sighed and got to her feet, too. "I suppose so. Just think about what I said." Glancing toward their front door, Belle saw a tall woman in a printed housedress, with frizzy yellow-gray hair and red lipstick. She was sweeping their front porch with a broom, accompanied by a white hen.

"Oh no. It's Miss Yoakum." She looked Corky's way. And Corky knew why. "Kathryn . . . ," she said.

Corky let out a sigh of sighs. "Yes, ma'am."

Miss Delilah Yoakum, avid hen owner and six-foot-tall neighbor, lived down the dirt street behind their house, where Corky still rode their old horse, Goldy. She'd been Corky's elementary music teacher. Until, that is, the autoharp incident. After teaching for forty years, she now spent her time raising hens, whispering her memories, and sweeping her dirt driveway into the dirt street in front of her house. At school, where she had worn her hair coiled in a bun and had a manner just as taut, she was famous for sweeping the music room's floor. It had been a bit of an obsession, since she was also teaching the children folk dances, being quite light on her feet for such a big woman. Unable to either sing or dance, Corky had hated everything about Miss Yoakum's class except the times the teacher brought her new chicks to school for the kids to pet.

How and why Miss Yoakum lost her mind when Corky was in fifth grade—spending an entire day playing the World War I song "Over There" nonstop on the autoharp—was a matter of High Cotton conjecture, since Miss Yoakum had no relatives to ask. The consensus was that she had a sweetheart who didn't return from the Great War, so she never married and instead moved to High Cotton to teach music. But nobody knew for sure. And in the years since the unfortunate autoharp incident, every now and then, having been a founding member of the Baptist church's Women's Missionary Union ladies' group that historically met at Belle Corcoran's house, she'd remember it was Wednesday and sweep her way over to the meeting. The WMU, of course, had made it a priority to be sure she was cared for, since it was the Christian thing to do. But so did the entire village, churchy or not. Officer Tommy Tilton was always returning her hens to her. And when Miss Yoakum began calling Corky's father at the drugstore to order groceries, Cal would just send the list over to the Pak&Pay grocery across the street. Then he'd have the drugstore delivery boy deliver them to her on credit, deeming it a small expansion of his "Service to the Sick."

"Delilah, hello," Belle said, opening the front door.

"Belle," Miss Yoakum responded, the hen at her feet giving a little cluck. "Am I late?"

"So sorry, dear. The meeting is over. Kathryn will escort you back home if that's all right."

"Well, if she must. Where is she?"

"Hi, Miss Yoakum," responded Corky.

"Hi, yourself. I'm not going anywhere with you. You're not Kathryn Corcoran. She's chubby and can't sing."

Corky rolled her eyes at her mother, who appeared to be suppressing a chuckle while also somehow giving her daughter the eye to do the right thing. Sighing, Corky burst into song. After the chubby remark, Corky wanted badly to sing "Over There." But, glancing at her mom, she chose "Amazing Grace" instead.

"Amazing g-r-a-ace, how sweet the s-o-und . . ."

Miss Yoakum made a face. "You can't sing at all. You're Kathryn Corcoran, all right. What happened to your fat cheeks?"

With another adolescent eye roll, Corky led Miss Yoakum off the porch, the white hen, head bobbing, following them toward the sidewalk.

"Miss Yoakum, should I pick up your hen?" Corky offered.

"Henrietta won't like it. But you can take this," she said, handing Corky her broom. And off they went, Henrietta strutting close behind.

As they passed Goldy's corral and turned onto the dirt street this side of the Poindexters' kitsch-cluttered front yard, she felt Miss Yoakum staring at her. For a block and then two, she kept it up, Corky feeling more uncomfortable with each step until finally Miss Yoakum spoke.

"Why the long face, Kathryn?"

"I . . . wanted to make a new friend," Corky heard herself admitting. "And I think I hurt her feelings."

"What did you do?" asked Miss Yoakum.

"I gave her a book. And it offended her, I guess. But I didn't mean it to."

"Ah yes." Miss Yoakum nodded. "A book, like music, is very personal. You bring yourself, your own story, to everything you read. It's a book's boon and bane. But it's also its raison d'être—its reason for being—to meet you where you are. Exactly like a great piece of music."

Corky looked Miss Yoakum up and down. She was making sense.

"That looks like my broom," Miss Yoakum suddenly said. "Who did you say you were again?"

And we're back, Corky thought. She handed Miss Yoakum her broom, happy to see they were finally in front of her little house, overgrown yard and all.

"Here we are, Henrietta," Miss Yoakum said. "Thank you, child, whoever you are. Ta-ta."

Corky watched until both music teacher and chicken disappeared around the back of the house. Turning around, she walked slowly home, pondering what Miss Yoakum had just said. *Bringing your own story to a book?* Until that moment, she wasn't aware she had a story to bring to anything. Glancing back toward Miss Yoakum, who had reappeared to sweep her dirt driveway, Corky thought about Miss Yoakum's doozy of a story. *But . . . what's America's?* Corky wondered. Yet, even as the thought was forming, Corky, experiencing a dawning realization, glanced in the direction of the railroad track, and knew.

There is a young moment when the world can suddenly reveal that it doesn't revolve around you. This was Corky's moment. Grasping in inches the concept of what she'd one day know as *empathy,* Corky began to understand why America was upset. She glanced toward her house, thinking of the old photographs of her parents hanging along the front staircase, ones she'd passed her entire life without a thought. Now she wondered about *their* stories. She thought about Mrs. Poindexter and her lawn ornaments . . . and Cliff, the cheerful one-armed Texaco gas station attendant who once had two arms . . . and Earl and Velma and Velvadine and her librarian friend, Miss Delacourt . . . Corky took a deep breath. *Everybody's got their own story,* she realized as she locked eyes with the driver of a passing car . . . *and they're swirling around me every moment of every day.*

All she had to do was be open to seeing them.

7

Around 5:00 p.m., Mack poked his head into Corky's room. "Roy Rogers and I are going over to Papa Cal's. Want to come?" he asked. Mack knew full well what Corky thought about Papa Cal. He was just messing with her.

"I've got plans," Corky answered.

"Oh, you do, huh," he said, surprised. "C'mon, Roy. It's just you and me."

Corky's friend Marilou Moon had asked her to go to the American Legion's talent show fundraiser that night since Marilou's dad was in it. Corky didn't much care about seeing what would be considered the "talent" of High Cotton performing anything. She was secretly hoping to see Tad. And see him she did, at least the back of his blond head, three rows up, sitting with his mother.

Opening the show were Marilou's father and three other upstanding members of the Legion doing a barbershop quartet of "Good Night, Ladies," wearing 1920s outfits complete with straw hats and fake mustaches, Mr. Moon's having a mind of its own and falling off midsong. Next was Lynda Lou Rutherford, a girl in her class, who played Chopin's Polonaise, her recent piano recital piece, and only goofed up once. That was followed by Mrs. Leona Quattlebaum, a soprano in the First Baptist choir, who sang a reedy rendition of "Ave Maria," straining at the high notes. And those were only the ones Corky remembered. They were all so boring, she focused on Tad's blond hair and thought about whether she liked French kissing or not.

Just then, though, Mr. Noah Boatwright IV walked out on stage wearing black face paint, ridiculously white lips, and white gloves. He looked like an escapee from an old-fashioned minstrel show, the kind packed with stereotypical songs and routines that were once widely performed despite their racist themes. The confused crowd hushed and then became even more confused as he nodded at the piano player and began singing "Ol' Man River," the legendary song from *Show Boat*, the first integrated musical way back in 1927. Having heard it in Miss Yoakum's class, even Corky knew "Ol' Man River" was meant to be sung only by a Black dockworker. And here was Noah IV, the rich, very White descendant of a post–Civil War cotton plantation owner, belting it out off-key. Corky couldn't take her eyes off his earnest, greased-up face as he gesticulated like an opera singer. After he finished, there was a lull followed by polite clapping that died away while he kept taking bows. Soon, but not soon enough, he got off the stage as a bunch of little ballerinas from Miss "Hi" Jinx's ballet school rushed around him in tutus to do an elementary school version of *Swan Lake*.

After the show, just as the sun was going down on the long summer day, Corky walked with Marilou back to the Moons' car to wait on her parents, Marilou's mother having gone backstage to help Marilou's father with his rented barbershop outfit and mustache. Corky strained to see Tad again in the crowd filtering out from the Legion Hall. And there he was. Tad and Mrs. Boatwright were scurrying to keep up with Mr. Boatwright, back to his normal face . . . and he was striding straight for *her*.

"Miss Corcoran!" Noah IV said, stopping in front of Corky. "What's this about a Southside girl playing with our church softball team? My son Bubba said it was *your* idea."

Corky was taken aback. It was the first time Noah IV had ever acknowledged Corky's existence. *It was Pastor Pete's,* she wanted to answer, but, eyeing Tad, she figured, why not take the credit for what could finally be a winning game for the Baptists?

"Yes, sir," she said proudly.

He leaned into her face, so close that, despite it being dusk, Corky could see the remains of the blackface grease paint behind his ears. And he was scowling. "It's not right, young lady. It's going to stir up trouble in our nice, quiet town. And it'll be your fault!"

To say that surprised Corky was proof of how clueless her young self was. She should have been intimidated, which was, no doubt, Noah IV's intent, but she had spent her entire childhood having adults tell her she was misbehaving, so that didn't faze her. No, she was more worried about what that might mean for her future chances of being kissed again by his youngest son. Plus, from her view, it seemed more than a little ridiculous for him to be against a Black girl playing softball with them when he'd just been up on stage acting and *looking* as if he'd like to be Black himself. All she could do was stare after Mr. Boatwright as he marched on, followed by his mousy wife, Tad glancing back at her with a pained look on his face.

"What was that about?" Marilou said. Realizing Marilou hadn't heard the whole thing, Corky shrugged and got in the car with her to wait on Marilou's parents.

Back home, Corky headed to find her mom and dad, who were both sitting in the kitchen dining area. Cal was chowing down on the steak dinner he always ate after closing up the store.

"Where's Mack?" Corky asked.

"On a date, it seems," Belle answered. "How was the talent show?"

"Boring," she griped, plopping down in her chair, "until Mr. Boatwright sang."

Her father looked up from his steak. *"Boatwright?"* he grumped. "What's he doing in the American Legion? He didn't serve in the war."

"He was in the show," Corky explained, making sure not to mention his chastising her in the parking lot. "He did a solo."

Her dad rolled his eyes. "Ruining the church choir isn't enough for that man? What did he sing?"

"'Ol' Man River,'" Corky said.

Hearing that, her father almost choked on his steak. *"Ol' Man River'?"*

"Yeah, with his face all blacked up," she said.

"'Ol' Man River' in *blackface?*"

"Oh no," Belle moaned. "He didn't . . . Not in this day and age!"

"That's what Marilou's mom kept saying on the way home, too, and told Mr. Moon they should have stopped him," Corky went on. "Mr. Moon said they'd already pocketed his big donation before Mr. Boatwright asked to sing. Then he said Mr. Boatwright just showed up with that stuff on his face tonight without telling anyone and 'nobody says no to a Boatwright in this town.'"

Cal Corcoran started belly-laughing. "'Ol' Man River' in *blackface!* Oh, dear *GAWD* . . ." He laughed so hard, he had to catch his breath, and he kept on for a good, long time. Corky couldn't remember when her father had laughed that hard. As a kid, understanding nothing at that exact moment except her father's laughter, she recalled thinking that was a good way to end the day.

In her bedroom an hour later, Corky was in her pajamas waiting for the lights to go out in her parents' room. When they did, she opened her bedroom door a crack, waiting for Roy Rogers.

During the summer, Roy slept on a mat in what would be called a mudroom if it had been up north. It was a separate part of the house's big, old kitchen that served now as a laundry room connecting to the back door, where her mother said an antique icebox once stood when the house was first built in 1900. The friendly town iceman would drive up to the back, grab up a big block of ice with huge clamps from his wagon, and stick it in the box. The people from whom her parents bought the house in the '50s had ignored the old, unused icebox on the back porch once they had ushered in the future by buying a kitchen refrigerator. Belle, however, had disposed of it immediately. Now, the empty place was Roy Rogers's summer sleeping spot away from the mosquitos and wasps, as well as his winter spot during the coldest nights. After the house's lights went out, though, Roy had started creeping up the stairs to push open Corky's door and join her, scooting under her bed. In the morning, at the first sound of Corky's parents stirring, he'd sneak out the same way he came in, back to his downstairs sleeping spot. Corky always thought they were pulling a fast one on her parents. Only after she was grown did she realize they probably looked the other way once Mack left home, enjoying such things the way parents do.

In a minute, Roy Rogers did sneak into her room, and Corky gave him a hug. With Roy at her side, she gazed out her open screened window, thinking big thoughts about this whole odd day. From her window on the back side of the house, she could see Goldy's corral, the Poindexters' house, the corner with its streetlight—the only still working one on her street. Yet she couldn't see much else since shade trees blocked the rest of her view, including their front yard. During the summer, she liked gazing out the window with Roy before bedtime. Most nights were quiet, nobody driving by to break the peaceful feeling, the only sound being the cicadas and their summer chirping. In less than a minute, though, she saw Sunny and Sandy Beach's top-down convertible Corvair pass under the streetlight. "Mack Corcoran! Yoo-hoo, MACK, *yoo-hoo!*" they giggled and whooped toward the house before vanishing down the road.

Right behind came Bubba Boatwright in his silver Corvette, just far enough back for the girls not to notice, vanishing into the dark as well.

For a full minute, all went back to being so quiet that Corky didn't think much about an old truck going the same direction as Bubba and the Beach Sisters, noticing it only because its muffler was rattling. But, as if it had rounded the block, the same loud truck came by again. It had slowed down so much, it was moving at little more than a crawl. Corky squinted for a better view. As it passed under the streetlight beyond the horse corral, she saw it was a decrepit flatbed with what looked like slat side rails. She'd never seen it before. When you live in a tiny town, you pretty much know not only the people but all their cars, especially since nobody bought anything but Chevys and Fords and the occasional Cadillac, if you were a Boatwright. Before it passed out of sight, Corky also noticed one of its red taillights was broken.

Still, she didn't think much of it . . . until the noisy flatbed truck went by *again*, circling the block from the other direction. And that, for the first time, gave her pause.

Corky stiffened and Roy Rogers came to attention. Sniffing the greasy, oily smell wafting up to his powerful canine nose from the flatbed, he gave a little protective growl and moved close to his girl.

She waited to see if the flatbed truck circled again.

When it didn't, Corky relaxed. She shook her head at herself, thinking, *Maybe Mr. Boatwright has gotten to me after all.*

8

Dogs have always had a world of their own. But in a time and place with no leash laws, like 1964 High Cotton, their world could be as big as they wanted it to be. Any time could seem a good time to trot around the neighborhood to meet and greet their fellow residents, be they canine, feline, or human.

So, the next morning, Roy Rogers woke up at dawn. Scooting from under Corky's bed, he slipped down the stairs to his back-porch spot and curled up to wait for his girl's mother to appear. After a while, he felt her pet him on the head to wake him up again, his dog bowls full of food and water. After he wolfed down his breakfast, she opened the back screen door, and out he went, sniffing the early morning air before heading off on his usual rounds.

He trotted south, in the direction of the highway. At the first corner, he turned left and, within a few blocks, saw his ladies. They were nice ladies who called him by name, so he always dropped by to pay his respects. It seemed the neighborly thing to do since they enjoyed seeing him and giving him a dog biscuit. As usual, they were drinking something from their own small dog dishes with handles, while chatting across their picket fence.

He trotted over.

"It'll be fine, Agnes," the one with the biscuit in her apron was saying to the other. "It's only a softball game. And it'll be good for the girls."

"Well, if you say so, Cordelia," said the other. "I only worry about our church being ready for it. You know how people are. WMU ladies aside, Etta Mayweather's not the only one."

That made the biscuit lady sigh, at least until she had the pleasure of spying him. "Good morning, Roy! Here for your dog biscuit?"

Roy wagged his tail and, remembering his manners, sat down as she pulled it from her apron pocket. "Here you go!"

He swallowed it whole and trotted away.

Passing the school and the library, he headed for the church. At the church's corner, he turned left again just as the church's human, who also knew his name, was getting out of his smelly motion machine. But something new was happening. A doughy older human had pulled in beside the church's human in another motion machine, one shiny and big and hardly smelly at all. As that human got out of his machine, Roy sensed something he didn't like: *anger*. The doughy human was mad about something. Roy kept his distance, trotting into the street to avoid them both as the angry man slammed his shiny door, threw up his hands, and started yelling. "Pastor! My son told me you're letting a Southside girl play on our softball team! Have you lost your *mind*? Mark my words, it's going to start up trouble in our nice, quiet town—*more* trouble! I just had to warn Cal Corcoran about what I heard was coming at the drugstore. And now *this*! Your high-minded ideas are all well and fine until one of our beautiful stained-glass windows is broken by juvenile delinquents. And may I remind you I just paid for that new Noah's ark window!"

Trotting away, Roy decided he did not like that loud, angry human. He'd never accept a biscuit from him.

Taking another left past the church, Roy knew he shouldn't stay in the street because of the motion machines, but he liked the feel of the warm morning asphalt under his paws. Roy sniffed the air. At a stop sign up ahead sat a bad-stinky old motion machine. Snuffling to try ridding his snout of the stink, Roy paid it no mind as he passed, continuing his trot on the warm asphalt as the passenger-human was saying something to the driver-human, which he also paid no mind.

"Darryl . . . hey . . . hey . . . see that dog? That's Corky Corcoran's dog, the mutt that growled at me at the school when I was breaking in the other day. *Quick!* Swerve at him—hit him if you can. Nobody's looking. *Do it!*"

Careening around the corner, the stinky clunker headed straight for an unsuspecting Roy.

At that exact moment, though, Roy heard a cat hiss. There, under a tree on the street's edge, sat the sassy cat that hissed at him every morning just to razz him. Roy sprinted over the curb straight for the devil-cat, chasing it up a tree. And just as the cat scrambled onto a limb to razz him from above, he heard the stinky clunker smack the curb behind him and bounce to a stop inches from the tree. Back on the sidewalk, Roy cocked his head at the humans, who were now yelling at each other.

"*Damn* it, Dwayne, I coulda bent the damn axle hitting the curb to miss the damn tree. You know we don't got no shocks!"

"*Nuts!* And you didn't even scare the dog, Darryl. I'll have to get him myself later."

And as the stinky clunker squealed away, Roy trotted on.

Heading into his morning round's homestretch, Roy stopped this side of his last street corner to visit a Chihuahua that always whined at him since it had the misfortune of having humans who built a fence to keep it from its freedom. Roy could tell the tiny dog was lonely, its humans obviously not giving it enough attention. So, out of the goodness of his canine heart, he trotted around the garbage can in the driveway to "chat" with it. And as he and the little dog were barking up a conversation, the garage door opened and out came one of the little dog's humans, a woman Roy sometimes saw there, and she was angry, too. But it was a different kind of angry. More like growling, it seemed to Roy. Striding past them, arms full of men's clothes on hangers, she kept up her growly sounds as she dumped them all into the garbage can and spit on them, after which she wiped her hands in some sort of gesture that seemed to mean something and slammed the lid down louder and growlier. Then, after marching back into the house, she came out carrying a suitcase. Roy knew that meant the Chihuahua's human was leaving, and he hoped, for the little dog's sake, it wasn't for long.

Heading home, Roy trotted to the next corner and turned left down his street.

But as he passed Mrs. Poindexter's house, he suddenly stopped in his tracks to sniff the air . . . He could still smell a whiff of the greasy, oily, black exhaust fumes from the rattling old truck that had made his girl tense the night before, and he sensed, without knowing how, that it was an omen of some sort. He growled. His doggy intuition was telling him to watch, wait, worry. Sniffing the air again, he couldn't smell it anymore. He sniffed here, there, and everywhere for it, ready to follow its offending trail. He sniffed under the streetlight. He sniffed along Mrs. Poindexter's yard. He sniffed across the street to the fenceless field and back to the streetlight again. But he couldn't latch on to the full scent; it had been too long.

Giving the air one last good sniff, he let rip a mighty bark, telling everyone what he was thinking. Then he trotted past Goldy in her corral and entered his own backyard.

On a usual morning, he'd splay out under his favorite backyard shade tree until one of his humans needed him. But that morning, watching his girl and her mother get into their motion machine, he stayed put, nose up, standing sentry, readying for what he felt in his bones was coming . . .

9

All small Texas towns have a Dairy Dip of some sort. High Cotton's homemade Dairy Queen came into being in the mid-1950s when the baby boomers started growing up, and there was money to be made off them, even in High Cotton. A spot was needed for these new "teenagers" to drive to and hang around. A much younger Coach Trumbull, looking for ways to augment his meager teaching salary, and having four of these teenagers himself, built the walk-up soft-serve ice-cream stand with its big "Smiling Swirl-Top Cone" sign that beckoned night and day. It offered no inside seating. You placed your order via its walk-up or drive-through windows. And it was a hit from the beginning. There were only so many times the High Cotton equivalent of a greaser with a hot rod and his poodle skirt–wearing girlfriend could circle the limited streets of the town. They needed a place to park and gawk. And that stayed the same as the '50s turned into the '60s, the desire to see and be seen being endemic in all teenage DNA, with ice cream and sodas as the delicious draw.

The Dairy Dip was also wisely situated between the school and the sports fields that lined the highway, the better to foster business from those either commiserating or celebrating. And Coach Trumbull, a better businessman than a coach, was determined to have the place visible from both football and baseball stands. Above the little hut, the bulb-lit sign outlined a painting of the curlicue soft-serve delicacy that was its specialty: the aforementioned famous smiling swirl-top cone. As soon as the Dairy Dip's success was assured, he'd added the asphalt circular drive around the stand-alone shop, which became part of the drag every High Cotton teenager with a car included in any nighttime carousing.

By 1964, while a bit weathered, the Dairy Dip was still standing, still making ends meet for the coach, and still serving the same soft-serve ice cream and watered-down soft drinks the morning that Belle and Corky drove by in the Corcorans' station wagon, taking Corky to the drugstore for her soda-fountain lunch shift.

As they passed, Corky looked up at the Dairy Dip's smiling ice-cream-cone sign. Staring at the deliriously happy-happy cone, Corky said, "Are we happy?"

Belle glanced at Corky. "What brought this on?"

"Dad was laughing last night about Mr. Boatwright. He doesn't laugh much."

"That laugh was coming from a whole other place, dear. Trust me."

"It's just that I don't recall us laughing much. We used to."

"Well, things have gotten busy . . . ," Belle said, her voice trailing off.

"You were fighting the other day, weren't you?" Corky said.

"Oh, sweetheart. It wasn't really a fight. It was more of a discussion."

"You played 'Clair de Lune.' Just like you did when Mack and Dad were fighting."

"I did?"

Corky nodded. "You always play it when you're sad or mad."

"I play it because it's beautiful," Belle corrected her, "and because it makes me happy, not sad."

"But you had a fight, didn't you? What about?" Corky pressed.

Belle sighed. "If you must know, I want to get a job. You are almost in high school. But your father doesn't want me to work."

That stopped Corky. "Are we okay? Is the drugstore okay?"

"Yes, yes, we're fine. It's just . . . I want to do something else, a part-time job maybe, once you start high school. And your father doesn't think his wife working will look good for business. Actually, he said people would ask the same question you just did, so I guess he's right."

As they waited at the town's single traffic light across from the drug-store, Corky gazed beyond the store, across the tracks. Thinking about America, she then asked, "Why don't we have any Southside friends?"

"We do."

"No, Mom, we don't. Willy doesn't count."

Belle sighed again. "The way the world is . . . it's just not easy."

Corky looked her mother's way. "Are you and Evangeline friends?"

That seemed to catch Belle totally off guard. "It's not really proper to be friends with people you are employing. Plus, we just met."

"But you like her."

"Yes, I very much do."

"So, you could be friends."

"Well, yes."

"Do you think Evangeline and America are happy?" Corky asked next.

"I hope so," Belle said. "Once Evangeline's husband gets a new job, I'm sure they'll be happier."

The light turned green. As they crossed the downtown highway and Belle parked the station wagon by the drugstore's side entrance, Corky still had questions. "Why don't you make me call her Mrs. Willcox like I have to with all the other adult ladies I know?"

Belle paused. "You're right. You should."

"I hope she stays awhile." Corky studied her mother and asked what she'd wanted to ask for years. "Why don't you keep any help Dad sends you for very long? They say you're hard. That's the scuttlebutt. Nobody knows I hear, but I hear."

At that, Belle fumed. "Kathryn Corcoran, I swear you don't have a filter! We need to work on that."

Corky cocked her head. "Why? What's a filter? Are you mad? That wasn't a good question?"

"Enough questions, young lady. Go on in now. You wanted to do this. So, do it well. Straighten your skirt and blouse, behave, and don't ask any irritating questions." Corky got out of the car and straightened her clothes. "That's better," Belle said. "You look very nice. See you later."

As soon as Corky entered through the side door, Earl called her over to the main counter in front of the prescription area. The seven- or eight-year-old Black boy was again standing there holding out a quarter. "Katie, this young man would like a strawberry ice-cream cone. Would you get it for him?"

Corky nodded and did so with pleasure.

"Good morning, Katie!" Velma and Velvadine said in unison as Corky hustled behind the soda fountain and began scooping the cone.

"Isn't that just the cutest outfit she has on?" Velma said to Velvadine. "You look so grown-up in your pretty blouse and skirt."

"At least her skirt's not as long as your granny dress," Velvadine said tartly, glancing down at her sister's hemline.

"You know my ankles get cold at work, Velvadine!" Velma said back as Corky finished scooping.

By the time Corky returned to the soda fountain after delivering the cone, Noah Boatwright IV had plopped his derriere on his usual stool for his usual grilled-cheese-and-three-Coca-Cola lunch, spreading out the *Fort Worth Star-Telegram* newspaper on the fountain's counter like he owned the joint. She frowned at him, but he didn't even notice, back to not acknowledging her existence. She even slapped down each new Coca-Cola on the fountain's marble counter with a decided attention-getting attitude.

No response.

As people came and went while Noah IV ate his lunch, some stopped to tell him what a mighty fine rendition of "Ol' Man River" he'd given at the American Legion's talent show. He thanked them one by one, buying each and every fan a Coca-Cola and inviting them to sit down and tell him more. After it happened several times, Corky began to suspect word had spread about the free Coke. One man she knew from church took Noah IV up on the free drink, and when his frowning wife appeared to collect him after shopping, she overheard their whispers:

"Ernest Bodine, how could you encourage that man? That's all my friends are talking about this morning, his horrid blackface at the talent show! And him a Baptist deacon!"

"It was a free Coke, Abigail," the husband said, snickering. "I ain't passing up a chance to get anything free from a dang Boatwright."

As Noah IV kept buying Coca-Colas for each new admirer, Corky noticed Dr. DuBose up on the prescription area talking furtively with her father, just as he had her first day. To make things even more mysterious, Dr. DuBose also, once again, glanced her way behind the soda fountain.

If that wasn't mysterious enough, Noah IV, after receiving his last fan's accolades, stopped by to talk to her father again, too, doing his own second round of furtive talking and glancing back to where she stood. Remembering Noah IV's warning after the talent show, she began to worry that it was about America playing with their softball team. But, if so, why would Dr. DuBose not like it?

Coach Trumbull entered the store, and that got her mind off her dad, Dr. DuBose, and Noah IV. The coach strode over to Mack, who was shelving nearby, and they began their own furtive talking. Quickly, Corky opened a Dr Pepper and scuttled closer. She was going to offer it to one or the other if she had to, but all she really wanted to do was eavesdrop.

"I started chewing on this today, Mack, and I hate to admit I don't know where to start," Coach Trumbull was saying. "In fact, this morning I got so frustrated that I just picked up the telephone and called the one man who knew for sure what I could do for her: Coach Ed Temple."

The man he was referring to was the one who'd famously discovered Wilma Rudolph, Edward Temple, her Tennessee State University track coach, as well as the 1960 Olympic women's track team coach. That impressed both Mack and Corky, and not just because Coach had tried calling Wilma Rudolph's coach. They were impressed because he'd made a long-distance call.

On a weekday.

In 1964, calling long distance was an event. Since there was no internet yet, information gathering often took days or weeks, still ruled as it was by the library and the letter. And while almost every home had a telephone, everything to do with them was quite pricey—especially long-distance calls. They were reserved for special occasions or bad news, and even those were usually placed at night when long-distance rates were lower. Plus, making a long-distance call was quite a production. You dialed *zero* for the operator. The operator would perform the complicated trick of dialing the number for you, connecting to operators in other towns. Then the phone company charged for how long and what time of day you talked, along with what type of call you were making, "person-to-person" being the most expensive.

So, unless a person was as rich as the Boatwrights, no one ever placed a long-distance call in the middle of the day in the middle of the week. That Coach Trumbull did so was a testament to what he thought of America's talent. As Mack had guessed, the coach had seen what he'd seen, and his coaching soul couldn't let such a sight go.

"I even tried *person-to-person*, hoping to catch the man, damn the expense," Coach Trumbull went on. "But he's gone for the summer, working with this year's Olympic team. Nobody was even in his office. So, I left a message with the university's operator. Maybe he hears all the time that someone's discovered the next Wilma Rudolph. But I doubt it. I'm leaving for baseball camp this weekend. If I haven't heard anything from Coach Temple by the time I'm back in August, I'll try a letter, I promise." He patted Mack on the shoulder and left.

"What else did he say about America?" Corky asked.

Mack went back to his shelving. "I'll tell you at home."

"But I brought you a Dr Pepper," she said, holding it out.

"Not now. I'm not thirsty."

So, taking a swig of the Dr Pepper, Corky returned to the fountain.

After the lunch rush, her father called to her, "Katie, the delivery boy's about to leave. He can take you home."

Corky went outside to wait. As soon as she was out the door, Tad Boatwright whizzed up on his bike, shooting her that dang half grin. "Hey, Mollylynne's Spin-the-Bottle party's tonight right after dark, don't forget," he said, slowing as if he might stop.

That very moment, though, the delivery boy came out. "Ready?"

"Meet me at the schoolyard after you get home," Tad whispered, pedaling away.

All the way to the Corcorans' house, the delivery boy was talking about something, but Corky didn't hear a thing, thinking about another schoolyard kissing practice with Tad.

Readying her lie, Corky called out as soon as she came through the front door: "Mom! I'm going to the schoolyard to practice soft—"

Before she could finish, she heard what sounded like someone falling down the stairs. Corky ran to the back stairs and saw Evangeline hovering over her mother lying on the landing.

"MOM?"

"Help me get your mamà to the couch," Evangeline said to Corky. Her mother was groaning. Angrily. "This leg. It'll be the *death* of me."

After they helped her mother through the hallway and onto the living room couch, Evangeline sat down by her side, patting her hand, and Corky loved her for it. *I should be doing that,* Corky thought. Yet even as she was worrying about her mother, she was also thinking about Tad Boatwright. Feeling guilty, she forced herself to lean over and kiss her mother on the cheek.

"My goodness, Kathryn," Belle said. "Don't worry. I'll just have a couple of bruises, I think."

Even though she could see that her mother was probably okay, Corky felt tears rising. It was the scare that got her. When she was in the fifth grade, her friend Sadie Springer's mother suddenly died. Corky's parents gave her the choice of whether or not to go to the funeral with them. She chose to go. It was her first funeral and the only dead body she'd ever seen . . . and she couldn't get over that the motionless body lying in the casket before her was the nice person who'd smiled at her in church only the week before. When they went through the line at the graveside and Corky was standing in front of her friend, it was the only time in her young life she couldn't think of anything to say. Finally, Belle saved her by reaching down and hugging Sadie.

With that memory vividly in mind, Corky stared down at her mother lying so still on the couch. So, when Evangeline went to get a hot towel for Belle's forehead, Corky sat down by her, studying her mother's face for the first time in as long as she could remember. Even though she wasn't great at picking up signals, Corky knew sadness when she saw it, just like she had with America in front of their bookshelf a few days before. And she was suddenly thinking about their talk in the station wagon that morning. Corky had never questioned whether her mother or father was happy. That wasn't what she'd asked her mother as they passed the Dairy Dip's happy ice-cream-cone sign. She'd asked if *we* were happy.

Belle patted her knee. "Weren't you just asking to go to the school-yard to practice softball with your friends? I thought I heard you say that before I fell."

Corky paused. Telling her injured mother a lie felt like a big, fat sin. But she did it anyway. "Yes, ma'am."

"Go ahead. I need to rest. Evangeline's here. And take Roy Rogers. He's going to follow you, anyway. I think it may be time to put up a fence. Just be careful. And let's not tell your father about my fall, okay? Not just yet. I'll tell him in good time."

Changing into pedal pushers and tennis shoes, but leaving on her nice blouse after Velma's compliment about it, Corky left. With Roy Rogers bounding along beside her, she hustled toward the school.

Tad, though, wasn't there. She started to wait awhile until she noticed Dwayne Bumgardner's hooptie parked on the far side of the schoolyard. Dwayne was probably trying to break in again and had scared Tad away, she figured. Grabbing Roy's collar, she decided not to stay, either. But to keep up her lie to her mother, she knew they'd better take their time returning. So, she and Roy meandered around the library and the church and back to the library. With more time to kill, she glanced in the direction of the highway. She was no more than three blocks from it, but she never walked all the way there unless she was going to the drugstore and could use the stoplight. She'd been taught it wasn't safe. On her walks home, she usually angled away from it, even though she could see the highway every time she came to a new corner. Today, though, she found herself angling toward it. So, when she and Roy got to her street, she was only a block from the highway near the Northside cemetery's entrance. Selecting a good place off the pavement, she and Roy sat down. As cars whizzed past a block away, she stared across the highway. There were the railroad tracks. There was the Southside cemetery. There was the dirt street leading over the tracks and into the "other" High Cotton. Over there, somewhere, lived America and Evangeline and hundreds of other High Cotton people she'd rarely seen and would never know. With Miss Yoakum's moment of profundity still on her mind, Corky was suddenly contemplating how big the world was. And, as she stroked Roy's large head, she found herself lost in imagining what America was doing right that very minute.

Finally, she shook herself from her reverie and headed with Roy back home.

Coming through the front door, Corky went to find her mother, who was in the kitchen fixing dinner as if nothing had happened.

"Mom . . ."

"I'm all right, sweetheart. Now go tell your brother supper will be ready soon and not to forget to wash up. He's out feeding Goldy. And remember, don't tell your father about my fall today."

Corky headed to the corral, still full of her deep thoughts. Glancing in the direction of Mollylynne's house just around the corner, her thoughts now included Tad and first kisses. As Mack brushed Goldy, she leaned on the split-rail fence to watch.

"Was Lorelei your first kiss?" she suddenly asked her brother.

Mack shot her a none-of-your-business look and kept brushing. But Corky already knew the answer.

When Mack was in the eighth grade, a new family joined the neighborhood right after New Year's Day. Loraine and Lee Jones, along with their eighth-grade daughter, Lorelei, moved into the house on the other side of the Corcorans from the Poindexters, making her literally the girl next door. Mack noticed. Corky remembered how everybody in her world immediately loved brown-eyed Lorelei, including Roy Rogers, always a good sign since Roy was a terrific judge of character. In a matter of days, Mack had a best friend who, by the end of the school year, had turned into his first date/girlfriend/kiss and all that went with it. They fought and made up constantly, Lorelei being as strong-minded as Mack, both just beginning to understand anything and everything around them, as adolescents do. Otherwise, they were inseparable.

"They're perfect for each other," Belle had said to Cal after having the Jones family over for dinner. "Lorelei's good for Mack."

"*Good* for him?" Corky's dad had laughed. "Don't let him hear you say that, or he'll drop her like a flaming-hot potato."

"Well, she is. She's as levelheaded as they come for her age, despite their little spats."

Corky's favorite Lorelei memory, the one that cemented her own adoration of the girl next door, was a late spring afternoon when she followed Roy Rogers through the hedges between their two houses to find Mack and Lorelei sitting very close to each other on the Joneses' porch swing. Roy bounded over, lying down exactly where the swing couldn't hit him. Nine-year-old Corky, however, was another matter.

"Go away, Bug," Mack quickly said.

"Would you like to swing with us, Corky?" Lorelei countered.

Corky nodded.

Lorelei scooted away from Mack, leaving a space just big enough for Corky. Hustling over, Corky flopped in between them, to her delight and her big brother's chagrin.

For two years, the pair was a steady couple in between their constant breakups and makeups that had the other girls boomeranging between hopes raised and hopes dashed enough to give them all vertigo. On it nicely went until the middle of their sophomore year, when the Joneses moved to Houston. Mack moped for weeks. Belle, though, made a point to keep up with the family, always knowing what was happening to their former neighbors, even after Mack and Lorelei slowly quit writing each other, life going on as it does when you're a teenager. By his senior year, Mack had a new girlfriend named Cissy McCloud, whose best attribute was still being in High Cotton. Roy Rogers had never once acknowledged Cissy's existence, and that spoke volumes to Corky's way of thinking. All Belle ever said about her was "Well, she's not Lorelei," usually with a sigh.

As Mack kept brushing Goldy, Corky glanced over her shoulder toward the Southside. Contemplating the size of the world again, she climbed up to sit on the corral's split-rail fence and said, "You ever wonder what other people are doing right this very moment?"

Mack kept brushing.

"Like, what do you think Lorelei is doing?" Corky went on. "Do you ever think about her? I do. I miss her."

Mack paused. ". . . Why all the questions?"

"Mom said you went on a date last night. With who?"

He shot her another none-of-your-business look. And Corky again knew the answer. "Cissy McCloud," she guessed, leaving a bad taste in her mouth.

"Yes, Bug. Cissy's home."

Corky made a face. Cissy was a girly-girl who wore makeup. Cissy talked down to her. More to the point, Cissy was a Methodist. Corky had been told the two broke up when they went off to college, Mack to the University of Texas, Cissy to Southern Methodist University. "But you split up!" she blurted.

Shooting her yet another none-of-your-business look, Mack only said, "Go on inside, will ya? Tell Mom I'll be there in a bit. I need to finish."

Resting the brush on Goldy's flank, Mack watched his sister head to the house.

Actually, he *was* finished, but he didn't want to go in just yet. He did miss Lorelei. And he *did* think far too much about what she was doing at any moment of the day. It had been three years since she'd moved away. They'd barely been sixteen. *So, what's the point?* he thought. Yet even while he was telling himself that, he could feel himself growing warm at the very thought of her. He knew it was no good to keep feeling like that. *She's probably not even the same person,* he told himself. But he wasn't ready to file her away as just his first girlfriend, because he knew the moment he did, she would become only a memory, not his first and last and only love, which he'd been sure she was when she'd lived next door. So, when he missed her most, like now, he would try remembering a fight they'd had over something stupid, hoping that'd calm him down. It never did. Instead, he'd always wind up inside his own favorite Lorelei memory—the time she decided to help with his pitching.

She had wandered over as he was about to put his glove and a bucket of balls into the trunk of the old '57 Chevy his father had just bought him. He was heading to the school's baseball field to practice his fastball since his dad had stopped him from using the oak tree.

"Why do you love baseball so much?" Lorelei had asked him as he'd opened the car's trunk.

Setting the bucket into the trunk, he'd shrugged. "I don't know, I just do."

Crossing her arms, she leaned against the car. "I read that the hardest thing to do in sports is hit a baseball. Is that true?"

"Depends on who's throwing it," he answered. "If it's me, I like it being hard."

"Did you know that baseball is the only sport in which errors are counted as actual statistics?" she went on. "I mean, that's brutal!"

"Why are you reading about baseball?" he'd asked.

"You, of course," she said, shrugging.

He smiled at her, gripping his leather baseball glove. "It's not the stats I like. It's what you do to get the stats: hitting, stealing, throwing, striking, batting, and, oh man, the strategizing. And no clock. It isn't over until it's over. Gawd, I love it. All of it. Even putting on my cleats makes me happy."

"It's sort of boring to watch, though," she'd said next.

"Are you kidding?" he'd shot back. "Play it and see if it's boring."

"Okay, then, throw it to me," she said, grabbing his glove out of his hands.

"What?"

"Pitch it to me, why don't ya?" Lorelei had said. "I'll help."

"You don't know anything about pitching!"

"I watch baseball with my dad. I'm smart. I have eyes. What would it hurt?"

"You. You'll get hurt," his cocky younger self had said, puffing up. "I throw hard."

"Oh please. I can catch a ball." She walked back to her side of the Corcorans' front yard and squatted down like a catcher. "Ready."

He wound up and pitched. It went wide.

"Huh," she'd said, throwing it back and crouching down again.

"What?"

"Maybe you're trying too hard. Throw with your whole body, not just your arm."

"You sound like Coach."

"See? Smart. Do it."

He did. It zipped. Perfect. And *hard* . . . so hard, Lorelei lost her balance and fell backward with a yelp. He sprinted over, thinking she was hurt. Instead, laughing at falling, she'd bounced up and kissed him full on the lips . . . *hard* . . .

Goldy stomped her hoof, popping Mack out of his memory.

"Oh, sorry, girl," Mack said and gave her one last slow and luscious brush along her entire back that made her shiver with delight. Patting her neck, he sighed quietly, put up the brush, and went in to dinner.

As he sat down at the kitchen table, his mother looked at him oddly.

"What?" he said.

"You forgot to wash up after being out with Goldy, Mack. My goodness."

"Sorry, was thinking about something," he mumbled and went to do so.

Belle turned to Corky. "And what is going on with you, Kathryn?" she asked, watching Corky poke at her green beans. "You haven't taken a bite of your food. Do you feel well?"

No, Corky almost said. *I do not.*

Because Corky was thinking about something, too: Tad at Mollylynne Morehead's bottle-spinning party after dark.

With each poke of her green beans, she had been plotting what she might do to be there, and it made her head ache, being as bad at plotting as she was at lying. She could try sneaking out; it was only around the corner. But she had yet to learn the fine art of sneaking out of anything, being as bad at sneaking as she was at plotting and lying. Before leaving town, Mollylynne's mother had made a point to tell Officer Tommy Tilton that she and her soon-to-be-ex-husband were going to be gone overnight, leaving Mollylynne to mind the house. Later that evening, on one of his sweeps by the Moreheads' house, Tommy Tilton would notice boys sneaking in the back door and decide to investigate, and that would break up the party before even one bottle could be spun. But Corky couldn't know that yet, so she kept poking at her green beans.

After they finished supper, she helped her mother with the dishes and wandered upstairs.

Mack was in his room, stretched out on his bed, chucking a baseball straight up in the air just to catch it and chuck it again, which was what he did when he was thinking.

So Corky went over and leaned on the doorframe. She wasn't there to admit to Mack he was right about her giving America the book; she was hoping never to tell him that. And she didn't want to think about parties and kisses a minute longer. No, she had other questions, lots of them, about all the new ideas she'd been having since meeting America.

"Why don't we have any Black friends?" Corky began. "Why do they all live over there and we live over here? And why does Daniels' Shoe Store have people from the Southside buying shoes separate from us?"

"All good questions," Mack said, still chucking the ball. "Keep asking them."

"Mom says not to, and you're telling me to keep it up?"

"I guess I am."

Corky thought about Noah Boatwright IV's talent show warning again. "Could America get in trouble playing with us? Are we doing something bad?"

Mack caught the baseball and sat up. "No, not bad."

"But in the book . . ."

"That story was thirty years ago. That's not now."

Corky frowned. "Well, what is now?"

Mack fumed at that one. "Now could be better, and it will probably get worse before it gets better. But our worse is not the worse that's in that book. Okay?"

Corky's frown deepened. "Last Sunday at Papa Cal's, I read a newspaper story to him about a lunch counter sit-in. He said he hoped Dad burns the store down before he lets one of those happen at the soda fountain. 'It ain't right!' he hollered, whacking the table. I jumped."

"Bug, don't worry. Some people are still fighting the Civil War. But this is High Cotton. Seriously. It'll be all right. Nothing big ever happens here."

Corky glanced at Mack's framed All-State baseball award. "Tell me what else Coach Trumbull said, okay? He's going to help America, isn't he?"

Mack's expression went south.

"What's the matter?" she said.

He gripped the ball in his hand so hard, she half expected it to pop. "Know how Wilma Rudolph got discovered?" he said. "Coach told me. She was an All-State basketball player for a big Black high school in Tennessee. They called her Skeeter, she moved so fast. Coach Temple, the track coach at Tennessee State University that Coach Trumbull called today, happened to see her play when she was fourteen and invited her to his track camp. He'd had more members of his women's track team, the Tigerbelles, go to the Olympics than pretty much anybody else," he went on. "So she wound up at the 1956 Olympics while she was still in high school, then to Coach Temple's university, then the 1960 Olympics, and got the damn gold medal as the fastest woman on earth."

"Okay," Corky said, not quite getting his point.

"Bug, what I'm saying is she had huge breaks."

"But . . . Coach Trumbull called Wilma Rudolph's coach."

"Yeah, but we won't know until he gets back whether the message got to Mr. Temple."

"Can't Coach Trumbull still help, anyway?" Corky pushed.

Mack shrugged. "I don't know. He did say he saw an Abilene girl's track team on the cover of *Sports Illustrated* last month that he might try, although he said it was a private team and they all had bouffant hairdos, whatever that means. He also said if he didn't hear anything from Mr. Temple, he might just film America doing the hundred meter and send that to him. We just gotta wait."

Corky, still confused, kept on. "So, you do still think she's good enough to get to the Olympics?"

Mack sat back heavily against his headboard. "You saw what I saw. She's got a gift. Whether she gets to develop it, I don't know. That's the first thing with anybody, getting a chance."

"But . . . that would mean that some people never do. Some really, really talented people."

"Yeah, Bug," he said. "That's exactly what it means."

"But that's not right!"

"No, it isn't." He paused, adding all but under his breath, "Plus, while I can't imagine it, she may not really want to. And you got to have the *want-to*."

That puzzled Corky. "Why wouldn't really, really talented people want to?"

Mack fumed again. "Could be a million things. Maybe they're lazy. Maybe they take their talent for granted. Or maybe they're just plain scared."

That puzzled Corky even more. She started to say so.

But Mack looked out his window and went quiet. She knew that look. He was through talking to her.

So, she went downstairs to watch TV until bedtime. After watching a couple of her favorites, she heard her dad come in the back door. At first, her parents were talking quietly as her mother served her father his steak. But then the voices got loud.

Corky turned off the TV. Her parents were arguing again.

"They offered you a job? Why?" Cal was saying.

"Because the position opened," Belle answered. "It's important work, and they think I can do it. And it's only part-time, Cal. For now. Only later might it—"

"We've gone over this, Belle!" Cal interrupted. "People will gossip that the drugstore is not doing well. No other business owner's wife in town works."

"Mrs. Daniels does," Belle pointed out.

"Mrs. Daniels doesn't count," Cal countered.

"Why not?" Belle said.

"Because she's Mrs. Daniels." Cal sighed. "Why can't you understand? Our livelihood could suffer. It's just not good for business."

"But it'll be good for *me*," Belle said. "Why can't *you* understand?"

"Being the man of the house, I have to make the decisions best for us all. I'm sorry, you just can't. *No*."

"Cal . . ."

That's when they both noticed Corky standing in the doorway, and the conversation stopped.

Her father went upstairs without another word, and her mother went into the living room, barely looking her way. Corky followed to find her sitting on the couch, staring at nothing.

So Corky put "Clair de Lune" on the record player and sat down beside her.

They listened together to the opening of the beautiful music. Then her mother sighed and patted Corky's leg. "Kathryn, have I ever told you why I have this record?"

Corky knew it was the only one her mother ever played, but she'd never questioned why.

"Remember how I told you I moved here when your father was a high school senior and I was a sophomore?"

Corky nodded.

"On his first trip back home from college his freshman year, your father said he wanted to impress me," her mother began. "But he didn't have any money. He was rooming with a musician named Gerald, so your father asked him what was the most beautiful piece of music in the world. Gerald showed your father this record of 'Clair de Lune' by a Frenchman named Debussy. He told Cal it meant 'Moonlight.' Lord knows what he had to trade for it, but his roommate was right. I'd never heard anything more beautiful. It sounded like an exquisite dream."

"That's why Mack and I had to take piano lessons?" Corky said.

"Yes, that's why, and why your father bought that used baby grand. And there it sits." Her mother smiled wistfully as the recording's dreamy crescendo sweetly swelled. "But I still have the record. And I still think it's the most beautiful piece of music I have ever heard."

Hearing that, a memory floated before Corky's mind's eye . . .

She's four years old. Her mother and father are dancing in front of her to this music. She stands there watching, wondering why they're holding each other so close and moving so funny, barely moving at all. Are they okay? Being herself, even at the age of four, she asks, loudly: "ARE YOU OKAY?"

They both jump. Laughing, her father sweeps her up in his arms and swings her around and around . . . as her mother smiles and smiles . . .

Corky glanced upstairs, where her father was surely sitting in his easy chair reading one of his pulp Westerns.

Her mother noticed. "He loves us, dear. Never doubt that."

An hour later, Corky was in her pajamas waiting for the lights to go out in her parents' room. When they did, she opened her bedroom door a crack. Soon, Roy scooted into her room and Corky gave him a hug. Trying not to think about spinning bottles, she gazed out her open window with Roy Rogers, just as she'd done the night before. Like clockwork, there went the Beach sisters in their top-down Corvair, yoo-hooing for Mack, and right behind cruised Bubba in his silver Corvette.

After that, things got so quiet again that she dozed off leaning against Roy Rogers's big noggin and began dreaming about bottles *spinning spinning*, closet doors *closing closing*, and lips *touching touching . . .*

Popping awake, she checked the time: 11:00 p.m. And she began entertaining the first incredibly bad decision of her percolating new adolescence: *What would it hurt if I snuck over to the party for a minute to see Tad? It's just around the corner. I'll come right back.* Never mind she'd never done anything remotely like this before. Never mind if she got caught, her parents would never trust her again. And never mind she'd never gone out by herself at night anywhere. *My parents will never find out . . . ,* she reasoned. *But what if they do?* Just as she was about to talk herself out of her very bad idea, she pictured herself in the thrilling, dark closet, kissing Tad—*who is probably right now in the closet with Mollylynne Morehead.* And that last thought made Corky jump up; throw on her shorts, T-shirt, and sneakers; and tiptoe down the front stairs. "Stay!" she whispered to Roy, who'd followed her downstairs. Just as she was about to ease open the front door, though, she and Roy saw a car roll to a stop against their front curb in the full-moon-drenched night. It was Bubba Boatwright's Corvette again.

Stumbling out of the car, Bubba began doing something that made Corky's eyes almost pop out of her head. He was unzipping his pants.

Roy began to growl.

Gross! Is he about to pee in our yard? Corky thought, shutting her eyes, the moonlight far too bright not to see specifics.

"Hey, Mack!" Bubba yelled as he peed. "Mack Corcoran!"

Corky opened one eye to see him zipping back up.

"Hey, M . . . Miss Goody Two-Shoes!" Bubba sputtered. "C'mon out and fight me like a . . . a . . . m-m-m . . ." Instead of finishing his sentence, he fell backward, landing on his butt in the street.

Roy growled again, louder.

"Roy, hush!" Corky whispered, sure he was about to bark and wake up the entire house.

But as they watched, Bubba pulled himself to his feet, got back in his Corvette, and swerved slowly away.

Glancing upstairs, Corky held her breath. The house stayed quiet. But, of course, Tad, in her overactive imagination, was still inside the closet with Mollylynne.

Her better angels were counseling her to go back to bed.

She did not.

"Stay here!" she whispered to Roy and slipped out the front door, which she had never noticed creaked quite so loudly.

She was barely off the front porch, though, when she heard Roy hassling behind her. "How did you do that!" she hissed, unaware of the loose doorknob that Roy could nose open any time he wanted. Fuming at her dog, who was now sniffing the air, Corky gazed back at the still dark house, trying to decide what to do.

And that's when she heard the sound of the truck.

Grabbing Roy's collar, she hustled them both behind the nearest bush and squinted up the street through the moonlight. There on the south-side curb of the Corcorans' house, the side without a streetlight, sat what looked like the same flatbed truck from the night before. It seemed to be idling with its lights off, the muffler clattering away. She waited to see if the driver was there to visit the neighbors who lived in the Joneses' old house. But nobody got out.

She glanced back at the house. *Should I tell Mom and Dad?* she thought. But what would she say? It was just a truck. It wasn't doing anything weird compared to Bubba pissing in her front yard . . . although it rather looked like it had been watching that, too. *No, that's too weird,* she told herself. *Bubba's always doing something stupid, and Mr. Boatwright's still just making me paranoid, that's all.* The truth was she wasn't even sure what she was being paranoid about. And she sure didn't want to be teased when it turned out to be nothing. Besides, if she did tell her parents, wouldn't she have to explain where she saw it? *Oh, well, I heard a noisy truck while I was sneaking out to go to a party, Mom.* She could just lie and say she saw it from her window, but that would be a lie on top of a lie. And that was the problem with lies; they usually begat other lies, and you had to keep them all straight, another reason she was a lousy liar. Too much work. It was enough to make her want to just stomp over, ask whoever was in the truck to state their business, and be done with it, which she was aware, even with her underdeveloped teenage prefrontal cortex, wasn't all that bright.

So, her heart pounding, she and Roy waited behind the bush. And waited. And *waited.* It felt like an eternity, as such waiting always does. Growling and sniffing, Roy surely thought so, because Corky was now struggling to keep him behind the bush with her.

Suddenly, Roy let rip a mighty bark and simmered all the way down. Corky could still hear the flatbed's rattle, but it seemed to be dying away. She peeked around the bush. The strange truck was gone.

And, up in her parents' room, a lamplight turned on.

Dang it, Roy! Grabbing Roy's collar, Corky hustled them back inside and quickly through the hallway into the kitchen.

"Kathryn?" she heard from the top of the stairs.

"I'm just getting some . . . uh, milk, Mom."

"It's late. Go on back to bed now. And check the front door, will you? I thought I heard it creak open. The knob needs adjusting again."

In a minute, Corky and Roy returned to her room, Corky into bed and Roy under it.

Roy fell fast into untroubled sleep, already doggy-snoring.

But Corky lay there for a very long time staring into the dark, her mind awhirl with too many percolating, spinning, rattling new thoughts.

10

The next day, Belle stood staring out the kitchen window lost in thought, as had become her habit the last few months. The dishes had long been washed, but with a dish towel still in hand, her mind was on her "discussions" with Cal. She was feeling a certain restlessness again, the odd sensation she'd been experiencing for a while. How could she make her husband understand if *she* didn't? It was a problem that seemed to have no name. She had everything she'd always wanted, a beautiful family, a good husband, no financial worries. Yet at this point in her life, something felt missing.

Evangeline passed through the kitchen to return a broom to the porch. On her way back, a load of clean laundry in her arms, she was softly singing a sweet, lulling song to herself in what sounded to Belle like French, and it mentally transported her to New Orleans. Via train.

"Dodo titit, dodo titit, krab nan kalalou . . ."

"Is that a Haitian lullaby?" Belle asked.

"Oui," Evangeline said as she kept walking toward the stairs. "Sleep, little one, sleep, little one, crab's in the gumbo . . ."

Belle smiled. "Evangeline, what's it like in Haiti?"

"Hot," Evangeline said over her shoulder. "Sticky."

"Do you miss anything about it?" Belle asked.

"Coconuts off the tree," Evangeline answered. "And Lalo, *gwo*. Very good."

"Lalo," Belle repeated. "And that is?"

"Spicy beef on jute," Evangeline explained.

"Jute. I assume you can't get that over here," Belle said.

"*Non.* But it's O-K. We got BBQ."

Belle laughed. "That we do."

Evangeline turned to study her. "You feel O-K today?"

"After yesterday's fall? Yes, just a few bruises. I can't thank you enough for your kindness." A bit embarrassed, she shook her head slightly. "This leg of mine, oh my."

Evangeline gave her a sympathetic smile and turned back to the stairs.

"Could I tell you something?" Belle suddenly said, surprising herself.

Evangeline stopped. *"Oui."*

"I'm . . . uncomfortable with having help," she admitted.

Evangeline suppressed a chuckle at hearing the obvious stated. *"Oui,"* she said again.

"I don't want to feel like a cripple, but Cal treats me like a china doll. Plus, I grew up in a small house. So, this"—Belle waved at their big house—"has never felt quite right. I know it's a good thing . . ."

"An American thing," Evangeline added. *"Oui."*

"Very much *oui*," Belle answered, trying out the French with her Texas accent.

And that pleased Evangeline, making her grin.

Belle paused. "Evangeline, may I ask . . . Have you heard from your husband?"

The grin vanished. Evangeline shook her head. *"Non."*

"Cal is a good judge of character," Belle responded. "From what he's said about your husband, I have no doubt things will work out."

For a moment, the two women locked eyes gently, kindly, sharing an understanding of things beyond words.

Then Evangeline turned and headed upstairs.

Glancing back out the window, Belle felt the odd restlessness again. She hung the dishcloth over the sink and called up the stairs, "Evangeline, I need to go out. You okay here for a while?"

"Of course. You go," she heard Evangeline answer.

With that, Belle grabbed her purse and left.

Upstairs, Evangeline began to fold clothes from the laundry basket, at first briskly and then slower . . . now the one staring out the window, lost in thought.

After the lunch hour was over, Corky was ready to go, still thinking far too much about the night before. Since the delivery boy was out doing his rounds, Corky began walking home. She headed, as usual, across the downtown main street's highway to pass the library before she'd turn left and walk the handful of blocks to her house. But when she got to the library, she spotted her mother's Chevy station wagon on the street up ahead. And Roy Rogers was hanging out the side window.

Curious, she decided to find out where they were going if she could catch them. In a few minutes, she found the station wagon parked in front of the First Baptist Church, and standing sentry at the front doors was Roy. He bounded over to her.

"What's going on, Roy? Where's Mom?" Corky opened the big front doors to the church's sanctuary and peeked in. When she saw her mother sitting in their usual pew, she eased through the doors. "Stay!" she whispered back to Roy as she closed the door, then walked down the aisle and sat down by Belle. *"Mom?"* she whispered.

"Oh. Hello, dear."

"Are you okay?"

"If you're worried about my fall yesterday, I'm fine, just a few bruises. I was tired, I guess. What are you doing here?"

"What are *you* doing here, Mom?" Corky asked. "And why is Roy Rogers here?"

Belle looked back as if expecting Roy to bound down the aisle. "Ah, well, I've been coming here for a while, usually while you're in school. And every time I'd leave to go back home, there was the dog sitting outside the church door. Somehow, he'd figured out where I was, as he does. So, after it happened several times, I just gave up and started taking him with me. He's being a good boy out there, isn't he?"

But Corky wasn't satisfied. "Is everything really all right?"

"Yes, of course," her mother answered.

"But why do you come here?"

"Oh, just to think."

Corky looked around, uncomfortable. "And pray?"

Belle smiled. "Well, that's rather the same thing if you do it right, isn't it?"

"What are you thinking about?"

"It's private, Kathryn."

"Okay, but what is it?"

"Sweetheart, that's what *private* means. You keep it to yourself."

"But why?"

"You and your questions," her mother said, shaking her head. "It's just that adults, especially women, sometimes need time to themselves. Away from everything. That's all."

"Is it about Dad?"

"No, no, dear."

"So . . . you aren't catting around like Mollylynne Morehead's parents?"

Belle laughed out loud at that, quickly popping her hand over her mouth since she was in church. "First, young lady, how do you know about Mollylynne's parents? And second, don't worry, your father and I are fine."

"But you were fighting."

"That happens with married people even if you love each other. You'll find that out soon enough. Now, answer my question."

"Mollylynne told people at school that her daddy was catting around. That's why her parents were out of town last night, because her daddy's off with his 'floozy' and her mom's gone to Reno for a divorce." *And that's why Mollylynne was having a Spin-the-Bottle party,* Corky almost added, still not that great at lying.

"Oh my," Belle said. "Well, I suppose that's somewhat healthy for Mollylynne. I hope. But don't you repeat it. And don't make me laugh out loud again since we're in the church sanctuary," she said, patting Corky's leg. "Now, if you're going to stay, sit here with me silently. Think you can do that?"

No, Corky thought as she nodded yes.

"All right. Try to think just your thoughts. It's good to learn how to sit with them a little now that you're getting older. You don't have to close your eyes. Just look around. Look at the nice stained-glass windows. That should help."

As they sat there a moment in the silence, Corky tried. She peeked at her mother, who had her eyes closed. So, she stared up at the choir loft: boring, not helpful. Then the baptistry above it: boring, too, and still not helpful. Then she looked at the stained-glass windows, which were colorful and pretty, but she'd already memorized them from so many Sundays in church. Her favorite was the new one of Noah's ark with all the animals that Corky figured Noah Boatwright had donated because of his name. But it just made Corky see him in blackface singing "Ol' Man River" only to stick his white nose in her face afterward. Even when she tried concentrating on her favorite part of the window, the giraffes entering the ark two by two, she was still thinking about Noah IV. And that wasn't helpful. At all.

Ugh, she thought.

Corky peeked back at her mother. Remembering Miss Yoakum's words—*everybody's got a story*—she was thinking again of the framed pictures along their staircase at home. Not the ones of her and Mack, but photos of her parents when they were first married. And that made Corky realize she didn't know much about her own mother because she rarely talked about herself. In fact, she didn't know anything at all about her mother's family, since her grandparents died before she was born.

So Corky heard herself say: "Tell me a story."

Belle almost laughed again. "You can't sit quietly, can you?" she whispered. "And aren't you a little old to be asking me to tell you a story?"

"No, I mean . . . tell me a story about when you were my age."

Belle's eyebrows popped high. "My, you are growing up. Well, what story should I tell you?"

"Anything."

She thought for a moment. "All right, I'll tell you about the time I rode the train all the way to New Orleans when I was thirteen."

Corky perked up. That sounded good.

"Or I could tell you about my first kiss."

Corky studied her mother. That seemed a bit suspicious, coming out of the blue, even as her lips tingled at the very thought of Tad. *Does she know?*

"Well?" Belle asked. "Which would you like to hear?"

Corky shrugged, now a bit worried. "Either."

"Good," Belle said, smiling, "because it's the same story."

And that perked Corky up so much she realized she was sitting on the edge of the pew staring her mother's way, forgetting all about her frets.

"You remember where I was born?" Belle began.

"Sweetwater."

"That's right. Sweetwater, out in West Texas. Have you heard of the Great Depression and the Dust Bowl?"

"Sort of."

"I was born right after the Depression hit, and life was hard. My father and mother were over forty when I was born, old enough to be my grandparents, really. You remember me telling you that, too, right?"

Corky nodded.

"My mother's family were farmers caught in the Dust Bowl up in the Texas Panhandle. Even from where we lived in Sweetwater, we could see the brown skies north of us when the dust storms were bad," Belle explained. "All my aunts and uncles and cousins on her side died horribly from what they called brown lung from breathing too much of it. But when I was born, my father got a railroad job working in Sweetwater, just far enough away for us not to be caught in the worst of it. And he was able to hold on to his job during the Depression when so many others couldn't. That's how we got to High Cotton by the time I was a high school sophomore."

"And you met Dad and got married."

"Well, yes. But that's a story for another time; let's just say he kept coming home for the summers from college until I graduated." Belle smiled, patting Corky's leg again. "Anyway, when I was thirteen, we were still living in Sweetwater. My mother had pampered me after I survived polio with this stick leg of mine. Daddy did not. Even with my weak leg, he never let me think I was going to be an invalid, although I certainly felt like one," she said. "Did I ever tell you he named me?"

Corky shook her head.

"*Belle* means 'beautiful' in French, and I was feeling anything but beautiful. So, one day, he said, 'Why don't we go see my relatives in New Orleans, my beautiful Belle?' Ever the charmer, he winked at me and held up two overnight train passes." Belle chuckled. "My very Baptist mother didn't approve, mostly because she didn't like my New Orleans relatives. They were Catholic and, therefore, a 'bad influence.' But that trip was the most amazing experience I'd ever known. I'd been sick for so long. I could easily have died or been paralyzed. Even with my weak leg, I couldn't gripe. Yet I recall worrying about what my life was going to be like. My leg was always going to show with the dresses I would wear for the rest of my life. So, being thirteen and suddenly caring how I looked, I started avoiding leaving the house at all. That's when my railroad daddy decided to show me things beyond my little dusty town's limits. He knew that the only way to not be afraid of the world and people different from me was to go see it and go meet them," she went on.

"And, oh, from the very first moment we pulled out of the train station, it was exciting. The train's clickety-clack rocking and rolling was hypnotizing as we passed through town after town, people waving at us as we sped by." Belle sighed, full of memory. "We even had our own compartment as the sun went down, the lights of the passing towns flashing by. I could barely breathe, much less sleep, it was that wonderful. The only way I finally let myself close my eyes was by telling myself I'd be coming back home on the same train. But I had no idea what I was about to see. New Orleans was like going to another country, it was so different. And so was my father's family. They all spoke this mishmash of English and French that sounded just sublime."

"Like Evangeline?" Corky asked.

Belle cocked her head. "The sound of it, oh yes, although I'm sure it's somewhat different, being Haitian. Every time she speaks, I think of that trip." She turned to look at Corky. "In fact, have I ever told you my maiden name? Do you know what it is?"

Corky realized she didn't know that, either.

"It's La Couer. It means 'of the heart,' and my father's family all certainly seemed to very much be so. They were as poor as us, but they were a very romantic bunch." She shook her head, smiling broader. "In fact, everyone and everything in New Orleans seemed romantic, the city so old, so beautiful, so French. Having just turned thirteen, I was at the exact right age to think that was thrilling. Then I met one of my cousins' young friends. His name was Jacque," she said slowly with an accent. "I thought him very romantic, too. He was blue-eyed and blond and had this impish grin . . ."

Uh-oh, Corky thought.

". . . and one night while I was there, he caught me by myself in their little courtyard and kissed me on the lips, a sweet peck."

A peck! Corky relaxed. With all that French buildup, she feared her mother was about to tell her it was a French kiss. If she had, Corky would have been absolutely certain her mom had spies everywhere and somehow *knew* about Tad.

Belle was still talking. "The kiss was nice," she said, leaning toward Corky. "All first kisses are nice." With that, her mother paused longer than usual, bouncing Corky right back to fretting. "But, oh, sweetheart, that trip opened my eyes to how much more I could do as *well* as how much bigger the world was than Sweetwater, Texas, just like Daddy hoped. For years even after I married your father, I dreamed sweet dreams of far-off places. But after we had you and your brother, I knew that seeing the world wasn't realistic. Instead, you know what I did?"

Corky shook her head.

Belle grinned. "I 'saw' the world through the library. I once told Raynelle that. You know what she said?"

Corky shook her head again.

"'There's no frigate like a book to take us lands away'—Raynelle was quoting a famous poet. And it's true."

Corky screwed up her face. "What's a frigate?"

Belle chuckled again. "A fast, old-timey ship. It's a metaphor. Do you get it?"

Corky smiled, nodded.

For a moment, Belle gazed off dreamily. Glancing back at her inquisitive, growing girl, she said, "Want to know a secret?"

Corky couldn't nod fast enough.

"A few years back, I saved enough money from the weekly allowance your father gives me for the house to apply for a passport. For twenty-five dollars, I can look at it and dream of all the places in the books I've read."

"Wow, you've got a *passport*? Where is it?"

Belle shook her head. "No, no. Even your mother gets to have a few secrets of her own. And don't you go looking for it, either. One day I'll show it to you. But, remember, no one knows about it except you and me."

"Not even Dad?"

"Not even Dad." Belle hugged her. "Now, let's go home." When they both stood up, Belle looked down at Corky's feet. "Kathryn Kay Corcoran, are you wearing your tennis shoes? Oh, for heaven's sake! I told you not to."

"Nobody can see them," Corky tried. "I'm behind the soda fountain. And my Sunday shoes pinch!"

Belle sighed. "What am I going to do with you? C'mon, let's go get Roy Rogers."

On the way home, as Corky petted Roy's head, stuck as it was over the front seat from where he perched in the back, she snuck glances at her mother. She was just as beautiful as she'd always been. But now, well, now, with little secrets and big stories all her own, she was suddenly . . . interesting.

That night, Roy joined Corky upstairs again, and the two of them watched out her window as Sunny and Sandy Beach's Corvair drove by, followed soon afterward by Bubba Boatwright's Corvette. But, to Corky's great relief, no strange truck appeared to make her feel strange, too.

Instead, all was wonderfully quiet.

So quiet that her thoughts turned to trains and secrets and kisses and frigates and passports for lands far away until she drifted off to bed, hoping to dream sweet dreams of her own.

11

In the Corcoran family, there was something called the Curse of July.

Or so Gladys, Papa Cal's wife, had named it before she died.

In July.

Corky never knew her, but she knew of the Curse. Papa Cal made sure of that, announcing it every summer day preceding the dreaded month to every available family member for as long as she could remember. Supposedly, members of the clan who migrated to Texas four generations ago—on both grandparents' sides—had died exclusively during the hell-hot summer month of July, usually from natural causes, but sometimes going to their final reward via accidents or illnesses during that month as well.

That's why Mack was standing in Corky's doorway. Papa Cal always made him promise to remind the family each time Mack saw him.

"Beware the Curse," Mack said wryly. And Corky knew he would do it each morning probably until August, like her own haunted alarm clock.

She just rolled her eyes and crawled out of bed.

Since it was Saturday, she was really looking forward to working behind the soda fountain for the lunch crowd. Lots of people would be coming in, and that meant her friends might, too, and she was excited to show off her soda-jerk skills. Her original plan was to get her mother to take her to the store earlier than usual, but she waited because she thought there might be a chance that America would show up at the house with Evangeline.

Finally, Corky asked her mother, "Is Evangeline coming today?"

"No, dear, it's Saturday. Why?"

There was no way Corky was going to tell her mother about giving the library copy of *To Kill a Mockingbird* to America and now feeling a need to apologize for it. "No, just wondering."

"I'll take you to the store again so Roy won't follow. Are you sure you want to be there longer today?"

She nodded.

She was going to have a good day, a fun day, even if it killed her.

At the drugstore, she rushed to stand proudly behind the fountain, where the Stamper sisters were already working.

"Look at you in another cute dress, Miss Katie!" Velma said sweetly. "You should wear dresses all the time."

"Hard to ride her horse in a dress, Velma," Velvadine said, winking at Corky.

"I'm just saying she looks very ladylike," answered Velma.

"Yeah, ladylike—maybe sidesaddle will make a comeback, you never know." Velvadine smirked, handing a Dr Pepper to Teddy Underwood, a regular customer who daily occupied the lunch seat as far away from Noah Boatwright as geographically possible. "Whaddya think, Teddy?"

Known for rarely uttering a word, Teddy took a swig of his Dr Pepper and responded with a carbonated burp, wiping his mouth on his sleeve.

"My sentiments exactly," said Velvadine.

One of Corky's school friends sat down on a fountain stool for an ice-cream cone with her mother, and Corky showed off her scooping skills, knowing she was inspiring jealousy and thoroughly relishing it. With the Saturday shopping crowd, though, the downside was she would also see half of the WMU ladies' group from the church, most of them surely making a point to stop their shopping to embarrass her by commenting on how ladylike and grown-up she looked. And that included Mrs. Solomon, who had just sat down and ordered a Coca-Cola with a glass.

"Miss Corcoran." Mrs. Solomon solemnly nodded as Corky opened the cold Coca-Cola bottle for her and presented her with a clean glass.

"Mrs. Solomon." Corky solemnly nodded back.

"You look very ladylike today in your Sunday best, Miss Corcoran," Mrs. Solomon added as she poured her Coke into the glass to drink it, ladylike.

"Why, thank you, Mrs. Solomon," Corky responded very politely, wishing she'd had the presence of mind to spit in the glass.

A few minutes later, at straight-up noon, Noah Boatwright IV appeared for his grilled-cheese-and-triple-Coca-Cola lunch, spreading out his newspaper on the fountain's counter. As usual. Corky gave him the stink eye when he ordered, but Noah IV was still not acknowledging her existence. She slapped down each new Coca-Cola on the counter, much as she'd tried the day before, once so loudly that her dad actually came down from his prescription area perch to look her way, and that pretty much stopped her from doing it anymore. Yet Mr. Noah Boatwright IV remained oblivious. Worse, that day, even more people suspiciously seemed to be dropping in just to compliment him on his rendition of "Ol' Man River" at the American Legion's talent show and, again, he thanked them by buying each and every one a Coca-Cola of their own, inviting them to sit down and keep talking. Corky kept busy opening Coca-Cola bottles and handing them to his "admirers."

As Noah IV was acknowledging another new admirer, the radio's music program paused for its noon news update:

Our top news stories this hour:

Betty Friedan, acclaimed author of *The Feminine Mystique*, praised women being added to the proposed Civil Rights Act, suggesting it could address her book's famous "problem with no name . . ."

Chanting "We won't go," 12 men burned their draft
cards as 1,000 students gathered in New York City to
protest the escalating war in Vietnam . . .

Jack Ruby has been convicted of the murder of
Lee Harvey Oswald, the alleged assassin of President
Kennedy . . .

In Mississippi, 3 civil rights workers are missing
and feared murdered during Freedom Summer's voter
registration drive. Many believe the Ku Klux Klan is . . .

"Turn that depressing thing off! We're trying to have a conversation here!" Noah IV ordered. "Now, tell me again, what part of the song did you like best? Let's get you a Coca-Cola."

As she served the new drink, Corky noticed Dr. DuBose step his big self up onto the prescription area to talk with her dad. And, just like the day before, he glanced her way behind the soda fountain before leaving.

As she watched Dr. DuBose go, Noah IV and his admirers left as well, but not before Noah IV stopped by the main counter, motioning her dad down to talk again, too. And like Dr. DuBose, he glanced back yet again her way.

Seeing that, Corky was convinced the two men had to be talking to her dad about their softball game, even though that sounded crazy. Why would two grown men be mucking around with their only softball game of the summer? She knew why Noah IV didn't like it. He'd stuck his face in hers to tell her so. But why would Dr. DuBose object?

While Corky worked to wrap her mind around what any of it meant, Coach Trumbull came marching in with a sack in his grasp. He strode over to Mack, who was shelving nearby.

"Mack," he said, "I'm on my way to camp. Give these to America and don't take no for an answer. They're the cleats she wore at the track. You know how I keep track shoes for you boys to use, and none of the boys, for my entire career, was ever as fast as America. Maybe if she has these, she'll run this summer on her own, and I can tell Coach Temple that if he does call back. I put a note in there explaining that the school system loans these to all our runners. But, between you and me, after what I saw, I wouldn't let any other kid use this pair anyway. They're hers now, whatever happens. It was an honor to see her run." He handed the sack to Mack. "See you in August."

As Coach Trumbull left, Corky watched him pass Reverend Washington coming in. She perked up. Reverend Washington was the Southside minister Pastor Pete had called from their house to persuade America to play in the softball game. Corky knew who he was in the same way she knew most of the important adults in her tiny town. She'd always liked his big laugh. And he laughed a lot. After nodding to her father, who'd returned to the raised prescription area, she watched as he almost bumped into Noah IV heading toward the side door. They were talking. Considering all that had just happened, Corky had to hear.

She casually inched closer.

"Mr. Boatwright, I hear you did a fine rendition of 'Ol' Man River' at a talent show," Reverend Washington said.

Boatwright paused. "Some seem to think so."

Corky saw a flash of something cross Reverend Moses P. Washington's face. "Well, now, if you ever get a hankering to come over and sing with our choir, we don't do show tunes, but we occasionally do mighty fine spirituals, and we'd love to have you. Sounds like you might enjoy it."

Sputtering a moment, Noah IV finally found his tongue and mumbled something about his obligation to the Northside's Baptist church as he scurried around the big pastor and away. Reverend Washington, chuckling to himself, strode over to the main counter to pick up a prescription from Earl. When he walked back out the side door, Corky decided to follow.

"Reverend Washington?" she said as they both stepped outside.

"Yes, young lady?"

"I'm Corky Corcoran. Pastor Pete called about America playing in our softball game from my house."

"Ah yes. What can I do for you?"

"Thank you for helping America play with us."

"Well, you're very welcome. I rather like the idea. Did you know that I played a game of scrub baseball when I was about your age on that field with your father?"

If Corky's jaw could have dropped to the sidewalk, it would have over such a breach of Northside-Southside propriety. She didn't know what to say but: ". . . What?"

Reverend Washington, being giftedly loquacious as part of his calling, went on to tell her more about her father as a kid than she'd ever heard before. "I believe it was around 1932," he began. "That was the summer your school built that baseball field. It was brand new, and a few of us from the Southside couldn't keep away from it. We thought it a thing of beauty up next to our school's sandlot, which didn't even have a backstop, much less official bases or shiny new stands. We were all around eleven or twelve. From our side of the railroad track, we'd sneak over there when nobody was looking. We just wanted to hang around it, not really play on it. We knew better than that. No, just looking at it made us happy." Reverend Washington sighed. "I suppose that was the last summer of our childhood, really. It was the Great Depression. Most boys only a little older than us, on both sides of town, were expected to work in some way. We knew that was probably the last summer we could do as we please, so we spent our days playing sandlot baseball and admiring your school's new field.

"One day we noticed we weren't the only ones who wanted to hang around it. A bunch of White boys, including your young daddy, Cal Jr., were already there doing the same thing. And they'd started up a game of scrub. You ever play scrub?"

Corky nodded.

"You can play scrub with six players, but it isn't much of a game, as you know," Reverend Washington went on, "so the four of us came closer, showing ourselves, in hopes they got the hint. Besides myself, it was Jimmy Meadows, Joey Hicks, and Ambie DuBose. You know

Dr. DuBose, I'm sure. He was one of our group, just as rowdy as we all were."

Pausing to chuckle, Reverend Washington shook his head. "Knowing him back then, you'da never guessed he'd work his way into becoming a bona fide medical doctor, nossir. Course, nobody would've guessed I'd straighten up enough to be a preacher, either!" At that, he outright guffawed. "Anyways, when we showed ourselves, your daddy was the one that called out, 'Hey, we need some players.' Well. It took us about two seconds to get on out there and start playing. A couple of the White boys left, one of them, I recall, being Noah Boatwright IV, but we still had enough for a real good scrub. At least until the policeman rolled up. You should have seen us scatter!" And this time, he guffawed even louder.

"Yes, that was quite the summer." Reverend Washington laughed. "I can see your daddy now, bat on his shoulder, hovering over home plate. He was a good boy, and I'm happy to see he turned out to be a good man, doing his part to keep our town healthy. Now, you and America have fun out there, and let's hope everybody plays nice. It was ever so much a pleasure to meet you, Miss Corky Corcoran. I hope to see you again." And he ambled off toward the Southside.

Of course, what Reverend Washington couldn't tell Corky was the rest of that day's story:

A twelve-year-old Noah IV did leave, declaring that he "ain't playing ball with *them*," as did the other White boy. But the rest stayed, and for about an hour, they played scrub—four Black boys and four White boys—until the police cruiser appeared. Out from it came one of High Cotton's three policemen in the '30s, a man named Hiram Tilton, Tommy Tilton's great-uncle, whose job he believed was to enforce the Jim Crow laws, and that included scrub baseball.

As the Southside boys disappeared across the tracks, Officer Hiram Tilton forced all four White boys into his 1931 Ford Model A police car and took them, one by one, to their homes, advising their parents to march them out to their respective woodsheds and give 'em a good whipping. The law of the land was segregation, he'd said . . . and that meant you kept everything separate for the boys' own safety as well as for the safety of the Southside boys, he'd said . . . Life was tough enough living during these Hard Times without making it harder for them all to live together, he'd said.

And the last of his young deliveries was Cal Jr., Corky's father-to-be, to Corky's grandfather, Cal Sr.: Papa Cal.

At the sound of a car pulling into their dirt driveway, Cal Sr. and his wife, Gladys, came out of the house's back door. As Hiram Tilton and Cal Jr. got out of the patrol car, Hiram hitched up his pants and walked Cal Jr. over to them. "Gladys. Cal."

"What's going on, Hiram?" Gladys said, wiping her hands on her apron. "Why's Cal Jr. with you?"

Hiram Tilton stated his spiel about the hardness of life, the law of the land, and the safety for boys on both sides of High Cotton, ending with the whipping order.

To which Corky's grandmother Gladys said, "We'll do no such thing, Hiram Tilton!"

Hiram turned to Cal Sr. "Calvin, you know I'm right."

"I'll handle it, Hiram," Cal Sr. said as Hiram left. "Let's go, boy."

"Calvin, no!" Gladys said, planting her hands on her hips.

"Go back inside, Gladys," he said as he clamped a hand on twelve-year-old Cal Jr.'s shoulder and began marching him to the woodshed.

As they neared, though, they saw Willy already there chopping wood. At that moment in time, Willy and Papa Cal were in their prime, muscled from daily hard labor and ramrod tall in stature. Looking their way, Willy stopped chopping. Setting down the axe, he wondered what Cal Jr. had done this time, the woodshed whippings not all that unusual for a growing boy during the Depression.

But as Cal Sr. and a hangdog Cal Jr. came closer, Cal Sr. stopped to stare at Willy, who was staring back curiously at them. And, without explanation, Cal Sr. turned around and headed back to the house, defying Hiram Tilton's edict to punish his Northside boy for playing with

Southside boys. In that moment, the law of the heart had won out over the Jim Crow law of the land.

Outside the drugstore, Corky was so taken aback by Reverend Washington's story that she could do little more than watch the Southside preacher go. Then she remembered the track shoes. Rushing back inside, she saw Coach Trumbull's sack by Mack, grabbed it, and rushed after the preacher. "Reverend Washington! Reverend Washington!"

He turned back to her. "Yes, young lady?"

"You heard how fast America is, right? About how we timed her at the school, and she's as fast as Wilma Rudolph?"

"Oh yes. Everyone's heard. I assume that's why Pastor Pete wants her to play with you, am I right?"

Corky nodded. "Coach Trumbull left these track shoes for her so she could get used to running in them this summer for her big future and all. There's a note inside from him, I think. But we don't know where she lives."

Reverend Washington smiled. "I'll get them to her."

Thinking about the library book and remembering her Miss-Yoakum-inspired big thoughts, Corky said, "Would you also tell America something for me?"

"Certainly, if you'd like."

Looking around, she came up close and whispered her message in the pastor's ear.

"And she'll know what that means?" the good reverend said.

"Yessir."

"Okay, young lady."

Smiling, Corky hustled back behind the soda fountain just as Teddy Underwood finished his Dr Pepper with a last big burp and ordered another. As Corky grabbed him a new one from the Coke box, she saw Bubba Boatwright push open the front doors and head straight for Mack, who was stocking nearby.

Corky froze, Dr Pepper still in hand.

"Hey!" said Teddy.

"Oh, keep your shirt on," Velvadine said, coming up behind Corky to watch the Bubba-Mack drama unfold.

With Corky and Velvadine looking on, Mack set down the box of jars in his hand and stood up eye to eye with Bubba. Bubba started talking low, obviously steamed about something. And when he didn't stop, Mack, narrowing his gaze, leaned into Bubba's face until they were nose-butting close.

Corky jerked her head around to see if her father had noticed. He had.

"Mack!" Cal called down from the prescription area, shooting him what both of his offspring knew was a stink eye to end all nonsense.

Mack turned his back to Bubba, picked up the box of jars, and moved closer to the fountain. Bubba kept on talking, and Mack kept on ignoring him until Bubba finally stomped out the store's front doors and screeched away in his Corvette.

"What was that about?" Corky whispered to Mack, Velvadine leaning near to hear the answer.

"Just his usual Bubba crap," Mack said as he went back to shelving. "Forget about it."

On Corky's way home after the lunch crowd died away, her mind full of Coach Trumbull, America, and the softball game, not to mention finding out her father had played scrub baseball with the town's future Black doctor and preacher, Corky stopped by the library. She wanted to see the *Sports Illustrated* cover with the women's track team on it that Coach Trumbull had mentioned. Plus, she needed to ask Miss Delacourt a question.

"Hi there, Corky," Miss Delacourt said as Corky swung through the library's front door. "Have you finished the book I gave you?"

"Almost," Corky lied. "No new frigates today," she added.

"Frigates?" Raynelle laughed. "Ah! 'There's no frigate like a book.' You're quoting Emily Dickinson! I'm impressed. Okay, what do you need today?"

"Could I see last month's *Sports Illustrated* magazine? I just want to look at the cover."

"Certainly. Let's find it." Miss Delacourt walked over to the magazine rack, and Corky followed.

"Miss Delacourt, do you have a library police?" she asked as the librarian began to thumb through the magazines on the shelf.

"What? No."

"You don't go after books overdue?"

The librarian chuckled. "Of course not, sugar. You just pay a fine."

"What if a book never comes back?"

"Well, that's a whole other thing. Corky, did you lose *To Kill a Mockingbird*?"

"No, no. I promise I'll bring it back before it's due . . . It's just that I have a new friend. She's from the Southside."

"Really?" Miss Delacourt said as she kept thumbing through the copies. "Is it the girl who's playing with your church softball team?"

Everybody in town really has *heard,* Corky thought. "Yes, ma'am. And she thinks there's such a thing as the library police."

The librarian frowned. "Why does she think that?"

Corky almost let slip the truth, lying still too annoyingly complicated. Instead, Corky said, "She likes books and she doesn't have any. So, I told her, 'Well, at least you can go to the library.' She looked at me like I was nuts, Miss Delacourt. And I realized I couldn't remember ever seeing any people from the Southside in here."

Miss Delacourt hesitated at the uncomfortable point of fact. "Ah . . . yes, well, that's a library policy set up long ago under the Carnegie library rules in Jim Crow states, and, I hate to say, not under our control." She paused, smiling back at Corky. "Not yet, anyway. But maybe very soon." Her hand landed on the right magazine. "Here it is," she said, pulling out the May issue of *Sports Illustrated*. "Well, would you look at that!"

she said, eyeing the cover of the glitzy private Abilene track team as she handed it to Corky. "Isn't that something! I don't think I've ever seen women on the front cover of *Sports Illustrated*."

"Coach Trumbull says it's the first time, that it was probably a stunt to get attention."

"It got *my* attention." Miss Delacourt laughed. "Look at all that makeup! And those bouffant hairdos. How do they run in those?"

Glancing at the women on the cover, Corky opened the magazine and read the cover's caption:

> The blonde, brown, and redheaded runners compete while wearing these hairstyles seen here—the bob, the beehive, and the flip. Teasing helps add volume, and Aqua Net hairspray holds it all in place. Even during homestretch sprints, the sprinters claimed their hairdos don't budge . . .

She showed it to Miss Delacourt, who laughed again. "Oh *my*."

Corky stared at the girly-looking White runners and tried to imagine America wearing a bouffant hairdo in order to join the club. But even being her usual optimistic self, Corky knew that wasn't going to happen. She handed the magazine back to the librarian.

"I think I'll read that article myself," Miss Delacourt said, setting it aside.

Watching her for a moment, Corky blurted, "Miss Delacourt, are you married?"

"Well, no, I'm not."

"Why not?"

"Corky, sugar, some questions aren't exactly appropriate to ask."

"That's what Mom says, too, and I'm supposed to apologize."

"You don't have to do that."

"Okay," Corky said happily and went right back to the topic. "So, you have to work?"

"Corky . . ." Miss Delacourt gave up. "Yes, I suppose I do."

"If you had a husband, would you still work?"

"Yes. I love my job."

"So, then, you're a *working girl?*"

The librarian cocked her head. "Do I look like a working *girl* to you? Think now."

Corky wondered if this was a riddle. "You're working."

"Yes . . . and . . ."

"And you're a girl."

"I'm female, but I'm not really a girl. You're a girl. What am I?"

"Oh! You mean you're a lady."

"In a sense, yes, I'm a lady if I happen to be acting polite and ladylike as society expects, which I usually am, but not *always*. Just like you, Miss Corky Corcoran. All ladies are women, but not all women are ladies, just like all gentlemen are men, but not all men are gentlemen. So, better put . . . ?"

"Oh, a woman," Corky answered.

"There you go. Words matter, sugar." Miss Delacourt eyed her. "Is this about your mother?"

"How did you know?" a surprised Corky answered. "It's just that my dad says it's not normal for women to want to be working girls—I mean, want to work."

Miss Delacourt leaned close. "Here's the thing to remember about *normal*. In big times of change, *normal* is what is being changed. And I can feel that something big is coming. You and your young girlfriends, sugar, are going to be the ones who benefit from it most, wait and see." She smiled. "And, Corky, about your mother. Do you know she is quite remarkable?"

Corky froze, wondering if this was another riddle or, worse, a trick question.

"Your mother can sell anything, anytime, to anyone. I've never seen a thing like it," Miss Delacourt explained. "Every year, to keep our Carnegie library endowment, we have to raise ten percent of our operating funds, and as High Cotton's population dwindled over the last several decades, it became a perennial problem, until your mother came along. That entire children's book section that you've loved so much? After you were born, she single-handedly raised the funds for it. She even learned the Dewey decimal system on her own. And there's so much more. The salaried job we've offered her is to be my assistant either full-time or part-time, her choice, because we want her as part of our staff any amount of time we can get her. She's that good."

Corky again didn't know how to respond. She wasn't used to seeing her mother as anything but her mother, but more than that, she sure wasn't used to hearing compliments about her.

"Now," the librarian said next, "about *To Kill a Mockingbird*. You say you're almost finished with it?"

Corky nodded.

"Do you like it?"

"Very much. But there's that word my mother called you about: *rape*. What does it mean?"

Miss Delacourt sighed. "Did Belle not explain it?"

"Not yet."

"You should ask your mother again."

"That's what Mack said."

Miss Delacourt paused. "Why don't you look it up in *Webster's Dictionary*? And if you still have questions, I'll help you broach it with your mom, okay?"

So Corky looked it up. And, as she read the definition, she decided she would *never* ask Miss Delacourt questions about it, much less her mother . . . Although she suddenly, devastatingly understood far more than she wanted to about the trial in *To Kill a Mockingbird*.

As she left the library in a big hurry, Tommy Tilton was passing in his police cruiser on his usual rounds headed for the school. He waved at her, slowing down. "Hey, Young Miss Corcoran. Want a ride home today?" he called to her.

"No, but thank you," Corky said, waving again, wanting to walk that day more than most. Still thinking big thoughts, now even bigger, Corky turned the corner and headed toward home. She was so deep in thought, it took her several blocks to notice that somebody in a car was following her. When she saw who it was, she fumed and kept walking. "Stop it, Dwayne," she called over to Dwayne Bumgardner in his beat-up, stinky 1952 Chevy hooptie rolling along beside her. "I didn't tell anybody anything. I'm not scared of you."

Dwayne grunted. "Maybe you should be."

She blew him a raspberry.

He kept creeping along beside her.

She stopped and plopped her hands on her hips. "What do you want?"

"I hear you got yourself a Southside girl playing on the church softball team."

"Yeah? So? You never come to church. Why do you care about our softball game?"

"It ain't about church, ugly. You think you're better than me, don't you?"

"Clearly I am," Corky answered. "You're in my junior high class and you're old enough to drive a car."

Dwayne's face turned red. Bringing up the fact that he kept failing because he was dumb as dirt hit a nerve. "Well . . . well . . . ," he sputtered, "what if you find a burning cross in your front yard, smart-mouth?"

"Then I'd know it was you, stupid. And where'd you get that idea, anyway?" she said and began walking once more.

"You ever hear of the Ku Klux Klan?" he called out his window.

She rolled her eyes. "There's no Ku Klux Klan in High Cotton. And there's not been any in Texas since Ma Ferguson beat that KKK guy for governor back in 1924," she said proudly, remembering her sixth-grade paper on Ma Ferguson, the first female governor of Texas.

Corky had received an A-plus on that Texas history paper entitled "Ma Ferguson Ran the KKK Right Out of Texas," and her mother had taped it to the fridge for a week.

Dwayne snorted. "I wouldn't be too sure about that."

"Oh yeah?" Corky said back over her shoulder as they kept moving. "You gonna start your own KKK chapter?"

"Maybe I will."

The next thing both of them heard was a short whoop of a siren. Rolling up behind them was Tommy Tilton in the High Cotton police car.

"Ooh, Dwayne. You in trouble?" she razzed, relieved to see Officer Tilton nearby. "You better be glad Roy Rogers isn't here. I'd sic him on you."

Dwayne shot her a nasty look. "Yeah? Try it. I'll run him down."

And the look in his eyes made Corky worry for the first time, not for herself but for her free-range dog.

The town's patrol car pulled up even with Dwayne's open window until Dwayne finally stopped. Instead of getting out, Tommy just called over, "Hi, Dwayne, whatcha doing?"

"Nothing."

"Glad to hear it. Why don't you get along now and do it up the road?"

Ducking his head, Dwayne slowly drove away.

Tommy called to Corky on the sidewalk: "Miss Corcoran, may I give you a ride home now?"

"That's okay."

"I'll use the *siren* . . . ," he coaxed, knowing that'd get her. So, she hopped in the cruiser's back seat. As they took off, he glanced at her in the rearview mirror. "You're mighty quiet for you. Everything all right?"

"Dwayne just said he was going to run over Roy Rogers," she blurted.

"He did, did he? Hold on."

Tommy whipped around the corner, whooped his siren, and pulled Dwayne over again. This time, Tommy got out and strode over to

Dwayne's window, and Corky leaned out the cruiser's window to hear every word.

"Okay, Dwayne. Listen up and listen good: If anything ever happens to that girl's dog, I will come looking for you, understand? In fact, if I were you, I'd do my best to make sure Roy Rogers stays good and healthy for the rest of his life because if *anybody* hurts him in any way, I'll come looking for you. There are a half dozen citations I could write you up on right now—on this heap of junk, and I'll be happy to slap 'em on you with gusto, cowboy, if I ever see that dog do so much as limp. Got it?"

Dwayne's face went south. "Yessir."

"Good. Now get along." Tommy got back in the cruiser, and off they went toward the Corcorans' house, siren whooping as promised, at least until they reached her corner, where he was smart enough to turn it off. As she got out in front of her house, Tommy said to her, "Maybe you shouldn't walk home for a bit."

"Why?" she asked.

"Oh, I've seen some vehicles around town that I don't know. Hey, I just heard about your new church softball team member," Tommy added, his tone turning all upbeat and happy. "I'm told she can run like the wind, yessir. Can't wait to see." He smiled big at her . . . a little too big, the kind of big smile that adults smile when they really don't feel much like smiling but think they should look like they do. "You be careful now."

Around the corner, Tommy steered his old police car slowly and carefully. Being worn out, the engine of the black-and-white 1955 Ford Fairlane police cruiser was sputtering. Tommy sighed. The town didn't have money for a new cruiser, so he did what he could with what he had, which was the theme of his entire policing career.

Over the last half century, High Cotton's population had shrunk so low that the town had struggled to afford a police force. By 1964,

Tommy Tilton was High Cotton's lone policeman and had been on his own for years. He'd been the only applicant when the town decided it needed to keep at least one policeman in a cruiser if for no other reason than giving out speeding tickets in the time-honored way of small-town speed traps, offering High Cotton sorely needed income. The rest of the time, his job was to cruise High Cotton's streets looking official and dissuading young, high-spirited teenagers from misbehaving—if he could catch them, that is, since he couldn't be everywhere at once.

Actually, to Tommy's way of thinking, the high-spirited kids were no real problem. There were the juvenile delinquent types like the Bumgardner brothers, Darryl and Dwayne, who he was always tailing, knowing they'd be doing something sometime they shouldn't be. But, as for the rest of the kids, since a tiny town only has a few streets to cruise, the local teenagers just needed ways to let off their adolescent steam. For instance, he knew the Beach sisters had a thing for Mack Corcoran and would be stalking his house a little now that he was home from college. He also knew Bubba Boatwright had a thing for the Beach sisters, so Bubba'd be right behind. Plus, there was always Bubba's drinking-and-driving problem, which Tommy was having to handle far too frequently lately.

Otherwise, High Cotton was a nice, peaceful little town.

There was a problem with a nice, peaceful little town, though. If something big ever *did* happen, it could easily catch the town's lone cop by surprise. Lately, when he had glimpsed some strange vehicles several nights in a row during his evening rounds, Tommy wasn't quite sure what to think. It was probably nothing. People get new or "new-to-them" vehicles all the time. But since he was acquainted with pretty much every driver in High Cotton, he'd have expected to get an earful from the proud new owners about said vehicles on first sight of them. However, the first sight of these unfamiliar vehicles was just a glimpse of a strange truck here and a peculiar old car there. Worse, each glimpse was under the cover of darkness and never quite close enough to one of the town's few working streetlights to get a good look. The truck seemed to be a flatbed and the car a jalopy, maybe an old Studebaker. But he couldn't be sure. The sole clue he really had, in case something big did happen, was that he'd only spotted the vehicles on *this* side of town—the northwest side. Since the Boatwright mansion was up on the western rise above town, he had a hunch it had something to do with Bubba Boatwright. If so, the situation would surely be made worse by the carte blanche the Boatwrights enjoyed in High Cotton. He checked his watch. If his hunch was right, he'd soon need to be on the lookout for Bubba returning from drinking at the Broke Spoke. Considering the bad blood between Bubba and Mack Corcoran, he'd decided to patrol nightly between their two houses for a while, fearing what a drunk Bubba might haul off and do. *That boy is on the road to perdition,* Tommy thought, and not for the first time.

As Tommy cruised on, pondering the situation, the old black-and-white cruiser gurgled, lurched, and died right in the middle of the street.

Tommy cranked the starter and stomped on the gas until the engine roared back to life. Before it had the chance to die again, he headed quickly downtown.

"Back to the garage," he grumbled.

Pulling into Cliff's Texaco station, Tommy slapped the car into park and checked his watch again, worrying about missing his nightly rounds.

Cliff gave him a big one-arm wave. "So, Officer, whaddya got today? You got a new problem or just the same old ones?"

Glancing west, Tommy, a fan of the famous '50s TV game show, fumed and said, "That, Cliff, is the $64,000 Question."

12

A few minutes later on the Southside, Reverend Washington knocked on the door of the small, cream-colored, square house a block over from his church.

America opened the door. ". . . Brother Washington?"

"America, I have a package for you." He handed her the sack Corky gave him. "I am told it has a note inside."

Opening the sack, America recognized the track shoes and pulled out the note to read:

> *America,*
> *Here are the cleats you used at the track in hopes you will run this summer. Use our school cinder track with my permission. If you can't, dirt roads will do. The school system buys these for our track team to use. And I would have you on mine if I could. I am proud to say I saw you run.*
> *Coach Trumbull*

She looked up at her pastor.

"Is it good?" he asked.

She couldn't answer. She didn't quite know how. But the pleased, wide-eyed look on her face made Reverend Washington smile. "I also have a message for you from Miss Corky Corcoran. She says that she 'didn't understand and now she does.' I hope that makes sense to you."

For a moment, America looked away. Glancing back at the big man, she nodded.

"Pastor?" Evangeline appeared from the kitchen.

"Evangeline, how are you? Is everything going okay?"

Evangeline sighed softly in response.

Reverend Washington smiled again. "Ladies, if you need me, you know where I am." Opening the picket fence's little gate to leave, he waved at them as they closed the front door.

Still holding the sack, America waited for her mother to ask what was in it. Evangeline didn't. That was exactly what had happened with the sneakers. It wasn't like her mother at all. But America knew why. Her mother was waiting to hear from America's father about his job search. America watched her wander back to the kitchen, where she paused in front of the kitchen wall phone as if willing it to ring.

"Mamà," America said, standing in the doorway.

"*Oui?*" her mother mumbled.

"Would you like to try on the Sunday dress I made you? It's almost finished," America tried.

"No, not tonight, *chéri.*"

At that moment, the kitchen phone rang.

Evangeline grabbed the phone receiver. "Rayford?"

America headed to her room down the short hallway. Passing their Singer sewing machine in its closed treadle cabinet, she ran her free hand over it lovingly. Then she went on into her room, leaving the door open a crack. Still holding the sack of running cleats, she gazed over at the new sneakers in her closet and couldn't help thinking how odd it was that everyone was suddenly offering her shoes.

"How did things go?" she heard her mother ask from the kitchen. America strained to hear more but caught nothing until finally she heard her mother ask, "When will you know?" A very long pause followed until Evangeline suddenly said, "If not, how will we get by?" And she heard her mother quickly correct herself. "Oh, I didn't mean it that way, *chéri mwen*! We'll get by. We always get by, don't we?"

Hearing her mother hang up the phone, America eased the door shut, sat down on the edge of her bed, and closed both hands around the sack.

In the kitchen, Evangeline dropped into a dinette chair. Picturing her husband in a strange town trying to make things right again, she found herself thinking of the first time she had called a lanky, young Rayford *chéri mwen*: "my love." As they walked along the Galveston seawall, he'd asked her to marry him. Having learned just enough Haitian Creole to flirt with her and fall in love, he'd said, "*Marye mwen, bebe!* If I get the railroad job, will that be enough for you to say yes?"

She'd answered: "*O chéri mwen . . .*"

It had been enough. Through everything since, *he* had been enough. And she knew that he would always be enough. Getting up, she went into their bedroom, lay down, and stretched an arm out to touch his empty side of their bed. And the sweet *chéri mwen* memory calmed her enough that she fell into a deep sleep for the first time in days.

In her room, America could hear her mother's soft snoring. Knowing how worried and exhausted her mother had been, she was glad to hear it, but she couldn't sit still thinking about all she'd just heard. And just like the night she'd started Corky Corcoran's library book, her entire being was once again shouting: *Go.*

Taking the track shoes out of the sack, she put them on. Careful not to scratch the floor with the metal cleats, she instantly was back at the track in her mind, running like the wind. That's the way the shoes made her feel. Like she could all but fly. Slipping them off, she tiptoed in her sock feet out the back door. Then, popping the cleats back on, she sprinted down her Southside dirt street, running as hard and fast as she could go.

As she passed the schoolyard, the high school boys playing baseball on the small, dusty field hooted and hollered and whistled.

"America! *Americaaaaaaaa!*"

When they kept on, she yelled back, "You're nothing but foolishness, all of ya! Leave me be!"

Every boy laughed, except one. That boy, a tall, burly teenager named Leon, who everybody called Lion, grabbed a bat and whacked the baseball hard and straight to drop right in front of her.

"Ooooh, Lion's sweet on America," one jeered.

"Oooooooooh," the other boys joined in as Lion, ignoring them all, stared at America to see what she'd do.

The ball rolled toward her feet and she picked it up.

Lion trotted coolly in her direction. "Guess I hit it too far. Don't know my own strength sometimes," he called her way.

"Get the ball back, would ya, Lion?" yelled one of the boys. "We're in the middle of a game here!"

Lion, smiling his best smile, held up a hand, expecting her to toss the ball. Instead, eyeing the dusty sandlot, America bounced the hardball in her palm.

"C'mon, America, give it back!" one of them yelled.

America kept bouncing it in her palm.

Lion noticed as he came close. "Wanna play?"

"Don't be *stupid*, Lion. Everybody knows girls play softball. They can't handle hardball!" yelled a mouthy boy named Jacob, who the other boys called Jabber. "And what she doing with cleats on, anyway? That's stupid, too—everybody knows girls don't run, neither."

America narrowed her eyes at Jabber. "Want to race?" she called to him.

"*Ooooooh.*"

Jabber came closer. "What do I get when I win?"

"IF you win, you get the ball back," America said. "WHEN you lose, I keep the ball."

"HEY, that's MY ball!" yelped one of the boys.

"And you *all* leave me be," America added.

"Hold on . . . *All* leave you be?" asked Lion.

"Easy-peasy," said Jabber, puffing up.

Jabber lined up by America on the dirt street, and the other boys rushed over to watch. Smiling slyly, she pointed to the corner of the schoolyard about fifty yards away.

He nodded.

"Ready. Set. GO!"

Head back and spine straight, America sprinted once again like the wind, getting to the corner before Jabber had barely made it halfway.

Without breaking stride, she pitched the baseball back perfectly, not to a very surprised Jabber but to a very impressed Lion. And, as she kept on running, a big, wide, proud smile broke across her face.

Five hours later and fifteen miles up the Fort Worth–Decatur highway, Bubba Boatwright sat at the bar in the Broke Spoke Tavern. Established in 1846, when the Decatur highway was nothing more than a rutted wagon path, it looked, smelled, and sounded as old as it was: creaky, dank, and dark. The ancient bar with a dozen rickety barstools and two small tables filled up the entire room, the floor looking more like dirt than sawdust.

Already halfway through his second sixer of Lone Star beer, Bubba was muttering. Again. And the bartender, along with the other regulars, had already had enough of Bubba's latest whining.

Rolling his eyes toward the two men sitting at the far end of the bar, the bartender griped, "You still talking about that softball game? We've heard it all several damn times this week."

"A Southside girl . . . a *Neeee-gro*," Bubba went on, grossly overpronouncing the polite term used in '64. "And, OF COURSE, All-State Golden Boy Mack Corcoran is the team's COACH. G'dammm Goody Two-Shoes . . ." He burped. *"Neee-gro,"* he repeated, liking the way his mouth felt when he said it. *"Neeeeee-gro . . ."*

"You've had enough, Bubba." The bartender folded his arms. "Better get on home now."

Sliding off his barstool, Bubba stumbled out of the tavern, passing under a threadbare Confederate flag tacked above the door.

The two men at the other end of the bar upended their beers and left as well. Out in the parking lot, one man reached into a dented Studebaker jalopy for a pack of cigarettes and got into the passenger seat of an old flatbed with side rails and a broken taillight driven by the other.

And when Bubba drove away in his shiny, silver Corvette, they followed.

After the summer night finally turned dark, Corky sat in her upstairs room, waiting patiently for her parents' lights to go out. When they did, she cracked the door for Roy Rogers. In a minute, as usual, Roy appeared and joined her at the window to watch the street under the spray of the corral corner's working streetlight.

As expected, the two soon saw Sunny and Sandy Beach's top-down Corvair drive by, with, as expected, Bubba Boatwright's Corvette trailing behind.

But as Corky and Roy watched, the Corvette slowed, weaved, and rolled to a stop, bumping over the curb, Bubba's head landing on the steering wheel's earsplitting horn.

Everyone except Belle went running outside. And there was Bubba, snoring, head still on the blaring horn, with Roy Rogers trying to bark it silent.

Corky's father stopped the blaring by pushing Bubba's big head off the horn and back on the headrest.

Mack fumed. "He was probably swigging at the Broke Spoke."

"He's been coming by a lot," Corky said, patting Roy's panting head. "Every night since Mack's been home."

"What? Why?" their father said. Letting go of Bubba's head, it landed once again on the horn with the same blaring result. Cal quickly pushed the still snoring Bubba sideways, went back to the house, and called High Cotton's cop. Within a couple of minutes, Tommy Tilton appeared. Since the Corvette was only scuffed, Tommy, Mack, and Cal pulled the passed-out Bubba from the Corvette and stuffed him in the patrol car so Tommy could take him home. And everyone went off to bed except Corky and Roy.

Turning off her bedroom lights, Corky sat back down with Roy in front of her open window, and the two of them quietly, sweetly listened to nothing but the sound of the summer cicadas for a good long while. Leaning against the big dog, Corky dozed off until, hearing the sound of a truck, she jolted awake.

She scanned the street, but didn't see a car or truck anywhere. *Did I dream it?* she wondered. Even Bubba's Corvette was already gone.

But rolling slowly under the corral corner's streetlight came Dwayne Bumgardner's hooptie.

Dang it, Dwayne, why are you coming by? Corky thought, watching it disappear from her window's view as it headed toward the front of the house.

Growling, Roy's ears perked up, and he bounded down the stairs to the front door.

Now what? Corky thought, rushing after him.

When Corky got to the door, she saw through the door's glass panel that the hooptie was parked across the street, and, standing by their curb, both wearing long-sleeved, hooded sweatshirts on the hot summer night, were the Bumgardner brothers, Dwayne and his taller brother, Darryl. Dwayne was holding what looked like a homemade wooden cross, and Darryl seemed to be holding a gas can. As Corky watched, Dwayne pushed the cross into the front yard's dirt and struck a match while Darryl sloshed gasoline on the cross. Darryl, however, sloshed a little too enthusiastically, splashing Dwayne's sleeve, which made Dwayne jerk and drop the burning match. Which happened to touch his splashed sleeve on the way down.

So, instead of setting the cross on fire, Dwayne set himself on fire.

With a yelp, Dwayne ripped off the burning sweatshirt and stood there bare-chested for a shocked moment staring at his equally shocked brother.

As Corky started to rush upstairs to tell her parents, she saw Tommy's police cruiser coming up the street. Within a matter of seconds, Tommy had slammed on the cruiser's brakes, jumped out, stomped on the burning sweatshirt, and, with a glance at the still dark house, ordered both up against his cruiser. Corky cracked open the front door to hear.

Gazing back at the house, Tommy waited for a light to come on. When it didn't, he turned back to the brothers. "Boys, if I had a jail, you'd be in it after this stunt. You watch yourselves, or I'll ring up the county sheriff, who's got himself a dandy one, you hear me? I got a good mind to do it right now. Either of you say one word, and I'll do it." Then he commanded Darryl to get in the cruiser's back seat with the cross and ordered Dwayne to follow in the hooptie.

Watching them all pull away, Roy gave a mighty bark.

"Shhh, Roy!" Corky whispered, quickly popping the door shut.

"What's going on *now*?" Corky heard her father's muffled voice call down the stairs. "What's the dog doing at the front door?"

"He heard something, I guess," Corky answered, glancing through the door's glass panel to make sure everything was back to normal.

Roy let rip another mighty bark.

"ROY, hush up!" Cal called down. "Keep him quiet, young lady! I've got to get some sleep. It's past midnight, for crying out loud!"

"Yessir," she said, grabbing Roy's collar in a futile effort to look as if she could make him do anything he didn't want to do. *"Roy, c'mon now,"* she whispered. *"Up with me or you'll have to sleep on the back por—"*

But Roy was already bounding up the stairs to Corky's open window, growling and whining as if something was still riling him, something that he alone could hear . . . until Corky thought once again she heard a far-off truck rattle.

Oh no, she thought. She listened hard but heard nothing more. Suddenly, just as he'd done after the clattering truck disappeared on the night of the bottle-spinning party, Roy let rip one last mighty bark and simmered all the way down.

"Katie!" she heard her dad's voice call from her parents' bedroom.

"Yessir!" she called back.

Roy had already curled up under Corky's bed. But Corky watched and listened by the window a while longer until, finally, she made herself get on into bed. Still stuck on all that had just happened, she fought with herself about whether to tell her parents about the brothers and even maybe hearing the truck from the other night. If she woke her parents up again, they'd be grumpy and want to know everything, she'd tell them too much, and they'd overreact, maybe not letting her play in the game. *Especially if Noah IV and Dr. DuBose really were talking to Dad about it,* she thought. Or they might tell Tommy, and he'd think the truck had something to do with America, too. *Then he might stop the game altogether,* she realized. And if there were no softball game, she might not ever see America again.

No, Corky decided. Mr. Boatwright's weird warning, on top of Darryl and Dwayne's monkey business, was just making her imagination play tricks, that was all. *Besides,* she reminded herself, *didn't Mack say nothing big ever happens in High Cotton?*

And that young decision would haunt her for the next fifty years.

13

The next day was Sunday. As they did every Sunday, Corky's father went to work, and her mother and Corky went to church. Mack would have begged off, but he knew better that morning, considering his tenuous situation with his parents. So, at church time, the Corcorans, minus their Sunday-working father, filled their usual pew.

The average Baptist church service doesn't have a liturgy to speak of. The church sanctuaries don't have icons or symbols or any such things covering their walls, proudly so, at least not in 1964, not even a cross. If a church was prosperous enough to have stained-glass windows, those might have a smattering of such things on the beautiful glass, but that was it. What they had, what they relied on as their only real weekly ritual, was full-throated singing and a rousing, good Bible-quoting sermon to light the spiritual fires under their members. Therefore Baptist pastors, especially in small towns, lived or died—figuratively speaking—by how well they could preach. And Pastor Pete was a pulpit-pounder. He was the kind of Baptist who would have felt right at home in a nineteenth-century tent revival, and it sometimes seemed the service was still crafted that way. You had some good hymn singing, and you had an offering, and you had a choir special or a solo by one of the more talented choir members. But it all led up to the sermon. And that morning, Pastor Pete was biting at the proverbial bits to get to his sermon, rocking on his heels and belting out the hymns introducing him.

Leona Quattlebaum sang a reedy rendition of "How Great Thou Art," much like the "Ave Maria" she sang for the American Legion's talent show, straining as always for the high notes. As she finished, everything went quiet, the congregation waiting for Pastor Pete to begin.

And begin he did. To Corky's delight, his sermon was about the softball game. For the first time in her young life, Corky was tickled to hear an adult spouting scripture to her, because they all had to do with what she, Pastor Pete, Mack, and Coach Trumbull saw America do at the school track.

Pete first read Isaiah 40:31: "'But they that wait upon the LORD shall renew their strength; they shall mount up with wings as eagles; they shall run, and not be weary; and they shall walk, and not faint.'"

He followed that with 1 Corinthians 9:24: "'Know ye not that they which run in a race run all, but one receiveth the prize? So run, that ye may obtain.'"

And he even added Psalms 37:23: "'The steps of a good man are ordered by the LORD: and he delighteth in his way.'"

And, boom, he started into the sermon's topic.

"Brothers and sisters, I had the honor of watching a potentially world-class, God-given talent in action last week. I have never been so moved at seeing such a remarkable display. And this week we are going to have a chance to do something special to support that gifted fellow High Cotton resident and allow you to see it, too. Not only are we going to have a rousing good time playing girls' softball with the Methodists as we do every summer for both our boys and girls. But this week we will do something that will go down in our church's annals as momentous crosstown Christian cooperation. We have gotten the permission of our Baptist brethren from the Southside of our small city to let this remarkable, young woman, a member of their congregation, play with us!" At that point, he paused, having to squelch a slight smile. "And, I must mention, it will also offer a wonderful chance for us to finally break our long losing streak." Then he stood up ramrod straight and went on. "And the Lord will delight in our ways, I truly believe."

A murmur rippled through the congregation.

"Now, I know some of you are a little worried about setting such a precedent," Reverend Pete went on, waving a hand. "But are we not to be witnesses? To let our light shine for all to see? To spread our arms and take in the world around us in the name of Christ Jesus Our Lord and Savior, who himself said, 'Suffer not to let the children come to me?' After all, is this not a purpose of everything we do, including softball?"

The murmur rippling across the congregation now had a certain grumbling aspect. And there, smack dab in the middle of the sermon, Amos Quattlebaum, one of the church's deacons, raised his hand. "Pastor?"

This had never happened before. Pastor Pete was being interrupted in the middle of his sermon. Pete adjusted his horn-rimmed glasses, hiding his irritation. ". . . Yes, Brother Amos?"

"She's not going to be coming to church, is she?"

The crowd's murmuring grew louder.

"No need," Pastor Pete answered. "As mentioned, she is already a member of our fellow Baptist church here in town. And God is at softball games, too."

"Well, okay, but—"

Pastor Pete interrupted him. "Now, Brother Amos, surely you don't have a problem with this talented, young girl playing with us, do you? After all, wouldn't Jesus play softball with her?"

From the hesitant look now on Amos Quattlebaum's face, that point hit home. "Well, sure . . . I guess."

Since Corky was lingering on the thought of Jesus playing ball with them, she didn't hear the next few seconds of Pastor Pete's reply, but whatever she missed seemed to be doing the trick. Everyone had quieted down. They were buying it. Pastor Pete could *preach*, even about softball. Plus, some of the congregation had already seen the movie based on *To Kill a Mockingbird*, which had been playing in Fort Worth for over a year at that point, with legendary actor Gregory Peck as Atticus Finch, defy-er of all things unjust. Once people of even slightly noble convictions see Gregory Peck playing such a man, they don't forget it, and those movie-loving church members weren't going to be called un-Christian or racist in front of each other. All, that is, except Deacon Noah Boatwright IV, who didn't care what others called him because he was a Boatwright. When he saw things go quiet once more, he dispensed with Amos Quattlebaum's courteous hand-raising and popped to his feet in the choir loft behind the preacher.

And the mood turned.

"It's wrong, I tell you, Pastor!" he all but shouted. "Things are fine the way they are! We'll be asking for trouble from those who don't like it! How are you going to feel after one of our beautiful stained-glass windows is broken by rock throwers and other town rowdies without your high-minded ideas?"

Two more deacons, taking their lead from Mr. Boatwright, chimed in.

"Amen!" one said.

"Amen!" echoed the other.

"Now, Brother Boatwright—all of you—I promise you are worried over nothing," Pastor Pete answered, turning sideways to address Noah IV in the choir loft behind him without turning his back on the congregation. "It's only a softball game, after all, isn't it? Think what Jesus would think. *Do* what Jesus would do. 'Know ye not that they which run in a race run all, but one receiveth the prize?'" he repeated from the Corinthians scripture. "Let's win the prize, brothers and sisters!" he added, confusing some who wondered if he meant winning the crosstown Christian goodwill prize or winning the softball game after their embarrassing decade-long losing streak. To stop all further discussion, he ended his usually lengthy sermon and said to the congregation, "Why don't we all bow our heads in silent prayer for a few minutes and let the word of the Lord sink in before the invitation hymn 'Just as I Am.'"

Pastor Pete turned his back to the choir and Noah Boatwright IV. Noah IV sank back into his seat and stopped talking, but it was the kind of stopping that you just knew wasn't really stopping at all, his face telling a story his mouth was not.

Mack, sitting beside Corky, was smiling broadly, enjoying the entire show. He knew full well what was being stirred up and was relishing every second of it. In a few minutes, after no one came forward while the invitation hymn was being sung, Pastor Pete led them all in the benediction to end the service.

On the way out the church door, the crowd jostling to get home to their ham or roast beef dinners, Tad bumped up against Corky, slipping her a note scribbled on the back of a church offering envelope: *Meet me at the schoolyard again?* Grinning, he looked back as she read it. She shook her head and made the saddest face she was able to muster, which wasn't hard because she was very, very sad. This was Sunday. On Sunday afternoons, after their roast beef Sunday dinner, she had to go read the newspaper to Papa Cal.

Tad looked disappointed, too. But he started talking to Mollylynne Morehead, who'd been punished for the Spin-the-Bottle escapade by having to go to church with her sourpuss grandmother, Mrs. Etta Mayweather. And Corky felt her stomach drop.

Thirty minutes later, inside the Boatwright mansion on the small rise over-looking High Cotton, the male members of the Boatwright family sat around the long, antique, English walnut dining table that the first Noah Boatwright had bought in 1877 for his new mansion, complete with a por-trait of himself that hung behind the head of the table where his great-grand-son Noah IV now sat. They were waiting for Mrs. Noah IV to bring in the roast beef dinner she'd put in the oven before they left for church. The boys, Bubba and Tad, knew what they were in for, since the family was between cooks. As their mousy mother placed the burnt roast beef and the milky mashed potatoes on the table, the boys looked back and forth at one another. Even the rolls were burnt, and they were just "brown 'n serve" from the gro-cery store. While they weren't in any big rush to act like they were actually going to eat their mother's cooking, the boys were still antsy to get it over with. But they had to wait for their father to stop brooding over what had happened at church and say the blessing. This familial ritual had little to do with religiosity, and it wasn't much of a meaningful tradition as traditions

go. The mealtime prayer had been handed down for four Boatwright generations: Noah IV, being the current paterfamilias head of the household,
was expected to say grace over each meal just as Noah III had done and
Noah II before him, back to the town founder and mansion-builder himself,
the elderly Noah Ulysses Boatwright I, whose new young wife, being more
superstitious than religious, thought it wise to give a nod to the possibility
of the Almighty since she married Noah I for his money and rather wanted
to be sure he stayed so blessed. For almost a century, not a bite of food was
partaken at that long antique table without pious words being said over it.
So it was and so it remained until the moment that Noah IV finally looked
down at the burnt slice of roast beef his timorous wife had just placed on his
plate, jumped to his feet, and cursed.

"God*damn it!*" he said, taking the Lord's name seemingly in vain.

Cleaning up his language had been his one failing as a now pious
Baptist deacon, but since he was a Boatwright, he didn't much care.
Besides, he meant the curse literally. He truly did want God to damn
it, although not the food. He wanted God to damn not only his being
disrespected by his own pastor in front of the Sunday-morning congregation but also his pastor asking a Southside girl to play with their
Baptist team without getting permission from his deacon board so they
could have rightfully nipped it in the bud. "Who the hell does he think
he is, preaching at us about Jesus playing softball? Jesus wouldn't play
softball!" he hollered. "Why can't people leave things the way they are?
Something bad is going to happen. Mark my words!" And the more he
bellowed, the more his mousy wife cringed and his sons looked busy,
even to the point of eating the burnt meal on their plates.

Noah IV turned and stared up at the portrait of Noah I. It wasn't
easy being the only adult male Boatwright in the town his great-grandfather founded, he was thinking. *Wait, NO! The town we'd owned!* he
corrected himself. *It was part of his original thousand-acre farm, was it
not? Why, this town wouldn't even be here if it weren't for us! They owe us!*

And that was Noah IV's truth. Learning nothing on his own, Noah
Boatwright IV had inherited his forefathers' values as much as their

property, having been given everything and believing he deserved it all. But something deep inside made him suspect he had no real power anymore in "his" town, not even the reverent respect the Boatwright name had always elicited. Now that all the land was sold except for the mansion, the only thing he had left was money. And the money, to his surprise, wasn't enough. "I have power! I do!" he roared. "And I'll prove it." Grabbing his Cadillac keys, he headed out the front door, calling back, "I'm going to stop this right now!"

Across town at the Corcorans' house, Belle fed her family their own decidedly not-burnt Sunday roast beef dinner. For a while, they sat around sated and satisfied, bellies full of roast beef and potatoes and dinner rolls and sweet iced tea. Then her dad got up and began looking for the delivery truck's keys, and her mother started wrapping up a part of the dinner to feed both Papa Cal and Willy. Corky knew not to sigh. She'd already been reprimanded for that far too many times. She just went on outside and climbed into her dad's pickup, waiting to go to her grandfather's.

Papa Cal's house was on the far northeast side of High Cotton, a bit out in the country. A decade earlier, after Noah Boatwright III died, Noah IV had sold off the remaining farmland, all but ten acres surrounding the mansion, to live off the boatload of money. Since Corky's father was already doing dandy financially after buying the drugstore, he bought Papa Cal's shotgun house's acreage for his father's golden years. Since that day, nothing much had changed except the town got smaller and Papa Cal and Willy got older, too old finally to drive a tractor, much less plow a field or pick cotton. And the land they'd farmed was as depleted as they were, all three forced to go fallow together.

At the house, bouncing to a halt in the truck, Corky and her father headed for the back entry, where Papa Cal and Willy were sitting in two easy chairs in front of the rabbit-eared TV. Both were over eighty. Papa Cal still had a head of white hair, while most men his age were bald as a billiard ball. Plus, he still had the build of an outdoor farming man even though he hadn't done a lick of farming in Corky's memory because of his dwindling eyesight. As for Willy, he'd worked as a hired hand on Papa Cal's patch of Boatwright land for his entire long life. He was the skinniest man Corky had ever seen, and yet, until recently, he had also somehow been the strongest. You couldn't tell there were any muscles on his whole sinewy body, especially at his current age, but boy, were there. He used to pick up Corky's pudgy little self just for fun, acting like she was light as a feather, and she was surely not. And could he ever whistle, the kind of whistle a tomboy would have loved to do, the loud, two-finger-on-the-lips *whrrrrWHTT* through the teeth that you'd hear at baseball games or see in the movies. Corky practiced with him for hours, yet she never mastered it. But, while he could still rip out a great whistle, his sod-busting years had now left him about as arthritic as a working man could get, moving slowly and painfully when he was forced to move at all.

Corky and her father had walked in right in the middle of one of Papa Cal's and Willy's crying jags, which happened sometimes. When Corky asked her dad why they did that, he said, "They're just old, Katie."

"Why are we still here, old friend?" Papa Cal was whimpering.

"I don't know, Mister Cal, I don't know." Willy shook his head as both their eyes welled up with old-man tears.

"It's almost July. Maybe this is the year," Papa Cal said. "Maybe this July will finally get me." Referring to the July Curse, like his warnings to his grandchildren, was a summer event, brought up every Sunday until August, especially during crying jags.

But seeing Corky, Papa Cal was suddenly all frowning swagger. "Cricket, what's this I hear about a Southside gal playing ball with you?" How he heard things stuck in his house all day, Corky had no idea. "You gonna let her?" he said to her dad.

"I don't know, Papa," Corky's father said back to him. It was what he always said to Papa Cal to avoid any sort of actual conversation.

"Don't you do it. God wouldn't have made us different colors if we were supposed to be mixing them," Papa Cal went on, totally ignoring the fact of Willy sitting beside him. Plus, his bringing up God always confused Corky since he never went to church, being one of those people who evoke the name of the Lord only when it suits their argument. "Why are people trying to change things?" he was still going on. "All these young'uns stirring up trouble. They should just let things be. It's worked fine all these years, right, Willy?"

"That's right, Mister Cal." Willy always agreed with him, even when Corky suspected he didn't.

"If you don't let things be, they can bite you in the ass. Right, Willy?"

"That's right, Mister Cal."

"Snakes in the grass, Sister," he said to Corky. "You gotta watch out or they will bite you in the ass. It's just like that."

Her dad sighed. "Papa, Belle sent you and Willy your suppers. Yours is in the kitchen and Willy's is still in the truck. I'm going to take Willy home while Corky reads the paper to you, then I'm going back to work. Mack will pick her up later."

As Willy and her dad pulled out of the driveway, Corky grabbed the Sunday edition of the *Fort Worth Star-Telegram* she'd brought from home and started flipping through it, choosing what to read.

Reading to Papa Cal every Sunday was the first time she ever read the newspaper, and while she didn't much like having to go to Papa Cal's, she loved reading the news. It would usually go like this: He'd laugh big at the funnies, harrumph at the news, and nod at the baseball scores. After a few articles, though, he'd stare toward the window as if watching his memories, and that was Corky's signal to stop reading.

"Papa Cal," she'd say, "what do you see?"

"Nothing. You know I can't see," he'd snap. "It's what I hear."

"What do you hear?"

He'd never answer. So, she'd often stop reading for a moment, close her eyes, and listen: *Birds. Dogs. Wind.*

Finally, she'd hear Papa Cal sigh, and that was the signal he was finished with whatever memory he was watching. And they'd spend the rest of the time listening to any ball game that happened to be on the TV or radio.

It was the same that Sunday. Corky began contentedly thumbing through the pages to choose her articles to read aloud. During that summer, as it had been for the last few years, the newspaper covered stories about the Civil Rights Movement aplenty, from lunch counter sit-ins to marches to the Civil Rights Act that was about to be signed into law in just a few weeks. The marches were like all marches, although the March on Washington for Jobs and Freedom with Martin Luther King Jr.'s famous "I Have a Dream" speech at the Lincoln Memorial in front of 250,000 people did kick it up several notches. However, the lunch counter sit-ins touched daily life for the vast majority of Americans, lunch counters being as ubiquitous as soda fountains in 1964, sometimes being both, as it was in Cal Corcoran's drugstore. As Mack had learned his freshman year at UT, the sit-ins were a form of civil rights protest in which both Blacks and Whites, mostly students, would quietly sit down together at lunch counters like the ones in the popular Woolworth's five-and-dime store chain and politely ask to be served. They began in earnest in 1960 with varying degrees of success, depending on one's definition of success. Sometimes the participants were quietly served, and sometimes the lunch counters quickly closed. In 1964, sit-ins were still happening, some nationally organized, some local, as the Civil Rights Act neared reality that very summer. And that meant they were still being covered in the newspapers.

Having heard both Pastor Pete's sermon and Papa Cal's opinion of America playing softball with them, Corky was feeling righteously disobedient. Just to get Papa Cal's goat, she began reading only the stories about civil rights.

"After a fifty-four-day filibuster," she read, *"President Lyndon Johnson now has the votes to pass the Civil Rights Act of 1964 in the US Senate. The act will effectively end the application of Jim Crow laws, as it will prohibit discrimination on the basis of race, color, religion, sex, or national origin . . ."*

Papa Cal grunted. "Read something else."

Corky flipped to her next choice.

"Today marks the anniversary of the fastest woman in the world, Olympic gold-medalist Wilma Rudolph, participating in a civil rights protest in her hometown of Clarksville, Tennessee, to desegregate one of the city's restaurants," she read. *"That very day, the mayor announced the city's public facilities, including its restaurants, would become fully integrated—"*

"Move on!" Papa Cal said, louder.

"Today also marks another civil rights anniversary, this one of the lunch counter sit-in that shocked the nation: Last year, Tougaloo College students and faculty staged a sit-in at Jackson, Mississippi's Woolworth's lunch counter in which the participants, both Black and White, were attacked by a violent crowd who burned them with cigarettes and kicked some to the ground," she read. *"One White participant was dragged out by her hair—"*

"Stop reading those right now!" Papa Cal ordered. "Find something else, or I'll have your daddy tan your little hide for not minding!"

So, she read him a story about the Warren Commission on the Kennedy assassination and another about the plans for the fall's State Fair of Texas, skipping the part that announced the upcoming Juneteenth state fair celebration of the day in 1865 when Black Texan slaves heard they were free. But it took all she had and the portent of her dad actually tanning her hide at her age to keep her from adding it back in.

As she was about to start safely into the baseball scores, though, Papa Cal stopped her flat.

"Hear that?" her grandfather said. "I think that's a rattler headed for the corner of the house."

"I don't hear anything," Corky said.

Getting to his feet, he surprised her by actually answering. "Learn to listen, Sister," he said. "When you lose your sight, your ears get real sharp. You can learn a lot by listening. Stand up. Close your eyes."

She stood up and closed her eyes.

"What do you hear?"

"Not much, a few birds somewhere," she admitted. "What do you hear?"

"I can hear Eli Stubbs three houses down when he goes outside to fart instead of doing it in front of the missus. That man can fart. I can hear a tractor over in the Pearsons' field half a mile away. It needs a tune-up." He turned a little to the left. "And that bird singing, now that's a mockingbird."

"How can you tell?"

"It's doing different calls of other birds, one after another. That's why it's called a 'mocking'bird . . . wait . . ." Papa Cal jerked his head toward the far part of his mowed backyard near the grown-up fallow field. "There it goes again. Closer!"

"What? The mockingbird?"

"No, I just heard a rattlesnake rattle in the tall, weedy grass!"

"I don't hear it," Corky said.

Papa Cal cussed. "I asked your father to get that brush cleaned out up against the house, but he hasn't done it. And after that big wind last week, I bet we got leaves scattered between the house and the tall grass out in the field, just like them rattlesnakes use to get to the house. Willy was going to do it today, but we clean forgot. And now I hear a rattler slithering this way."

"Papa Cal, you can't hear a snake slithering," she said.

"Don't you tell me what I can hear! I can hear it, I tell ya," he said, then pulled a little 410 shotgun from behind the back door. "Go kill it." He held out the gun. "Willy and I keep it loaded. You're ready to go." When she didn't take hold of it, he thrust it her way where he blurrily thought she was standing until she finally took it for fear of him fumbling enough it would go off. "There!" he said, pointing to the back steps. "I hear it slithering right now!"

Corky held the gun away from her. "I don't want to, Papa Cal!"

"What's a matter, you scared?"

If that taunt had come from a childhood friend, it would have been as if Papa Cal was double-dog daring her and hard to resist. But this was her grandpa. "Yes!" she admitted.

"What's wrong with you? I'd do it myself, but I can't, and we can't wait. That critter's just biding its time. It's already taking up residence in the brush by the back steps, I tell ya! Got to kill it before it settles in under the house! It's a snake in the grass! You don't stop 'em when you catch 'em, they might stop you."

"Papa Cal, you just got 'snakes in the grass' on your mind because you mentioned it when Dad was here," she tried, desperate.

"You think I'm foolin'? There it goes again. Get on out there!"

Corky poked her head out. While Papa Cal was right about the wind-blown leaves all over the mowed area, she saw no slithering. She looked at the corner of the house. There were some overgrown weeds, but she didn't see any snakes. "Can't we wait for Mack?"

"No. I hear it now. Didn't I teach you to shoot?"

It wasn't a good memory for Corky. Papa Cal had put up a target when she was ten. After she had proudly hit the target dead center a dozen times, showing a bit of natural skill with the small shotgun for a beginner, Papa Cal pointed to some birds screeching a few yards away. "Try shooting those pesky dang crows in the tree," he ordered. And she did. Over a half dozen crows dropped to the ground, flopping in their death throes. She recalled her ten-year-old self being on the verge of puking at what she'd done. Until she noticed something even worse . . . There among the dead crows was also a dead mockingbird. And seeing that, she couldn't keep the tears from coming. Papa Cal had rolled his eyes. Only Willy had come over and patted her on the head. "It's all right, li'l Cricket," she remembered him saying. "You keep that tender heart." After that, Corky had promised herself that she would never shoot at a living thing again. And now her grandfather was ordering her to shoot at something she couldn't even see?

"Time to kill it, Sister!" Papa Cal yelled, pushing her onto the back steps and stumbling out behind her. "Hear it?"

"No!" she moaned. "What am I supposed to aim at?"

"The weeds by the corner of the house. That's where I heard it slither."

"But—"

Papa Cal grabbed the little shotgun from her hands, aimed it at the corner, and fired. "Missed! *&@%$!" he cussed.

"How do you know?" Corky said. "Maybe you got it!"

"No, I'd know. I just pray the goddamn thing hasn't slithered under the house to get me later." Papa Cal held out the gun. "Here."

Corky took the little 410.

"Help me back in the house and reload it."

"No, Papa Cal!"

"Fine! Then put it back behind the door. I'll load it again myself later somehow if I have to."

When she did, Papa Cal pointed at the phone. "Now, call your father."

Corky dialed the drugstore, handed Papa Cal the phone, and Papa Cal unloaded on Corky's father. "That brush has got to be cleaned out!" Papa Cal yelled into the phone. "You promised you'd get it done and it ain't done. A rattler's probably under the house right now waiting!"

She could hear her dad sigh. "Papa, I promise Mack will work on it tomorrow first thing."

"And while you're at it, you need to give Sister a switching for not minding me."

"Okay, Papa. I'll discuss it with her later."

"*Discuss?* What good's that gonna do? She needs a spanking. She kept reading whatever the hell she wanted and wouldn't shoot a rattler I heard at our back door!"

Her dad sighed again. "Okay, Papa, okay. Put her on the phone."

When Corky took the phone, her father said only this: "Young lady, you will be going back early in the morning with Mack to help clear out that brush for your grandfather. Now give the phone back to him."

"Yessir," she said and handed the phone receiver back to Papa Cal.

"You going to be all right on your own tonight, or do you want Willy to come back and sit with you?" Cal asked his father.

Papa Cal grunted. "Don't need any help to get myself to bed. Been doing it fine for eighty years without you. Mack coming real early?"

"Yes, Papa, Mack'll get there real early, and Corky has volunteered to help," her dad said. "I've got to go. I have customers waiting for their medicine."

Hanging up the phone, Papa Cal sank back into his easy chair, trying not to look shaken. "Let's just listen to the game. No more reading."

That was fine by Corky. And for a nice, long time, the Texas Rangers baseball team filled the gaps in the welcomed silence.

Soon, Mack showed up. And as she and Mack left, Corky heard Papa Cal shuffle over and lock the back door, as if he thought the snake was going to turn the knob and barge right in. Since nobody locked their doors in High Cotton, she recalled it being just another strange Papa Cal thing, like rattlers everywhere.

On the way home, Corky told Mack the whole story, starting with the righteous newspaper article choices she had read to Papa Cal. "There was even one about Wilma Rudolph."

Mack chuckled. "You're such a brat."

"Then he wanted me to shoot a rattlesnake I couldn't even see, Mack," she went on. "He shoved that shotgun he keeps behind the door at me. And when I wouldn't shoot, he grabbed it, aimed at the house's corner himself, and pulled the trigger like a blind, crazy person!"

Mack paused. "He's keeping that 410 loaded? *Damn*. It's nice he didn't shoot himself in the foot—or *you*. I better tell Dad about that."

Corky crossed her arms. "Why does Willy put up with him? I don't understand."

"You never heard that story?" Mack said.

Corky rolled her eyes. "Yeah, yeah, Willy once saved Papa Cal from a rattler." Papa Cal loved to crow about the time that Willy, from forty paces away, drew a bead with his .22 on a rattler that was coiling up to strike Papa Cal: "Blew him to smithereens, blood and rattler guts everywhere!" Corky had heard that story hundreds of times, always figuring the rattler got bigger and farther away with each telling.

Mack shook his head. "No, not that one. You know how one of Willy's arms doesn't hang quite right?"

"Yeah."

"Right after Willy started working as a hired hand for Papa Cal, seems Papa Cal saved Willy's life when a tractor he was driving overturned in a muddy ditch during a sudden downpour, pinning Willy under it. The ditch began to fill, and the water around Willy's head was rising so fast that Papa Cal had to do something or Willy was going to drown right there. After he tried everything he could think of, and Willy's head was all but underwater, somehow he pushed the tractor off Willy just enough to pull him up from under the muddy water, and carried him, crushed arm and broken leg, all the way to his pickup and down to the doctor." Mack glanced over at Corky. "That's why."

Corky made a scoffing *phhht* sound with her lips. "C'mon, that can't be true. Did Papa Cal tell you that?"

"Nope," he answered as they pulled into their driveway. "Willy told me. And you know how little Willy talks. They had each other's backs, Bug. Hard to shake that."

Mack got out, slammed the door, and headed inside. "You coming? We've got to go back to Papa Cal's at the crack of dawn, remember."

More than a little confused by this new story about her grandfather, Corky slowly followed.

At dawn the next morning, Mack and Corky dragged themselves out of bed, threw on some work clothes, stumbled out to Mack's car, and headed to Papa Cal's, both so sleepy neither said a single word the entire way over.

And just as they pulled into the driveway, they heard the sound of a shotgun blast . . .

14

Mack slammed on the brakes, and they both ran toward the sound. They found Papa Cal lying off the back steps clutching his already swelling leg, his shotgun dropped in the grass.

Quickly checking for any sign of the rattlesnake, Mack and Corky somehow got their grandfather into the back seat of Mack's car and careened to High Cotton's little hospital.

Within a few minutes, they were sitting in the waiting room as their mother and father rushed in. Her dad went to find out what was happening while her mother came over and hugged Corky. But Corky didn't feel as if she deserved a hug. It was a day she would experience real guilt, the kind grown-ups feel and carry with them. And she would feel it twice before the day was over.

That evening the girls' teams had scheduled one more practice before they played the softball game at the end of the week. The Methodist girls were to practice at 6:00 and the Baptist girls at 7:00 before it got dark. Corky and Mack had planned on getting to the field early, Mack wanting to "scout" a little, and Corky worrying if America would be coming at all. As kids do, she was more worried about America and missing practice than Papa Cal, maybe because she couldn't quite face that she hadn't shot at the rattlesnake . . . and that was because she didn't really believe it was there.

As they sat in the waiting room, her mother pulled her closer and said, "Kathryn, if you're still set on playing that softball game, I need to tell you that when Evangeline came to work this morning, she said she wasn't sure America was going to play."

"What?" Corky pulled away. "She's got to play! I'm sorry for what I did!"

Hearing that, Belle narrowed her eyes at her daughter as she'd done many times before. "What did you do, young lady?"

Corky didn't want to tell her mother about giving America the library book, so she said: "You told me I should try to be more sensitive to others, right? It's about that."

Her mother sighed. "Well, Evangeline said she was going to leave it up to her since she is sixteen. So, you may still see her and you can apologize, if you get to go. We need to see how your grandfather is doing before we make any decisions about tonight."

Her dad appeared and updated her mother in whispers.

As they talked, Corky heard her mother say to him: "No, don't worry. I trust Evangeline. She called America to come over and help finish quickly."

Corky jumped up. "Evangeline is still at the house and America is there, too? Mom, I have to apologize. Now. *Right* now. Please!"

Her mother studied her for a moment. "Well, all right. Just go, do what you think you should do, and come right back. You hear?"

Corky rushed out the door. If America had helped Evangeline, they could already be finished, so she ran the handful of blocks to her house as fast as she could. When she got there, nobody was around. Not even Roy Rogers. Corky glanced down the street toward the highway. And there was Roy, trotting toward the road and the train tracks, tail wagging away.

"Roy!" she called. She started jogging after him. But as she got closer, she saw where he was going and why. Up ahead of him were America and Evangeline heading home, Evangeline in her housedress and America in her cutoff overalls. Roy Rogers had decided to follow them.

Corky began to run again, hoping she could catch them all before they crossed the highway and the tracks. She tried calling to them, but being too close to the highway, the passing cars drowned her out. All she could do was watch them cross. There went Roy as if he'd done it a hundred times before, and, for all Corky knew, he had. So, going against parental and community norms, Corky crossed the highway and railroad tracks. Gingerly, she stepped over the cinders and the metal rails, glancing down the arrow-straight tracks leading off to the horizon both ways. And then she stepped over to the Southside. Corky wanted to call to them again. But the moment she was over the railroad tracks, she couldn't make herself yell, as if doing the forbidden made her mute.

So, she just kept following.

That was when the wind shifted, and Roy Rogers, catching his girl's scent, trotted happily back to Corky's side. Corky knew she probably should grab his collar and head home. But she didn't. She hadn't apologized to America.

So, she kept following them, with Roy tagging along beside her.

For four Southside blocks, she watched Evangeline and America as they walked past the Zion African Methodist Episcopal Church, the Mount Olive Baptist Church, and the Southside Public School with its chain-link-fenced playground, sandlot ballfield, and single rusty swing set.

Watching some high school boys playing baseball, she stared at the school for a beat too long, and, when she looked around, America and Evangeline had disappeared. Rushing ahead, she didn't see them anywhere. Roy thought Corky was playing a game. He nipped at her heels until his nose caught America's and Evangeline's scents, and he trotted after his new friends, who'd turned the corner. Corky rushed to the corner. There they were. They were passing a small, cream-colored, square-shaped house with a yard full of knickknacks and whirligigs to rival Mrs. Poindexter's. And as soon as the two were in front of the next house, which was exactly the same as the first one except it was as unadorned as the other was cluttered, Evangeline opened the picket-fence gate.

Roy barked.

America whirled around to see Corky standing on the street corner and Roy Rogers bounding her way. Since her mother had already entered the house, America stopped Roy and gazed at Corky on the corner. She motioned to Corky to wait as she opened the house's front door and called inside, "Mamà, I'm going for a run! I'll be back in a minute." With Roy Rogers in tow, she jogged to where Corky stood.

"What are you *doing*?" America said as Roy nuzzled her hand.

"I wanted to apologize in person," Corky blurted. "I'm sorry I wasn't sensitive about the library book. I didn't understand what was happening in the parts that made you mad. Did Reverend Washington tell you?"

"Yeah." America sighed. "I'd already figured that out. It's okay."

"Mack told me you might not like it," Corky added. "You don't have to finish it."

The two stood there in silence.

Desperate to keep talking, Corky blurted the first thought that came to her. "Why didn't you let us bring you home the other night?"

America paused. "I guess . . . after seeing your big house, I didn't want you to feel sorry for us in our little rental. Until I met you and your family with all your books and everything, I never thought a thing about it. But that day, I did."

Corky gazed at the pristine cream-colored house with its picket fence, front porch, and rocking chair. "I *like* your house."

America studied Corky. "You really mean that, don't you?"

"I do," Corky said. She caught America studying her even closer. "What?"

America, despite herself, smiled.

"Did you make that, too?" Corky asked, noticing the blouse America was wearing with her cutoffs, another pretty one.

Glancing down at what she was wearing, she nodded.

"How do you *do* that?" Corky said.

America shrugged. "It's easy."

"No, it's not," Corky said. "You are so *good* at stuff."

"C'mon," America said. "You shouldn't be over here. You need to get back to your side of town."

"I can get there on my own," Corky said.

But America was already headed toward the tracks. "Let's go, Roy Rogers." Roy trotted beside her, tongue hanging out long and happy.

Hustling to keep up, Corky realized America was leading them away from the Southside school, where the high school boys were playing baseball. As she was wondering if it was on purpose, she noticed a tall, burly boy staring rather longingly in their direction.

"Who's that?" Corky asked.

"Pay 'em no mind. They're nothing but foolishness," America said.

"Even that one? I think he likes you."

America glanced around and saw Lion. "Why would you think that?" she asked, slowing.

"I'm learning stuff this summer," Corky responded.

At that, America sped up but smiled, slyly, to herself.

Corky caught up to her. "Are we friends?"

America kept moving. "I like you, Corky, but you don't really wanta be friends."

"Yes, I do. I'm really, really sorry about the book."

"It's not that."

"Is it because I ask too many questions? Am I being annoying?"

Corky noticed America's eyebrows go up the way Mack's did when the answer was yes. "Okay, okay. Beyond that, is it because I'm thirteen and you're sixteen? All the older girls I know are stuck-up and boring, but you aren't."

"It's much more than that. You know what it is."

"No, I don't."

"You say you don't, but ya do."

"No, I really don't," Corky answered.

America slowed again. "*Why* do you want to be friends?"

Corky's hope skyrocketed. "I've always wanted a big sister. We could talk about things. Like books. You could finish *To Kill a Mockingbird* and tell me what else you didn't like!"

America turned full around on that one. "That's *not* a good idea."

Corky screwed up her face. "Then, is it about you being Black and me being White? If it is, why can't we talk about it? I mean, that's stupid. It's just skin," she said next. And the moment it was out of her mouth, Corky recognized the new look on America's face. It was the one people gave her after she pushed too hard and before she heard something she might not like. Corky braced herself. Instead, America's face changed again, registering a rolling mixture of frustration, uneasiness, and affection, ending with the look Corky first saw in front of their bookshelf: sadness.

"Corky, just . . . c'mon," she finally said and strode away.

Corky trotted to catch up. "We could talk about something else. Like softball. Or Roy Rogers," she said as Roy trotted between them. "Or the Olympics! You're as fast as Wilma Rudolph!"

"I don't know about that," America mumbled.

That made Corky stop dead in her tracks. "What are you talking about? I saw it! Mack saw it! Coach saw it! The *stopwatch* saw it!" she said, rushing back up beside America.

America fumed. "I love running. But what good is it?"

"What *good* is it? To be as fast as the fastest woman in the world? To go to the *Olympics*?" Corky gawked, hustling to keep up. "I don't understand."

"I mean, how do they get by?" America said, still hearing her mother's words on the phone with her father. "Those Olympic athletes—they don't even get paid, do they? How do they get by?"

"Paid? I don't know. I guess not," Corky mumbled. And it was true. In the '60s, the Olympics was still an amateur-only competition. Olympians had to be pure amateurs, unsullied by money. They could not benefit financially from their Olympic sport unless perhaps they won gold, which might allow them to profit off their success with sports endorsements, Wheaties box appearances, and the like. But only after they quit the Olympics for good.

To Corky, though, who had no concerns about getting by, worrying about making money made no sense at all. Being the best in the world was all that mattered.

As if trying to get away from the whole topic, America upped her pace yet again.

And that confused Corky even more, until she remembered what Mack said about the *want-to*. "Are you *scared*?" Corky blurted.

"*NO* . . . !" America exclaimed. ". . . Maybe." She hesitated a step as if surprised by her own answer.

They were at the railroad tracks.

"You are!" Corky hustled right up to her. "But why?"

"Stop asking questions, Corky, just *STOP*." The look now on America's face gave Corky pause. It was the same exasperated look Mack always shot her when, having had enough, he'd tell her anything to make her go away.

So Corky decided to ask the one thing she really wanted to know ever since watching America run like the wind at the school track. "Okay, okay, but one more. Please?"

America rolled her eyes. "Will you stop if I do?"

Corky nodded.

"All right."

"What does it feel like to run that fast?" Corky said, eyes wide, hopeful. "You're the only one who'll ever be able to tell me."

America softened, Roy nuzzling her hand.

"I'm not sure I can," America said as she began to softly rub Roy's head. "I don't know if I have the words."

"Please?" Corky repeated, this time almost in a whisper.

America paused, as if conjuring how to express the inexpressible. "It's all kinds of things at once," she began. She looked past Corky. "It feels like . . . like I can move as fast as the world is turning and I can feel it through my toes . . . Yet it's also like I'm somehow stopping *time* and I'm the only thing moving and any moment I could lift off like a bird, as if I've got wings on my feet . . ." With a far-away gaze, America was suddenly smiling the smile Corky had seen at the track, the one Corky would always see in the years to come. "And inside me, the whole time," America went on, the smile broader, dreamier, "I feel this huge, blessed *bliss* . . . like . . . like . . . at any moment I just might burst into some kind of Almighty *glory* . . ."

It was the first time Corky had heard America sound like church. Corky had heard the word *glory* all her life, in hymns and Bible verses and sermons, meaning everything from praise to adoration to splendor to thanks. But not until that moment did she really hear all of what it could mean rolled into one big, beautiful act of athletic explosion. And she got it. The tomboy still inside Corky felt as weak in the knees as she ever did kissing Tad. For an instant, she felt as if she were running along with America, and it was almost too much for her growing little soul to absorb. Corky gasped. "I wish I could run like you, I wish I could play softball like you . . . I wish I could *be* you!"

And that shook America out of her soft trance. She laughed. Ruefully. "You're the *strangest* White girl I've ever met."

"You're the *only* Black girl I've ever met," Corky answered.

With that, America gazed at Corky with a knowing look. The chasm that stretches between thirteen and sixteen is a wide one—at that age, the gap as wide as a decade, every day, every minute, changing you where you stand. America could see it. Corky couldn't, not then, not until much later. From where Corky stood, even with so much between her and America, from years to train tracks, Corky still thought that America was smarter and kinder and more talented and grown-up than any other teenage girl she knew. That's what it feels like to meet your idol, and that's what was happening without her knowing it. Corky was idolizing her, the kind of deep, pure adolescent idolizing that knows no boundaries. In the same way she'd idolized her mother for her beauty and Mack for his baseball skills, she was now, as a brand-new teenager, idolizing America for all the things she wanted to be. And no railroad tracks were going to stop that. Corky decided, right then and there, she'd make America her friend.

"Go on, y'all," America said, nodding in the direction of the Corcorans' house.

As Corky took Roy's collar and stepped across the tracks, heading over the highway, America called after her: "I'll get that book to you quick as I can." Turning around, she headed over the railroad track in a run.

"Are you coming to the last practice tonight?" Corky called after her. "Are you still playing with us?"

But America had already sprinted away.

Two blocks beyond the tracks, America stopped, threw her hands on her hips, and walked in circles for a moment. She had heard Corky, but she was once more thinking about her father off searching for a new job. Each glimpse of the railroad tracks did that to her. She did have fun at the last practice, yet with everything so up in the air about whether she'd still be in High Cotton that summer, much less her being the only Southside player, she didn't know if she would go to the practice or not. What was the point? Head down, worrying about the future, she almost tripped. And that just made her mad. Looking around, she saw that Corky had disappeared up her street, so America wandered back to the railroad track. Toeing one of the railroad crossties, she thought about her parents' phone conversation and couldn't shake an unsettled, fearful feeling that suddenly made her as mad as when she almost tripped. She glanced down the highway. From there, she could see both the baseball field and football stadium beyond where she'd raced on its track for the coach and his stopwatch. *Use our school cinder track with my permission,* his note had said.

Pivoting, she raced back to the house, grabbed her track shoes, and slipped out again, pulling them on.

At the railroad track, she crossed and sprinted along the highway's gravel shoulder past the baseball field to the stadium until she was standing again on the cinder track. She should have been a little scared or at least anxious in a place Southsiders weren't welcome. She was not. Looking around to make sure she was alone, she took a big breath and ran. Just ran. Like the wind. Blissful. Head back. All glory. Around and around and around until she was so tired, she bent over her knees to catch her breath. Finally, she trotted out of the stadium. Passing the baseball field, she smiled, took a quick lap around the infield, and then crossed back to the Southside.

Enjoying the moment, she didn't see the boy step out in front of her until she almost bumped right into him.

"Hi."

It was Lion.

America rolled her eyes, veered around him, and jogged away.

"C'mon, America, hold up!"

She stopped.

Quickly, Lion trotted to her. Standing up as big and tall as he could muster, he said, "I'm going to walk you home."

She raised an eyebrow. "You are?"

"I am."

She smiled coyly, pleased despite herself. "How about running me home?" Grinning, she sprinted away, full again of all glory.

"Okay, that's not fair!" And he sprinted after her.

By the time Corky had put Roy Rogers in the house and returned to the hospital, Papa Cal was in a room. Dr. Alexander the Younger was talking to her parents. "The antivenom is working. We were more worried about his heart and his age. It was lucky he didn't accidentally shoot himself. If the swelling goes down as we expect, he can go home tomorrow. You can see him now if you want. By the way," the doctor said as he and Cal headed toward Papa Cal's room, "he keeps going on about how since this isn't July, he can't die yet. What's that about?"

Belle turned to Corky and Mack. "Just go on home."

"Can we go to practice?" Corky asked.

"Yes, yes," she said.

"Mother," Mack said, "what about Willy?"

"Oh dear," Belle said. "Yes, I'll talk to your father about bringing him to sit with Papa Cal."

So, Mack and Corky went home, dressed for practice, grabbed Roy Rogers, and headed to the ballfield.

As Mack drove, Corky glanced at her brother. "I'm sorry."

"For what?" Mack said.

"You know."

"Bug, Papa Cal had no business shooting that gun. If it makes you feel any better, I'm now assigned to checking the 410 every time I leave Papa Cal's to make sure it's empty. A snakebite is bad, but shooting off his foot is a helluva lot worse."

Corky nodded, not feeling better one bit.

As they pulled up to the baseball field, they saw the usual dogs and the usual parents but were surprised to see lots of other people in the stands just for another practice.

"Wow . . . ," Corky said.

Word had obviously spread about America.

Pastor Pete pulled up in his Chevy Nova behind them and called to Mack. So, Mack went over. They talked a moment and Pete pulled away.

"Where's he going?" Corky asked, getting out of Mack's car with Roy.

Mack frowned. "His deacons just called a special meeting."

Corky thought nothing of Mack's frown, though. She was thinking only of softball. As she and her brother joined some of the other girls waiting near the backstop, her attention was on the Methodist team still practicing. Mack's attention, meanwhile, was on the crowd. As he studied the stands, he saw Bubba Boatwright climb to the top to do his usual stalking of the Beach sisters, who were already there to do their usual stalking of Mack. But as Bubba sat down a few rows behind the sisters, Mack saw him do a double-take toward the third-base line. He seemed to be looking in the direction of two scruffy-looking strangers leaning on a gray jalopy. And Mack got a bad feeling. He glanced back up at Bubba. "Swear to God, if anybody causes trouble, I'm gonna . . ."

Mack paused midsentence; Corky noticed and looked in the direction Mack was staring. There, on the top row above Bubba and the Beach sisters, sat Cissy McCloud. Cissy waved ever so coyly at Mack, making Corky roll her eyes as Mack climbed up the stands to her. Just then, though, she saw Tad climb into the stands to sit down by Bubba. And Corky's eye roll turned into a nervous tingle.

At 7:00 p.m. sharp, Mack and the Baptist girls took the field, and the Methodist girls filed into the stands. They were staying to watch, including big Anna Mae Mulroney, all sitting with their pastor-coach, Reverend Doug Gifford, who was chewing his Dubble Bubble double-time.

The Baptist girls began warming up. And just as Corky started worrying about America, she came trotting across the tracks and onto the field.

Roy Rogers bounded over to greet her, barking happily, but Roy was the only one making a sound. Everybody went silent watching America jog across the baseball diamond, and that should have made America jumpy. Instead, in true athletic fashion, she took a glove from Mack, jogged to the outfield, and focused entirely on roving. And, with Roy by her side, did she ever rove. Even Roy was soon tuckered out, his tongue hanging down long and sideways. America had never played more than recess softball, she claimed, but it sure didn't look like it. And much of the curious crowd seemed starstruck. Once, they even clapped. Standing at home plate, Mack hit a pop fly to right field, an easy one since it was for little Thelma "Peanut" Ledbetter. Thelma was shaking in her boots, literally, since she'd actually worn her little, red cowboy boots to practice. And she missed the ball completely, which was not surprising. The surprise was that America appeared behind her and caught the ball right before it touched the ground. The spectators clapped and Thelma gave her a big hug.

The more they practiced and the more America ran and jumped and caught and shone like the great raw-talent athlete she was—like watching Wilma Rudolph play softball—the more worried the

Methodist girls looked, Anna Mae the only one still looking cocky. Finally, Reverend Doug huddled his team, led them in a quick prayer, and they left.

For the rest of the hour, the Baptist girls ran around trying to emulate America. When they couldn't, they laughed and cheered her on until even America began to smile bigger and bigger, especially when she ran the bases like a hurricane.

As the sun slowly set, Mack decided they'd had enough, and the girls all ran over to trot off the field with America. Mack glanced toward where the scruffy strangers had been leaning against the gray jalopy. They were gone.

He turned to the team. "Time for ice cream, girls." And everybody headed to the Dairy Dip.

After quickly putting Roy in the car, Corky rushed to catch up with America, sticking as close to her new friend-to-be as she could.

"I'll grab the equipment bag and be right there," Mack called to them. "America, we'll take you home like we did last time. It's almost dark."

As the group streamed across the Dairy Dip's circular driveway to line up at the walk-up window, Bubba Boatwright drove by in his Corvette. Its fancy detachable top was off, and Tad was in the passenger seat. Corky's stomach fluttered as she waited to see Tad's cute half grin that would make her want him to kiss her again.

But when Corky moved closer to America to let the Corvette pass, Bubba shot America a look of pure hate.

Tensing, Corky glanced at Tad and her stomach dropped. He was looking at America exactly as Bubba had.

"Told ya," Bubba muttered to his brother. And as the car rolled past the girls, Bubba called Corky a vulgar racial slur just because she'd had the nerve to befriend a Southside girl. As Tad looked her way, Corky forgot to breathe. Because what she saw in his eyes wasn't the puppy love she was feeling. She saw the same look of pure hate. And it was . . . now aimed at *her*.

It shocked her. In her confusion, her percolating adolescence turned her innocent crush on Tad into something darkly desperate.

And Corky took a step away from America.

Instantly realizing what she'd done, Corky stepped back, hoping America hadn't noticed. But she had. She'd seen and heard everything. Corky could see it in America's eyes, her face slowly registering this new hurt.

And America was now the one stepping away.

As the import of that hit home, Corky glimpsed her own fickle, two-faced soul. She began to say something, anything, to fix it.

But then Mack came striding their way, equipment bag in hand. And as the Corvette rolled by him, Bubba spit the same slur at Mack.

Mack whirled around. "What did you say?"

"You heard me," Bubba said.

Dropping the bag, Mack pulled a baseball bat from it and marched toward the Corvette. "Come say that to my face, Boatwright, you racist son of a bitch. Or I swear to God I'll mess up your shiny Corvette."

Bubba pulled the Corvette over and got out. Mack dropped the bat. Bubba took a swing and missed. Mack started to throw the next punch. But, instead, Mack slapped him.

Since everybody knew Noah Boatwright IV was a child-beater-turned-Baptist-deacon after being seen slapping a young Bubba many times over the years, Mack must have known that slapping Bubba would get to him better than any kind of punch. And Mack was right. Bubba's jaw dropped. As his eyes filled with furious tears, Bubba threw a wild punch. Mack ducked and punched Bubba full-on in the stomach.

Bubba went down like a box of rocks.

The Corvette's car door flew open, and Tad went running to Bubba.

"Let's go," Mack ordered Corky, picking up the bat and equipment bag.

Working hard to process all the moving parts of everything that had just happened, Corky finally pulled her eyes away from Tad, who was still helping Bubba to his feet. Only then did she realize that America wasn't there.

"Where's America?" Mack said.

They both looked toward the train tracks across the highway.

"Ah damn," Mack groaned. "She heard Bubba."

But Mack didn't know what Corky knew. He didn't know what she'd done. And Corky burst into tears.

"Bug," Mack said, "don't worry about Bubba doing anything. He might be rich, but he's still white trash that talks out of his ass. He's got to have somebody feeling worse than him to feel good himself. He'll just go out to the Broke Spoke and cry in his beer. And that'll be it."

Corky wiped at her eyes, but Mack's words didn't matter. All that mattered was what she had done. She hated it. She'd hated it the moment she'd done it. *Why did I do it? Because I wanted to kiss Tad again?* It was the first time Corky thought maybe she didn't know herself very well. Or, worse, she didn't know the person she was turning into. She dried her eyes on her sleeve and gazed toward the railroad tracks. After this, she just knew America wouldn't play in the game, and who could blame her?

On the way home, Corky kept thinking about Bubba and Tad and other people in her High Cotton world she thought she knew. She'd just stopped being friends with a boy she'd known and liked her entire life. At the very same time, she'd hurt a girl she hoped to have as a friend for the rest of her life. The dynamics of what had just happened were far beyond her experience to handle. If she didn't know Tad Boatwright, what *did* she know? And what did she know if she didn't know *herself?* Suddenly aware that the sum of all she didn't know seemed now to be the size of the known universe, she could barely breathe. As they came to a stop in their driveway, Pastor Pete's car pulled in behind them before Mack, Corky, or Roy could get out.

"How's your grandpa?" he said, hopping out and slamming his door.

"He's in a room and they say he's resting okay," Mack answered, getting out of the car. ". . . Why are you here?"

Adjusting his glasses, Pastor Pete took a deep breath. "I left the meeting early. The deacons just voted to not let America play, Mack."

Mack exploded. *"What the *#**$#*!"* He actually said a few words Corky'd never heard him say. And he said them to their minister.

Pastor Pete, though, didn't seem surprised. "I know, I know, Mack! But what am I supposed to do? I have to abide by my deacon board. This was all my big idea, and I'm sorry."

But Mack wasn't through. "Every last girl on that team loves America. If they took a vote, *they'd* all vote to let her play with them. And make no mistake, each one of those girls is watching *you* closely, Preacher."

"Are you preaching to *me?*" Pastor Pete said, suddenly testy. Corky had never seen her pastor testy. The guy was always Sweetness and Light to the point of annoyance. Then he sighed. "Fine, you are preaching to me. And you *should*. But my hands are tied. Look, it was Noah Boatwright. He pressured the others."

Mack laughed darkly. "I already knew that."

"Ahhh Lord," Pete groaned, running a hand through his hair. "What am I going to do? We have to find a way to tell her beforehand."

"We?" Mack grunted. "You mean *you*. I'm sure not going to tell her she can't play. Besides, there isn't any way to tell her. We don't even know where she lives. She made me let her out in front of one of the churches over there."

With Roy hassling over her shoulder, Corky opened her mouth to tell them she knew, but snapped it shut. She couldn't admit she'd gone to the Southside by herself. Plus, why would she want to help tell America something that would hurt her more?

Pete closed his eyes. "This just keeps getting worse. I guess I could call up Reverend Washington at Mount Olive Baptist. He'll know where she lives."

"How are you going to tell him something like that?" Mack pressed. "And even if you did, what if he can't tell her in time? What if America just shows up? Would you stop her from playing?" To lay it on even thicker, Mack added, "Don't you *ever* want to win one of these games?"

Pete paused at that, shaking his head. "Oh no, no. They could fire me."

"They're Baptists, Pastor Pete. They can do that anyway, for any reason," Mack reminded him.

Pete shook his head yet again at that bit of truth. "I *so* hate this. I guess if she shows, I'll have to explain we didn't have a way to let her know . . . Oh, dear God in Heaven, I just can't. I can't tell her she can't play if she shows! What am I going to do?"

"Wait, did you say you left the meeting early?" Mack asked.

"Yes, I had to come to tell you, and I need to go see your grandpa. They're all still there at the church. All but Noah Boatwright. Seems he primed the pump yesterday, going by every deacon's house. He only came tonight to make sure they voted 'right' and was leaving the discussion of some finances to them. Why?"

"No reason," Mack quickly added.

"I suppose it's in the Lord's hands," Pete mumbled, looking as if he were on his way to hell. "I better go on by and see your grandfather before it gets too late."

As Pete pulled out of the driveway, Mack got back in the car.

"What are you doing?" Corky asked.

"You and Roy go on in. Tell Mother I had to go do something and I'll be back in a while."

"What are you going to do?"

"Help 'the Lord's hands.'"

Corky set her jaw. "I'll help, too."

"Corky, no. You'll make it worse."

"I can't make it worse. It's already worse."

"No," he said again.

No had never been an acceptable word in Corky's world in the same way she didn't like to be told what to do, not even by her brother. She tended not only to keep asking questions after she was told *no*, but also kept doing things she was told not to do, despite the consequences.

Learning the hard way seemed to be her signature move. "I have to go. I have to!"

Mack fumed, narrowing his gaze. "All right. But you and Roy are staying in the car. You hear?"

She nodded, knowing full well she would not.

At the church, she watched him disappear in the side door. Telling Roy to stay in the car, she followed her brother inside. She heard voices coming from behind the closed door of the Adult Sunday school meeting room. She hustled near. With her ear to the door, she heard Mack speaking to the chairman of the deacons, who happened to be Mr. Harold Springer, Sadie's father.

"I saw her run with my own eyes, Mr. Springer. I swear she's Olympic material. She's that good without even any training! How would you feel if your daughter was incredibly gifted and just because of the color of her skin was told she couldn't use her God-given, Olympic-quality gift to play in a church softball game?"

From what she could hear through the door, she could tell Mack wasn't quite getting the response he wanted from that ploy, probably because Mr. Springer could not conceive of Sadie being Olympic material of any kind.

Corky strained to hear more for another few moments, the tone of the voices making Corky figure with each passing second that Mack's way wasn't working. Things got quiet. Far too quiet. So, despite what Mack might do to her, Corky busted in.

"What if America IS that great?" Corky said to all the men around the table. "What if she ends up in the Olympics, and you were the ones who said she couldn't play with us? Coach Trumbull thinks she might be the next Wilma Rudolph! Don't you want to see it? Don't you want to say you were the ones who helped her? *Don't you?*"

Mack grabbed Corky's shoulders, spun her around, and shoved her back out the door. "And BY the way," she went on as he pushed, "how come there aren't any women deacons? They're the ones who do all the real work around here!"

Mack closed the door on her, but opened it again just to hiss, *"STAY!"*

So, she stayed. Ten minutes went by. The men's voices behind the door turned low and muffled. And just as she started to bust back in, Mack came out.

"What happened?" she said.

He grabbed her around the neck in a chokehold and, in the parlance of all big brothers, began rubbing her head hard, delivering noogies.

Corky hated noogies.

"Well?" Corky said when he finally let go.

"They asked me whether Coach Trumbull really thinks she is Olympic material. They had a little trouble believing what they were hearing around town, especially with Boatwright in their faces. So, I said yes and added that there was a slight chance that Coach was sending a scout to come watch."

"But Coach never said that."

"No, but it could happen," Mack said. "If not at the game, it sure could sometime. So I lied. After that, I suggested that the deacons take a secret vote to give everyone a chance not to feel the Boatwright Wrath. And that vote was in favor of letting her play."

"But what about Mr. Boatwright?" Corky said.

Mack laughed, deeply pleased with himself. "He'll think twice before he leaves a deacons' meeting early. But listen up. You cannot tell Mother about this. These men will take the credit for changing their minds once they do see America in action. And that'll be just fine."

They drove back to the house, and Mack kept the car running as Corky and Roy got out.

"Where you going now?" Corky asked.

"Got a date. Tell the parents."

A little later, watching out her upstairs window with Roy by her side, Corky didn't see Bubba, the Beach Sisters, the strange truck, or Tommy Tilton in the police cruiser. Ears perked, Roy sniffed the night air and, to Corky's relief, called it good. No barks tonight. Wanting this bad day to finally be over, she got into bed and closed her eyes, thinking about how the day had at least ended a little better. But try as she might to feel good about the deacon meeting's outcome, her mind was stuck like glue to the last, new hurt, *her* hurt, on America's face.

15

Parked at their high school make-out spot off the country road over-looking High Cotton, Cissy and Mack were necking like old times, both working up quite a hormonal sweat, until Cissy nibbled on Mack's neck.

"Ow," Mack said.

"Wimp," Cissy said back.

And that made them go back at it hotter and heavier.

Then Cissy did it again, this time sucking with gusto. Wincing, Mack touched his neck. "Shit, that's going to leave a mark."

Cissy leaned near. "Do you care?"

Mack answered by pulling her nearer to go at it yet again.

They heard a car coming. The road was rarely traveled, stretching past the Boatwright mansion before heading its winding way back to the highway. Parked off the pavement, they weren't in danger of anything but being seen, so they sat up to wait until the car passed.

When the car's lights faded away, Mack pressed back close to her. "Why did we break up? I don't remember."

Cissy pressed closer still. "Right now, you don't want to remember."

"How long are you home?"

"Just until next week. I'm going to summer school."

Mack fumed. "You get to be in Dallas and I'm stuck in High Cotton."

Cissy slid back against the car's passenger door. "At least you're in school. You hear about Ralphie Tankersley in our class? He got drafted the instant he dropped out. And my father says any day now they're going to start sending ground troops to Vietnam."

"Yeah, well," Mack confessed, "school's not going that good."

Cissy sat up. "Mack Corcoran, don't tell me you're *failing*!"

"No, I'm . . . just working on something."

"Baseball." Cissy sighed. "What if that doesn't work out? You can't get by on your good looks. You've got to have a degree. Did you at least finally decide on a major?"

"Now I remember why *you* broke up with *me*." Mack screwed up his face. "Not yet."

"Not yet," she repeated.

"It's just all those required courses I'm not interested in . . . ," Mack said, trailing off.

"So? You still need a major. And don't say PE."

"What's wrong with PE?"

"Nothing, if you want to be Coach Trumbull making ends meet with an ice-cream shack." Cissy sniffed.

"Well, what's *your* major?" Mack said.

Cissy rolled her eyes at the absurd question. "Everybody knows mine's not important. I'm a woman."

"Hold on." Mack studied her. "Are you dating someone else?"

"I'm dating lots of someone elses, silly. Like the saying goes, that's what college *is* for us girls—getting an MRS degree!" Cissy said with a laugh. She glanced down the hill at High Cotton. "It's getting late. Maybe you better take me home."

A few minutes later, at Cissy's house, she opened the car's passenger door to get out. "The parents have plans for me for the next couple of nights. So, Thursday night? I leave Friday." Cissy leaned over and grabbed his face. "Oh, that handsome face of yours. We *do* look marvelous together." She gave him a long, passionate kiss and scooted out the car door. "Choose a major, a good one," she said, heading toward the house. "Finance. Premed. Prelaw. You know, something that is sure to make a lot of money. Then we'll see."

Mack sat there a moment waiting to cool down before he could drive away, the kiss having revved him right back up.

On the way home, he took High Cotton's main street/highway, deserted at this hour of the night except for cars passing quickly through town on their way to either Decatur, Fort Worth, or points beyond. He wasn't quite ready to go home yet, so he just drove. Soon, he found himself pulling to the curb by his favorite High Cotton spot, the bronze Aloysius Homer Dowd memorial plaque in front of the high school. There, on a night exactly like this one, he'd had that first kiss Corky had asked about, followed by a much longer second kiss during which Lorelei placed her hand over Aloysius's etched face so he couldn't watch. Sitting in his car, Mack grinned at that memory until brown-eyed Lorelei turned into green-eyed Cissy, the steamy press of Cissy's lips still heavy on his. And that made him gently sigh. For old time's sake, Mack got out, walked over, and tapped the sign's image of High Cotton's only famous son, as he had done all through his school days.

"What do you think, Aloysius?" he said to the baseball player's etched face. "Did your girlfriend ever tell you to go into finance instead of baseball?" He sighed again, this time not at all gently. "Maybe she's right. Maybe everybody's right. Maybe it's time to grow up, choose a major, and go to class, or I might end up drafted like Ralphie," he mumbled. "But . . . then what's a dream for?" Looking up at the stars, he remembered a quote he'd seen at the college practice fields where he'd been working on his fastball: "The dream is free. The hustle is sold separately." He sure as hell was hustling. *Maybe the UT coach will help settle this, at least the dream part,* he decided. *That is, if he'd hurry up and call about whether or not I made the team.*

Blowing out a big breath, he got back in his old Chevy. From there, he could see the school's baseball field a block over, the Dairy Dip sign casting shadows across it. So, he sat there gazing toward the field that had raised him as much as his parents. *Gawd, these were good times. The best times,* Mack thought. *How could finance or prelaw ever beat that?*

A sadness swept over him. Compared to the problems of the screwed-up world, he knew his problems were small. But they were his. And he couldn't ignore them much longer. As mad as he was at his father, Mack was aware of how much his father's adult decisions had paved the way for him to be sitting there wishing for his own dreams to come true. Yet he felt caught in a loop: Even if he made the UT team, he knew it really wasn't over. If he went whole hog for his dream and it went bust, he could still end up like Ralphie Tankersley, since he didn't care about his classes at all. On the other hand, if he applied himself to some major he didn't like, he might become wealthy and have Cissy with all the thrilling things she did so well. But apart from those things, he couldn't help wonder . . . *Would I be happy?*

Grappling with such existential questions was beyond his abilities that late, especially since he was still feeling the effects of Cissy's last lusty kiss. So, he gave up for the night, started his '57 Chevy, and headed toward the highway to go home.

When Mack turned onto his dark street, he noticed what looked like truck lights turn in behind him. He thought nothing of it until the truck came up inches from his bumper, stayed there for two full blocks, and careened around him so close that Mack had to swerve off the street into a neighbor's yard not to be hit. Slamming on the brakes to keep from crashing into a parked car, he whacked his head on the steering wheel before coming to a complete stop. Dizzy, he stumbled out of his car and looked around.

The truck had vanished.

He felt his forehead. A knot was already forming.

At the Corcorans' house, Corky jolted awake to the sound of someone creeping up the stairs. Roy growled, ran out of her room, and the growling stopped.

Corky peeked out.

Across the hall, in the big house's upstairs bathroom, Mack had turned on the light over the mirror and was checking a swelling, red bump on his forehead.

"Mack?"

"Shhhh! Keep it down!" he whispered, glancing toward their parents' bedroom. "It's past midnight. On the way home, I got run off the road. Guess the guy was drunk."

"What's that?" Corky asked, pointing to several big, red splotches on his neck.

The accepted term for such marks after a date was a *hickey*, a piece of information Corky would not learn until high school. "None of your business," Mack said, turning his head to see them before going back to examining the bump on his forehead. "At least my car's okay. Good thing it wasn't a ditch I had to swerve into. Damn truck."

Corky stiffened. "Was it a flatbed truck? With a noisy muffler?"

"I don't know, I was too busy swerving. Go back to bed, Corky. And don't tell Mom and Dad. I'm in enough trouble."

"But it wasn't your fault."

"Yeah, well, they'll make it mine, the way this summer's going. So, keep it shut," he said, examining the hickeys.

"Mack, listen, I need to tell—"

Before she could go on, Roy whined.

"Hush, Roy!" Mack hissed. "Go on, you two. You're going to wake them up! *Go!*"

Back in Corky's room, Roy went under the bed and was instantly snoring. Corky slipped under her covers, seeing the strange flatbed in her mind, its broken taillight flashing off and on like a stoplight. She wished she'd told Mack.

And with that worry, she was back to thinking about what had happened at practice, her mind wandering to first kisses and first betrayals. Corky felt her tears rising once more, seeing the hurt look on America's face again. For a long time, she lay awake, staring at the ceiling and feeling as bad as she could ever remember. Finally, exhausted, she fell asleep and began to dream . . .

She is standing at the railroad tracks along the highway in the dark. On the other side, America is running as fast as the wind, as fast as all glory, until she sees Corky and slows to step over and return the copy of To Kill a Mockingbird.

But a train is coming. A fast train, whizzing by, clickety-clack-clack-clack.

After it passes, America is gone.

But the book is everywhere, its pages swirling loose and tattered with the swoosh of the train-whipped winds.

16

The next morning, feeling the double whammy of two doses of adult-size guilt, Corky could barely drag herself out of bed. With Mack gone to drive Papa Cal home from the hospital, she was back to her usual morning routine of feeding Goldy. So, she trudged out to the corral.

Deep in thought, Corky stood by the trough holding the pail of oats as Goldy waited. Goldy noticed she was not paying attention to the important task before her and swished at Corky with her tail.

"Sorry, girl," Corky said, filling the food and water troughs, and offering Goldy her daily carrot. She turned to stare in the direction of the railroad tracks. What happened at practice the night before would not let her go, and she desperately needed to find a way to apologize to America—again. If she didn't at least try, odds were that America wouldn't play in the game. And she had to do it now, as fast as she could, because the game was only three days away and there'd be no more practices.

So Corky hatched a plan.

Back in the house, Corky found her mother. "Mom, I have to go to the store early. I'll ride my bike so Roy Rogers won't follow."

"Not in your dress, you won't," said her mother, as Corky was hoping she would. "And you know Roy would follow you anyway. Your father is letting you work earlier this morning?"

"Yes . . . yes, ma'am," Corky lied.

"I'll take you. Go put on your dress."

As Corky got out of their station wagon at the store, her mother said, "Remember, I have my volunteer work at the library this afternoon. So, get a ride from the delivery boy or walk home."

Corky waved at her mother as the station wagon disappeared down the street. Pivoting, she headed in a fast scoot over the railroad tracks behind the store, passing the Mount Olive Baptist Church on her way to America's house. She opened the picket-fence gate and hesitantly went in. But when she got to the front steps, she couldn't make herself knock on the door. Instead, she hurried back to Mount Olive Baptist Church. Taking a deep breath, she stepped through a door marked "Office" at the back of the steepled, white building and interrupted a surprised Reverend Moses P. Washington.

"Hello, sir."

Reverend Washington cocked his head her way. "Well, hello, Miss Corky Corcoran. We meet again. What can I do for you today?"

"Could you get another message to America for me?"

"Perhaps. What should I tell her?"

Corky hadn't thought this part through. She chewed for a second on what such a message should say. "Please tell her that Corky is, again, so, so sorry for what she did this time. And that she is begging her to come and play with us anyway."

"Anything else?"

"I'd rather not go into details."

"Ah." He nodded.

Piano music began to waft into the office.

Reverend Washington smiled and got to his feet. "Well. You're in luck. Come with me. You can tell her yourself."

Inside the church sanctuary sat America. She was at the upright piano on the far side of the sanctuary playing a pop song, working out the chords.

Standing in the doorway with the reverend, Corky was flabbergasted at the sight. "What *can't* you do?" she heard herself blurt.

America's head jerked around at the sound of Corky's voice. She started to bolt, but saw Reverend Washington standing behind Corky. The good reverend was giving America the look Corky often got from her mother, the one that said: *Do the right thing.*

So, America eased back down on the piano stool, eyes on the keys.

"I'll leave you two ladies to talk," said Reverend Washington, returning to his office.

Corky, now full-on embarrassed, found herself unable to say what she wanted to say. Instead, she said, "Were you playing 'Hound Dog'? The Elvis song?"

"It wasn't Elvis's first," America said. "It was Big Mama Thornton's."

"I didn't know you could play the piano," Corky tried next.

America continued to stare down at the piano keys. "A little."

"Did you take lessons? I took lessons, and, boy, was that a waste of money," Corky kept on.

"Got it from Mamà," America mumbled. "She plays by ear. She picked it up as a girl in Haiti, where there was a street piano outside her building."

A long, awkward pause followed.

Finally, Corky spoke. "I didn't know where to find you."

"The last few days, I've come here to play while Mamà is working without me." America raised her eyes. "What do you want, Corky?"

"I . . . don't know what happened after practice last night. That wasn't me, least not the me I know. I hurt you because I kissed Bubba's brother, Tad, and I wanted to kiss him again, I think. I was wrong, and I knew it was stupid the moment I did it. And I *never* want to kiss him again," Corky exclaimed. "But I don't understand . . . Why would Bubba even say what he said in the first place?"

America shot her the same incredulous look she had when Corky suggested she use the public library. "You're asking *me*? *I* sure don't understand it—I've *never* understood it. It just *is*." America dropped her eyes back to the piano, her hands now clenched.

Seeing that, Corky felt even worse. "Well . . . it shouldn't be." All out of steam, she plopped down on the front pew, as close to America as she risked. Then, in a voice so soft she hardly recognized it, she said to America, "Please play with us. If not for me, for the other girls. They love you, and they didn't do anything stupid because they kissed a stupid boy."

For a moment, America didn't answer. "I need to think about it."

"Why? Because of me?"

"Mamà hasn't ever liked that I'm playing in the game, worrying about trouble. After last night, I think maybe she's right."

Corky frowned, confused. "What trouble? It's just a ball game. And Mack says Bubba's just white trash that talks out of his ass."

America turned and gaped at her. "You really *don't* understand a thing, do you? You're still such a *kid!*"

"I know!" Corky said. "But how can I not be if you won't talk to me?" And Corky said once again, this time even softer, "Please, please play with us."

America fumed. "Why do you care so much?"

Suddenly embarrassed by how much she looked up to America, Corky answered, "I just do, okay? You're so good at it. You catch so good! And you can run faster than anybody else, maybe in the world! The rest of us can only dream of being that good! And when you're that good, don't you just have to try? Don't you have to do what's inside you?" Corky was now almost mad at her. *"Don't you?"*

Fighting to stay calm, America had placed her hands over the piano keys. But hearing that, she brought them down hard and loud, matching the sound she felt inside.

Corky jumped, recognizing the signs. She'd pushed too far.

Dropping her hands into her lap, America muttered, "You know nothing about *nothing*, Corky Corcoran."

The two of them looked as if they both wished they hadn't said a thing. For several uncomfortably silent moments, they sat, unmoving, America staring at the piano keys, Corky staring at America.

Afraid that any second America might bolt, Corky looked around for something to keep her talking. But as she took in the small church's old-timey interior, she was instantly fascinated by its beauty, so different from her church's bland, modern insides. The Southside church had no expensive stained glass, just rows of clear, open windows, but there behind the pulpit was color galore. She stared at the baptistry framed by the painted mural of a river flowing across the entire wall. Corky was entranced. "America, your church is . . . oh wow. I mean, is that a river?"

With that, America softened, raising her eyes to look at the baptistry. "Yeah. It is."

"Were you baptized in it?" Corky asked.

"No." Getting up from the piano bench, America sat down on the front pew by Corky to better admire the baptistry's mural. "But it *is* great."

"Compared to ours, for sure. Ours is just a big, white bathtub with curtains."

"I was baptized in the ocean," America said, staring at the blue-painted water.

"That's even *better*," Corky said. "In Galveston?"

America nodded. "We've lived in four different towns since leaving Galveston. So, I guess Mamà and I feel most at home in church."

Corky thought a moment. She was always going to church, but she sure never felt like it was home. "I'd like living in different towns like you. You meet lots of new people all the time," Corky said. "Sounds terrific."

"And I'd like staying in one place all my life like you, never having to say goodbye to the new people you like," America said. "That sounds terrific."

Corky snuck a glance at America. Taking a deep breath, she said, "If you don't want to play with us, it's okay."

They sat there for another long moment, the two of them silently gazing at the mural together, as if the river itself were flowing around and through them.

Finally, America broke the silence. "I can't ride a horse."

"What?" Corky mumbled.

"You asked what I can't do."

Corky perked up. America was making a deal. And she knew all about deals.

She smiled conspiratorially.

America smiled slyly back.

"What time does your mom finish at our house tomorrow afternoon?" Corky asked.

"She told me about 4:00," America answered.

Corky popped to her feet. "Come to the house at 3:00." And to America's great surprise, Corky leaned over and hugged her neck before rushing out the door, headed lickety-split back to the drugstore.

Following her out of the church, America walked to her rental house. In her room, she reached under the bed and pulled out Corky's library book, eased down on the bed, and brushed her hand over its pristine cover. Then, remembering what Corky said about the rest of the story, she hesitantly opened the nice, new hardback and began, again, to read.

Meanwhile, forcing herself to walk slowly so as not to sweat through her dress, Corky snuck back over the railroad tracks and through the drugstore's side entrance, which made her almost bump into Dr. Ambrose DuBose.

"Button up your shirt, son!" Dr. DuBose had just stepped down from the raised prescription area, where her father stood, and was looming over a Southside teenager who was now fumbling with his buttons. As the good doctor left, Corky glanced up at her father. He seemed to be thinking hard about something as he watched Dr. DuBose go.

Corky couldn't take it anymore. When he turned back to typing an Rx label in his big manual typewriter, she popped up by her dad and blurted, "Have Dr. DuBose and Mr. Boatwright been talking to you about the softball game?"

Focused on the Rx label, Cal Corcoran barely looked around. "Hmmm? What softball game?"

Confused, Corky could only stare, first at him and then at the fountain, where she could have sworn the two men had been gazing back at her. *If it isn't the game, what the heck have Dr. DuBose and Noah IV been talking to my dad about?* she wondered.

"Katie, go on now," her father ordered. "I'm busy."

The next two hours Corky spent working behind the fountain before walking home were uneventful. And that was a good thing. Because when she got home, Corky found a note from her mother:

> *Kathryn,*
> *I've taken the job. Tonight, the library is open late.*
> *Supper is on the stove with instructions on warming it for*
> *you and Mack before I get home. Come to the library by*
> *3:00 p.m. and take a letter to your father for me.*

At 3:00, Corky and Roy Rogers rushed up the steps of the white-columned Carnegie library and pushed through the front doors. Belle looked up from the librarian's main counter. "I'm working now, Kathryn. No time to talk. Here, take this to your father," she said, handing Corky a sealed envelope. "And what is Roy doing in here? Both of you, go on now! I'll see you tonight."

Corky didn't move. "Mom?"

Belle smiled. "Everything's fine, sweetheart, I promise. *More* than fine. You'll see."

17

The thing about old houses is not only what they've seen but also what secrets they might be keeping. If walls could talk, they'd often tell some mighty fine tales. If the Corcorans' walls could talk, they would tell of Phinneas T. Rigby, the man who built the stately two-story house in 1900. He was the prosperous bachelor owner of a local pub named Rigby's Saloon who stayed legally prosperous until Prohibition in 1920. After that, he sold illegal hooch he created in what moonshiners called a *copper pot still*, using cornmeal, sugar, yeast, water, and sometimes raisins or prunes for added zest. And since the town's imbibers trusted him to never put in poisonous substances such as manure or paint thinner for extra kick like other moonshiners, his widely known "cottage industry" was a huge success that almost rivaled his saloon years. He'd tried making bathtub gin, but the quality wasn't up to his standards, which was true for most gin made in bathtubs at the time, all agreed. So, he stuck to the pot-still method and made a minor fortune. Of course, this created a problem about where to hide that fortune, since he couldn't use the banks for obvious reasons. He had to get inventive about where to stash it all. The Corcorans would discover one of the places inside the house, but only because Belle, in her later years, would finally decide to replace the ugly wallpaper in the living room where they had hung an unremarkable Norman Rockwell print to cover a slightly torn place over the sofa. There, between the studs, were four bulging bags of silver dollars where the saloon-owner-turned-bootlegger had stashed them, putting up the ugly wallpaper himself right before he died in 1929, telling no one.

The other place was out in the horse corral. In a lean-to shed he'd added to the corral, Phinneas kept his moonshine still, along with buried bags of the lesser coins he'd made off the neighbors by selling single drinks for a dime a swig. And there were many, many neighborhood swiggers since even the Broke Spoke Tavern had to shut down during Prohibition years, selling only its own, less trusted, moonshine out of the back. Actually, the dime bags were how Phinneas Rigby had died. After one too many swigs of his own hooch, he decided to sit down on a stool and count his money, dropping an entire bag of dimes in the dirt near the handsome, high-spirited white stallion he'd built the pen for. The young stallion had taken umbrage at him for getting too near his back hooves while dime-scooping and had kicked the life out of him. After his death, the remaining hooch and yet-to-be-buried dime bags were quickly pilfered by his best customers. Until, that is, the house sold that same year to a young couple with a plow horse and a big family who wondered why they kept finding Mercury head dimes each time they raked the poop from the corral.

Decades later, Corky and America, dressed in their sneakers and cutoffs, stood by that same corral admiring the aging palomino paint mare that the family had adopted for young Mack a year after adding Roy Rogers to the family. For continuity, Belle had asked young Mack if he wanted to call the mare Dale Evans, since that was the name of Roy Rogers's famous wife. Mack had said no, that he wanted to name her Trigger after the TV cowboy's famous palomino. However, the mare, who'd already lived half her life, knew her name. It was Golden. So, she refused to acknowledge Mack or five-year-old Corky's existence when they called her Trigger. Finally, Mack compromised and began calling her Goldy, and that was close enough for the mare.

"Her name is Golden, but we call her Goldy," Corky explained to America, telling her the entire story. "She'll answer to both."

"Golden . . . ," repeated America. "I like that. I'm going to call her Golden."

"She hasn't been ridden in a while, but that's because she's so old, not because she's ornery," Corky explained. "I'll hop on with you. She'll like us fine."

America reached out and stroked Golden's blonde mane as Corky kept talking. It was the same soft, brushlike stroke she used to touch the fancy encyclopedias on the Corcorans' bookshelf. "Want to know why I wanted to ride a horse?" America said as she continued to stroke the palomino.

"Because this is Texas?" Corky guessed.

America shook her head. "Because my great-grandfather was a cowboy."

"Really?" Corky tried to picture that.

America nodded, still stroking. "My father said he'd worked the Chisholm Trail, taking cattle right by here to get to the trail up the road. Papà is a man of few words. He doesn't talk much. But he told me the whole story, and that meant he was proud of it."

"Wow," Corky said. "How'd he become a cowboy?"

She shrugged. "Papà said he was already a cowboy working with livestock all through the Civil War right up to Juneteenth," she said, referring to the day Union troops landed in Galveston to read the Emancipation Proclamation, ending slavery. "After that, being a free-man, he'd just kept on cowboying. Papà said the Chisholm Trail opened up about that time, and it had lots of Black cowboys driving cattle up to Kansas. My great-grandpapà did it most of his life, he said, and even got good at rodeoing, too. So, I just wanted to feel what it was like."

Corky beamed. "Well, let's do it."

As Corky put the bridle on Goldy and knotted the reins, she pointed toward the little lean-to shed beside the horse trough, where once Phinneas Rigby had worked his moonshine still and where now the Corcorans housed their saddles and bareback pads. "Want to ride saddle or bareback?" Corky asked. "I think Goldy likes bareback best, not as much weight. *Bareback*, for us, is with a pad and girth. It's just a little harder to get on after you're off. There's a bit of a trick to it if you're not by a fence."

"I choose what Golden likes best," America said.

"Bareback it is." Corky popped the pad on Goldy and cinched the girth. "Want to use the corral fence?"

America paused. "Show me the trick."

"Okay. Mack was good at it when he got about my age. Me, not that much yet, but I'm working on it."

With her left hand, Corky grabbed the reins and a handful of Goldy's mane near the shoulder. With her right hand, she grabbed hold of Goldy's withers, her bony shoulder ridge right in front of the cinched pad.

"One, two, three," Corky said and tried flinging herself onto the horse like Mack did. She didn't make it. "Trying again. One, two, three, hmpggh." Corky swung up a leg and the leg came right back down. "Shoot! Not today," she said and started to lead Goldy over to the fence.

"Let me try," America said. Taking the reins and a handful of the lower mane with her left hand, she grabbed the withers with her right and swung herself gracefully up onto Goldy as if she'd been doing it her whole life.

"Oh great. You're even good at *this!*" Corky griped, laughing. Leading Goldy to the split-rail corral fence, Corky stepped on the lower rail and popped behind America. "Let's go!" Corky said. "Lead her out of the pen with the reins. Kick her a little, just taps, so she knows you want to go. As soon as we're on the road, using the reins, turn with both your hands and your legs in whatever direction you want to go."

So America did. In a minute, they were all on the dirt street with America practicing left and right, and Goldy nicely obliging. Proud of herself, America sat up straight as they ambled along the road. "Does she ever run?"

"Not anymore," Corky said. "Mack broke an arm on her when he was twelve, racing across the field in front of our house. Goldy stumbled on a rock or something. He went straight over her head, and *bam*. But you can kick her all day now, and she'll insist on nothing more than a trot, and only if she feels like it, which is never. I've tried. In fact, half the time I don't even tie her up when I get off anymore. She usually just stands there waiting for me."

Hearing a car coming their way from the Corcorans' house, they looked around. It was Sunny and Sandy Beach's Corvair, top down. The sisters had spotted Corky and America riding Mack's horse down the dirt street and drove straight for them. Passing them, the Corvair stopped a few yards ahead.

As Goldy, America, and Corky approached the convertible, Sandy's and Sunny's eyes darted back and forth between America and Corky.

Reaching around America, Corky tugged on the reins to lead Goldy safely to the other side of the street.

"Hi, Sandy and Sunny," Corky called to them as Goldy came to a stop on her own.

"Oh, yeah, hi," said Sunny, her eyes stuck on America.

"We're looking for Mack," said Sandy.

"Oh, we know," answered Corky. "But I don't think he does."

"You're funny," said Sandy. "Where's Mack?"

"At my grandfather's with my dog. But I'll tell him you 'called.'"

Sandy cocked her head. "You're Mack's little sister. Didn't you used to be fat?"

Sunny was still staring at America. "Wait, I know you. You and your mother cleaned our house once."

"Oh yeah!" Sandy chimed in, now looking at America, too. "And your mother can't speak American very good."

Hearing that, America threw a leg over Goldy's mane, slid down, and stepped over to the Corvair, towering above the two girls sitting in the convertible.

Worried about what was going to happen, Corky eased to the ground, letting go of Goldy's reins to step closer. She held her breath.

America opened the Corvair's door, leaned toward the two, and repeated what Mack had said to her the day they'd all met: "Want to race?"

Corky breathed again as Sandy and Sunny both looked at her for translation. "I wouldn't," Corky said, shaking her head.

"Hmmph," said Sandy, slamming the car door and floorboarding the Corvair in an attempt to zoom away, creating more back-engine noise than speed.

America looked back at Corky, and they both started laughing.

At that moment, though, the Corvair backfired, either scaring Goldy or making her recall her youth, because she began to chase after the loud car on a dead run.

Stunned, America and Corky stared at the old horse racing away. Then they both scrambled after her.

Corky lasted only two long blocks before having to bend over her knees to catch her breath. When she looked up, she saw America sprinting closer and closer to the mare until she caught up, grabbed Goldy's reins, and slowed her to a stop.

"What are you doing with Mack Corcoran's horse, girly?" came a wobbly voice from the nearest yard. Miss Delilah Yoakum, brandishing a broom she'd been using to sweep her dirt driveway, her hair wilder than usual, was marching full tilt toward Goldy and America.

"It's okay, Miss Yoakum!" Corky called, huffing and puffing up to them.

"Who are you?" Miss Yoakum demanded.

"It's me, Corky—Kathryn—Corcoran."

"No, you're not. Kathryn Corcoran is a chubby little girl who can't carry a tune. Get away! I'm calling Tommy Tilton."

"No, no, it's me, I promise. Remember how I walked you home from the WMU meeting last Wednesday? Listen, I'll sing." Corky sang another few bars of "Amazing Grace," which was enough for Miss Yoakum to lower her weapon.

"That was horrible," Miss Yoakum said. "It *is* you, Kathryn Corcoran. My, have you changed, except for your bad singing. But what's this girly doing with your brother's horse?"

"Catching her fast as liquid lightning, that's what," Corky said, glancing proudly at America as she moved toward them, leading Goldy. "We'll be on our way now, Miss Yoakum." Turning to America, Corky said, "You drive."

Unable to suppress a smile, America did the bareback mounting trick once more, landing on Goldy's bareback pad. Looking around, Corky saw an empty water bucket at the corner of Miss Yoakum's yard. "May I borrow that bucket for a minute?"

"I don't see why not," said Miss Yoakum.

Corky took it over beside Goldy, turned it upside down, and stood on it. America held out her hand. Corky grabbed it and swung up behind. With a wave back at Miss Yoakum, off they went.

As soon as they were back at her horse corral, Goldy trotted straight in and the two girls hopped down.

"Thank you, Miss Golden," America said to Goldy, patting her neck.

"There's a better way to thank her that she loves," Corky said as she took off the bareback pad and eased the bridle over Goldy's ears. Hanging both in the shed, Corky grabbed a comb and a brush from a shelf. "Do you want to brush her mane or back?"

America pointed to Goldy's mane.

Corky handed her the comb, and America began running it through Goldy's golden-white mane, lovingly untangling each little snarl. Meanwhile, after Corky wiped the sweat from Goldy's face where the bridle had been, she used the brush to massage her back, Goldy giving a little shiver of delight.

When Corky finished, she watched America sumptuously sliding the comb along the mare's long mane one last time, finishing with a quiet sigh. Corky took in the sight of the two, committing it to memory as the best moment of that perfect day. She glanced at America's long braid. "Want to braid some of Goldy's tail like a show horse? The hair comes out all curly when it lets go."

America nodded, her face as open and happy as Corky had ever seen it, and that thrilled Corky to the bone. Corky took a little of the tail, separated it into three sections, and waited for America to take over. America expertly whipped them into a braid and laid it lovingly down on Goldy's big buttocks.

"Now, because she feels so good," Corky said, "watch what she does after all our hard work. Stand back."

Goldy shivered all over, folded her legs underneath her, and with her chin touching the ground, rolled over on her side to rock back and forth before popping up on her legs and shaking off all the dirt, like Roy Rogers would shake off water.

Watching Goldy, America belly-laughed. It was the first time Corky had ever heard her laugh that freely.

America turned toward Corky. "Thank you."

Corky grinned. "Friends?"

This time America gave in. "Friends."

"What's the Haitian Creole word for friends?"

"*Zanmis.*"

"*Zanmis,*" Corky repeated. "I like the sound of that."

The two stood there for a nice, awkward moment until America said, "Turn around. This has been bugging me since we met."

Corky turned around. Pulling off the rubber band around Corky's ponytail, America began whipping Corky's hair into a braid as well. "It's *penyen ti très* Mamà's way," she said. "Just a few full strands, if no oil."

"The Beach sisters were snotty," Corky muttered as America braided.

"There," America said as she finished, setting the braid down on Corky's neck just as lovingly as she'd done Goldy's.

"Miss Yoakum, too."

America sighed again. "It doesn't matter. None of it matters. I probably won't be here much longer."

Hearing that, Corky suddenly remembered how they'd met. Less than two weeks earlier, she was overhearing her dad's phone call about making a loan to America's father, who was out *looking for a job*. It seemed eons ago, Corky realized, the America she met then not the America she knew now. Somehow, with all that had happened since, Corky had forgotten that America was going to move. At first, sadness washed over her at the thought of America leaving just as they finally were real friends. As was her young habit, though, Corky immediately hatched a plan that could fix everything. Why couldn't Evangeline work permanently for her mother? And why couldn't her dad help America's father find something, anything, here? *It could happen*. But first, her dad had to meet America and see how great she was. *That way, he'd understand*, Corky told herself as she turned to America and blurted, "Come to the store tomorrow before noon, just for a minute. Please, please, *please*? It's important!"

Before Corky could pelt her into submission, America gave her a sidelong glance and agreed.

Energized by the slightest possibility that America might stay, Corky beamed as she ran new water into Goldy's water trough. And as a contented Goldy began pawing the dirt by the trough, something silver and glinty caught Corky's eye. Navigating around Goldy's leg, Corky reached down.

It was a Mercury head dime.

"Wow, look at this," she said. "Dad and I collect old coins from the store's cash register for fun. And this is a really old one, 1929. They stopped making these in 1945. See? They have a picture of Mercury with a winged headdress on it since he's—"

"The god of speed," America answered. "That was in my seventh-grade textbook."

"Here." Corky held out the dime to the only goddess of speed she knew. "It'll be a good luck charm. For the game. And the Olympics." When America hesitated, Corky grabbed her hand, popped the coin in her palm, and held it there until America closed her fist around it.

After giving Goldy a few last pats, the two headed toward the house, and the closer they got, the more they heard music. Corky could clearly tell the music was "Clair de Lune." But it was different. And she realized what it was. The music wasn't coming from the record she was used to hearing. It was coming from the piano.

As they stepped into the house's front hallway, they could see their mothers in the living room, Evangeline sitting at the piano, her hands roaming the keys, while Belle stood in the curve of the baby grand wearing a rapturous look that Corky had never seen before.

"I can't believe you can do that by ear!" Belle was saying to Evangeline. "Oh, how I'd love to be able to play."

Evangeline stopped. "You can, *zanmi*." She tapped the baby grand's empty sheet-music shelf. "This way."

Belle waved the idea away. "I'm too old."

Smiling at that, Evangeline began playing the opening strains of "Clair de Lune" again just as America and Corky entered the living room. Seeing them, Belle put her finger to her lips to keep the two daughters quiet as they came closer. And in that way, for the next few minutes, the four of them experienced the beautiful music together.

18

Every life has a smattering of days that change everything. For Corky Corcoran and her family, this day and the next would prove to be the kind of days that make you who you are, that push you and those around you into fears realized and lives never imagined.

And, as such days do, the first one started much like the ordinary day before it.

As usual, Mack fed Goldy and left early to do his Papa Cal and Willy chores before going to the store to stock. Corky, as usual, had her bowl of Frosted Flakes cereal and glass of Welch's grape juice. She played with Roy Rogers, as usual, taking care not to mess up her braid, which still looked pretty darn good; she was looking forward to showing it to Velma and Velvadine. As usual, at 11:00 a.m., her mother announced it was time to drive her to the drugstore. And Corky was excited to go, as usual, but more so that day since America promised to come by in order for Corky to execute her big plan to keep America in High Cotton.

But the moment Corky got out of their station wagon and her mother pulled away, the usual turned unusual.

Very unusual.

First came Earl out the side door. He marched to his parked pickup, grabbed a sawed-off shotgun from its gunrack . . . and took it inside.

Seeing that, Corky hesitated. When she entered the side door, Earl was standing at the front counter as if he'd been there all along. A little

Black boy was holding out a quarter for an ice-cream cone, and there was no sign of the shotgun.

"Katie, honey, would you please get this boy his strawberry ice-cream cone?" Earl said to her.

Heading to the soda fountain, she noticed Dr. DuBose up in the prescription area talking to her dad again, and there was something unusual about it, too, although she couldn't quite decide what. She now knew they weren't talking about her softball game, but something still bugged her about it. As she scooted behind the fountain's counter, she glanced at the old, faded sign hanging above the soda fountain, which had been there since before her dad bought the store: "We Reserve the Right to Refuse Service to Anyone." And she thought for the umpteenth time how stupid it was that she had to deliver the ice-cream cone to the little boy who was standing right over there, just steps away. But she went ahead and began scooping.

The usual suspects were already occupying most of the counter stools, including Noah Boatwright IV, who was eating his grilled cheese, reading his *Fort Worth Star-Telegram*, and had almost finished the first of his three Coca-Colas. He was still not acknowledging her existence, and Corky decided she was fine with that. But as she finished scooping the ice-cream cone and was about to take it over to the front counter, she looked down. Under the fountain's counter was Earl's shotgun. She felt a chill. Why would her father ask Earl to bring in a shotgun, and why put it here? *Is he going to shoot someone?*

But before she could notice anything else different, a van marked "New Hope College"—the Black Presbyterian junior college in the next town up the Fort Worth–Decatur highway—parked right in front of the drugstore's big plate-glass windows. Corky watched the students pile out. For a second, the small group clasped hands in a prayerlike, unbowed way, then one by one entered the store, moving toward the soda fountain. As they passed, Mack, who was on his knees stocking shelves near the door, jumped to his feet.

Taking the last swig of his first Coca-Cola, Noah IV saw the Black students coming his way and all but choked on it, spitting it across the stool sitter next to him. At that point, the stools emptied, and the regulars, including Noah IV, melted into the furthermost aisles.

Ice-cream cone still in her hand, Corky glanced up at her dad and Dr. DuBose. They were staring at the students moving through the aisles, and they did not look one bit surprised. Her dad turned to Dr. DuBose as if he was expecting the big doctor to do something.

And he did.

Dr. DuBose descended from the raised prescription area and strode toward the soda fountain. Straightening up as tall as his big girth allowed, he marched to the lead student, who was heading toward the first stool, a skinny, young man with his chin high, as if bolstering his courage. But instead of the good doctor joining the Black students' cause for their civil right to be served, Dr. DuBose stepped in front of the student leader and proceeded to stare him down.

The student stopped, Dr. DuBose's girth so formidable that it forced the student to step back. The two locked eyes as the melting cone dribbled down Corky's arm, and she suddenly understood Dr. DuBose's *not in my town* remark she'd overheard a few days back. Dr. DuBose and Noah Boatwright *weren't* talking to her dad about her softball game. They must have heard about *this*. Tiny High Cotton, Texas, was having its first lunch-counter civil rights sit-in. And Corky wished to the Lord Above that she didn't know anything about them, because what she knew was not good. All the images of what she'd read to rile Papa Cal on Sunday appeared before her young eyes, especially the one in Jackson, Mississippi, that had also just been on the TV news again, complete with footage, due to its one-year anniversary. She remembered how the news film showed the gathering White crowd pushing against both the Black and White college students sitting calmly on the stools. She remembered how the mob started dumping drinks on the students' heads and laughing as others covered them with mustard and ketchup. And she remembered how things suddenly turned violent as the students were attacked, some pulled down to the floor and beaten, the mob taking jars off the shelves to pummel them. She even remembered a guy burning a female student on her arm with a cigarette and laughing while he was doing it. Corky was twelve when she first saw the original version on the TV a year ago, and she couldn't unsee it, even after her mother had quickly turned off the set.

With all those images rushing before her eyes, Corky could only stand there gaping.

"KATIE, COME HERE!" her dad ordered, waving her toward him. *"NOW!"*

The little Black boy who'd wanted to buy an ice-cream cone had wisely disappeared, so, dropping the cone into the sink, Corky rushed to watch from behind her dad. She also noticed that Velma and Velvadine suddenly had an interest in manning the front counter, Velma nervously twirling a strand of long, red hair with her fingers, and Velvadine adjusting and readjusting her big glasses, leaving only Earl . . . and that hidden shotgun . . . behind the soda fountain.

And there, still in front of the first stool, stood Dr. DuBose staring down the skinny student leader, who was no doubt trying to grasp why a big, important-looking Black man was standing in his way.

At that very moment, Corky saw America appear at the glass front door. She was grabbing one of the door's handles when she noticed the Black college students surrounding the soda fountain—and froze.

Oh no, no, no! Corky wanted to shout to her. *This isn't why I wanted you to come, I promise!*

Time seemed to stop. Corky held her breath as all the people in the store looked back and forth between a tense Earl and the two Black men staring each other down. Everyone was waiting for the next moment to arrive, for someone, anyone, to make the first move.

And when the next moment arrived, it was Mack who did the moving.

Mack wasn't looking at the two men staring at each other. Nor his father in the prescription area. Nor the waiting anxious college students surrounding him. He was looking at America frozen outside the front door, her face gradually registering what was happening. When she finally let go of the handle and sprinted back toward the railroad tracks, Mack kicked the stock boxes out of his way; strode to the skinny student leader in front of Dr. DuBose; locked eyes with him for a long, telling moment; and sat down on the second fountain stool, waiting for the student leader to sit down on the first.

The skinny student looked back and forth between Mack and Dr. DuBose, who was still standing between him and the stool. Carefully, he eased around the big man and sat down by Mack.

With that, the doctor just stood there as if he couldn't believe the student had defied him. But these were college students from up the road who knew not Dr. DuBose. So, when the rest of the college group streamed past him to fill the remaining fountain stools, Dr. DuBose's face dropped. He stood there for another stunned moment before storming out the store's side door.

Corky peeked up at her dad. He was staring at Mack, his face full of fury and disappointment. She glanced over at Earl, who was standing at attention behind the soda fountain waiting for a signal from her father before either serving the students or closing down the fountain. Then, she peeked down at the regulars all bunched up in the nearest aisle, the one dedicated to Black hair products. Grabbing a big jar of Satin Sheen hair straightener, Noah IV hissed up at her dad, "*Corcoran!* Do something!"

Corky gazed at Noah IV's face, contorted with anger, and realized this might have been the way the Jackson, Mississippi, violence began . . . with an enraged man standing in the aisles picking up a jar or a bottle of something and heading back to the counter stools to express his displeasure at the nerve of anyone Black sitting on "his" stool. And she also realized something else. Earl didn't have his shotgun under the soda fountain counter to shoot anybody sitting on the stools. He had it there to stop any such enraged souls from losing their heads and starting something ugly.

Noah IV inched closer to the prescription area. "Corcoran! You *hear* me? *Do* something!"

And Cal Corcoran did. Staring down at his son sitting among the Black students, he did the only thing he could have done.

He nodded at Earl.

And Earl served them all.

All the students ordered Dr Peppers and ice-cream cones, except for one, who, deciding to be different, ordered a banana split with extra whipped cream.

While the students ate their treats, the fountain regulars, including Noah IV and his jar of Satin Sheen, just watched.

And to Corky's huge relief, that's all they did.

Finishing his ice-cream cone, the skinny student leader sitting by Mack looked at his watch and gazed out the store's big plate-glass windows as if looking for something. Finally, he paid for his purchase and stood up. Then the whole group did the same, leaving as quietly as they'd come.

Within thirty minutes, it was over.

As the students piled back into the college van, no one in the store moved. After a minute, though, the fountain regulars, a bit shell-shocked, went on their slow way, including Noah IV, who walked out the side door with the Satin Sheen in his hand and had to come back inside to return it. In seconds, nobody was left inside except Earl, Cal, Corky, the Stamper sisters, and Mack.

Mack stood up from his stool. Corky came out from behind her dad and watched her brother turn and gaze up at their father.

But Cal refused to look at him.

As the van was preparing to pull away, a reporter and photographer from the *Fort Worth Star-Telegram* seemed to appear out of thin air. Corky rushed toward Mack. "How did they get here so fast?" she asked, glancing at the newsmen.

Mack gave Corky one of those looks that adults give to children when they ask the obvious. "Bug, they were tipped off."

Noticing the reporter scribbling in his notepad while the photographer snapped pictures of the departing van along with exterior shots of the store, Corky scurried over to the front doors to watch. The reporter came through the doors and straight up to Corky. "Hey, kid. Tell me what happened."

So, she did. But, to her surprise, he asked more questions.

A whole lot more.

Corky cocked her head. "You sure ask a lot of questions. I've been told not to because it's irritating."

"Oh yeah?" he said. "How else do you learn things?"

Corky grinned. Right then and there, she decided she wanted to be a reporter.

He handed her his card. "If you think of anything else . . ."

But her father strode up and took the card. "Sir, that's enough questions for the child."

The reporter winked at Corky and gave her another card. "Look me up after you go to journalism school."

The reporter moved on to bombard Earl and the Stamper sisters with the same questions, and her dad said, "Katie, give me that one, too."

"I won't call him, I swear," Corky said, wanting badly to keep it.

He fumed. "Earl?" he called toward the soda fountain.

"Yeah, boss?"

"The delivery boy's out delivering. Take Katie home, would you?"

"Yeah, boss."

"Mack!" Cal said next. "Get your butt up here. *Now*," he ordered as he disappeared into the store's office.

Walking toward the side door to go home, Corky heard the first of what was going to be an extremely heated conversation between her father and Mack and was glad she was going to miss it:

"What did you think you were doing?"

"Trying to keep anything bad from happening and, by the way, doing the right thing."

"I'm trying to run a business here, son, the business that feeds us! That pays for your wasted schooling! Don't you tell me what's right and wrong."

"Are you going to close the soda fountain?"

"That's not your concern! I'll do whatever I have to do."

Corky's stomach flipped. Her dad might close the fountain like many other places did when they couldn't continue to "refuse service to *anyone.*"

As she followed Earl through the side door, the same one Dr. DuBose had stormed out only a few minutes before, she thought about both her dad and the Southside doctor. She knew why her dad did what he did. What else could he do after Mack got involved? But why had Dr. DuBose done what he'd done? In the years to come, her older self would continue to be puzzled over why he hadn't taken the students' side. All she could ever figure was that for her father and the doctor, both men of their times—seeing themselves as guardians of a separate peace long established and hard earned—things must have seemed fine the way they were. Perhaps Dr. DuBose also thought that what his Southsiders would have to go through to make things better was just too painful. That day, though, young Corky could only wonder as she got into Earl's truck, eyeing the empty space on the truck's gunrack where the sawed-off shotgun had been.

At home, as Corky walked through the back door and headed up to her room, she could hear her mother on the phone with her father. *We'll be in the papers tomorrow,* she kept thinking, grasping for something good to think about now that High Cotton's one and only sit-in had ended peacefully, even if she did keep seeing Noah IV with that jar of Satin Sheen hair straightener in his hand.

Corky's mother must have felt sorry for her, because there, as she pushed open her bedroom door, was Roy Rogers. Sensing a problem the way dogs do, he jumped up on the bed and lay down alongside her while "Clair de Lune" wafted up the stairs, her mother hoping the pretty piano music could help soothe her little girl. Soon, Corky fell asleep, the feel of Roy's warm fur lulling her like good medicine while the record played on.

And, as such things mingle into memory, when grown-up Kate remembered the drugstore sit-in, it would be as if its soundtrack had been Belle's beautiful, dreamlike piano music.

Mack didn't come home that night until the wee hours of the morning. Avoiding his father, he'd gone straight from work for his last summer date with Cissy since she was leaving the next day for summer school. But Corky didn't know that and worried. So, when she and Roy woke to the sound of Mack sneaking up the stairs at 3:00 a.m., they both waited for him to get to the top.

"Mack . . . ," she whispered, cracking her door open.

"Shhh!" he hissed, putting a finger to his lips and nodding toward their parents' room. And he slipped past into the dark. Corky watched him go, wanting to talk about what he did that day. It would have to wait until tomorrow.

But tomorrow held its own drama, the kind that, for some, would forever change the direction of their lives.

19

The next day was the day of the big softball game. For Corky, there'd be no working at the drugstore even if she wanted to, since her father closed the soda fountain for a day out of an abundance of caution. High Cotton residents, of course, came anyway to gawk and talk after seeing the article and a picture of the store in the *Fort Worth Star-Telegram* that morning. Or so Velma and Velvadine would tell Corky later, along with how many dozens of ice-cream cones they missed selling to them. The reporter had even quoted Corky. Under any other circumstances, that would have made her proud as punch . . . and it still secretly did, although she was smart enough to keep it to herself as she cut out the article and stuck it with the reporter's card in her desk drawer.

After the excitement of seeing her and her dad's name in print wore off midmorning, though, Corky spent the rest of the day fretting about whether her father was going to close the soda fountain. Or "burn it down," as Papa Cal had suggested.

But as the day got closer and closer to the softball game, any more fretting, at least about that, would have to wait. There was a ball game to play—*the* ball game—along with yet another reason to worry whether America would show. After all, America surely must have thought the sit-in was why Corky wanted her to come. So, if she didn't play, it would be Corky's fault again.

But she held out great hope America *would* show, trusting that when you discover you're good at something, you can't help but want to do it when you get the chance. Mack felt it with hardball. Corky felt it with softball. So, America, despite everything, must be full to bursting with the feeling.

At about 5:00 p.m., Corky got dressed in her chosen duds for the game and waited on the back steps with Roy for time to pass.

Finally, just before 6:00, Mack appeared from Papa Cal's, where their dad had banished him for the day. As Mack loaded the baseball equipment bag into his car, Belle kissed Corky, wished her luck, and held Roy Rogers's collar so he wouldn't try to follow.

"Mom," Corky said, "want to come to the game? We just might win this year."

Belle smiled. "Well, I hope you do, but it's probably best if I stay home with Roy." It turned out that Belle Corcoran had a mama-bear streak, surprising everybody, especially her children. At Mack's first church softball game in the fifth grade, he'd wrenched his ankle so bad colliding with the second baseman that he couldn't stand up. Before either pastor-coach could get to him, Belle, defying her limp, was at Mack's side trying to pick him up and take him home. It had embarrassed young Mack enough that he'd banned her from all games thereafter, at least until he grew past the point of being picked up by his mother. So Corky wasn't all that troubled by her mother's absence since who knew what was going to happen in this crazy summer game that might make her mama-bear side kick back in.

As they drove toward the field, Corky kept looking at Mack, who had a new hickey on his neck and who had yet to say a word about the drugstore sit-in.

"Dad's mad, isn't he?" Corky finally tried.

He cut his eye at her. "What do you think?"

"Why'd you do that?" she said.

"I think you know."

"Is Dad going to close the soda fountain?"

He sighed. "Maybe. Depends on what happens next."

Corky frowned. ". . . What's going to happen next?"

"Nothing, I so damn hope and pray."

A chunk of silence sat between them after that until, almost to the field, Corky said what she feared most: "Do you think America will come to the game after yesterday?"

"Well, Bug," Mack said, smiling wryly, "if she doesn't, we're dead meat."

Texas summers are legendarily scorching. The church softball games had to be played either in the morning, which nobody wanted to do, or right before dark. Early evening was when both boys' and girls' church games had always been played, but not too late due to the matter of the lights being turned off for the summer on the town's only baseball field. After dark, the only light would be from the Dairy Dip's big sign, which cast its glow only to about half the baseball field's diamond and parking area.

Neither game, though, had ever lasted that long, so nobody much worried about it.

At the ballfield, Mack and Corky hopped out of the car, Mack grabbing the equipment bag, and headed toward Pastor Pete, who was already on the field by home plate, a box at his feet. "Look at the crowd!" Pete said, rocking on his heels, happy as a clam in mud, since the deacons were not, after all, stopping him from letting America play. "This is going to be *great*."

The girls' church softball game never had a crowd. The spectators were rarely more than a spare parent or two who didn't mind the pain of the girls' poor play. But from the looks of the stands, half the town had heard about the Baptists' ringer and came early to see what all the fuss was about. Of the two separate stands—home and visitor—the home team's stand was already full and the parking lot was filling up, too, cars and trucks parked way down near the football field, all but out of sight. Corky was also surprised to see faces she didn't recognize. A lot of the strangers were standing out against the four-foot chain-link fence past the third-base line, just like men from the opposing team's town did for the high school baseball games during the year. Since the girls were just playing other girls in town, much less it being church softball, that was new, too. She looked at Mack. He was frowning in that direction. Just as she was about to ask him about it, Marilou and Prudence came running over to her, all shrieks and squeals. They were about to play a *game*! And all three girls ran to join Pastor Pete at home plate.

When most of the team had arrived and gathered around him, Pete couldn't stand it any longer and opened the box he'd brought. From it, he pulled a shirt that said "1964 Softball Summer Champions," and that made the girls gasp and giggle.

"This is the year, I can feel it!" Pastor Pete crooned. "And if it isn't, well, the T-shirts are still correct, because you're all champions in the Lord's eyes! So, everybody's getting one after the game no matter what!"

And that inspired another round of the Baptist girls' gasps and giggles.

The biggest annual problem for the Baptists was always the same one. Most of the Methodist team girls, year in and year out, could actually play. This year, though, the newest Methodist players, a bumper crop of fifth graders, were questionable. The Baptist girls, on the other hand, were, as always, challenged in all areas. They had no chance. They *never* had a chance. Until America. So, their hopes for the first-ever Baptist girls' win were higher than the High Cotton water tower hovering over the field.

Tommy Tilton pulled up in the town's old police cruiser and got out. He was still wearing his police uniform, out of not only expedience but also for its perceived authority, even for officiating at a girls' church softball game. In his official capacity for the next couple of hours as the game's one and only umpire, Tommy would have his hands full. A few years back, he even started bringing a whistle, just in case things got out of hand considering he was doing this by himself, even though baseball umpires historically did not use them. He hoped just the sight of it might help his cause, forgetting he was still wearing his holstered police-officer sidearm. Since nobody had ever seen him draw the handgun from its holster in the entire history of his time as High

Cotton's cop, it really wasn't much of a deterrent. But just like his job as the town's cop, he took his umpiring seriously and truly committed to the role.

Besides the Baptist girls not being very good players, they also weren't very good at remembering the rules, especially since the only softball they got to play the rest of the year was recess scrub softball. So, Tommy spent much of his time as umpire reminding the girls that they couldn't do whatever they were doing. Their summer game's rules were a hodgepodge of elementary playground rules, local church-game rules, and official slow-pitch softball rules taken from an old manual Tommy checked out each year from the library to consult. So far, though, he'd never needed to. But he liked to be prepared. Since the pitchers were the pastor-coaches for either team, the most important local rule for the girls' game was that the two men could not participate in a play beyond the pitch, as it had been for the entire decade of the game's existence.

This year, however, the rules, both local and official, would not only matter but soon come into play. Dramatically.

While Tommy set each base sixty feet from home plate, as per slow-pitch softball regulations, both teams chose an outfield for warming up. As they pitched to each other, the Baptist girls stared at the growing crowd, nervous as a bag of cats, all of them knowing full well the crowd was there to see America.

Scanning the highway anxiously looking for her friend, Corky could barely breathe.

"Is she coming?" Marilou whispered to Corky. "She's coming, right?"

And, as if Marilou had conjured her, here came America just as she'd done for their practices, sprinting across the tracks, the highway, and onto the field. And Corky breathed again.

The Baptist team girls started jumping up and down, waving and calling to her. Mack pitched her a glove, and she joined Corky and the girls warming up.

But both teams' girls had a hard time concentrating, noticing even more people arriving, and from where: the Southside. Streaming across the railroad tracks, the Southsiders filled up the entire empty visitors' stand. And unbeknownst to America, in the middle of the crowd were Lion and his baseball pals.

It was an amazing sight. For the first time in the history of High Cotton, the citizenry of both sides of the town's railroad tracks were in the same place, watching the same game, a situation so unheard of that some who saw it called it a bit of a miracle. All the girls stopped to watch the drama unfolding, including Corky. And then she spied . . . Willy. Her jaw dropped as she saw Willy's old, bony self slowly, painfully climb the stands and take a seat. And she never loved him more. She almost ran over to him. Instead, she smiled and waved. He smiled and waved back. And something about seeing him sitting there smiling her way proudly and sweetly made the last four days of Papa Cal, the rattler, and the drugstore sit-in come flooding over her. Corky felt her eyes well up with big, fat, sloppy tears. She furiously wiped them away before anybody saw, struggling mightily to keep her soggy, young dam from bursting wide.

It was 6:00 p.m. Time to play ball.

The girls headed to their respective "dugouts," which were just benches inside the chain-link fence enclosures on both sides of the field, the Baptist team using the one along the third-base line. But the Baptist girls were too nervous to sit down. Instead, they all milled around in front of their dugout with "Coach" Mack, waiting for the coin toss that would start the game.

However, just as Pastor Pete was creating a spot in front of the high school field's pitcher's mound for the two pastors to pitch their softballs to the girls, Noah Boatwright IV yelled Pete's way, waving him over to where he stood behind the chain-link backstop with Bubba and Tad. As Pastor Pete hesitantly headed toward Noah IV, Marilou Moon's father, who'd already grabbed a seat behind the backstop to watch Marilou catch, jumped up and hurried toward Noah IV as well.

Both Corky and Marilou noticed.

Nonono, Corky thought. *Mr. Boatwright found out about the deacons' secret vote.* Corky yelled to her brother, pointing at Noah IV. "Mack!"

Looking up, Mack immediately sprinted to Noah IV, who was already talking to Pete, and the more he talked, the lower Pete's head dropped. Mack threw up his hands. But Pastor Pete just stared at the ground.

So, together, Corky and Marilou slowly came closer.

"This is *bullshit,* and those deacons are nothing but *spineless, baptized* bullshit!" Mack was saying, so mad he was flinging spittle.

"Don't do this, Boatwright," Mr. Moon said.

"We voted again, Moon. You had your say," Noah IV answered as he and Tad walked off, leaving only a grinning Bubba to climb into the stands to watch the game.

"Daddy?" Marilou said.

"I'm sorry, sweetie," Mr. Moon said to Marilou through the chain link. "It's about what happened at the drugstore yesterday. I voted against it."

Raising his head, Pete took a deep breath and stared at America, who was smiling and laughing along with the other Baptist girls huddled as near as they could get to her.

"America's already *here!*" Mack pressed. "What are you going to do?"

For a moment, Pete stood adjusting and readjusting his glasses, watching America. Then, clenching his jaw, he finally muttered, "Nothing. I'm doing nothing."

At that, a shocked Mack almost hugged the guy, and a beaming Mr. Moon returned to his seat.

As the pastor-coaches, Pete Hockenheimer and Doug Gifford, joined umpire Tommy Tilton on the pitcher's mound for the coin toss, Mack searched the home stand's crowd until he found Bubba in the top row, relishing the jackass's coming surprise.

"Okay, men," Tommy said to the two pastor-pitchers, "here's my yearly reminder. For the girls' game, you two are pitchers *only* and cannot participate beyond pitching. And, as per girls' rules, the game will be six innings unless the game goes long, at which point we revert to time instead of innings before sunset. Got it?"

Both pastors nodded.

Tommy tossed the quarter, and Reverend Doug called heads. It was tails. So, the Methodists became the "visiting" team and would bat first, giving the Baptists last bat.

Tommy took his place as umpire behind the plate.

"*PLAY BALL!*" he yelled, the crowd clapping and hooting.

And the game began.

1st INNING
SCORE: 0–0

As each Methodist batter came to the plate, the Baptist fielders started up the traditional hazing chatter of all youth baseball, calling, "*Batter, batter, batter, batter.*"

It didn't faze them. In quick fashion, the Methodist girls loaded the bases. So, the Baptist girls tensed as tenth-grade left-hander Anna Mae Mulroney stepped up to the plate twirling her bat like the big home-run dog she was. She was as slow as molasses on a stick, and she knew it, so she always went for the fence to lower the odds everyone would see her try to run.

But as Pastor Pete readied to pitch, Roy Rogers loped onto the field and straight to Corky at shortstop.

"Dang it, Roy!" Corky scolded. "How do you always do this?"

"Roy Rogers, come here!" Mack hollered, running over to grab Roy's collar.

"Should we call Mom?" Corky said, noticing how happy Roy was to have found them.

"No time. We'll need to put him in the car," he said.

"But it's still hot. Let him stay in the dugout with us. *Please?*" Corky begged.

Tommy came over. "Mack, we've got to get going. Daylight's burning." Corky held on to Roy's collar as Mack jogged to the dugout, pulled the thin cotton cord from the equipment bag, tied it around Roy's neck, and led him to the dugout.

"Sit!" Mack ordered, tying the cord around the dugout's bench leg.

Roy sat.

"Stay!"

Roy stayed, at least for the moment, since staying would be more about the strength of the tether cord than Roy's obedience, which was always in question.

And the game started again.

Anna Mae immediately whacked Pastor Pete's pitch over the fence. As the Methodist runners scurried across home plate, Anna Mae did her famous slow-walk around the bases.

That quick, the score was 4–0.

"It's okay! We'll catch 'em!" Pastor Pete encouraged his little team, clapping. When the next batter hit a grounder, though, what followed was a comedy of errors by the nervous Baptist girls: Second baseman Lily Sue threw the ball over the head of first baseman Onezy . . . Scrambling for it, Onezy threw it back over *Lily's* head . . . Retrieving the ball, Lily threw it to third baseman Prudence, who missed it *completely*. But as the runner headed for home, Prudence grabbed the ball and slung it to catcher Marilou Moon . . . and to the surprise of everyone, the ball hit Marilou's glove perfectly just in time to tag the runner out for Out #1.

Jumping to his feet behind the backstop, Mr. Moon hollered, "Way to go, sweetie! Two more outs!"

With a little help from the Methodists' own nervous new batters, fifth graders like Thelma, the Baptist girls got them for Outs #2 and #3.

"SIDE OUT!" Tommy announced.

The Baptist girls were up to bat.

Reverend Doug sauntered to the pitcher's mound, smacking a wad of gum the size of Texas in his cheek as he passed Pastor Pete. Ignoring both his rival and his gum, Pete yelled more encouragement to his little band of fumblers as he joined them in the dugout, Roy Rogers deliriously happy to see them all.

The top of the Baptist batting lineup was Onezy, Twozy, Corky, and, in the cleanup position, America.

Onezy and Twozy both hit dribblers that got to first base before they had a chance to, for Out #1 and Out #2. But Corky hit a line drive the shortstop missed, and made it safely to first base.

America was up.

Staring at the far-off fence, America raised her bat. Reverend Doug threw the arching pitch, and America connected, the ball whooshing over the center fielder's head to roll near the fence. As the outfielders ran after it and the spectators watched in awe, America zipped around the bases for an in-the-park home run so fast that she had to slow down rounding third to allow Corky to cross home plate in front of her.

The Baptist girls screeched in delight over scoring *two* runs in an inning—a *first*—as Roy Rogers barked to show his solidarity.

Next, Marilou hit a grounder and got on first base. But then Lily, having an exceptionally late swing that rarely ended before the ball was in the catcher's glove, swished three times for Out #3.

"SIDE OUT!" announced Tommy. "INNING OVER!"

2ND INNING
SCORE: 4–2

"Batter, batter, batter, batter," the Baptist infielders chanted again as the Methodists came to bat. The top of their lineup packed the bases again. And, as Anna Mae, twirling her bat, stepped into the batter's box, a male voice rang out from the third-base line spectators:

"Put your weight behind it, chubby!"

This was new. Catcalls had never happened at their little summer softball games. But if it bothered Anna Mae, she took it out on the ball. Anna Mae did, indeed, put her weight behind it, socking the ball over the center-field fence with ease. And once again, as all the runners crossed home plate to score another four runs, Anna Mae did her famous slow-walk around the bases for four more runs.

Watching her, Mack had an idea he shared with a nodding Pete.

Meanwhile, the bottom of the Methodist batting order, still nervous, quickly repeated their strike-out performance for Outs #1, #2, and #3.

"SIDE OUT!" Tommy announced.

As the Baptist team headed for the dugout, Mack met America coming off the field. "I'm pretty sure Reverend Doug is going to start walking you," he whispered. "So, Pastor Pete will try to walk Anna Mae. She'll still swing for the fence if she can reach the ball. But she'll be off-balance enough that anything she hits should bounce in your neighborhood. So, when that happens, I want you to sprint to Anna Mae and tag her slow-walking self before she even gets to first base. I bet the farm you can do it."

America nodded.

"And if you do get walked," Mack added, "I've got another idea."

The bottom of the Baptist batting lineup, Sadie, Prudence, and Thelma, were up next, and their skills were not a pretty sight. First came Sadie, who, scared of the ball, was famous for running from it. Each time Reverend Doug pitched her a ball, she jumped out of the batter's box.

"C'mon, Sadie! Swing!" Pastor Pete coaxed. "It doesn't matter if you hit it. Swing!"

Sadie, though, kept jumping out of the way. After three more tries, the pitcher, Reverend Doug, threw up his hands.

Tommy came to the mound.

"Why aren't you calling her out?" Reverend Doug griped.

Tommy sighed. "*Rev*, with all due respect, these are just girls, some of them very young, and the whole idea is to let them learn about sportsmanship and have good, clean fun. Isn't that what you said the game was for when we started these summer games? Why don't we walk her? It might get her to swing next time. Agreed?"

Fuming, Reverend Doug rolled his bubble gum to his other cheek, reined in his competitive juices, and nodded.

"Take your base!" Tommy called, and Sadie skipped happily to first base.

Next up was Prudence, who, unlike Sadie, *always* swung: Out #1.

Little Thelma followed. Her batting complication was that she closed her eyes. Three blind swings later, she struck out for Out #2. After that, Onezy got on base and hopes rose. But then Twozy fouled a ball off, which the catcher easily caught in the air for Out #3.

"SIDE OUT!" announced Tommy. "INNING OVER!"

3RD INNING
SCORE: 8–2

"Batter, batter, batter, batter," the Baptist girls started chanting again, if less enthusiastically. As usual, the first three Methodist girls got on base, and Anna Mae came to bat, expecting to hit it into orbit, bringing them home.

Instead, Pastor Pete tried to walk her. And, as Mack prophesied, Anna Mae was not going to be walked. She leaned her big bulk toward the outside pitch, sticking out her bat as far as it would go, and smacked the softball anyway: a loopy blooper over second baseman Lily's head.

So, America put Mack's plan into action. As Anna Mae made her lumbering way to first base, America scooped up the ball, turned on the jets, and touched first base for Out #1 before Anna Mae had gotten halfway there.

But, to the crowd's delight, America kept running, rushing past Anna Mae toward home plate, ball in hand, to keep the other three girls from scoring. Tagging out one girl for Out #2, she scared the others back to second and third bases.

Meanwhile, Anna Mae stood on the first-base line in apparent shock. Tommy ordered her to her dugout, and she stomped off the field.

Yet all was for naught. Before the last Methodist fifth-grade batter finally struck out for Out #3 to end the side, three of them got on base—and that allowed both runners America had scared back to second and third to score anyway, upping the score even higher.

"SIDE OUT!" Tommy announced. "SCORE: 10–2!"

The Baptist girls, glum despite Pastor Pete's peppy clapping, were again up to bat.

At the dugout, Mack pulled America aside. "When Reverend Doug walks you—and he will—here's the plan." Mack leaned close to explain.

Corky, up to bat first, hit a wobbly fly and despaired. But the new center fielder, who was playing a real game for the very first time, not only missed it but got flustered enough that she bobbled it twice. As Corky rounded first and rushed toward second, the still-flustered fielder overthrew it so wildly, the ball hit the chain-link fence near third base.

Both the catcher and third baseman dashed for the ball while Pete and Mack whipped their arms like human windmills, signaling Corky to keep running.

So Corky rushed toward third.

But, as she slowed to hop on the base, the girls scrambling for the ball collided, and instead of retrieving the ball, they began arguing about who got in whose way.

Rushing over, Reverend Doug urged them to retrieve the still very live ball. *("GET IT! GET IT!")* Meanwhile, Mack and Pastor Pete were all but taking flight windmilling their arms, signaling Corky to go home: *GO, GO!*

And as Corky ran across home plate, the sweetest sound she heard from the stands wasn't cheers or whoops or applause but Willy's familiar two-finger whistle, shrill and loud and satisfyingly long. Just for her.

Feeling mighty-mighty after that, Corky hustled to the dugout to be greeted by all her teammates and, to her surprise, a loose and happy-about-it Roy, his tether cord's knot having unraveled after three innings of tugging and jumping. Corky quickly tied it back with the only knot she knew, a granny knot, and not a very good one, looking around to see if Mack had noticed. He hadn't. So, she hugged Roy, whispering, "Sit. Stay. Good boy," the last of which being all that Roy heard.

America was back up to bat.

As Mack predicted, Reverend Doug threw four perfect outside pitches to walk her.

"America," Mack called to her as she took her base.

Standing on top of the first-base bag, America nodded.

Marilou, the next batter, came to the plate. Reverend Doug threw the pitch. Marilou swung, missed . . . and America stole second.

As everyone gasped at what America had done, chaos momentarily reigned.

Almost swallowing his Dubble Bubble, Reverend Doug stormed to Tommy. "You can't *steal* in slow-pitch softball!"

"Yes and no," Mack called, trotting over, Pastor Pete in tow. "The rules say that stealing is permitted as long as the runner does not leave the base until the ball reaches home plate."

From his back pocket, Tommy pulled out the girls' youth softball rule book he'd checked out of the library and thumbed through it until he found the rule. "Yep. That's what it says."

"But nobody's fast enough to try that!" Reverend Doug blurted, and everybody within hearing distance turned to look at America. "We need to update our local game rules," he grumbled.

"Sure. Not for this year, though," said Tommy.

"But you've seen her run," Reverend Doug said. "If she can steal, it'll kill us!"

"And your point?" said a beaming Pastor Pete.

Reverend Doug harrumphed. "I'm not worried, Hockenheimer. Look at the score."

"BATTER UP!" Tommy hollered.

On the mound, Reverend Doug took a deep, zen-like breath, a practice he used during competitive moments, human nature co-opting his best Christian intentions. Eyeing America on her stolen base, the Methodist minister-coach-pitcher glanced to the heavens and pitched to Marilou.

Marilou swung and missed.

And America stole third.

The catcher had barely gotten the ball out of her glove before America was standing on third base.

Once again, Pastor Pete beamed.

And once again, Reverend Doug breathed deeply in and calmly out.

With two strikes against her, Marilou stared at America on third base. America smiled at her. Marilou smiled back, and when the ball came her way, she clipped it. As the ball rolled toward the pitching mound, she remembered to run.

Reverend Doug gaped at the ball coming his way. "Grab it, somebody!" he hollered.

Wasting precious seconds, none of the Methodist girls could decide who should do so.

"Anybody! For the love of jeepers!" Reverend Doug yelled, stepping out of the ball's way. "Throw it HOME!"

By the time one of them did, it was too late. America had crossed home plate to the sounds of the whooping, hollering crowd.

Her teammates showering her with back pats, America sat down in the dugout dirt beside Roy's tether, letting Roy Rogers lick her face to celebrate.

As the crowd noise died down, though, Corky thought she heard another catcall. She didn't hear this one clearly, but something about the tone made her feel like she'd felt when Bubba hissed the ugly slur at her and America. It came from one of the fence-line spectators again, and it reminded her of how fence-line fans at Mack's high school night games were sometimes noisy and drunk. She hoped she was hearing things.

But Tommy had heard something, too. He stopped the game.

"TIME OUT!"

Officer Tilton marched over to chat with the heckling strangers. Marching back, he passed Mack at the dugout. "Out-of-towners," he told Mack. "They'd heard about America somehow, and a couple of them have had a little too much to drink. I reminded them this is a girls' church softball game and to watch their language."

That satisfied Corky. But Mack kept thinking about Bubba's double-take at the last practice after Bubba spied the men leaning on the gray jalopy. Glancing at the stands, he caught Bubba gawking at the fence-line strangers and then *ducking* behind the nearest spectators.

What the . . . , thought Mack.

"PLAY BALL!" Tommy yelled.

"Okay, girls! Time to chatter!" Pastor Pete said, clapping to encourage his team. "Let's hear it!"

With Marilou on first base, skill-challenged Lily, Sadie, Prudence, and Thelma were up to bat next. Lily struck out for Out #1. Then Sadie ran away from yet another four pitches, and Tommy allowed her to walk. Sadie skipped again to first base, and Marilou moved to second.

But then Sadie got confused: The next batter, Prudence, grazed the first pitch, making it plop onto home plate, roll a few inches, and stop. Surprised, Prudence sprinted toward first base. Grabbing the ball, the catcher looked back for Tommy's fair-or-foul decision. Meanwhile, confused little Sadie, having already taken two steps off first base, *froze.*

"FAIR BALL!" Tommy called.

With Sadie still standing frozen off first base, the catcher threw the ball to the first baseman as Prudence sprinted safely by. So, the first baseman just reached over and tagged Sadie for Out #2.

Sadie slumped her bewildered way off the field, and Pastor Pete squelched a moan. Because little Thelma was up to bat.

Eyes closed, Thelma swished three times and struck out: Out #3.

"SIDE OUT!" announced Tommy. "INNING OVER!"

4TH INNING
SCORE: 10–4

The fourth inning was the fastest on summer softball record. The Methodist batters, at the top of their lineup, were sure they'd get on base. Instead, the first batter hit a fly ball to America: caught. The next batter hit a line drive to Corky: caught. The next one hit a pop fly to Twozy: caught.

Three up, three down.

"SIDE OUT!" Tommy announced.

The Baptist girls were now at the top of *their* lineup.

But Onezy and Twozy both hit foul balls near the first baseman: caught and caught. Then Corky hit another pop fly to the same fielder, who was no longer flustered: caught.

Three up, three down.

"SIDE OUT!" announced Umpire Tilton. "INNING OVER!"

But with only two innings to go, things were about to get very interesting.

5TH INNING
SCORE: 10–4

"Batter, batter, batter, batter."

Up first for the Methodists was Anna Mae.

Pastor Pete once again tried to walk her. And once again, Anna Mae wasn't having it. He threw the ball wide but not wide enough. Anna Mae leaned out and swatted it, the ball landing behind Twozy in left field.

America then did exactly the same thing as she'd done before, but from the opposite angle. Roving near center field, America raced over, scooped the ball up, and sprinted toward Anna Mae, who had almost made it to first base. Rushing past the pitcher's mound, America ran up behind Anna Mae and tagged her an instant before she put her big foot on the bag.

This time, Anna Mae wasn't shocked. She was furious.

"Don't touch me!" she hissed, whirling around, her nose in America's face.

Surprised, America turned to leave, and Anna Mae, sticking out her big barrel leg, tripped her.

America stumbled. A gasp went up from the crowd. And, like they'd seen major leaguers do on TV, all the players rushed onto the field. Chaos ensued. And as the Baptist girls pushed in close to tell Anna Mae what they thought of her, little Thelma took the opportunity to kick her in the shin hard enough to make the big girl howl.

Tommy lifted the whistle he had worn, unblown, around his neck at every game for ten years and blew it.

The crowd went silent.

Tommy stopped the game for a full minute to allow everybody to calm down and clear the field. Finally, he yelled: "PLAY BALL!"

Anna Mae was only Out #1, so the Methodists were still at bat. Being understandably overexcited, within minutes the new, little fifth-grade batters committed Outs #2 and #3.

"SIDE OUT!" Tommy announced.

The angry Baptist team entered their dugout. The only one happy was Roy Rogers, who greeted them as if they were all home from the war. The girls knew they had to get runs quickly since the yearly game was never more than six innings, and the sun was already going down.

America was up first. Reverend Doug again walked her. To no one's surprise, when the next batter, Marilou, swung and missed, America stole second base.

"Watch her!" Reverend Doug called to his infielders before the next pitch, knowing she'd try stealing third. Twice more, Marilou swung and missed. Twice more, he whirled around to see that America hadn't moved. He frowned her way; America smiled back.

The next batter was Lily Sue with her ever-late swing. This time, though, her bat topped the softball, rolling it toward first base. Zipping past her slow-moving ball, she hopped triumphantly onto the first-base bag. "Way to go, Lily, baby!" her mother whooped from the stands.

And still America had not moved.

Sadie Springer was up next. After running away from four balls in a row, Tommy again let her walk, to Reverend Doug's growing vexation. Sadie skipped once more to first base, Lily moved to second, and America moved on to third without having to steal.

As she watched, Sadie was having deep thoughts. Feeling bad about getting confused last time, she wanted to make up for it. While she was afraid of the ball and extremely fuzzy on the actual rules of the game, she still loved playing so much, she wished she could be as good as America in spite of being extremely poky. It was why she skipped. She could skip faster than she could run. Remembering how cool America looked while stealing, she decided to try stealing, too, despite the fact that there were no unoccupied bases to steal.

Of course, no one knew this but Sadie.

When the next batter, Prudence, missed Reverend Doug's pitch, Sadie began skipping toward second base as if she didn't have a care in the world, despite the fact that Lily Sue was standing on it. The Methodist infielders gaped, not knowing what to do. Their pitcher-coach had yet to see what was happening, so the catcher took it upon herself to throw the ball to the first baseman, thinking logically that Sadie would see the error of her ways and turn around.

Wondering why everybody was shouting, Lily Sue finally looked to her left. Here came a skipping Sadie. Not knowing what else to do, Lily ran toward America on third.

And that's when America broke for home.

By the time Reverend Doug grasped the situation, America had already touched home plate, scored, and was trotting to the dugout.

Outraged, he rushed to Tommy, pointing back at a satisfied Sadie standing on second base and a surprised Lily on third. "Are you going to let those steals stand?"

"Well," Tommy began, "they did all tag up before their first steals. And the catcher did have possession of the ball and could have been throwing it back to the pitcher, which allows for the steals, as the rules state."

"This is nuts! We need to change our local softball rules right *now*," Reverend Doug said.

Tommy fingered his whistle. "Nope, *Rev*, not for this year. I'm allowing the girls their stolen bases."

Throwing up his hands again, Reverend Doug breathed in, deeply zen.

On the next pitch, Prudence hit a grounder toward third base and made it safely to first. Meanwhile, Sadie proudly stood on her stolen base, thinking how much she'd enjoyed stealing it. Watching as the next batter, Thelma, swung blindly at the pitch, Sadie decided she'd steal another and began skipping to third base, unconcerned about poor Lily since the last time had worked so well.

This time, however, the catcher was ready. She threw it straight to the shortstop, who tagged Sadie skipping by for Out #2.

Still at the plate, Thelma looked toward Mack by the dugout.

"It's okay, Thelma!" Mack called while Pete squelched another moan. "Keep your eyes open and hit it!"

Little Thelma tried hard to keep her eyes open. But she clamped them shut and swung two more times for Out #3.

"SIDE OUT!" announced Tommy. "INNING OVER!"

6TH INNING
SCORE: 10–5

Glancing up at the sky, Tommy turned to the crowd and made an announcement. "The game is going long, and it'll be dark in a few minutes," he said in his loudest umpire voice. "So, we are reverting to time to finish the game. It is now 7:40. By exactly 8:00 p.m., we will end the game, win, lose, or tie. Okay, one last time: PLAY BALL!"

The Baptist girls anxiously took the field because the Methodists were at the top of their batting order with a five-run lead. One by one, they loaded the bases, waiting for Anna Mae to bring them home.

Confidently twirling her bat, Anna Mae walked to the plate and waited for the pitch. Pastor Pete again tried to walk her, yet he did such a poor job this time that Anna Mae smiled. As she slugged it high, high, high into right field, all three Methodist runners tagged up and ran confidently toward home plate.

Watching it disappear over her head, little Thelma stumbled back to see America speed behind her, dive for the ball this side of the fence, catch it beautifully, and pop up on her feet with the ball deep in her glove.

Anna was . . . *out*.

"WHOA! Triple play!" Mack yelled to the team. "TRIPLE PLAY!" But that didn't mean a thing to the Baptist girls since they'd never seen, much less made, a triple play.

As the Methodist runners passed home plate, certain they had scored, Reverend Doug shouted: "NO, NO! BACK!"

The confused runners didn't understand what their coach was yelling, having never seen a triple play, either.

Suddenly, all the coaches were screaming at the very same time.

"BACK TO YOUR BASES!" Reverend Doug shouted. *"FAST!"*

"TOUCH BOTH BASES WITH THE BALL!" Pastor Pete and Mack shouted. *"FAST!"*

America ran to second baseman Prudence, handed her the ball, and Prudence stomped on the base.

A roar went up from the Baptist fans.

Mack and Pastor Pete, still screaming, were pointing now at first base.

Prudence ran and handed the ball to first baseman Onezy. Stomping on the base, Onezy held the triple-play ball high.

"SIDE OUT!" Tommy announced.

The Baptist fans went wild.

"TRIPLE PLAY!" the crowd started chanting.

"TRIPLE PLAY!"

"TRIPLE PLAY!"

The Baptist fielders strutted their stuff into the dugout. The score, though, was still 10–5; the clock was ticking; and the sun was going down.

Mack called the girls together for a pep talk. "Listen up. It may sound like we're behind by a lot, but we're not. We only need one really good inning. So, let's go get it!"

And the bottom of the last inning began.

Onezy, Twozy, and Corky each got quick singles, loading the bases. America grabbed her bat and approached the plate.

"Surely he won't walk America now," mumbled Pastor Pete, eyeing Reverend Doug.

But he did, even though it meant giving up a run. As America took her base, Corky moved to second, Twozy to third, and Onezy crossed home plate.

The score now was 10–6.

And the bases were still loaded.

"Why did he do that?" groaned Pastor Pete. "He better not be slowing down the game on purpose!"

Reverend Doug was betting the next batter, Marilou, would strike out. Yet Marilou didn't. She swung and missed twice. But on her third try, she connected. Soundly. The ball hit the pastor-pitcher's leg in the air and dropped, squiggling off the mound.

Reverend Doug yelped, grabbing his calf. "Get it! Quick-quick!" he shouted at the second baseman. She tried, but Twozy and Corky had already crossed home plate.

Meanwhile, America had rounded second. By the time the baseman scooped up the loose ball, America was standing on third.

"Damn!" swore the Methodist girl, kicking at the dirt.

"Shake it off," Reverend Doug said, rubbing his leg, "and watch your language, young lady."

As America's teammates cheered, Roy whined, straining at his tether with America so near.

The score was now 10–8 and the clock was still ticking. The next few moments would be critical for making High Cotton Summer Softball history.

With America once again ready to score, up to bat were Lily Sue, Sadie, Prudence, and Thelma.

Realizing the bottom of the Baptist batting lineup was the team's last hope, the Baptist fans got quiet. Lily Sue stepped into the batter box and swished three times, striking out. But as the catcher threw the ball back to Reverend Doug, America decided to steal home.

With that, four things happened at once:

1) Caught up in the last moments of a game he desperately wanted to win, Reverend Doug lost his head, forgot he was playing a girls' softball game with rules he himself had written against his participation, and did what any adrenaline-pumped, old, minor-league ballplayer might do. Seeing America sprinting home, he threw the softball to the catcher: *hard*.

2) The young catcher, seeing a sizzling softball coming right at her, wisely jumped out of its way. The ball whizzed past Tommy to wallop the chain-link backstop, the crowd gasping.

3) Seeing America sprint by, Roy tugged so hard at Corky's weak granny knot that it let go. Bounding out of the dugout, he rushed to nip at America's heels in high doggy spirits just as she was about to score. Stumbling, America fell in the dirt, inches from home plate. Quickly, she rolled onto the plate while Roy hovered over her, licking her face.

4) Runner Marilou slowed to stop on third. But seeing the fun America was having with Roy on home plate, and noticing that the catcher didn't have the ball, Marilou kept running and dove right on top of America, Roy dancing around them both.

Back to his senses, Reverend Doug rushed toward his shocked, little catcher. "I'm so, *so* sorry, sweetie!" he tried. "You okay?"

"Boo!"

"Boo!"

While the crowd jeered, Mack, Pete, and Corky ran toward the home-plate pile, Mack to help the girls to their feet, Corky to grab Roy's tether, and Pastor Pete to remind Tommy that Reverend Doug had broken their pitcher-participation rule.

"He can't do that!" Pastor Pete yelled.

"No, he cannot," Tommy responded. "Baptist girls get the runs!"

As they all trotted back to the Baptist dugout to the screaming joy of their teammates, Tommy turned to a cowed Reverend Doug and said, "Pull yourself together, *Rev.*"

The score was now 10–10 and the time was 7:52, only eight minutes left to play before the game would be called on account of the darkness.

While the Baptist girls had only one out, they were now battling the clock. And next up to bat was Sadie Springer.

Pastor Pete checked his watch. "Swing now, Sadie! Swing! Please, please *swing!*"

On the pitcher's mound, Reverend Doug was still unwilling to lose or tie his first-ever summer game. So, he pitched a perfectly lobbed softball as soft as he could to Sadie, hoping she'd at least *try* to swing. And, for a moment, he thought it worked. Sadie wasn't running away . . . She was staying in the batter box . . . She was watching the ball . . . But, as the ball got closer, she panicked, turned her back, and the softball popped her square between the shoulder blades.

Reverend Doug threw up his hands yet again, and Tommy told her to take her base.

All the spectators checked their watches: 7:55.

"Go, GO!" Pastor Pete said, rushing Prudence to the plate. On the very first pitch, Prudence, having the game of her young life, hit a dribbler and made it to first base again, advancing Sadie to second.

That left only little Thelma up to bat with the clock continuing to tick.

The crowd audibly groaned.

Mack pulled Thelma over as she came hesitantly out of the dugout. Easing down on his haunches to look her straight in the eye, he said, "Thelma, honey, you are great no matter what you do, you hear? You always show up, and that's a gift. And if you keep playing, you are going to get better and better, I promise. So, listen to me. Stare hard at that ball coming to you, eyes WIDE open, and think of somebody you really, really don't like, somebody that makes you hopping mad. And as it's coming to you, picture that person's face on that ball and then whop the *heck* out of it! Whaddya say? Will you try?"

Thelma glared at Anna Mae in left field, picturing her tripping America.

"You picturing somebody?" Mack said.

Thelma nodded.

"Are you good and mad?"

Thelma, looking mighty fierce, nodded bigger.

"Okay!" Mack trotted over by first base, turned around, and pointed to his eyes that he'd stretched as WIDE as they'd go. When the ball started coming her way, Thelma kept her glaring eyes open, and for the first time ever, she lightly popped the softball. It rolled so softly down the first-base line that Thelma was running alongside it. The first baseman rushed to scoop it up, but when she turned around to throw it to tag Thelma out, nobody was there to catch it.

Thelma was safe on first base.

A roar went up from the crowd for little Thelma, who was jumping like a kangaroo up and down on the base to show her joy.

The time was 7:58.

Prudence was on second base, and Sadie—the winning run—was on third.

To the last rays of the sun sinking in the west, Onezy got up to bat. Reverend Doug pitched.

Onezy hit a grounder between the legs of the shortstop.

As the crowd held its collective breath, all eyes turned to third base, where Sadie, who had been confused most of the game, was staring at her teammates in the dugout, all shouting for her to run.

So, she ran in her excruciatingly slo-mo way . . . until, with the seconds ticking off, she started skipping. And as she skipped her way across home plate, Tommy looked at his watch. It was 8:00 p.m. on the dot.

"GAME OVER!" he shouted, raising his whistle and blowing it long and loud.

Everyone in the stands leaped to their feet, giving the girls an applauding, hooting, stomping High Cotton standing ovation while the rest of the Baptist team's girls rushed toward home plate to jump up, down, up, down together, screaming with softball happiness.

For the first time ever, the Baptist girls' team had *won*.

THE 1964 ANNUAL HIGH COTTON GIRLS' CHURCH
SOFTBALL GAME
FINAL SCORE: 10–11

Corky looked back for America, who was stepping out of the dugout with Roy. Corky ran over to hug her neck. And as America handed Roy's tether cord to Corky, the crowd clapped louder.

Mack noticed as he and little Thelma trotted toward home plate to join the rest of the celebrating girls.

"America!" he called to her. "They're clapping for you. *Wave!*"

America, embarrassed, stared up at the stands. Unable to make herself wave, she shyly smiled at the crowd from both sides of High Cotton, clapping—together—for her. She could feel her heart pounding as the crowd kept on clapping. And when she didn't move, all her teammates rushed back to the dugout to surround her and Corky. Still jumping up and down with joy, they wouldn't let her go until she jumped up and down with them. Finally, laughing, she did, and a barking Roy joined in.

It was almost dark, the bright Dairy Dip's sign quickly becoming the only light available, its faint glow reaching just a few yards past the ballfield's third-base dugout. The parking lot beyond would be in full darkness in moments. So the crowd began to trickle away, either to the Dairy Dip, the parking lot, or the railroad tracks heading back to the Southside, Lion and his baseball pals included. But not before Lion caught America's eye and grinned big her way.

Striding over to the Methodist dugout, Pastor Pete put out his hand to shake Reverend Doug's, which made Doug take another big, cleansing, zen-like breath before he finally shook it. Next, striding to the Baptist dugout, where the girls were still celebrating with America, Pastor Pete pulled out his box of T-shirts and handed the shirts to the girls, who all immediately put them on.

After that, Pete turned to the remaining crowd, and, in a pulpit-booming voice, announced: "Ice cream on *me* for everyone, including our Methodist friends, and our neighbors from the Southside still here!"

At the offer of free ice cream, yet another round of applause broke out, and even the Methodist girls and their minister decided to partake.

As a nice-size crowd of all denominations and all High Cotton addresses started lining up at the Dairy Dip for free ice cream at the walk-up window, Corky saw Willy heading toward the line. "America, c'mon, you gotta meet Willy!" And she rushed after him, leading Roy along behind.

"Hey, Roy Rogers! Hey, Cricket!" Willy called over the loud music now blaring from the Dairy Dip's speakers, patting them both on the heads.

"You've got to meet America, Willy!" Corky looked around and frowned. No America. "I thought she followed me . . ." Corky noticed Mack near the dugout in the shadows grabbing their softballs, bats, and gloves to shove back into the equipment bag. "MACK!" she yelled as loud as she could over the music. "Where'd America go?"

Before Mack could answer, from the loose bag rolled a hardball he'd missed when he'd changed out his baseball equipment for the softball game. Picking it up, he fingered it out of long habit. It was all he could do to not throw it, happy to be touching it instead of the big softballs. Stuffing the hardball into his jeans pocket, he yelled to Corky, "I saw her heading the other way. Maybe she had to get home, Bug."

As Roy sniffed the air, Corky thought about that for a moment. America leaving without saying goodbye didn't sound right.

Roy Rogers sniffed the air again. Detecting a familiar oily-greasy stench, he growled. It was the smell of the old truck that had upset his girl.

Corky looked down ". . . Roy?"

Whining, Roy jerked free of Corky's grasp and raced toward the darkening parking lot.

"*Roy!*" Corky darted after him, squinting through the remaining sundown light, trying to see what her dog saw:

Two figures were standing at the edge of the Dairy Dip sign's thinning glow. One of them was America. The other was a wobbly, obviously drunk stranger. America seemed to be arguing with him.

But when Roy was only inches from them, Corky saw that America wasn't arguing, she was struggling . . . The man, yelling at her, had clamped his fist around America's wrist.

Leaping, Roy Rogers latched onto the man's forearm.

The man howled but didn't let go despite Roy's jaws clamped deeply into his flesh. He kneed Roy hard. Roy yelped, rolled, leaped again, and the man kicked him before he could latch on. Roy hit the ground with a yelp and came up barking bloody murder as America kept struggling. It was all happening about as far away from Corky as second base is from home, and yet Corky couldn't quite believe it, hoping the fading light was playing tricks with her eyes. Then she heard another male voice shouting obscenities from the darkness beyond the drunk stranger and America. She tried to run faster, but she felt like she was barely moving, as if she were Anna Mae Mulroney moving at the speed of molasses.

"MACK!" Corky hollered toward the ballfield. *"MACK! MACK!"*

On the ballfield's side of the chain-link fence, Mack was still shoving softballs and bats into the bag when he looked up, heard Roy barking, and squinted through the dying light. For a second, all he could do was take in what he saw. Then he grabbed a bat and was suddenly in motion, vaulting the four-foot fence and racing toward the struggling pair.

Roy's barks turned desperate as the stranger began pulling America into the lot's growing shadows. It was now so dark that the rest of the parking lot beyond the Dairy Dip's glow was shrouded and the pair was standing in the last of the Dairy Dip sign's reach.

As Mack sprinted toward them, he saw them both vanish into the darkness . . . and America, still struggling, pulled them both back into the thin light.

Mack paused. He was too far away to help before America might be dragged back into the dark. So, he dropped the bat, pulled the hardball from his jeans pocket, took his pitching stance, and, aiming for the man's chest, threw the hardball as swift and hard as his All-State fastball. At that exact moment, though, America kicked the stranger in the crotch, making him double over—and Mack's perfectly thrown hardball, instead of hitting the man perfectly in the chest, hit him in the head with a decidedly sickening pop.

The stranger crumpled to the ground, and America began to run. But not toward Corky and Mack. She was running toward the highway and the tracks beyond.

"AMERICA!" Corky rushed after her, screaming at the top of her lungs as she got to the highway. *"It's ME!* Are you *okay?"*

But America was already across the railroad tracks. "Go home, Corky! *Just go home!"* America called back, still running.

"I'm sorry!" Corky yelled, stopping on the highway shoulder to watch America disappear into the dark. *". . . I'm sorry,"* she repeated under her breath. She was sorry for not telling Tommy or Mack about the strange truck. She was sorry for wanting to kiss a boy enough to hurt a friend. She was sorry for the way of the world, and for all the stupid sins of everybody in the world.

She was *so, so sorry* . . .

Hearing Roy barking again, Corky whirled around to see Mack rushing toward Roy, who was still hovering over the downed stranger lying half in, half out of the last of the Dairy Dip sign's glow. Grabbing Roy's dangling tether cord, Mack dragged him back to the Dairy Dip and Willy, who had seen it all and was coming Mack's way as fast as his old bones would let him. Before Mack could say a word to Willy, though, he saw Bubba Boatwright in his Corvette trying to sneak out of the parking lot. Pushing Roy's tether into Willy's hand, Mack kicked the passing door, making Bubba slam on the brakes.

"It wasn't me!" Bubba sputtered, staring past Mack at the splayed-out stranger. "I don't know who that guy is!"

"Yes, you do, you S-O-B! Talk or I swear I'll rip off this door. You know the guy, don't you?"

"No! Maybe . . ."

Mack kicked the door again.

"Okay! *Okay!*" Bubba said. ". . . I might have gone to the Broke Spoke a lot this week, and I might have been griping about the colored girl playing for our church team. And maybe I went on a little too long and had a little too much to drink . . ."

Still smelling the familiar oily-greasy exhaust and now hearing the sound of the truck that went with it, Roy Rogers let rip another mighty bark, yanking at the tether Willy was having to hold with both hands, the flimsy cord slipping.

"Roy!" Mack ordered over his shoulder. "Settle down!"

But Roy did not.

Jerking out of Willy's grasp, Roy dashed to the splayed-out stranger, whose boots seemed to be vanishing by inches into the lot's full darkness. Somebody in the shadows was pulling the human toward the stinking, idling truck.

"Roy! NO! Let 'em go!" Mack yelled as Bubba screeched away. *"Let 'em GO!"*

Instead, Roy Rogers, still barking, dashed headlong into the darkness.

Then so did Mack.

And, right behind, moving faster than an eighty-year-old had any business doing, dashed Willy.

Corky stared helplessly after them, only now making it back to where they'd all been standing.

"Corky?" she heard from behind her. There stood Tommy Tilton holding the ice-cream cone he'd finally gotten at the noisy walk-up window.

Pointing, Corky tried explaining it all in one breath: "Some guy tried to grab America and Roy Rogers ran after him and America kicked him in the nuts and Mack hit the guy with a baseball and there are more guys out there in the dark and now Mack and Willy are in there, too!"

Tommy dropped his cone and dashed to where Corky was pointing, fumbling to get his gun out of its holster. *"STOP whoever you are or I'll—"*

But before he could finish, they heard what sounded like a rifle shot.

Stunned, Tommy fired his pistol in the air. *"POLICE! Stop or I'll shoot again!"*

That's when they heard a thud . . . and a whine . . . and a horrible second of silence . . . Blinded by sudden headlights, they heard a screech of tires as a rattling truck whipped around and peeled out of the far end of the dead-dark parking lot, its broken taillight disappearing down the highway.

Then Corky and Tommy rushed into the dark, too.

When their eyes adjusted, they found Willy cradling Mack on the ground, Mack's hand covering his left eye, blood streaming through his fingers, and Roy Rogers standing sentry over them both.

"Oh, dear God . . . Mack, *don't move!*" Tommy said. *"You could lose your eye."*

As Tommy pulled out his walkie-talkie to call an ambulance, Corky hugged Roy and stared at Mack in Willy's arms, lying so still she thought he might be dead.

"Corky, are you bleeding?" Tommy was saying to her. Corky felt something warm running down her cheek. She wiped at her face where she'd been hugging Roy. Blood. She checked Roy all over, but couldn't find any wound.

The blood was someone else's.

20

Between the time that Tommy heard the rifle shot and fired his own handgun in warning, someone had whacked Mack so hard with a rifle butt to get away that the blow had detached his retina.

When High Cotton's version of an ambulance finally arrived, which was little more than a panel van with a hospital aide driving, Tommy and the driver debated how to move Mack without causing more trauma. Finally, they got him to High Cotton's little hospital, and the doctors at first thought they needed to rush him to either John Peter Smith Hospital in Fort Worth or Parkland Memorial Hospital in Dallas. But after consulting with the hospitals, they decided not to chance rushing him anywhere, since the only way to save his eye's sight had everything to do with him *not* moving in the hopes it would reattach on its own. So, Mack had to lie still, miserably, in a hospital room, with both of his eyes wrapped to keep him from moving for a full week. In 1964, it was all they could do.

After hearing Mack's account of his fastball hitting the drunk stranger's head, Tommy checked the area's hospitals. But he came up with nothing. He even checked morgues and funeral homes.

Still nothing.

Mack also told Tommy about Bubba's Broke Spoke Tavern rants, so Tommy next drove out to the roadside saloon. He remembered the faces of the game's hecklers and was hoping against hope to find them there. He didn't. So, he asked pointed questions of all the regulars and bartenders about Bubba and his rants, not to mention his underage drinking, since the legal drinking age in Texas was still twenty-one. But either those who overheard Bubba's rants weren't there or the customers and bartenders just didn't want to help a cop. Feeling the truth to be the latter, Tommy enlisted the county sheriff to go back with him the next day. Yet the Broke Spokers continued to plead deaf, dumb, and blind. So, he had no choice but to leave, noticing, as he left, the Confederate flag over the door.

The next night, when Mack felt like talking more, lying in his hospital bed blindfolded and motionless as humanly possible in an attempt to save his eye, he told Tommy, in his father's presence, all he could recall, including the double-take Bubba gave two strangers leaning against a dented, gray jalopy at the girls' practice.

"Could it have been a Studebaker?" Tommy asked.

"Maybe," Mack answered. "It just seemed like Bubba knew them."

When Cal heard that, he stalked out, with Tommy quickly following.

Driving Mack's Chevy they'd retrieved from the ballfield, Cal screeched out of the hospital lot. By the time Tommy arrived at the Boatwright mansion, Cal was already in Noah IV's face, both standing in the driveway between the Cadillac and the Corvette, Bubba cowering a few feet behind.

"Hand to God, I've never been to the Broke Spoke!" Bubba wailed.

"Go back in the house!" Noah IV shouted at Bubba.

"Don't you move a muscle!" Cal shouted back.

Tommy jumped out of the cruiser just as a distraught Cal, remembering how Mack said he'd made Bubba talk at the game, marched back to Mack's car and retrieved a baseball bat, threatening to take it out on Noah IV's Cadillac *and* Bubba's Corvette.

"*Cal!* Hold up!" Tommy yelled. He pulled Bubba aside and said something that must have scared Bubba a little straight, because he agreed to go to the tavern and identify anyone he recognized.

Noah IV puffed up. "You touch my son again, Tilton, and I'll have your badge!"

"Well, I'll be sure not to touch him, then," Tommy answered. "But you don't have a say in this, Mr. Boatwright, no matter what you think. Bubba's nineteen. An adult when it comes to being an accessory to a crime." Tommy turned to Cal. "I'll take care of this, Cal! I *mean* it. Go back to your boy."

When Bubba and Tommy got to the Broke Spoke, though, Bubba recognized no one, and that might have been his plan since he was still claiming to never have set foot in this particular den of iniquity, even after the bartender set Bubba's usual sixer of Lone Star beer on the bar before noticing Tommy.

Later, when Tommy reported the futile trip to Cal, all Cal said was: "I wish I'd taken it out on Boatwright's damn Cadillac."

Another week passed. Mack seemed to have a bit of blurred vision. But after more calls to specialists, the doctors had to inform Mack that at this point, he would likely see blurrily for a while out of the eye before it would lose sight permanently.

During the weeks that followed, Tommy figured out the connection between the vehicles he glimpsed at night in High Cotton, the heckling out-of-town spectators he reprimanded, and Bubba Boatwright's part in how those hecklers heard about America playing in the softball game. He even made time to check the area's mug shot books for the hecklers' faces. But his efforts to find the men would all ultimately come to nothing. After a few more fruitless visits to the Broke Spoke Tavern, still hoping to see the hecklers, the gray jalopy, or the flatbed truck, all Tommy finally could do was file reports on both America's and Mack's assaults in case any evidence turned up. But nobody was ever found to pay for attacking America or bludgeoning Mack for trying to save his dog. It was the worst kind of evil, the kind you can't see coming and the kind you can't see getting away.

Everybody in town had immediately heard, of course. Pastor Pete, who'd sat with Corky's parents at the hospital all that first week, was no longer thinking about softball except for the fact that his deacon board had warned him he was on thin ice for disobeying their vote. He gave his response the very next Sunday. Pastor Pete preached the sermon of his life in the way that only happens when bad things happen to good people and you've got a pulpit to fill. It was also one of the shortest sermons the congregation had ever heard him preach, as well as the most scripture-stuffed one. During the singing and offering and choir special that always led up to his sermon, Pete stayed quiet, barely acknowledging any of it. When it finally came time for his sermon, he rose and went to his pulpit, but he did not begin with pounding the pulpit, his voice rising, as usual. Instead, in little more than a murmur, he began with two quotes, one as a prayer and one that might as well have been the title of his sermon.

Closing his eyes, he quoted:

"'May the words of my mouth, and the meditation of my heart, be acceptable in thy sight, O Lord, my strength, and my redeemer.'"

Opening his eyes, he quoted:

"'There are none so blind as those who will not see.'"

Then he paused, straightened his glasses, placed his hands firmly on his pulpit, and began:

"I've just come from the bedside of Mack Corcoran. He may lose the sight of one of his eyes. I told that fine, young man that it's what you make of tragedy that makes you. Your response, whatever it is, can and will define the rest of your life. But it is also what I am telling myself. Tragedy often instructs in ways happiness cannot. And I want to share with you what the Lord has laid on my heart this morning.

"All of you have heard what happened after the game. Call it what you like, but what happened to America Willcox and Mack Corcoran, in my view, was Evil Incarnate," he continued. "And it began long before that night. I admit to the sin of pride and envy in asking a talented Southside Baptist girl to play softball with us in a show of crosstown Christian communion. In doing so, I tested our town's goodwill, underestimating the power of gossip and intolerance in the service of Evil Without and—I dare say—Within. I feel my own guilt and shame over my part in what happened. But I feel just as ashamed of our, yes, *our* larger part in what led to it.

"You may say, *Pastor Pete, I bear no responsibility in this!* But I think you do. We all do. Evil is all around us," he said, waving an arm, "even here in our little town. We forget this world is fallen. We forget that it's our duty to remember to be better, to stand up to Evil when it shows itself, even if it sometimes shows itself within our own hearts. In fact, that's the only kind over which we really have total control, the kind within us. It's also the kind easiest to make right."

Taking a deep breath, Pastor Pete then stood up as dignified as his skinny frame would allow to say what was next: "In the context of this tragedy and its connection to our softball game, I've been warned by certain people to watch myself, that obedience to a human deacon board is my job. But I think those certain people misspoke—"

Hearing that, Noah Boatwright IV jumped to his feet in the choir loft. "Now, you hold on a second, Pas—"

"Oh, for the love of *GOD*, Boatwright!" interrupted Marilou Moon's father from his third-row pew. "Let the man preach! SIT DOWN."

Shocked that anyone would speak to him like that, much less in church, Noah Boatwright IV sank slowly back into his seat.

Pastor Pete started again, this time leaning over his pulpit. "But I think those certain people misspoke. In the ten years I've been here, I've learned what my true job is. My job is to shepherd a flock that is trying to obey God. And sometimes that means telling the truth even when it hurts. So, I've looked into my own heart. And now I want *you* to look into *yours*. What does God ask of us? As the book of Micah says, To do what is 'just,' to 'love mercy,' and 'walk humbly' with our God. We are people of the Bible, are we not?" he asked, his voice finally rising. "*SO!* What did the prophet *say?*" He pounded the pulpit so hard it made most of the ladies jump.

"*'Be JUST!'*"

He pounded.

"*'Love MERCY!'*"

He pounded.

"*'Walk HUMBLY!'*"

He leaned even farther over his pulpit.

"Right now, what does your heart tell you? *NOT* what your neighbors, friends, or your upbringing tell you. What does *your heart* tell you? That feeling you have, the one that makes you angry or resentful or judgmental or petty or prejudiced. Doesn't it feel awful?" he said, making eye contact with every member. "It should! That's its *job*. I know right now what my heart is saying. And I pray you listen to what yours is saying, too. And if it isn't saying pretty much the same thing, well, I guess we're just back to where we started: 'There are none so blind as those who will not see.'"

Taking yet another deep breath, Pastor Pete paused one last time. "Remember, my brothers and sisters, as the scripture says, 'The truth will set you free.' May the words of Saint Paul be the ones we can all say one day to the angels: 'I have fought the good fight, I have finished the race, I have kept the faith.' AMEN. Now let us all stand and sing 'Amazing Grace' for our invitation hymn, listening with our hearts to the words of that grand old hymn."

By the next Sunday, Pastor Pete was gone.

As the reverend himself pointed out, he'd been there ten years. So, a slim majority of the deacon board spearheaded by Noah IV decided that a decade was a bit too long, that maybe he really had finished the race, at least in High Cotton, and perhaps *he* should be set free.

It split the church, of course. Baptist churches split all the time, and sometimes for much smaller reasons, so this wasn't news except it had somehow never happened in High Cotton. But the high-minded members who appreciated his last sermon all prayed Peter Hockenheimer went somewhere worthy of his personal revelation.

After that, everything else in town went back to normal, oddly so to Corky, since nothing at Corky's home was anywhere near normal. Since Cal Corcoran was the only pharmacist within thirty miles, even while his son lay very still in the hospital a few blocks away trying to save his sight, he had to go back to work.

Meanwhile, Corky turned her irritating questioning inward. *Why didn't I tell Tommy about the stupid truck?* she berated herself. *What if I were the reason for everything happening?* Corky felt so full of guilt that she thought she might explode. Yet how could she tell her parents now? What good would it do? Confession might be good for the soul, but it sure wouldn't be good for the souls around her. She just couldn't. America was right. She knew nothing about nothing, *less* than nothing. So, she kept on keeping all her nothing to herself.

Another week passed. Mack was told he could come home, but he had to stay in bed. So, he came back to his room with a bandage over his left eye with orders to continue keeping as still as he could for yet another week in a last-ditch hope to save the eye's vision. But his pitching days were over.

From that night on, Roy Rogers took to sleeping in Mack's room again instead of Corky's, still standing sentry over his boy.

On one of those nights, right after Mack came home, the phone rang. It was the University of Texas's head baseball coach. The UT coach had told Mack he would be letting him know of his decision by the end of June. It was the end of June.

After Cal talked to the coach awhile, explaining everything that had happened, he hung up the phone and sank into a chair.

"Cal, what is it?" Belle asked.

"Mack made the team," Cal mumbled.

Belle gasped. "*Oh, dear Lord.* How are we going to tell him?" She paused. "Do you want me . . . ?"

Taking a deep breath, Cal Corcoran stood up straight and gazed up the stairs. "No, it needs to be me."

The next morning, the delivery truck drove up the back driveway to bring a new person to help Belle care for Mack.

"Kathryn, go let her in," Belle said.

Corky opened the back door. The woman was from the Southside, short, middle-aged, and had on a nurse's uniform.

Roy Rogers rushed up to her, wagging his tail expectantly. After sniffing her all over, though, he trotted away.

Seeing that, Corky couldn't help herself. Two weeks had passed since the game, and it was as if America had disappeared into thin air the moment she'd sprinted across the dark tracks. Holding back tears, Corky rushed to her mother and blurted, "Where's Evangeline? Where's America? Why doesn't anybody *know*?"

Belle pulled her aside. "Bring your voice down, young lady. They probably left for her husband's new job."

"Are they okay?"

"I hope so."

"But where did they *go*?"

"We don't know. They didn't leave us a forwarding address."

"Why?"

"Maybe they'll send it later," Belle tried.

"But they didn't say goodbye."

Belle's face fell. "No, they didn't."

And then Corky couldn't help herself: "Mom, I feel bad because I saw something I should—"

"Kathryn, it doesn't matter." Her mother cut her off; she'd never done that before. "Feeling bad won't change things. Life doesn't always go the way you want it to. And most of the time, it isn't a bit your own fault." Glancing upstairs, she added, "It's time you learned that." Belle turned to the new helper waiting patiently for instructions. "I'm so sorry. Please tell me your name again?"

"Pearl."

"Pearl, thank you for coming. Let's go upstairs to meet my son."

Corky ran out the door. She headed down the street, over the highway, and across the tracks, as fast she could go, until she passed the little, square, cream-colored house with all the doodads and whirligigs and was standing in front of America's rental house. It was just as pristine as before. But the rocker on the front porch was gone.

So Corky ran to the Mount Olive Baptist Church. In a minute, she was knocking on the office door of Reverend Moses P. Washington. No one answered, so she headed for the sanctuary. And there he was. Standing under the baptistry, he was straightening the cane-backed chairs in the choir loft.

"Where did America go, Reverend Washington?" she said even before hello, slumping down on the front pew.

He sighed. "I'm sorry, child, I don't know. Her father was looking hard for a job, so he must have found one, and they had to leave without warning. They weren't here long enough for me to learn much more."

"But she didn't say goodbye!"

"I know. Goodbyes are not easy."

"But what if we never see her again?"

Reverend Washington smiled sadly. "If that is the case, I, for one, will be glad I had the privilege of knowing her at all." His face softened. "We heard about your brother. How is he?"

She looked down. "He may lose his eye."

A dark cloud seemed to pass over the reverend's face . . . dark with the threat of thunder and lightning. He said nothing for a long moment, as if collecting himself. In a voice low with feeling, he said, "Since Eden, there's always been a snake in the garden. That's the world we must journey through, one full of snakes willing to do wrong."

Corky had always been impressed by how preachers talked in pictures. Probably all that Bible reading. But, thinking of Papa Cal, her skin crawled at the mention of snakes. She'd heard enough about snakes that summer. And, frankly, even though she knew preachers thought a snake was just used by Satan in the Garden of Eden, she sure wasn't surprised a snake was what the devil chose. Still unable to shake her guilt over Papa Cal, she was now feeling guilty about causing what happened after the game, despite her mother's words. And she suddenly said out loud: "I think it was my fault."

Reverend Washington frowned. "What was?"

Corky hung her head. "Everything."

Hearing that, he sat down beside her on the front pew. "Well, you don't look much like a snake to me. Whatever you did or think you did, it was still finally snakes, just snakes, that chose to do wrong. Hear me now."

Corky hung her head lower.

"Did you hear me, child?"

Corky nodded. They sat there in silence. A nice moment passed. Not wanting to go just yet for reasons she couldn't quite say, she gazed up at the baptistry with its glorious river mural. "I like your baptistry. It's so much better than ours. Wish we had a river." She cocked her head, squinting. "Oh, and there are angels above it. I didn't notice them before."

The big man cocked his head. "Well, you might not have been looking for angels. Only if you are looking for them might you ever see one."

Corky stared up at this big, gentle, patient Southside man who she liked very much. She had a feeling they weren't talking about real angels anymore, but you never quite knew with preacher-pictures. And to her surprise, it made her suddenly miss Pastor Pete. "Pastor Pete is gone."

"Yes. I heard," Reverend Washington said. "But don't worry yourself about him. We serve the Lord, not the church. Pastor Pete will be fine."

Corky got up to go, but turned back toward him. "May I hug you?" she heard herself say.

The big man got to his feet. "It would be an honor," he said and spread his big arms to take her in.

She hugged the preacher hard and turned to leave.

As she disappeared out the door, she heard him call to her: "Stay open, child. Don't let the world close you down. God knows it's gonna try—and God knows it can do it. Stay open so your heart can do what it's supposed to do. If you do, I know it's going to be something good. Just like I know it for America."

Corky hurried out the door and back across the tracks. It would be the last time she ever crossed them.

After that, she asked everybody she knew about America, including her father, but they all told her the same thing: America's father must have gotten a job and they left.

Was the story true? Or was the real reason they left so quickly because of what happened after the game? Corky hated not knowing.

Velma and Velvadine were the only ones who told her anything new. With Mack in the hospital, they opened the mail for the drugstore until Corky's father came back. In the mail, her father got a package with no return address. Velma and Velvadine opened it, saw several stacks of twenty-dollar bills along with a note, and quickly sealed it back up to place on Cal Corcoran's desk. But not before they read the scribbled note:

> *TO: Mr. Cal Corcoran*
> *c/o Corcoran Drugstore*
> *High Cotton, Texas*
>
> *This should make us more than even.*
> *Thank you.*
> *Rayford Willcox*

It was from America's father. *He paid back the loan,* Corky thought, *and America was sure right about him being a man of few words.* She'd find out later that he'd left an envelope at Daniels' Shoe Store as well for the sneakers Mr. Dan had given America.

Talking to Velma and Velvadine, though, made her think about the soda fountain sit-in for the first time since Mack's injury. It had happened only a couple of weeks before, yet seemed so long ago. And what seemed so dramatic now seemed less so. Like everything else in town, nothing showed much sign of change. Since college was over until the fall, the college students didn't return, perhaps feeling their High Cotton job was done. Dr. DuBose kept dropping by, Velma and Velvadine told her, but never during the lunch hour anymore. And little Black boys still held out their quarters at the front counter. All they cared about was ice cream, not equality. Still, Corky kept waiting for something else to happen. It never did. Not that summer.

So, she lost interest in working behind the soda fountain. Instead, once Mack was home, she rode their palomino for days at a time, calling her not Goldy but Golden, as America had. And one of those days, watching Golden roll in the dirt after being brushed, she saw another glint of silver where she'd found the first Mercury head dime, the one she'd handed to America for good luck. It was another dime, this one even older. Picking up the coin, she closed her fingers around it and squeezed it tight.

The summer went on that way for several more weeks, Corky even avoiding going to the library. She'd have said it was because of Mack, but it wasn't. Finally, she went in to confess to her library friend that she'd lost the copy of *To Kill a Mockingbird*.

"I'm sorry, Miss Delacourt," Corky said.

Raynelle frowned. "What do you mean, sugar? You dropped it in the book-return box outside weeks ago, right after your softball game, I believe. You just forgot, I guess, with everything going on at home. In fact, you left something in it. It's an envelope with your name on it. People do that all the time. I didn't want to bother you with it until I saw you again, considering what your family is going through. Here you go."

The sealed envelope said: *To Corky Corcoran.*

Inside, she found a folded piece of school-ruled notebook paper. On it, in delicate handwriting, was this:

> *Dear Corky,*
> *Don't worry. I'm okay. Thank you for my ride on Golden. I'll never forget it. And I'll never forget you. I'm glad we met. I really hope someday we'll see each other again.*
> *Goodbye.*
>
> *Your friend,*
> *America*

And Corky burst into tears.

SUMMER 2020

COVID Pandemic Surge Halts Summer Reopening Hopes
Major League Baseball Playing before Stadiums of
Cardboard Fans
2020 Tokyo Summer Olympics Rescheduled to 2021
Black Lives Matter Protests Erupt in Major Cities

Kate Corcoran turns off the TV and slumps back against her couch. Having retired from her newspaper job right before the pandemic quarantine, she is officially deep in cabin fever. And with all that has happened in the last few months, her thoughts wander to another life-changing summer:

The summer of '64.

Kate pushes away the bittersweet memories and heads to her home office. She planned to try writing a novel when she retired, so she opens her laptop to finally begin, hoping it might help her mood.

Glancing at her bookshelf, though, her eyes land on her old, old copy of *To Kill a Mockingbird*, and the memories flood back. She gets up, goes to her bedroom, and rummages through her jewelry box until she finds a worn 1922 Mercury head dime.

Easing down on the edge of her bed, Kate absently rubs the old coin and sits with her childhood memories. As an adult, she knows how memories can be fickle and sometimes lie as time goes by. But she also knows that they are all anyone has to understand who they were and who they became, whether the memories soothe, thrill, wound, or haunt—and this chunk of her past has done all of those. However, quarantined in 2020, remembering that long-ago summer, she feels more than a bit helpless. There has always been something she could do about most everything, even if it is just writing about it.

After all, she's been a journalist her entire adult life.

She was also a thirteen-year-old tomboy named Corky.

And she decides to do something she should have done long ago.

Back in her office, she types "America Willcox" into her computer's search tab, hits return, and waits.

Nothing.

How many women our age could be named America? Kate wonders, putting her fingers back on the keys to begin a deeper internet search using all the journalistic web skills she'd honed over the last twenty years. She has the kind of clues that work for a deep-dive internet search: She knows America's age and full name in 1964. She knows America was baptized in Galveston and lived in four towns before High Cotton, and that her father, Rayford, worked for the railroad and her mother, Evangeline, came from Haiti before America was born. She's done harder searches—this is going to work.

But something makes Kate pause.

When I find her, I can't just go knock on her door because of the pandemic, she realizes, *and a phone call out of the blue seems deeply wrong.*

Closing her laptop for the moment, she reaches for her old copy of *To Kill a Mockingbird,* and from it drops a yellowed envelope with *To Corky Corcoran* written on the outside in faded fountain-pen ink. Opening it, she gently takes out the folded piece of school-ruled notebook paper and, for the first time in decades, rereads America's letter:

. . . I really hope someday we'll see each other again.
Goodbye.
Your friend,
America

And Kate knows what she needs to do.

Right now.

Rummaging in her rolltop desk, she finds a ruled, white legal pad, the closest thing she has to a piece of 1964 notebook paper.

Then Kate grabs a ballpoint pen, pauses to take a deep breath, and starts a letter to her childhood friend:

Dear America,

Today, as I thought of you, I've been thinking about lines. Lines that we stand in. Lines that divide us. Lines that, long ago, blurred for a moment at a little baseball field when, all together, we cheered the extraordinary in our midst. And lines others crossed to do wrong after such a moment of doing right.

The last time I saw you, you were sprinting over one of those lines: the High Cotton railroad tracks. Here and now, a lifetime later, I have this urge to tell you what happened after that moment. Why? That, I can't answer, except to say it's strange how close you can feel to someone after knowing them only a short time compared to people you never get close to despite knowing them for years.

But the people you come to love early, the ones who help shape you into the person you become, never truly leave you, I don't think. And as time keeps passing, those are the ones who come naturally to mind, the ones you'd love to see once more. My parents are gone now, along with all the town's adults we knew and the animals we loved. If you're still in this world with us, and I so want to believe you are, I bet you feel the same tug of mortality and its bittersweet urge to look back. You may not feel the same desire to connect after all this time, maybe not remembering me the way I remember you. If so, that will be okay. I know we aren't the same people we were when we were thirteen and sixteen. Yet I also know, deep down in the ways that matter, we are. We all are.

So, I want to tell you the rest of my story in the hopes, one fine day, I might hear the rest of yours.

From you.

I got your goodbye letter inside the library copy of To Kill a Mockingbird *that you turned in for me, but not until I finally returned to the library in August. I've always believed there was nothing good about goodbyes. I've never been good at them. I have actually lied at times to avoid them, using the "oh, this isn't goodbye, I'll see you later" ploy as I disappear to avoid the awful feeling of them. And I would have resisted ours. What I didn't know is that I needed yours. I had thought you didn't say goodbye. But you did, and while I still think there is little good about goodbyes, I know yours was, and it may be the only one I've ever known to be so.*

Unlike the end of a book that wraps up all the loose ends, though, real life, its loose ends dangling everywhere, always goes on. And life went on after that summer night. Each time I'd ask about you—and you know I kept asking, suspecting the adults weren't telling me the whole truth—I never found out anything new. Yet the railroad tracks were always there, always reminding me. Finally, to finish growing up, I had to let it all go.

Life went on.

Life went on for my brother, Mack, too. It almost didn't. On the night of the game, after that drunk

stranger hit the ground from your kick and Mack's bean-
ball, his pals began dragging the drunk's limp body into
the dark toward a waiting truck. Roy Rogers noticed and
rushed barking into the deep dark after them. So, Mack
rushed after him trying to keep our dog from being shot
or run over—and got stopped by the end of a rifle stock
in the eye. Despite all they could do, which wasn't much
in 1964, he wound up losing the sight in it.

I only recall one thing Pastor Pete said when he came
to visit Mack: "What you make of tragedy is what makes
you." But all I saw through my thirteen-year-old eyes was
that it didn't make him, it broke him.

That fall, Mack stayed home, dropping out of school,
a bit lost, Roy never leaving his side. For the months
he recuperated, his old girlfriend Cissy never came to see
him, and I think I was more pissed about it than Mack,
who I suspected liked her more for her hickeys than her
personality or intellect. His injury had done one good
thing: It made him 4-F for Vietnam the following year
as the draft's inductions skyrocketed along with the war.
That should have made him feel somewhat better, but
needless to say, it didn't.

Then one day during the Christmas holidays, another
girlfriend showed up seemingly out of the blue: his first,
Lorelei Jones, who'd lived next door. Mom, having kept
up with our old neighbors and worried about Mack's lin-
gering listlessness, had called her without telling anyone.
Following her up the stairs, I watched Lorelei approach
Mack's room as Mack lay in bed, staring out the window,
head turned to see out of his good eye. Roy Rogers danced
around her with long-lost joy, and, for a moment, she
took her eyes off Mack to hug Roy's big head. When she
stepped into his room, I watched a surprised Mack tense

as she sat down by him, tenderly brushed his overgrown black hair away from his wounded eye, and placed her hand on the side of his head until he let go and leaned into it. Then she closed the door behind them.

She stayed for a few days, making Mack get out of the house, taking long walks or rides with Roy and Golden, talking deep into the night in between long periods of silence that even I knew to leave alone. And after hugging us all, she was gone. But Mack was different after that. As Vietnam began to fill every newspaper's front page after the first American ground troops were deployed, he heard how college students, compared to working-class boys, were finding ways to avoid being sent overseas, from joining the National Guard to moving to Canada to espousing conscientious objector status, both sincere and insincere. So, by the next summer, he'd joined VISTA, the domestic Peace Corps, working as a teaching assistant in a Chicago inner-city junior high. From there, he went back to the University of Texas and got his teaching degree in history, and his black "pirate" eye patch somehow just added to his now tough good looks, making him an instant hit for the Dallas junior high students who'd be lucky to have him during his long career. Soon, he even wound up coaching the school's baseball team, his love for the game too much to lose as well. As for Lorelei, they continued their fiery, loving, tit-for-tat relationship long after she became a lawyer and took a public defender job in the city to be near him, challenging one another their entire lives. I've no doubt you'd have loved her as much as we have.

I've no doubt you've also wondered about the drugstore sit-in you walked into the day before the softball game. I never had the chance to tell you, but I didn't know about it. That was not why I asked you to come by.

Yet it did happen. For the rest of that summer, that fact seemed not to have made any difference, but, of course, it did. Sometimes just an act done on principle can leave a lasting mark. Things were changing, if very slowly, and even slower in places like High Cotton, as the new laws forced change on a level never before seen. Dad could have closed the soda fountain permanently, but he didn't. I'd like to think it was out of respect for Mack, but most likely, with Mack recuperating at home, he didn't have the energy to do much more than run the store the way it was, hoping for no more drama, but also surely hoping there'd be nothing he'd have to change.

But something did change: Dad's heart. While he was a man of his times, he was also a businessman. That fall, after Mom went back to her new part-time library job against Dad's wishes, Dad had an idea. If she was determined to work, he'd hire her. But not as an employee, as a partner, to sell Elizabeth Arden and Fabergé and Max Factor cosmetics to the town's ladies, who came and sat in the padded chair across from the soda fountain dreaming of looking like our mom. Mother didn't even wear makeup until she started the job, yet she became such a whiz that Dad had another brainstorm. Just a few weeks after the summer sit-in, the Dairy Dip started selling hamburgers, grilled cheeses, and banana splits, adding an inside dining stool area about the same size as the drugstore's soda fountain. They were vying for the lunch market. So, Dad let them have it, saying he was tired of seeing Noah Boatwright's face every day anyway. "Why don't we go modern?" he said to my mother, revamping the fountain area into an entire department of ladies' cosmetics to let Mom run. And that she did. It became a moneymaker far beyond what the soda fountain ever did. And she did it without giving up her part-time job at the library, which she said she loved too much to quit.

During all that, as if she'd been waiting to all-out blossom, she even found time to also begin taking piano lessons, just as Evangeline had suggested. And within a few years, she could play "Clair de Lune" and anything else she wanted to. On my first trip home from college, she was playing it when I came in the door. I stood in the curve of the baby grand exactly where, after our ride on Golden, you and I saw her listening to Evangeline play it by ear, my mother's face glowing with the most rapturous expression. And as she played it for me, I noticed she had that same transported look.

"Wouldn't you love to play that for Evangeline?" I suddenly said.

She paused and smiled. "Yes, I truly, truly would," she answered and finished the beautiful music with an elegantly joyous flourish as if just for Evangeline.

And life kept going on.

I'd left High Cotton as quick as I could for college and got there just in time for the massive escalation of the Vietnam War, the sit-ins and protests now about that, the new draft lottery on every male student's mind. I had a college sweetheart whose number came up 17, and the only thing that kept him from Vietnam were his gimpy knees from playing college football.

After graduation, I took the reporter's card I'd kept all those years, looked up the reporter, and was hired for an internship that turned into a job at the Fort Worth Star-Telegram. *Then I married my football-hero-turned-high-school-coach, who easily landed a job in the city, too.*

One day, around that time, after school integration finally, fully began in Texas, I heard that High Cotton's "consolidated" high school was offering track and softball teams for girls because of Title IX. It made me both happy and sad. But, soon, just happy, thinking of all the young Americas out there who'd now get their chance, not to mention all the Corkys.

With each passing year, though, as you well know, the news made us certain the world was going to hell— assassinations of Robert Kennedy and Martin Luther King Jr., Watergate, nuclear disasters, race riots, AIDS, and so much more.

But there was also the moon landing, Woodstock, the tearing down of the Berlin Wall, the first Black and female astronauts—and, of course, the women's rights movement. I'd like to say I was part of it, burning a bra or two, but I just benefited from it. Soon I was off the women's page onto a beat and, after that, a column. I wrote about school shootings and terrorist bombings and the horror of 9/11, as the world kept threatening but never fully going to hell.

And one day, far too quickly, I was old enough to retire.

And now, here I sit, thinking how this summer of 2020 is so like yet unlike the summer of '64.

I've thought of you with every new Summer Olympics. One time, two decades after I saw you run as fast as Wilma Rudolph, I tried to find you. I was given a column assignment to write about Los Angeles's 1984 Olympics, and as I studied the list of Olympic athletes, I noticed a women's track team member from California named Evangeline. And while she seemed to have no connection to you besides your mother's name, I found myself wanting to talk to you, not so much about the Olympics but wondering how you and your mother were. I wasted a few days searching, using all the limited pre-internet reporter skills I had. I found no trace of you . . . as if I'd dreamed it all. But one look at Mack told me that you and that summer were very, very real.

"Maybe she didn't have a birth certificate; that still happened some back then," Mack suggested in '84 when I told him about it. "More likely she got married and changed her name, don't you think?"

So, once again, I had to let it, you, go.

Until today.

Life has an awful habit of creating mysteries. And this one, the mystery of the last time I saw you—where you went, who those drunk strangers were in the rattling flatbed truck, and whether one had to do with the other—would just linger, never to be solved. But I've never quit thinking about my part in what happened, how I didn't tell Tommy about a truck stalking our house because of a childish fear he'd stop our softball game, and what that ultimately meant for you and Mack. I still feel it deeply without a way to make it right.

But all of it now seems bigger than our personal mystery, the lessons learned, the truths expanded. Over the years, as the world kept turning and continuing its threat of going to hell, I've thought of it as the way evil wins sometimes and in some ways, although not forever, even when it seems it will. And that is especially true for this summer of 2020.

Hope, as we get older, often feels like a thing reserved only for the young. But I've never liked that. Not one bit. So, here and now as I write this, I've decided to try one more time to search for you. The America I knew was so smart, multitalented, self-possessed, and full of potential that, if she were given even half a chance, I can't imagine

*her life not being a success in some profound or personal
way that I could uncover, and I can't wait to start my
search.*

*I know this is a long shot. After all this time, I know
I might not find you or, worse, I've waited too late. If I
never get a chance to mail this letter, I'll remember the
wise words of Reverend Moses P. Washington and be glad
I had the privilege of knowing you at all.*

But I need to try.

*And if I find you—when I find you—One Fine
Day, you'll open your screen door and you'll joke, Corky
Corcoran. What took you so long?*

*I'll laugh, hug your neck, and tell you that I missed
you.*

*And, as we chat, I will start to thank you for being in
young Corky's life that crucial, long-ago summer: for putting up with her pushy, clueless thirteen-year-old self yet
still becoming her—my—friend and for how my world
expanded by just knowing you for that short time. In
grand Corky fashion, I'll want to declare that our world
would be a better place if more Corkys and Americas had
had a chance to be friends. But I won't, at first, wanting
to hear about you. You might tell me that you made it
to the Olympics but were injured or placed out of the
medals. Or maybe that your gifted grandchildren will be
the ones who finally run as fast as the wind for you there.*

*Or possibly, probably, you'll tell me that the Olympics
was never your dream but ours. That instead you settled down somewhere with someone you loved and let
the world go by, peacefully claiming the life your mother
hoped for you when she named you. Or one of a hundred
ways your life, a full life, should have gone. I'll listen to
your story, whatever it might be, good, bad, or, as for*

most of us, something in between, and I'll feel privileged in the listening.

And, as we keep sharing our stories, I'll confess I checked out the original copy of To Kill a Mockingbird *and kept it, library fines be damned. Not because of it, but because of you.*

You'll laugh at that, no doubt bringing up the library police.

That's when I'll tell you I want to write my own novel.

Why do you want to do that? you'd surely ask.

And I'll tell you this:

Because while a journalist's job is to tell what is true, a novelist's job is to tell what is truth, to create a world in which you'd want to live, in which everything is just, even if only in the end.

So, if I find you—when I find you—I will say with all the faith and courage and joy I can muster: America, my dear old friend, I'm going to write a novel about us.

Lowering her pen, Kate rereads her letter and lingers over its promise . . . until she hears a bird singing.

She smiles, hoping it's a mockingbird.

Ready now to start her deep-dive internet search for America, Kate gently tears the letter from the ruled writing pad, and, as if guaranteeing her search's success, she slips it into an envelope and confidently sets it by her computer, waiting to be addressed.

With one more rub of the Mercury head dime for luck, she opens her laptop.

And begins.

SUMMER 2021

Summer turns into fall.

Fall turns into winter.

And winter turns into spring, the world still turning as life goes ever on.

As summer once again arrives, the front page of Kate's newspaper proclaims:

COVID VACCINATIONS BRING SUMMER REOPENING HOPE

Then, One Fine June Day, Kate's husband calls her away from working on her novel when their barking puppy, Rogers, announces a visitor at the front door.

"Who is it?" Kate asks.

"Come see, *Corky*," he responds, grinning as he opens the screen door.

He never calls me Corky, Kate thinks as she comes near.

Standing there, dressed in a beautiful, handsewn, tailored outfit, is a slyly smiling woman with graying hair pulled back in long, intricate braids.

And in her hand is Kate's letter, as if she's checking the return address.

Heart in her throat, Kate's eyes well up with tears as her childhood friend steps close and hugs her neck.

Savoring the small summer miracle of that moment, she sighs, the years melting away. Then, finding her voice, Kate "Corky" Corcoran says with a laugh, sweet and young:

"America Willcox. What took you so long?"

AUTHOR'S NOTE

A good novel is not *about* something, it *is* something, a wise editor reminded me. But, in one sense, historical novels are a hybrid of sorts, the setting telling a tale all its own. Winston Churchill, by way of philosopher George Santayana, is famously quoted as saying that those who fail to learn from history are condemned to repeat it.

Or as some anonymous wit put it: "Don't make me repeat myself." —History

I don't know about you, but I'd rather not repeat it.

While history can be dry, dry, dry, a novel has the ability to bring it to life through fictional characters' experiences, both true and truth, as Kate/Corky expressed. That was my goal.

A child of the '60s, I lived through the decade's changes. I grew up in one of those segregated towns with a railroad track as its dividing line. I watched via television and news reports as American women found their voice, ultimately benefiting from it like Kate did. And I watched Black Americans do the same: I witnessed the first attempt at school desegregation through "school choice" my senior year, in which students from the Black high school across the tracks could choose to go to our school. Five years later, I found myself teaching middle school for three years during full integration in Fort Worth. That's what the 1964 Civil Rights Act was about, slowly, surely raising consciousness to forward change that was going to be hard for some in the short-term but worth it for most in the long haul. And one of the worthiest changes is that Black Americans have, slowly, surely, gotten a full-throated chance to tell their stories in the same way women of all backgrounds finally have . . . in the same way I bet you'd agree that *everyone* should, even if it's just telling our stories to each other.

If you are my age, you experienced the '60s along with me. If you weren't born yet, I hope the novel offers a living, breathing view of those years to balance with the history you've learned and the world we now share. Sure, we're still divided in far too many ways, but nowhere near as much as we were, and remembering that fills me with hope. After all, by definition, progress is a forever thing, isn't it? And, more than not, a deeply individual thing. The moral of this novel, if it has one, is about the absolute miracle of friendship, how, if given half a chance, it can cross any divide and open new worlds. It's also about the miraculous ability that books and sports possess to draw those new worlds together. It was true then; it's true now. If this novel has done the trick of bringing to life for you the giant strides we now take for granted from that tumultuous decade of my youth, then the novelist is happy. Here's hoping we continue to live and learn, never forgetting the progress we've made for the progress we can still make in becoming more human in the best sense of that word.

ACKNOWLEDGMENTS

A truth that happens to also be true are the skills of Danielle Marshall and Jane Dystel, and my literary debt to them. *Thank you* doesn't seem strong enough, but thanks, you two. Also, loving thanks always to my spouse, Don, my first reader-supporter, and to Beaux, my sweet pup teacher of all things dog.

Beyond the essential official websites researched, a few of the touchstone books referred to or studied for background include Betty Friedan's *The Feminine Mystique*; Taylor Branch's *Parting the Waters: America in the King Years 1954–63*; the wonderful, image-laden Time-Life Books covering the '50s and '60s: *The American Dream* and *Turbulent Years*; Maureen M. Smith's *Wilma Rudolph: A Biography*; David Goldblatt's *The Games: A Global History of the Olympics*; Paul Dickson's *The Worth Book of Softball: A Celebration of America's True National Pastime*; ESPN's documentary *37 Words* (Part I), especially its remarkable interview with Gloria Steinem and Billie Jean King talking to each other about Title IX. And, of course, Harper Lee's *To Kill a Mockingbird*, an enduring classic of this story's times and any time.

And if you've never heard Claude Debussy's short, famous, absolutely gorgeous piece of classical music "Clair de Lune" (the only fondly remembered piece from my own childhood's failed piano lessons), you're in for quite an aural treat.

To end, thanks with deepest gratitude to the public libraries and their books that shape us and reshape us throughout life. May they forever freely do so.

ABOUT THE AUTHOR

Photo © 2019 Korey Howell Photography

Lynda Rutledge is the bestselling author of *West with Giraffes*, selected by Library of Congress–affiliated Texas Center for the Book as their 2023 Great Read. She's also the author of *Faith Bass Darling's Last Garage Sale*, winner of the 2013 Writers' League of Texas Fiction Award and adapted into the major 2019 French film *La dernière folie de Claire Darling* starring Catherine Deneuve. Her fiction has also won awards and residencies from Atlantic Center for the Arts, Illinois Arts Council, and Ragdale Foundation, among others. In her eclectic career before becoming a novelist, she was a copywriter, freelance journalist, film reviewer, book collaborator, and travel writer. After years residing in urban locales including Chicago and San Diego, she currently lives with her husband outside Austin, Texas.

For more information, visit www.lyndarutledge.com.